KU-749-452

# THUNDERER

9510090066495

*Also by Julian Stockwin*

Kydd
Artemis
Seaflower
Mutiny
Quarterdeck
Tenacious
Command
The Admiral's Daughter
Treachery (US title: The Privateer's Revenge)
Invasion
Victory
Conquest
Betrayal
Caribbee
Pasha
Tyger
Inferno
Persephone
The Baltic Prize
The Iberian Flame
A Sea of Gold
To the Eastern Seas
Balkan Glory

# JULIAN STOCKWIN

# THUNDERER

HODDER

First published in Great Britain in 2021 by Hodder & Stoughton
An Hachette UK company

This paperback edition published in 2022

1

Copyright © Julian Stockwin 2021

The right of Julian Stockwin to be identified as the Author of the Work has been
asserted by him in accordance with the Copyright, Designs and Patents Act 1988.

All rights reserved. No part of this publication may be reproduced,
stored in a retrieval system, or transmitted, in any form or by any means without
the prior written permission of the publisher, nor be otherwise circulated in any
form of binding or cover other than that in which it is published and without
a similar condition being imposed on the subsequent purchaser.

All characters in this publication are fictitious and any resemblance
to real persons, living or dead, is purely coincidental.

A CIP catalogue record for this title is available from the British Library

Paperback ISBN 978 1 473 69886 4

Typeset in Garamond MT by
Palimpsest Book Production Ltd, Falkirk, Stirlingshire

Printed and bound in Great Britain by Clays Ltd, Elcograf S.p.A.

Hodder & Stoughton policy is to use papers that are natural, renewable
and recyclable products and made from wood grown in sustainable forests.
The logging and manufacturing processes are expected to conform to the
environmental regulations of the country of origin.

Hodder & Stoughton Ltd
Carmelite House
50 Victoria Embankment
London EC4Y 0DZ

www.hodder.co.uk

*'The men are not yet created that can stand against British seamen when properly disciplined & led'*
Admiral Sir John Jervis, Earl St Vincent

**VENDÉE COAST**

La Chaume
Les Sables d'Olonne
Pointe de Tanchette
*Vendée*
Pertuis Breton
Île de Ré
La Rochelle
Pertuis D'Antioche
46°N
Île d'Oléron
Gironde River
1°45'W
miles
0 — 20

NORWAY
Lyngør
Christiansand
SKAGERRAK
Wingo
Gothenburg
Holmen
Jutland
Great Belt
Sound
Nystad
Rostock
DENMARK
NORTH SEA
SWEDEN
Stockholm
BALTIC SEA
Hanö
Danzig
PRUSS
56°N
18°E

INNER LEADS

Gunboats

58°38'N    Podargus

Najaden

Thunderer

Lyngør

Calypso

0                    0.5
nautical miles

SKAGGERAK

LYNGØR

9°008'E

Åbo

Kronstadt
• St Petersburg

GULF OF FINLAND

FINLAND

EUROPE
(NORTH BALTIC)

N
W        E
S

RUSSIA

• Riga

LIVONIA

0          100
miles

COURLAND

Moscow

• Tilsit

Borodino

Smolensk

Vilna

• Grodno

Napoleon's advance on Moscow

IA

# *Dramatis Personae*

*indicates fictional character

| | |
|---|---|
| *Sir Thomas Kydd | captain of HMS *Thunderer* |
| *Nicholas Renzi | Earl of Farndon, former confidential secretary to Kydd |

**Thunderer, ship's company**

| | |
|---|---|
| *Allen | accounts clerk |
| *Binard | Kydd's manservant |
| *Boxall | captain's coxswain |
| *Briggs | third lieutenant |
| *Craddock | Kydd's confidential secretary |
| *Forbin | midshipman |
| *Franks | writer |
| *Gubb | purser |
| *Hare | captain of marines |
| *Hobbs | sailing master |
| *Lawlor | gunner |
| *Luscombe | Kydd's servant |
| *Lyell | former captain of *Thunderer* |

| *Mayne | fourth lieutenant |
| *Opie | boatswain |
| *Roscoe | first lieutenant |
| *Sadler | surgeon |
| *Smale | second lieutenant |
| *Tucker | petty officer |

## Others

| *Anneke | Dutch agent |
| Arakcheyev | Russian general opposed to Speransky |
| Bagration | marshal of Russian army |
| Baste | French admiral commanding Boulogne flotilla |
| Berthier | French grand marshal and chief of Imperial Staff |
| Castlereagh | British secretary of state for foreign affairs |
| *Cecilia | Kydd's sister, Countess of Farndon, Renzi's wife |
| *Congalton | high-ranking member of British secret service |
| Croker | first secretary to the Admiralty |
| Davis | captain, *Blake* |
| De Tolly | Russian army commander opposing Napoleon |
| *Denisov | minor Russian noble |
| Dewey | port admiral, Plymouth |
| Duroc | Bonaparte's grand equerry |
| Everard | captain, *Jason* |
| *Faulknor | relieving captain, *Tyger* |
| *Fookes | MP, a.k.a. Prinker |
| *Houghton | rear admiral, Rochefort squadron |
| Hoby | adjutant general, Royal Marines |

| | |
|---|---|
| Holm | captain, *Najaden* |
| Hoskyns | commander, *Daphne* |
| Junot | French general, invader of Portugal |
| Kutuzov | grand marshal and commander of combined Russian forces |
| *Lebedev | Russian academician |
| Lord Liverpool | prime minister of Great Britain |
| Lord Eldon | lord chancellor |
| Lord Keith | commander-in-chief, Channel Squadron |
| MacDonald | French marshal laying siege to Riga |
| Melville | first lord of the Admiralty |
| Montand | Mecklenberg grand marshal under Napoleon |
| *Moreau | colonel of engineers in Bonaparte's invasion army |
| Moubray | captain, *Montagu* |
| Murat | King of Naples and marshal under Bonaparte |
| Pelleton | long-serving general in Bonaparte's army |
| Perceval | prime minister of Britain, who was assassinated |
| *Persephone, Lady Kydd | Kydd's wife |
| Robillard | lieutenant-in-command, *Podargus* |
| *Rochambeau | staff officer, corps of *ingénieur géographe* in Bonaparte's army |
| Rostopchin | governor of Moscow |
| Ryder | home secretary |
| Savary | chief of secret police under Bonaparte |
| Speransky | Russian statesman overthrown for his liberal views |
| Strickland | port admiral, Portsmouth |

# Chapter 1

Spring 1812, England

On the last stretch of road to his Devon estate, the balmy weather, the vaulting blue of the sky and the smell of sun-touched woodlands complemented the vista. With rising feeling, Captain Sir Thomas Kydd RN gripped the side of the swaying trap as it took a steep, sweeping corner – and there ahead was Knowle Manor. The vehicle swung through the gates and came to a stop before the ancient front door, but not before he'd caught the flash of a face at an upstairs window.

Lady Persephone Kydd ran down to her husband in delight, embracing him as though they'd been parted for months, yet they'd returned to England just days before. She'd accompanied him on his last voyage and taken residence in Sicily while *Tyger* had stormed the Adriatic.

'How was the Admiralty, my darling?' she managed breathlessly.

'Welcoming above the ordinary, Seph,' he replied, with a chuckle, 'the whole crew main anxious to meet the victor of

Lissa.' A squadron of British frigates had confronted a French fleet twice its size in the Adriatic and prevailed in the tradition of Nelson – an action that had caught the public imagination.

*Tyger* was now lying in Portsmouth awaiting survey of her wounds and, having reported to the Admiralty, Kydd looked forward to a well-deserved leave until called to London again.

Persephone's hand slipped into his, her smile dazzling, and his heart swelled with happiness. He paid off the driver, who gave a sketchy salute as the horse clopped away.

Kydd took his fill of the old mansion, its mullioned windows and quaint chimneys, the garden a riot of colour, with neat flowerbeds and canes in immaculate condition. He strolled along in a haze of contentment while he heard how the riding school had fared while she'd been abroad – quite ably, it seemed – how much progress there had been on the orangery – disappointing but understandable given the soft soil; and about the re-flooring of the dairy – nearly done.

'It'll be all about the village that you've returned,' she said proudly. 'I've a notion there'll be entertainments to show you off to the Cornwood and Ugborough folk, if not all the tribes to Exeter.'

Kydd squeezed her hand. 'I'll do my duty right enough,' he said softly, knowing how much she would enjoy the village gaiety. 'Um, you haven't word of a visitor arriving at all?' he added, in an offhand tone.

'Oh?' Persephone replied, puzzled. 'No one dares disturb the sea-hero at his rest, I believe.'

So, it had been too much to expect. His confidential secretary Edward Dillon was no longer with him, executed by a French firing squad. His place had been taken by a remarkable individual, Lucius Cavendish Henry Craddock, a Balkan refugee of English origins, who had been a merchant banker in Radonice. The man had lost everything, his home, his business and his family, his wife and children burned alive in the ravages of war. He'd found refuge in *Tyger*, and Kydd had taken to him, with his calm, worldly-wise perspectives even while in the extremity of his suffering. But did he have any right to expect him to continue in the position? The prospects for a captain's secretary in a man-o'-war were far inferior to those he might expect ashore.

Craddock had journeyed to Manchester to show himself alive and well to his relatives and no doubt had been offered a position in the family business more in keeping with his talents.

Meanwhile, Kydd was in no hurry to return aboard *Tyger*. While there was no crippling injury to his command she had been much scarred by shot-strike, which would take some time to heal. His competent first lieutenant, Bowden, would ensure that this was done and it had been a thoughtful gesture of the first lord at the Admiralty to direct that repair be carried out in Plymouth instead of Portsmouth, which enabled him to take his rest at Knowle Manor. And it would be most agreeable to discuss with Persephone how the sizeable prize money to come from his cruise of depredation should be spent.

Several days later a corpulent major of the South Devon Militia in full regalia, accompanied by two troopers, rode up desiring Kydd to review a march-past of the other valiant defenders of this vital part of the coast. The public, he added proudly, would be sure to take the liveliest interest since salutes by a detachment of the Artillery Volunteers and their guns might be expected.

Kydd had readily agreed: he had a deep respect for the

3

stirring pageantry the English knew how to display to the fullest. And Persephone would be proudly by his side.

It proved a popular affair. Folk flocked to the Wembury barracks, its parade ground on cliffs overlooking the sea, and thrilled to the colour and spectacle. Kydd addressed the soldiery from his dais in stout seamanlike terms. Then came a crash and the reek of powder-smoke as the little six-pounders made their salute. A civic occasion followed. Combe Tavy took it in good part when Ivybridge claimed a dinner in honour of the hero on account of its commodious church hall, close by Glanville's corn mill, into which the town council and other notables could be squeezed.

Kydd and Persephone were ushered to their seats in the crowded room. It took waiters an eternity to jostle their way along with salvers, the contents cooling rapidly. From outside came the raucous jollity of lesser mortals enjoying an ox-roast and West Country ale. Kydd knew where he would rather be. When he glanced at a perspiring Lady Kydd he guessed she would too.

In the following days he visited his tenants and heard how the harvest had failed for the second year in succession. And late rains had flooded the lower Erme causing considerable damage to the Flete priory. Other happenings had to be prised out of the good country folk, who felt that such could not possibly engage the interest of one who had faced the enemy in far places and triumphed.

The settled rustic rhythms of Devon reached out to Kydd and he felt them work on his soul, the cares and troubles falling away as each day passed into the next.

Then a letter arrived. In it, to his surprise and pleasure, he was advised that he could look forward to the style and title of baronet in public recognition of his valour and service to the Crown in the late engagement. 'Captain Sir Thomas Kydd, RN, Bart' would be his signature on documents from now on, and among other prerogatives, he would take precedence before any other knight in ceremonial occasions. Persephone glowed with pride: her husband had achieved greater honour than any in her family, and her still-cool parents must now render him due respect and esteem.

One evening after dinner, as velvet darkness stole in, Persephone broke into his thoughts. 'Darling,' she opened, in an odd voice, 'shall we go outside? I've heard that the comet is growing in spectacle and must portend something of significance. I want us to be together in witness.'

'Why, if that is your desire, my love.'

The 'Great Comet' had first appeared some months earlier, and while men of science were declaring it to be the brightest event in the heavens this age, the more superstitious were foretelling cosmic doom and an earthly disaster.

They moved out to the front lawn and gazed upwards at the star-field. The comet had grown in length: Kydd estimated it, with its curved tail, to be at least ten degrees long. It was a wondrous thing – an intrusion into the ordered celestial regularity from regions that lay beyond the stars.

'I shall remember this night as long as I live, Thomas,' she said softly.

'That something of great portent will happen shortly?' he teased.

'Yes,' she answered simply, and held him at arm's length. 'For this night will I always treasure as when I told you . . . my news.'

'Seph?' He caught his breath.

'Yes, my darling,' she breathed, her eyes still on the

splendour in the heavens. 'There'll soon be another in our lives to love and cherish.'

From that moment his existence changed for ever. A child – a young Kydd, one who would bear his name and his title. A baronet passed on his honour and, while not an aristocrat with a seat in the House of Lords, his newborn, should he be a boy, in the fullness of time could claim a knighthood by right. He would inherit Knowle Manor and whatever riches resulted from his recent and future prizes. To go on to who knew what in the years to come . . .

It required him to re-orient his place in the dimensions of life, and the days passed in blissful happiness.

# Chapter 2

The trap's grinding wheels sounded above the morning birdsong and the breeze and, to Kydd's delight, he saw his visitor was Craddock. The man cut quite a different figure from before: mature and dignified, he now had a Spanish-style beard to hide the scars of the flames, his grey-tinged sable hair styled in the new Romantic mode. He wore taste-fully cut plain clothes of the kind more to be seen around the London stock exchange, and his eyes had lost their pain-filled dullness: they were now sharp and alert.

'I hope I do not inconvenience, sir?' he asked quietly, remaining in his seat.

'Not at all, dear fellow!' Kydd said warmly. 'Do alight – we've a guest room waiting. That is, if you're—'

'So kind in you, Sir Thomas. I only came to enquire if—'

'Nonsense! You shall stay a space and take glory in the Devonshire countryside with us.' He beckoned his estate steward. 'Appleby, a hand with Mr Craddock's trap.'

Later, with both settled in comfortable armchairs, Kydd heard of his long journey north to Manchester and reunion with his kindred for the first time in nine years. There had been astonishment and relief at his deliverance, shock and sorrow at his loss. As Kydd had guessed, a position had been suggested, a partnership in one of the family's Baltic concerns, but Craddock had declined it. 'You spurned the offer? I find that a singular decision, Mr Craddock.'

'Harry, please.'

'What will you now, then, Harry?'

'Should you still have need for a private secretary it would be my honour and pleasure to serve you again in that capacity.'

Kydd couldn't hold back a smile but quickly smothered it. 'Well, in all decency, I should point out that your prospects—'

'My dear sir, as to that, I took the precaution before leaving of making due enquiry of your inestimable first lieutenant, Mr Bowden.'

'Oh! What did he say about me, pray?'

'You have no more loyal and devoted officer on board the good ship *Tyger*. His assessment, however, was truthful and revealing, you may believe. He told me that your run as a frigate captain has been long and meritorious but must end at some point. Beyond that there is little likelihood of a ship, for even as a senior captain you have no interest at work for you in the Admiralty, and with the seas swept clean of Bonaparte's fleets, frigates are, these days, where distinction and prizes are won. My prospects therefore are slender.'

Kydd chose his words carefully. 'Mr Craddock – Harry. If it is your loyalty to me as your rescuer that impels you to make the offer, then do stand disabused. Your services while in the Adriatic have been a more than adequate return and—'

'Thomas . . . may I?'

'Certainly, old fellow,' Kydd said warmly.

'I know enough of your character to believe you would extend your kindness to any unfortunate you might find in my position and this is not the reason for my offer. It is that while in *Tyger* I found I took to the life – the direct speaking and mutual respect I saw among high and low in our little floating town, the consideration of one for another, the joining together in common purpose against the foe, the lack of dissembling. I confess myself in no haste to return to the usual run of shore folk.'

'Then you are right welcome to the post, dear fellow. But there is the matter of remuneration, your entitlement. The post is personal to me and is no concern or obligation upon the Navy Board to meet the expense and therefore I regret that—'

'My good sir, please accept that my motives for applying are not of the customary nature. While you have command of *Tyger* it will be my pleasure to continue upon the sea life, and when that is regrettably past, well, I shall then consult my situation. Meanwhile there are offices I can perform that I'm sanguine shall prove of utility to you more in a private capacity – as your man of business, might I be permitted to say, or perhaps by way of secretary-in-confidence.'

'This I can believe,' Kydd said, with feeling, 'but again, any fee associated—'

'There will be no fee. Only . . . the liberty of calling you my friend.'

'Harry – you have it.'

'Then if you'll allow me . . .'

Craddock was back promptly, bearing a crusted bottle. 'In Manchester there's a fine cellar for shining occasions and if this is not one then I fail to see what is. Shall we?'

Persephone, sensing a line had been crossed, joined them and together they toasted the hour in the finest Armagnac.

They heard more of Craddock's past and his departure from the family merchant-banking concern at the age of twenty to plough his own furrow in the rapidly emerging

markets of the Balkans. His adventures in the Barbary king-
doms of North Africa and the ancient cities of Turkey and
the Levant enthralled them . . . and then the advent of the
French revolutionaries.

# Chapter 3

The letter's superscription was very odd: 'Colonel Sir Thomas Kydd, Royal Navy'. Either it was the work of a madman or one so removed from the ways of the navy as to believe the captain of a ship was in fact a colonel. But it was elegant creamy paper, and when Kydd turned it over the seal was unmistakably that of the office of the first lord of the Admiralty.

He opened it carefully as Persephone looked on. This was indeed a mystery: the acidulous first secretary to the Admiralty, Croker, would never allow such a blunder in his office.

It quickly became clear. The missive was a note of congratulation from their lordships at his appointment as colonel of marines, a purely ceremonial position but one that indicated his standing after the action in the Adriatic. Enclosed was an invitation to a dinner in his honour at Mansion House from General Hoby, adjutant general, Royal Marines, and the most senior of that clan in the country.

'Ah. I cannot pretend but that this is well timed. *Tyger* is near complete of her repairs and – save your presence, my dear – I've a yen to take in a mort of sea air after all my pampering. This gives me a chance to make my number with the Admiralty that I'm now enabled to await their orders for sea.'

Lady Kydd, in respect of her condition, would remain at Knowle Manor, content to know that her husband was accompanied by his devoted valet, Tysoe, and Craddock, and would be back before long.

The dinner was a fine event, the guests mingling delightedly with the hero of the hour who, it was said, would be back to sea shortly.

Kydd's speech was well received and the largely professional gathering offered interesting conversation. At the brandy and cigars, he heard the views of the adjutant general that the supremacy of the navy at sea had made opportunities for the ambitious Royal Marines officer now scarce and exceptional. Across the table an army colonel pointed out that consolidating an empire consisted in the main of dusty parade-ground drills in far-flung territories while waiting for an enemy who never came. And this was without the consolation to be had by a Royal Marine in a ship making port back in England: he knew some troopers in India who'd been there continuously for above a dozen years.

Kydd was tempted to make the observation that much of the lack of career distinctions stemmed from the fact that, unlike the navy, whose ships were to be found across the entire globe, the only part of the world in which land forces could in any way be termed active was the Peninsula. There, Wellington had quartered his valuable battalions behind the invulnerable lines of the Torres Vedras, and was not seeking distinction in open battle.

At one point there was general puzzlement at the fuming of the Americans over some imagined slight to honour, but the consensus was that this would not be any cause for armed intervention, let alone war. More concerning was the effect of Bonaparte's Continental System in locking off his entire realm. From the Atlantic to the Baltic, the North Sea to the Mediterranean, trade of any kind with the British was forbidden. Britannia's funding of the war, however, had always been grounded on a healthy commerce with her traditional partners.

A single word could best describe the situation in which the world was finding itself after so many years of war: stalemate. Napoleon Bonaparte was confined to the Continent, raging like a lion in a cage, and, even with his giant armies, unable to break out. On the other hand, with command of the sea, Britain was helping herself to an empire – but was a helpless spectator to events in Europe. And at any point in these parlous times the state of affairs could worsen and plunge Britain headlong into catastrophe.

The conversations died. These conundrums had been chewed over endlessly in wardrooms and nothing had changed the essence of what lay behind them all. With Bonaparte victorious wherever on land he marched, it would be the continuation of a wearisome war as far ahead as any could foresee. Other topics were equally dismal: the bad harvests, economic dislocation from steam engines and such, and the growth, like cancer, of new industrial towns across ancient lands.

With the evening drawing to a close, Kydd made a light bow to General Hoby, gave his thanks for the dinner, and bade him farewell. Others too, rose, leaving him with Craddock, while he waited for his cloak and sword to depart. Craddock had proved the ideal companion: cultured, elegant and with exquisite manners, he'd allowed Kydd to hold forth while his restrained contributions were interesting and to the point.

It was after midnight but Kydd felt restless. 'Shall we call at my club for a snorter before we turn in? There's people I'd like you to meet, Harry.'

It was raining by the time they reached the smoke-grimed Portland stone edifice that was Brooks's Club and entered its august portals.

'Tiger, dear fellow!' one passing member called to him, beaming with pleasure. 'So good to see you unharmed by your late encounter.'

Kydd crossed to shake the prime minister's hand. 'Quite untouched, Grenville. But Craddock here has good enough reason to curse the French.'

After a polite exchange they found a pair of armchairs and prepared to appreciate a particularly flowery cognac, unperturbed by the joyous shouts from a nearby gambling room.

Kydd learned more of his new friend. A more than fair judge of a good brandy, his life at the convergence of the wine trades of France, Italy and the more sombre German vintages from the north had him well placed to advise Kydd on the stocking of his cellar at Knowle Manor. They were pondering what might best grace the cabin stores of *Tyger* when they noticed the raucous hullabaloo from the gamblers had died away. Suddenly a wash of voices sounded as a cluster of figures issued out, led by a plump gentleman in outlandishly extravagant costume waving a chicken leg. His florid features lit up with pleasure when he spied Kydd.

'Yo ho ho, and it's Tiger, as they're not wrong!' The chicken leg was flung aside as the Prince Regent of Great Britain and Ireland advanced to greet him.

'Your Royal Highness,' Kydd replied, rising quickly and bowing.

'A right fine drubbing, I heard.'

'We gave 'em pause to regret their impudence, I believe, sir.' It had not been so long before that he'd made acquaintance of the mercurial prince, who'd been taken with what he saw as Kydd's salty and direct ways. After the illness of his father, the King, he'd become regent and the highest in the kingdom.

'Might I present to you Mr Lucius Craddock, sir – he it was I rescued from the Adriatic in particularly distressing circumstances and now swears to serve me as long as he may.'

'Craddock.' There was a keen look of appraisal and the gaze shifted quickly back to Kydd. 'Do I hear their lordships have rendered their appreciation in proper manner?'

'I believe they have, sir. Know that I'm now not only a baronet but a colonel in the Royal Marines.'

'A colonel only?' The eyebrows contracted in vexation. 'Surely to be raised to a general is more to be expected.'

'It's all I might ask at my humble station,' Kydd said modestly.

'Nonsense! Still in your old ship? A species of frigate, isn't she?'

'Yes, sir.'

'There you are, then! The rascals should give you a ship worthy of your deeds, Tiger! A big one! If you can smite the tyrant with a tiddler, then what commotion can you not stir up with a ship o' size?'

'No, no, sir,' Kydd said hastily. 'Believe that I'm most content with my brave barky.'

'Ha! They'll be taking care of their favourites, I'll be bound. Well, this is to say they picked a wrong 'un in me, dammit. I'll see you into one of 'em, never doubt it.'

Alarmed, Kydd blurted, 'Sir, I'm happy with my present command, you must accept. I'm—'

'Rubbish, Tiger! I'm not accounted king-in-waiting for

nothing. Leave it to me. Should I have to sink the whole pootling crew you'll have your mighty ship-o'-war. Trust me!'

Lost for words Kydd could only bow deeply.

'Have to go now, Tiger. Five hundred on the table and I'm down a gallows deal more. But I won't forget, you may depend on it.'

# Chapter 4

*Plymouth Hoe, Devon*

The vantage point overlooking the harbour was always at its best in the warmth of early summer, with couples promenading arm in arm, children playing, and old folk taking the sun, enjoying their view over a glittering sea where so much of England's history had unfolded.

Kydd had come to these grassy slopes in times past to ease his spirits and today was no exception. While Persephone and their cook, Mrs Appleby, took to the shops he paced along as if it were a quarterdeck before an action that demanded thought above the usual.

The Prince Regent had not forgotten. Just when Kydd had believed himself safe, a terse Admiralty letter had arrived, couched in words almost rude in their abruptness. He was forthwith relieved of the command of HM Frigate *Tyger* in favour of the officer named, to take effect on the date specified, some four days later. No mention of why or honeyed phrases of duty done, or any reference to a ship-of-the-line or, in fact, any further employment. It was personally signed by Yorke, first lord of the Admiralty, and therefore it was useless to complain or appeal. No other communication had been forthcoming. He was grounded solidly 'on the beach' with no ship and no prospect of one.

Was this a political gesture, a spiteful lashing out by Admiral Sidney Smith after his role in putting down the Sicilian plot had been overshadowed by Kydd's victory at Lissa? Probably not. The eccentric had lost most of his friends and influence in high places. Another? There were plenty of serving admirals envious of his fame and willing to take steps to bring this to an ignominious end but they would need extraordinary influence to persuade the strait-laced Yorke.

In the Plymouth port admiral's office Kydd had found they'd already been duly informed, and were preparing to continue the commission of the famous frigate under her new captain with never a blink of an eye to show they'd noticed the change.

It had all the hallmarks of an Admiralty affronted by what they would have seen as Kydd's blatant attempt to claw his way to the quarterdeck of a ship-of-the-line by invoking interest at an incontestable level, the Prince Regent of Great Britain. This would explain what amounted to his near-instant dismissal from *Tyger* and silence on the subject of any other command. And it would be an unanswerable reply to the interfering prince that no ship of a kind suitable for his hero was available at the present time, with the unspoken reality that there never would be.

In something between grief and panic he'd come to realise that his sea career was over. Even the days left to him in the ship he'd taken from mutiny to triumph were to be spent in a dockyard under repair, after which he must finally retire with his memories to the land. It was unbearable to know that the heave of a deck under his feet and the majesty of the deep-sea realm in all its mystery and allure were now firmly rooted in the past.

He'd thought about coming out fighting, harnessing the public respect and admiration so gratifyingly on show recently, not to mention the well of professional esteem he'd earned among his peers. The urge was savage and primeval but doomed. He had no highly placed friends who were in a position within the Admiralty to spearhead a fight-back in a public spectacle that would put their own promotions in jeopardy. Without someone to speak up for him in the councils of the great, things must inevitably take their course.

He'd quietly revealed the situation to Bowden, who after recovering, suggested taking *Tyger* to sea, her repairs so near complete, and rejoin in the Mediterranean as though the letter had arrived too late. But Kydd's visit to the port admiral's office would prove he'd taken receipt.

A stunned, shocked silence had descended on the ship and then a growing hubbub. Before long a stream of petitioners was knocking at his door. They were all after the same thing, something it was not in his power to grant, a circumstance that wrung him with misery for its being so doubly unjust. The sailing master, Joyce, with his peg-leg; Lieutenant Brice, now so firmly on the rung of advancement; gunner's mate Stirk, and his shipmates who'd been with Kydd since his own fore-mast days; Boatswain Herne, now grey and with the dignity of age, whom Kydd had seen climb *Tyger*'s rigging at Lissa in a storm of fire and shot. And the two midshipmen, bewildered and cast down, looking to find that what they'd heard wasn't so.

All had come to be recognised as a follower. It was a humane and effective gesture, the understanding that men long-serving under a captain they trusted would go on to form the core of an efficient and loyal ship's company in another ship. Any number of valued hands recognised as followers could go with their captain in this way, even up to an entire complement.

But there was a hard and fast rule that the procedure could not be considered a move but more in the nature of an exchange. For every follower going into a ship, that captain must provide a replacement crew member from the new ship to go back to the old. But Kydd did not have a new ship – and therefore no followers could be allowed him. *Tyger* would put to sea under her new captain with her company unchanged. The crew Kydd had forged from dishonour through uncountable perils of sea and enemy to form a ferocious instrument of war would be his to care for and lead in all *Tyger*'s adventures to come.

The relieving captain, Faulknor, had arrived promptly, accepting Kydd's distant welcome with ill-disguised delight, his translation from a workaday frigate in the North Sea Squadron to command of the most famous frigate of the day as sudden and unexpected as Kydd's loss of it. He'd gone through the necessary musters and handover routines as rapidly as was decently possible, clearly in awe of his situation but a seasoned captain himself, nevertheless wary and correct.

He'd been given the honour at the farewell dinner of sitting on Kydd's right hand, the familiar faces on either side pale, unbelieving. The meal passed off heavily, jokes of the usual kind falling flat for no one could put a reason to the extraordinary events, still less account for their legendary captain's lack of a future. Their parting gift – a silver hunter – was handed to him with a mumbled valediction. His reply was equally stilted. And then it was over.

Persephone had not attended, unable to face being witness

to Kydd's grief, but she was there by the dockyard landing the next day when *Tyger*'s officers and warrant officers had pulled Kydd ashore in his barge. She caught sight of tears in the eyes of more than one as they glided in to the jetty with a final toss of the oars, captain's coxswain Halgren making a faultless alongside, the last thing he could do for his captain.

All stood, removing their hats and standing motionless as Kydd stumbled away, up and around the corner where he broke down in her arms.

His last ties with the past were severed later that day when his effects were landed, and he'd asked Tysoe for his advice on their storage. His faithful manservant then asked that after these many years he be given release from service. Kydd had sadly agreed, promising an annuity for his loyal devotion that would allow him to see out his years in comfort back in Jamaica.

He hadn't the heart to go to London to petition for a ship, as he had those years ago, and instead sent a pleading letter asking that his recent service to the Crown be recognised with another command, but he held out little expectation.

And then, from this summer vista, he saw the saddest sight imaginable. To the right, emerging from the Hamoaze, instantly recognisable to any who knew her, was *Tyger*. Outward bound for Bermuda.

He gulped and watched for the hours it took in the light airs to dip her topgallants beneath the horizon, once staying about for the run to the Atlantic – was that a sadly clumsy mainsail haul? Probably Faulknor taking his time in a ship new to him. In her, men were securing for sea, the first dog-watchmen would be closing up, and in the first heaves of an open-ocean swell, the gunroom preparing for supper.

# Chapter 5

Less than a week later Kydd heard again from their lord-ships, a remarkably short time in the Admiralty's universe.

He'd lost his dear *Tyger*, his frigate and his being, but incredibly he was not to be cast ashore. Despite all his fears a no-doubt-reluctant Admiralty had found him a ship. And not any ship but the one that was most certainly needed on the long and stony path to admiral – a battleship!

These behemoths were at the pinnacle of naval command. Standing in the line-of-battle to withstand the worst the enemy could throw against them, they were the true wooden walls of England, and every action they fought would resound down the ages. In foreign parts the battleship was an unanswerable demonstration of the might of the Royal Navy to all who dared try to wrest sovereignty of the seas from Great Britain.

The captain of such a ship was a hallowed being, privy to plots and strategies at the highest, attended by ceremony and arcane prostrations. Above all, he stood alone as its lord and master, overseer of the greatest artillery batteries to be found on any battlefield, the monster guns carried on several gun-decks fore and aft in dreadful array. He, Tom Kydd, wigmaker of Guildford, had achieved the peak of naval command: a ship-of-the-line.

He clutched the paper for long minutes, gripped by the moment. Then stark reality set in. The cold distancing of Yorke and the absence of platitudes showed that the Admiralty had been compelled to concede to the Prince Regent's desire. The enjoinder that he should take command of HMS *Thunderer*, 74, was a skilful move. She was old. In fact she'd been with the fleet since before the French wars had begun in 1793. Kydd knew that she'd seen blockade duty off the French coast for years and would probably be weary, dispirited and drab. Neatly, the Admiralty were ensuring that the dashing frigate captain of popular imagination was getting the 'promotion' he deserved, a battleship, but at the same time ensuring he could never again range the ocean as a free spirit, or fly at a moment's notice to some distant sea to win yet more laurels in lonely splendour.

Now it was to be part of a standing fleet, with all others around him under the eye and direction of an admiral or commander-in-chief whose desires it was his to concern himself with, whose orders took supremacy over all others. Even to the fundamentals of how to fight – the hallowed Fighting Instructions that governed everything from in what manner to alter course as a line, to the details of signal procedures. There was no more room for initiative, for on-the-spot risk-taking, for daring thrusts deep into enemy waters, simply the duty to exist and thereby contain the enemy.

The chances of fame and distinction were swallowed in being only one of a larger whole, saving that if it came to a mighty fleet action it would be another matter entirely. But the likelihood of such a glorious clash was unlikely, given Bonaparte's reluctance to risk another Trafalgar. Kydd's fate, therefore, was precisely what was wanted: to slide swiftly and gracefully into obscurity with an equally rapid fading from the public consciousness.

It didn't have to be that way. At the moment he was the lauded victor of Lissa, one of the shining band of frigate captains who had made a name for themselves throughout the land. Why should he not now rest on his fame, graciously accept the plaudits and slip into history as one of the select band of immortals who had won imperishable glory on the quarterdeck of his own ship?

To continue in a ship-of-the-line would gain him little more and would have its own risk. The more he considered the situation, the bleaker he felt. He knew he was a natural frigate seaman with the qualities, professional and personal, that were required for such a command. Quite different and equally demanding qualities were needed for a sail-of-the-line: the possession of diplomacy, a cooler head and broader perspectives. What if he didn't have them, if in one or more he proved lacking, leading to a blunder of significance in the larger picture? Offending an ally, failing to see a strategical objective above a tactical, misreading a move by the commander-in-chief at the wrong time? Whatever else, he would be thought unfit for the position and honour of captain of a ship-of-the-line, a failure, and would be quietly retired.

It had happened to others, generally accepted as not their particular fault but rather an unfortunate lack in the requisite skills at that level. But, still, accounted a failure, never to be employed at sea again.

Better he didn't take the risk.

And there was the realisation that he was no longer making decisions for himself, or even for Persephone, but for his unborn child. Would it grow up in adulation for the father

24

who had won such renown in his trusty frigate or would it look upon one known as a hero in a small ship but a derisory failure in a more powerful one?

However, there was a passing but definite possibility he could one day become an admiral. Some with origins before the mast had already achieved this: Captain Cook, Benbow, Mitchell – even the notorious Bligh. Should he throw away any chance he had for fear of failing?

Command of a ship-of-the-line was a necessary milestone on the way. Therefore it all reduced to a simple question: did he want to become an admiral badly enough to risk every-thing?

Craddock's view was that, in his ignorance of the politics of what was happening, anything he could contribute might be misleading. But Persephone was of one mind: 'Dearest Thomas – know that I'd infinitely rather be married to one who reaches for the stars and falls than one who never tries for fret of disappointment.'

He'd take the gamble.

# Chapter 6

When HMS *Thunderer* put into Plymouth Sound, Kydd was at Knowle Manor bearing a hand with the glassing in of the orangery.

A message came from the dockyard informing him that the vessel was moored in Cawsand Bay, the usual anchorage for the bigger ships touching port only. His orders required him to assume command at once, wasting no time to rejoin the blockade squadron off Brest.

Early the next day, he took leave of Persephone and told Craddock he would send for him when the time was suitable. All his anxious fretting, his thoughts and worry over the weeks were now to become reality. He was about to step forward to claim his ship, his destiny.

Kydd had never served in a 74, apart from the ancient *Trajan* out in the Caribbean and that had been as a humble able seaman. Others he'd seen only from afar. He felt a surge of tension at the sight of the bulk and majesty of a full-blooded man-o'-war of the breed as the dockyard hoy rounded Picklecombe Point to open the broad bay. *Thunderer* was lying to a single bower anchor, her black hull relieved only by the line of a varnished wale along each gun-deck, enabling closed gun-ports with their black outside to reveal the fearsome 'Nelson chequer' now almost universally adopted by the fleet.

Her masts were varnished, her spars black and her sails entirely struck. He was curious to see whether, after some hours at anchor, her shrouds had been set up properly with no unsightly bights, the yards squared across and no Irish pennants showing from aloft. There were no concerns there – the first lieutenant and boatswain were doing their jobs – but he'd seen something else.

'Take me around, just the once,' he asked, slipping across a coin, his eyes fixed on the big ship. The lower gun-ports had nettings rigged below them and he watched as a long-boat emerged under her stern: *Thunderer* was taking precautions against desertion. Probably a wise measure, but was this notice of what awaited him after the indulgence of a crack frigate with an all-volunteer crew?

He saw as well, with a stab of pleasure, the massive two tiers of stern windows denoting a 74-gun ship. The upper one, his, had the traditional open captain's walk. And as they rounded the stern closer to, he took in the elaborate and ornate carving, particularly in the supports to the quarter gallery. She'd been constructed before the war when the old eighteenth-century decorative practices had not given way to the plain austerity of wartime builds. In fact, this captain had gone to some lengths to maintain her looks with gilding and point-work in red, green and white on varnish, these days an unusual and pleasing sight.

At her bows was the figurehead, a fierce Jove with a quiver of thunderbolts, one of which he was hurling at the imaginary enemy ahead. It was full-size and extended from the elaborate scroll-work at the beakhead nearly down to the waterline at her forefoot. She might be elderly but was far from drab, and Kydd's spirits rose.

'Take us in.'

As Kydd was in plain clothes in deference to a possibly undistinguished commander, it was necessary to hail the quarterdeck. After a discreet pause, they hooked on at the main chains and Kydd hauled himself aboard briskly. Stepping over the bulwark to the wailing of a single pipe he instantly saw there was no side-party, or welcoming group of officers. Around the deck men stopped what they were doing to stare. No doubt they knew who he was but were making no effort. This was the bare minimum ceremony entitlement for any naval officer.

In a sea-worn uniform an officer stepped over to greet him. Older and of slender build, the man's hard face was set. 'Captain Lyell, *Thunderer*,' he snapped, offering a brief handshake. 'Captain Kydd?'

Something in Kydd rebelled. 'Sir Thomas Kydd, late *Tyger*, frigate.'

'But not her captain at this time.'

'No.'

'Which is why you're greeted in the proper form.' The voice was husky, the manner almost aggressive.

Kydd was taken aback at the man's hostility. Some on deck had not moved since he'd come aboard, agog at the exchange. What was going on?

'Come to take the ship,' Lyell continued darkly.

'Er, my orders are—'

'Shall we step aft?'

Kydd took in that *Thunderer* was in a remarkable state of neatness and fastidious attention. This was a captain who cared for his ship. Unlike a frigate, in a ship-of-the-line the captain's quarters were situated aft on the quarterdeck, forming a poop-deck above for the handling of sail and signals. In this ship its entry was in gleaming dark wood – not stained and varnished but French-polished to a lustrous gleam, as was the interior.

Two chairs were set out beyond the table and, without taking his eyes off Kydd, Lyell sat in one with a brief gesture to Kydd to take the other.

A steward hovered but was brusquely dismissed, and the old captain impatiently leaned forward. 'Sir, allow me to make my position clear beyond any misunderstanding.'

Kydd was puzzled, unable to account for his attitude.

'I believe your actions, sir, are those of a poltroon and unworthy of any in His Majesty's Navy who desires to be known as a sea officer and gentleman.'

Kydd swallowed. 'I beg your pardon?'

'Interests and patronage are not unknown in the service but to seek to further your position by currying favour at court before all others is – is . . .'

So that was it. 'Sir. I'll have you know that it was neither my wish nor my supplication that impelled the Prince Regent to act as he did, which was prompted only by an incident that brought us together in the past. At no point did I attempt to—'

'Do spare me your justifications and excuses, sir. I have a duty laid upon me to yield command of *Thunderer* to you and I shall faithfully carry it out. Do you choose to begin the handover now?'

So Lyell was to be counted among those who believed he was thick with Prinny, the notorious rake now in effect wearing the Crown of Great Britain. Yet at the same time it didn't explain the bitterness, the personal animosity.

'I do. Your books of account, sir?'

'Mr Allen!' Lyell barked. A man in old-fashioned black

coat, breeches and spectacles entered gingerly, clearly primed for business. 'Monthly muster.'

Kydd knew that more naval officers had ended their careers running a-foul of the Navy Board in respect of their accounts than ever suffered from shipwreck and had made it his business to be acquainted with each one. 'I always find the open list to be more useful, don't you?' he came back. This was the original from which the muster-clerk received his information.

Lyell glowered, but nodded to the man.

Then followed the usual general accounts, slop book, sick book and others. There were also the more arcane ones – the latest report of surveys of provisions, an account of casks shaken, backstays shifted, and the all-important purser's certificate. There were so many ways to falsify and cheat, but Kydd made a show of inspecting vouchers and returns, receipts and expenses, knowing, however, that to do a proper job it would be necessary to match them with their accounting in the books, an impossibly lengthy task.

'Very good,' he said at last. He couldn't spot any shortcomings and was prepared to sign for these. Next would be the higher level: the order book, which listed every written order either issued by this captain to one under him or received from those above him. Then there were the letter books, copies of every communication entering or leaving the ship and giving a priceless picture of the efficiency or otherwise of the ship in staying on top of the ebb and flow of events of every kind. With the return of sailing qualities and the ship's log to date in the commission with various remarks and notes they would form Kydd's reading for the foreseeable future.

'The standing officers?' These were warrant officers who remained in the ship even when out of commission.

Boatswain, gunner, carpenter, each with a little empire down in the orlop and having within his charge stores worth a substantial amount and needing meticulous accounting – and for which he himself was ultimately responsible.

Their books were found and slapped down before Kydd, who was conscious of Lyell's smouldering resentment. He nevertheless took his time, sighting pages at random to check for consistency, for diligent and regular entries. They seemed in order but only a formal muster would establish their veracity.

The morning was wearing on but Lyell gave no indication of wanting to call a spell in their pains. It wasn't until the hands were piped to their noon meal that a natural break was offered. It gave Kydd a chance to look surreptitiously around the great cabin and take in where he would have his being in the future. It was of impressive size, with a stateliness in keeping with the ship, which he noticed was quite unmoving in the slight chop in the bay that would have had his frigate snubbing restlessly at her anchor. Around the walls the paintings, miniatures and wistful sea vistas spoke, in their amateurishness, of a loving hand. There was no requirement to step around furniture as was necessary in *Tyger*. The chairs, table and fitments were tasteful but neither extravagant nor out of keeping with the dignified age of *Thunderer*. However, there was no going over to explore the stern walk or the size of the bed-place.

'She's sea kindly?' Kydd asked.

'Your sea qualities are there. The first lieutenant will offer an opinion and the sailing master will give you his views at a later time,' Lyell said stiffly. 'You'll pardon, but I've much to attend to. I take it you're satisfied in the article of accounts?'

'I'd like to take a sight of the condition of the standing

rigging, if you please.' It would give him more than a few clues about how *Thunderer* was keeping the seas.

'You may, but not in my company. As I mentioned before, my time is spoken for, sir.'

'Then I'd like to speak with your officers in turn if this does not inconvenience.'

'It does. Their services I will require until I quit the ship.'

Kydd bit back a response to this pettiness, then asked, 'And when will that be, Captain?'

There was a deliberate pause. 'I will land at eleven forenoon the day following tomorrow.'

'And until then?'

'No doubt I will pass you when you board after that time.' Still the malice, hostility.

The formalities of a handover were largely completed. It might have been a congenial time to chat together over old times and adventures in *Thunderer*, but Kydd was being banished from the ship until the very last moment.

# Chapter 7

Two days later Kydd arrived at the Stonehouse steps, within sight of Barn Pool over the Hamoaze. It seemed so long ago that he'd moored his first command there, the little brig-sloop *Teazer*. Now he was about to take charge of one of the grand line-of-battle ships that had so often passed him in stately array without even noticing him.

Dressed in full fig, sword, knightly sash and star, he ignored the stares of passing seamen and dockyard workers. Senior officers were normally accompanied by their retinue of lieutenants, coxswain and others, but he was standing alone.

From Stonehouse Kydd couldn't see *Thunderer* moored past Mount Edgcumbe. He could only assume Lyell would leave at eleven but it was probable he'd land here, relatively private compared to the busy Millbay docks.

At a little over half past the hour a boat rounded Devil's Point with a naval officer visible in its stern sheets. It was Lyell, but the boat was a wherry, not a ship's boat, let alone a captain's barge.

Kydd fell back to allow Lyell to step out. The man affected not to notice him, paying off the waterman. With none to meet him, he stalked, face set, past Kydd without a single backward glance.

The wherry lost no time in taking Kydd aboard. 'Busy time f'r *Thunderer*, this forenoon,' the man at the oars said gruffly, watching Lyell with his eyebrows raised. 'Had his gear shifted earlier. Yez wants a boat for your'n, y'r honour?'

'No, thank you,' Kydd replied. That would be the job of a ship's boat. Settling down aft, he casually swept aside his cloak to allow his uniform insignia to be clearly visible. This time, there would be no ignoring who he was.

In mounting excitement, and with not a little trepidation, his eyes sought out the vision of his ship past the undistinguished point, his command. It would either make his career or break him. But, whatever the future held, there was no robbing the moment of its dignity, its consequence in his life. A battleship: his to reign over from the breathtaking and solitary height of senior post-captain.

And there she was! A massive, almost monumental sight, the sunshine picking out the gold leaf and rosin-enriched varnish, and the lazy swirl of her ensign aft and jack forward, both larger than whole sails in *Tyger*.

'Lay alongside,' he ordered, making an effort to bring his features to an appropriate severity. In the splendour of his full-dress uniform he came up the side, met once again by a single boatswain's call and no side-party. He was still not a captain until he'd read himself in, declared publicly the contents of his commission, whose parchment crackled reassuringly at his breast.

A group of officers waited on the other side of the deck, watching him carefully. Punctiliously, Kydd doffed his cocked hat aft in recognition of the quarterdeck and again to the officers, who returned the gesture. One detached from the group. 'Roscoe, first lieutenant,' he growled, with a brief bow.

The single most important person to Kydd in *Thunderer*'s company. A surprisingly young individual, but with hard, direct eyes and a well-toned body.

'Captain Sir Thomas Kydd. Appointed captain of this vessel. If you'll clear lower deck of the hands, Mr Roscoe?'

Kydd kept to himself, pacing slowly and expressionless while first one, then several boatswain's calls pealed out, fore and aft and at the hatchways, summoning *Thunderer*'s company to the upper decks to meet their captain.

As they mustered, a sea of men looked aft, every one a stranger, yet still an individual, possessing character and skills that on blockade he would have ample time to get to know. Some were blank-faced, others suspicious. A few showed frank curiosity. They would inhabit the same circumscribed sea world as he, would follow him into action or . . .

'Ship's company mustered, sir.'

There was nothing to be learned from Roscoe's neutral growl and Kydd drew out his commission. In a measured bellow he announced to the silent mass that he was appointed by the Admiralty to rule over them as lord and master with powers not to be seen outside an Oriental despot's realm. His very word would send them against slashing blade and roar of cannon. And under the Articles of War he could punish or court-martial any as he chose.

'Carry on, please.'

'Aye aye, sir.' Still the hard-featured, expressionless restraint from his chief lieutenant. But he was captain now and he'd make it his business to discover what ailed the man.

'I'll be aft and I desire that each of my officers in turn will present himself to me privately, yourself in ten minutes. We have five officers?'

'Four.'

* * *

35

The great cabin was near stripped of living appointments. All but the cabin-width table, one lonely upright chair and a nondescript armchair were left, the deck exposed with its black and white chequer and all lanthorns removed. Kydd burned with resentment. The least Lyell could have done was give warning of his small-minded action.

He flicked open the door to the bed-place. It was of princely size and he remembered that in a ship-of-the-line he should call it a stateroom. At least a cot was hanging there, though without any bedding, and a large chest with drawers dominated the forward bulkhead. Apart from that, the wash-place beyond was bare of basin, jugs and the usual gear. In its emptiness the compartment seemed filled with the lethal blackness of the two guns standing out in stark solidity, with which he would be sharing his sleeping space.

Furious, Kydd whirled about and went to the after end of the great cabin, to a pleasing decorative and well-lit screen with a door to each side. He opened one, stepping out into the six-foot recess of his stern walk and an outstanding view of the open sea and the shoreline. A warm early-summer breeze wafted in and he felt better, even as the row-guard boat slid into his vision below, progressing languidly past. He let the prospect enter his soul for a few minutes, then went back inside. A wave of desolation returned, and with it, the bleak realisation that he knew not a single person aboard. Not even a Tysoe: if Lyell had left his manservant he would certainly have been awaiting Kydd. As it was, even if he sent for his baggage there would be none to stow it and settle him in. Until he got a measure of *Thunderer* and her company he must take care of himself.

Laying his cloak, cocked hat and sword on the cot he prepared to receive his first visitor.

The knocks on the door were firm and just two in number.

'Come!'

Roscoe entered, his hat under his arm. Undeniably hand-some, dark hair in curls but swept to a discreet queue, he carried himself lithely and with presence.

'Do be seated, Lieutenant,' Kydd said mildly, indicating the upright chair. He was sitting in the armchair – awkwardly, for it was too small for his broad frame.

His first lieutenant's expression was difficult to make out – if anything there was a touch of defiance.

'You've seen some sea time, I'd say.'

'Sir.'

'Well?'

'Midshipman in *Indefatigable* 44, Captain Pellew. *Barfleur* 90, Captain Elphinstone. Fifth lieutenant in the same, fourth into *Canopus* 80, Captain James.' As though apologising he went on, 'And lieutenant into *Raven* brig-sloop, before making third into *Thunderer* in 1804, where I remained until made first in 1810.'

There was interest at work here. All except *Raven* were well known for active and distinguished service under pre-eminent captains. It was curious that he'd not claimed participation in any famous action. And that he'd served so long in *Thunderer*: there'd been fine captains and actions in that time, including Calder's before Trafalgar, then the great battle itself, and more since, such as the Dardanelles expedition, with the fiery Talbot in command.

What it added up to was disquieting. This long-serving *Thunderer* lieutenant had achieved the pinnacle – premier of a ship-of-the-line – and could expect advancement in the wake of his captain's elevation. Why was he not a follower? Not up to the job? Come to think of it, none of the other officers had moved along with the old captain into his new appointment. Had there been bad blood?

'You had no inclination to follow Captain Lyell, I take it,' Kydd said evenly.

There was a flash almost of contempt, which he let go without comment and waited for his reply.

'You don't know Captain Lyell.' The tone was flat, disdainful.

'No.'

'May I speak freely?'

'As it shall be respectful to your captain, Mr Roscoe.' The lack of even one 'sir' and the sullen mood grated on Kydd.

'Then know that, through no fault of his, Captain Lyell has been denied an action of distinction these last two years he's been in command of this ship. Instead of abandoning ambition and hope, he resolved to bring her to the forefront, the best and brightest in the squadron even as the old lady is one of many years and scars. He's a fine captain and I for one doff my hat to him.'

'But not to follow . . .'

Roscoe breathed deeply, his nostrils flaring. 'You said as I might speak freely. I will. His reward for these years? Their lordships gave him two weeks to be off the ship, that a favourite at court might be obliged.'

Kydd's lips thinned dangerously. 'I'd put a reef in your tongue if I were you, sir.'

'Not until I've said my piece. He's gone now – but not to a ship as we can therefore be followers. He has nothing. He goes to half-pay, and without patronage, no expectation of ever getting to sea again. No estate, no fortune – his wife in her grave these last seven years. He's to live with his sisters, all hope gone now. And . . . and all to—'

'Enough,' Kydd snarled, leaning forward. 'Stow your jabber! As a first luff your judgement's all to hooey. Have you thought that as owner of a first-rank fighting frigate it was my idea to be thrown into a scowbunking blockader near as old as I am?'

He regretted it immediately but it was too late. He tried to make amends. 'She's a grand old thing, I grant you, but I hail from a different breed entirely. A frigate!'

That didn't help matters. The real problem was that Lyell had not gone on to promotion as flag-captain or even the captain of a first-rate under an admiral and taken all his followers, including Roscoe, with him. For their loyalty to the old captain, they were now stranded in the ship in which they'd spent years serving in the trust that when Lyell moved up so would they.

Roscoe, sitting bolt upright heard him out, then sank back slowly. 'A frigate. Ah, yes – and if you think your ways are ours, then I pity us all.'

'I find your attitude, sir, impolite, disrespectful and unacceptable in a first lieutenant,' Kydd rapped. 'I'll ignore it the once, given your . . . disappointments. I won't tolerate it further – understand?'

'Sir.'

'And if you so wish it, I shall make it my business to allow you to make your departure from this ship as soon as you may.' He didn't know if he had the power to do this, but if Roscoe had such strong feelings that he'd behave so before a new captain it would be better for both of them if he went.

The eyes flickered but there was no other response.

'In that case you may remain in post – but only as you deserve it. The efficiency and well-being of this ship as part of the squadron off Brest is my prime objective and you, as my right-hand man, are crucial in this. If you fail, I will have no regrets in having you removed. After I see the last officer we shall meet again, when you'll inform me of the state of the ship, its manning and immediate needs. You may go.' Roscoe rose with exaggerated dignity, gave a short bow and made to leave.

'Oh, and send a boat to bring off my baggage, if you please.'

It contained his clothing, writing materials, undress uniform, items of personal grooming. As a matter of priority he had to find another Tysoe, but from where was not immediately evident. Nor was it clear how, before they sailed, he would find time to go ashore and collect items to furnish his living spaces.

After Roscoe had gone he leaned back in his chair. In a way the man had reason to resent Kydd's presence. The perceived court-dictated imposition on *Thunderer* had caused a stumbling block to promotions. And the superseding of Lyell had produced an injustice Kydd regretted, particularly after his own recent fear that he was about to share the same fate.

'Smale, sir. Second luff.'

Kydd hadn't heard the knock and the apologetic voice that announced the second lieutenant. 'Enter.'

A shorter, affable individual came in to present himself. Fair-haired, running a little to corpulence, his air of confidence heartened Kydd, who noted the faultlessly turned-out uniform and lace cuffs that reminded him of Lieutenant Dacres in his first command, *Teazer*.

'I'll know your sea experience, sir.'

'Oh. Joined up as mid in 1801 in the old *Theseus* under Bligh the Second and saw out the rest of the war in *Blackbird*, cutter. After Amiens it was . . .'

Kydd heard it through, a pedestrian career considerably helped along by Earl St Vincent in whose eyes, it seemed,

Smale could do no wrong. This Bligh was the second in the Navy List – perhaps six by that name were serving at the moment.

At the end Kydd asked, curious, 'Tell me, do you get along well with the first lieutenant, Mr Smale?'

Taken by surprise he hesitated. 'Oh, well, yes, I suppose so.'

'Does this mean you agree that Captain Lyell was ill-served by my appointing to *Thunderer*?'

Smale stared at him. 'Er, these things happen, um, as the needs and conditions of service demand.'

Kydd had his judgement of the man. He would trim to the wind wherever it blew. The man was well connected, a safeguard against unfortunate circumstances, so it was easy to gauge his motives.

'Do ask the third to attend me.'

Briggs was different again. Wary but controlled, he answered Kydd's questions carefully and with due thought. Again, long service in *Thunderer*. Something about his bearing, though, reached out to Kydd. Was it because of the cruel twist that had had him as passed lieutenant caught by the peace of Amiens and cast out of his ship still a midshipman? A harsh fate without even the half-pay that came with confirmation in the rank. He'd dealt with that by shipping out as able seaman in a merchantman to Canada and there, ironically, had been press-ganged by a brig-sloop at the sudden outbreak of the war with Napoleon.

He'd been aboard until, as invasion loomed, the ship had been recalled to England where the commander of the sloop, recognising his worth and qualifications, had set him on the quarterdeck as a midshipman once more. Moving quickly, he'd been confirmed as lieutenant and seen a thankless existence on the Toulon blockade. A wounding at Cagliari had had the inevitable effect of delaying his further progress through the ranks. He'd been in the ship some three years now.

*Thunderer*'s fourth lieutenant, Mayne, was, again, different from the others. Fair-haired and of slight build, his was a recent appointment as midshipman from another sail-of-the-line in the same squadron. He had an air of resentment, no pressing desire to shine at this, the start of his presumably chosen course in life. Answering in monosyllables, sometimes averting his gaze, he gave Kydd no cause for confidence in him as an officer.

Contradicting what he'd told the first lieutenant, he decided next to make acquaintance with the warrant officers. These would be of long service, and he must rely on them to maintain and operate *Thunderer* as a ship of war, able to stand effectively in the line of battle.

The boatswain, Opie, was one of the old breed of seamen, lined but muscular, holding himself obstinately, challenging almost, his voice powerful and deep. Kydd suspected he'd be barely literate but would stand for nothing and be obeyed instantly. He need have no uneasiness about this man.

Sailing Master Hobbs was probably the oldest man in the ship. His service was long and varied. From a fore-and-aft rigged cutter through a stint in the Transport Service and surveying under the legendary Hurd, he'd been seeing out what was assumed to be his last active sea post in *Thunderer*. Kydd knew the type – utterly reliable and knowledgeable. At the same time he would not be a risk-taker, his comfort in retirement his to wreck.

Another of the old school was *Thunderer*'s gunner, Lawlor. Unsmiling and deliberate, he chose his words with care. Just what was needed in one who was to take charge of whole decks of guns, the largest in the navy, with magazines fore and aft that could, in a fraction of a second's carelessness, detonate the ship and everyone aboard. His responsibilities were also the custody and accounting of stores in value many times a sailor's wages for life.

The carpenter, Upcot, a garrulous and fidgety man, did not stay long. He lived among his workshop and stores right forward in the bows deep in the orlop, and Kydd would seldom see him.

It was a different story with Sadler, the surgeon. Supercilious and aloof, he seemed to think his time in *Thunderer* was a penance for some medical sin and his patients a lower form of life. Should *Thunderer* ever be caught up in a fleet action Kydd could only pity those who went under his knife.

'Sir – sir!' A face peered around the door.

'Who are you, pray?' The individual had what appeared to be a permanent frown of agitation but his dress was that of an officer.

'Gubb, Sir Thomas, Jonathan Gubb, purser of this ship.' The recently promulgated uniform regulations bestowed a new respectability on the breed.

'Do you require to see me?'

'At your earliest convenience, Sir Thomas.'

'Very well, Mr Gubb. I'll send for you before the end of day.' A thought struck. 'As you may have noticed, I have no manservant or other. Can you oblige with a recommendation?'

'Um, this is an unusual request, sir, but I'll do my best.'

'And another thing. Later I shall need a sighting of the ship's books. Do tell the ship's clerk to oblige me.'

'Mr Allen? I'm afraid he's no longer with us, sir.'

'Not in the ship?' Kydd was astonished. 'But the regulations clearly state that—'

'Yes, sir. That all ship's books shall remain with the ship in the event of a change in command. The books are here, sir, but the clerk is not.'

'Then how the devil can I—'

'Discharged sick to Stonehouse hospital. By order Captain Lyell,' the purser said woodenly.

Had Lyell engineered his removal in pique?

To prepare to sail soon for the French coast Kydd needed an up-to-date state-and-condition of the ship, account of provisions and so forth to give him a picture of her sea endurance. He'd signed for them, but this was to their existence, not contents. Dillon would have had these unobtrusively out and available to him but he didn't have Dillon any more.

He swore, then remembered himself and dismissed the purser to give himself time to think.

He put off the first lieutenant once again and loudly demanded the presence of the midshipman who'd been in *Thunderer* the longest.

The lad who appeared was struck dumb by the summons, having to decide between appearing at once on command or borrowing gear to make himself presentable. He'd made the former choice, assuming Kydd would want punctuality before appearance.

'F-Forbin, sir,' he stammered, shifting from one foot to the other, a lanky youth of about seventeen.

'Forbin. I have a duty for you,' Kydd said sternly.

'Sir?' Whatever were the rumours about the famous frigate captain taking over their ship, clearly they would now grow in the telling.

'Until I say otherwise you shall take station on me all day, stand fast the silent hours. All other duties are hereby suspended. Clear?'

'Aye aye, sir.'

'Then duty the first. Take a boat crewed by trusties ashore and at this address call on the lady now staying there. This will be Lady Kydd, my wife.' He pulled out his new fob watch and consulted it. 'She is to feed you a cold pie while she prepares to return with you to *Thunderer* for a quick visit. Understood?'

# Chapter 8

With the line of command from himself through the layers of service to a decent noonday meal being broken by the absence of a manservant, a sullen purser's steward was set to rousing out a bite while Kydd waited for Persephone.

'Sweet love!' she breathed, when shown to his cabin. 'What has happened?'

'Naught but the previous captain venting his spite, so as you can see I'm in mortal need of cabin fitments. Can you make purchase of the needful?'

Practical and never to be discouraged, with the help of the carpenter and his folding rule, Persephone soon had her list and stepped ashore.

Gubb was not having success in finding a suitable manservant within the ship's company so Kydd demanded a man from the pompous captain of marines, Hare, who expected his summons to have a more martial purpose. A stolid, unspeaking corporal was the result and he was set to collecting Kydd's baggage and stowing it in the stateroom.

Finally able to see Roscoe, Kydd discovered the true state

of *Thunderer*. Two-thirds of provisions had been expended and she was in need of wood and water. And there were other matters: a sprung main topgallant yard needing replacement, the main hatch gratings stove in at one point, the chain-pump's leather valves in want of changing.

But the chief need was for men.

'Established complement 640, we've 591 on the muster book. Six run so far, a good few left as are "King's hard bargains", useless and—'

'Yes. Fifty hands wanting – this is a grievous shortage. When I've the time I'll step ashore and see the port admiral about some pressed men.'

'Aye, sir.' Roscoe's smile was wintry.

'Meanwhile, get Lambhay moving with our resupply, the gunner to report to me in detail his standings. I've every intention of sailing within four days, Mr Roscoe. Carry on, if you please.'

Until he could get his quarters squared away he couldn't rest so he decided to make first acquaintance with his ship. 'Forbin!' he blared. The youth had taken to skulking in the lobby in readiness and appeared promptly. 'With me, younker.' Kydd was in comfortable sea rig and, his cocked hat significantly under his arm to indicate an unofficial presence, they stepped off.

The captain's domain was the raised portion at the after end of the quarterdeck. From aft, going forward, was his great cabin, followed by his private quarters to starboard. On the other side was the lobby, or coach, which acted as the ship's office and workplace for administration. At this point, the half-deck, a door led to the open quarterdeck at the mizzen-mast, the ship's wheel and binnacle close ahead with, amidships, gratings to the upper deck next below.

The main ladderway was centred, broad and spacious for rapid climbing in action from below, and further forward, beyond the main-mast, was the open space over which the boats were stowed.

Seamen paused in their work at seeing the new captain on the prowl, but resumed industriously at a glance from Kydd. He stood still for a moment, then pointed to a petty officer driving men at some task, all of whom wavered on seeing him. 'Who's that?'

'Oh, sir, that's Tucker, captain of the foretop.'

Kydd called him over and the man loped across warily. Out of the hearing of his men Kydd accused, 'You're using a stonachie to start those men. I'll not have that aboard *Thunderer*, you hear me?'

It was more than a year since the Admiralty had forbidden the use of a rope's end on unresisting seamen but Kydd had never seen the point of it, believing it not needed for men doing their best, and building animosity and indignation in others.

The quarterdeck was connected to the fo'c'sle by gangways each side, a large open space over-topped by bare spars between: the boat stowage. Down through it Kydd could see the guns of the deck below. He had no need to look up into the rigging as he went: all ship-rigged vessels were similar, and except for size, *Thunderer*'s was no different from any other – three masts: mizzen, main and fore. On each was the main sail, the course, with a topsail above it, topgallant higher and royal the highest of all. The baffling maze of ropes from aloft was the operating machinery of each yard and nearly identical on each mast.

It was the scale that was different: the main-mast was near four feet through, a 'made mast' constructed from a number of timbers strapped together, a monstrous-sized piece that soared belligerently up to the fighting tops with topmasts beyond. It supported acres of sail.

The fo'c'sle was deserted, with hands preparing to store ship. Kydd was able to examine where the seamen took their ease, the jeer-bitts where lines were belayed, and gratings where the upwelling warmth of the galley stove from the deck below would be welcomed. The squared-off forward end reminded him of the times as a young sailor in seas the world over he'd laughed and sung with his shipmates into the starlit night, or sat with his tie-mate Nicholas Renzi exchanging the favour of plaiting each other's queues. Renzi was no longer at sea, having married Kydd's sister, Cecilia, and taken up his ancestral seat as the Earl of Farndon.

Moving down the corner ladder, they arrived at the upper deck, the highest deck that ran uninterrupted the length of the ship. It had guns ranged in an unbroken row into the distance on both sides, each the calibre of *Tyger*'s main armament. With the fourteen nine-pounders on the quarterdeck and another four on the fo'c'sle the impression was of indomitable might.

Forward was the fore-mast, and abaft was the complexity of the galley, its black-metal Brodie stove dominating, the cook and his mates energetically at work. Looking aft, past the centre-line gratings, hatches and ladderways, Kydd could make out the sweep of gleaming dark wood that was the wardroom bulkhead. 'I'll make visit there later,' he growled, and clattered down the ladder to the deck below – the lower deck, which mounted the battleship's biggest guns, the awe-inspiring three-ton thirty-two-pounders firing shot that could pierce three feet of solid oak at a mile range. A musket burned an ounce or two of powder but these beasts filled the air with rolling smoke from a ten-pound charge with a fierce bellow heard miles away. Broadsides from *Thunderer* would bring a devastating storm of ruin to an enemy, but in the thick of an action these spaces would be a near imitation of hell itself.

But the lower deck had another reality. It was for the seamen's rest, their sleep. Unlike the upper deck, which was open to the sky amidships with the boats on their spars, and therefore swept by the elements, it was completely enclosed, preserving warmth and dryness for the hundreds of hammocks crammed within it at night. Their messes would be rigged between the guns and a meal taken after their grog when the events of the day would be chewed over in their refuge and sanctuary. There was little doubt as to what would be the subject tonight.

He glanced down. The decks were spotless, the sides lime-washed to reflect light through the gun-ports, the racks of utensils hoisted out of the way. Next to them were ditty-bags where seamen kept possessions that meant a lot to them. The petty officers' messes were canvas-shrouded for privacy.

Kydd had no need to investigate in detail. He'd started his sea life with the seamen in a mess precisely the same and knew what to expect. What was becoming increasingly obvious was that in this ship the people had been cared for, their quarters clean and bright. This would be down to the first lieutenant under the captain's direction. Whatever Lyell and Roscoe's shortcomings he had to respect them in this regard.

The entire after end of the ship was partitioned off. This formed the gunroom, where warrant officers, midshipmen, various clerks and obscure functionaries took their meals and found their rest. Unlike in a frigate, where the gunroom also messed those from the quarterdeck, a ship-of-the-line boasted a wardroom where, with the exception of the purser and surgeon, the inhabitants were all officers.

Not wishing to trespass on these spaces for the moment, Kydd turned forward.

On impulse he crossed to the ship's massive side and bent to feel about below the lower gun-port sill where the deck met the hull at a waterway, the spirketting. He rapped it hard and it returned a reassuringly solid ring. This was satisfying, for it told of a sound hull. He'd never forget his first night at sea, in the old 98-gun *Duke William*, a sailor pointing out its spirketting as druxy timber, white-speckled spongy wood that seemed to make his whole wooden world suddenly shaky and precarious, about to fall apart before plunging for ever into the depths. *Thunderer* was old but apparently still in good shape.

As he paced slowly aft, men scurried away at his presence, leaving him to take in the spectacle of the massive bulk of the main capstan and the spacious main ladderway. It was so broad it was set parallel to the ship's side rather than across. Past another half-dozen guns, planted fair and square in the centre, were the huge riding bitts that now took the battle-ship's twenty-inch anchor cable about them before it led forward to the hawse and out to the anchor, fathoms below.

Intruding into this warlike setting was the homely sight of animals – a few goats, some sheep, two pigs. They were securely penned within a manger: meat on the hoof while enduring months at sea on blockade. In *Tyger* they had no need for such, for their adventures usually took them to parts of the world where fresh meat was easily obtainable, but *Thunderer* had to maintain herself on a hostile coast or go without. He'd noticed two chicken coops on the poop and more discreetly on the fo'c'sle, the eggs a treat for the officers.

The deck below was the last, the orlop. Below the waterline, it was the dark empire of boatswain, carpenter and gunner, their stores and equipment. The purser would make issue from his quarters and the surgeon hold daily muster of the sick list. In the middle were the cable-tiers where the great length of the anchor cable was coiled. There were also the fish room, the carpenter's wings, the lady's hole – but these could all wait.

'Very well. I'll return now. The midshipmen's berth another time.'

Kydd felt better after his brief foray into the inner world of his ship, even if it must have caused consternation in the various realms he'd trespassed on. The impression he'd gained was of an elderly but well-kept vessel, graceful even, her appointments near palatial compared to a frigate's. With the immense gun-power that was his to wield, it was a most respectable command. Any difficulties lying in wait for him would be human, not *Thunderer*'s.

# Chapter 9

L ater that afternoon the articles Persephone had found made their way aboard: a compact writing desk that fitted snugly against the forward bulkhead, a handsome long sideboard ready to stow his elegant entertaining glassware and china, with a matching pair of leather-bound armchairs. A discreet parcel turned out to be his cot bedding while another held a carefully packed trio of Cornish jugs and a gimballed mirror for his wash-place. A hurriedly scrawled note assured him that more was on its way, including cabin stores, which she was taking time to choose, given that *Thunderer* would be away for so long.

His living spaces were taking on warmth and personality. His servant, the veteran corporal of marines, patiently moved the furnishings and fitments about until he was satisfied, then left Kydd to address the dismaying pile of papers that the purser had brought for him. He worked into the evening, trying to achieve a sense of order, but without someone like Dillon to bring about a regularity of concerns it was heavy going.

As the boatswain's calls squealed out the end of the day

fore and aft he was ready to retire, his cot beckoning with the promise of softness and slumber. But as he lay in the unfamiliar darkness, sleep wouldn't come. As with every ship, sounds in the night were individual, disturbing until their source had been identified. The peculiar rhythm of creaks deep within her that followed a swell down the length of the hull had to be learned and absorbed before it could take its place in the subliminal background of consciousness.

His thoughts rushed on. He'd noticed that the men at work, striking down provisions and necessaries, were surly, bleak-featured. They'd served for months on blockade and were almost within touching distance of England, home and beauty but, like prisoners in a gaol, were being kept and guarded from their rightful freedoms ashore. Their duty now was to take aboard stores that would only extend their exile. In a few days *Thunderer* would put to sea and all this would be a bitter memory.

He rolled over restlessly. How was he to win them over? The officers had been aboard for years and were accustomed to a way that was not his, employing the people in smartening the ship as a means of giving point to their existence.

His thoughts turned to the officers and in particular his first lieutenant. In all probability he'd be obliged to get rid of him. The moral courage he'd shown when speaking of what he saw as the injustice to Lyell would be better displayed in deciding a course of action in battle. But how much chance was there of that? On blockade Roscoe's attitude would leave them both in a corrosive state of confrontation.

Smale promoted to first would be a feather-weight premier, waiting out his patron's advancing him. The third, Briggs, had the makings but was wasted in a ship-of-the-line, and his fourth lieutenant, Mayne, gave every sign of being useless and bitter with his lot.

Melancholy entered Kydd's soul at the thought of what lay ahead. Instead of being here, he could be in Persephone's arms, enjoying a bucolic idyll with all the comforts a retired baronet could expect.

But he'd been through it all so many times and with the same result. If she wanted him to try, damn it, he would!

# Chapter 10

'What's our state now?' Kydd asked Roscoe, the next morning, after the hands had turned to.

Without raising his eyes from the activity about the main hatch, the first lieutenant answered, 'Ah, a matter for the purser, I believe. And he's failed to report to me our condition so far this forenoon.'

Kydd held back a retort and sent for the purser. 'Our state of provisioning, Mr Gubb?'

'Oh, I can't tell you, can't tell you, I say,' he babbled. 'Altogether such a rush. No ship's clerk and the master is quarrelling with the bosun about the stowage, and I'm at my wit's end to know where the victuals are being struck down that my steward can take their reckoning.'

'Sort it out for him, Mr Roscoe,' Kydd snapped. 'I'll not tolerate delays. I'm stepping ashore to see the admiral concerning our departure and do not desire to disappoint him.'

Kydd didn't know the newly installed port admiral, Dewey, but he was not left long to discover his views.

'Your first command of a sail-of-the-line, I believe, Sir Thomas.'

'Aye, sir.'

'As desired by His Royal Highness, I've heard,' he went on, in a tight voice.

'No, sir, that is not at all why—'

'Don't take that tone with me, sir! We're all men of the world. We can see for ourselves how many ducks make five! If you've secured the attention of the court to advance yourself, then that is your business. Don't expect the admiration and respect of the service should you choose to indulge in such an unseamanlike manoeuvre.'

'Sir. I must protest at your—'

'You're reporting your ship in all respects ready for sea then, Captain?' Dewey leaned forward, his eyes boring into Kydd's.

'I'm unable to do that, sir.'

'Oh?'

'On assuming command I'm told by my premier that we're short above fifty men. I seek your help in making this good before I sail.'

'What do you expect me to do?' Dewey asked silkily.

Kydd swallowed his pride at having to beg. 'Your standing press, sir. Should you release to me a substantial number, I would be obliged.'

'I have none. There's your answer.'

'None?'

'No seamen worth the name. Possibly I could find some landmen but I've my doubts.' There was a triumphant finality in his manner.

'Then, sir, I ask permission to sleep out of my ship,' he said woodenly. Just one last night with Persephone before he left to meet his fate.

57

'Certainly not, sir. You've admitted to me your ship is far from ready for sea. How do you suppose this will aid your purpose? Hey? Hey?'

Controlling his rage, Kydd stamped out of the Mount Wise headquarters. Clutching the satchel of orders and communications destined for the commander-in-chief off Brest, he headed back to his boat. As he calmed, though, he felt his anger turn to a cold determination: he would be the one to come out of all this colours flying. Be damned to it if he didn't.

'Ah, Mr Opie,' he said breezily, as he stepped on to the quarterdeck. 'Just the man I hoped to see.'

The powerfully built boatswain loped forward, in his hand a hank of small stuff, line used for working a fine whipping over a splice, and a marline-spike clutched in a tattooed claw-like hand. 'Sir?'

'I thought I'd take a look at the barky's standing rigging.'

The big man gave a shy smile and touched his shapeless seaman's hat. 'All a-taunto, I think ye'll find, Sir Thomas.' He looked past him in an unsettling manner, which Kydd was about to remark on when he noticed that the boatswain's left eye had the milkiness of the unseeing he'd last glimpsed in Nelson.

Going to the mizzen shrouds Kydd nimbly leaped from the deck to reach above the seizings at the deadeyes. He peered into the strands and saw past the grey weathered exterior the heartening blackness of Stockholm tar deep within. As he came down he stopped at one of the upper deadeyes and bent to smell. This time it was the comforting stink of rancid butter. The boatswain was seeing the lanyards were free to ease through the carved holes of the deadeye to ensure an equal strain on all parts.

Dropping to the deck he met the questioning expression with a pleased grin and walked forward, testing the tautness of a stay here, a pendant there. At the fore-mast Kydd swung himself up and around on to the shrouds leading up to the massive fighting top. As he mounted he noticed Opie respectfully one rung behind, keeping him well within view.

Kydd tested the ratlines for their security and positioning. 'You've rattled them down?' he asked pointedly. To have the thinner lines crossing the thick shrouds at right angles to form a ladder to the tops, all neatly parallel with the waterline, gave confidence underfoot to men racing aloft and, besides, was a mark of a smart ship.

'I always does, first thing after the hook kisses mud, sir.'

Without the first lieutenant chasing him, Kydd mused. Opie and *Thunderer*'s captain would get along.

# Chapter 11

Storing appeared to be satisfactorily under way and there was no point in standing over the men while they worked. Sighing, Kydd returned to his papers. On the way into his sanctum he noticed the locked cabin on his right, the departed ship's clerk's, and a thought took shape.

He had now a reasonably good grasp of *Thunderer*'s layout below decks and it was crowded. Her 'establishment' when taken into service in the balmy days of peace was for so many sea and marine officers, so many warrant officers and other important persons. Each was given a place to call his own. And then with war came an inexorable increase in these numbers. If he wanted to bring his confidential secretary aboard, there was no cabin for him. The only spare was that of the non-existent second Royal Marine lieutenant but this was situated deep in the noisome orlop and was the smallest. If he wanted Craddock in *Thunderer* he needed to find something like the ship's clerk's accommodation.

Sooner or later a replacement clerk would be found who would claim his cabin, which was where it was so that the captain could call on his services at any time. That was exactly what he needed from Craddock.

A seductive idea took shape. He could have his confidential secretary on the establishment and therefore on the ship's books, and thus perfectly entitled to a fine cabin if he was at the same time a ship's clerk. Craddock would be introduced as his secretary, never as a clerk, the real work to be done by a writer, which he was allowed by his position.

In one stroke he would have trumped Lyell's spiteful robbing him of a critical cog in the wheel of operations and at the same time have at his side a secretary and friend.

*If* Craddock accepted.

By rights he must mess down in the gunroom with the warrant officers and midshipmen, perceived as less than an officer. A ship's clerk was responsible to the purser. The post was considered preparation for an appointment by the Admiralty as a purser. And the incumbent would be held to the dire provisions of the Articles of War.

Craddock would probably weather better than most the long days and weeks of boredom on blockade but was he up to enduring the misery of long gales and Biscay bluster that were the Brest squadron's eternal lot? Had Kydd the right to subject him to that? There would be no going back on the commitment. If he agreed, the next time he could hope to touch land would be in exactly the same place in some months' time.

Kydd penned a swift note asking him to visit; when he came aboard he would lay it all before him and leave the decision his to make.

Craddock arrived by return. He was dressed thoughtfully in a well-cut black frock-coat, and such was his presence, the Spanish beard, the maturity, that it was the officer-of-the-watch who stood at the great cabin door to announce him.

Kydd rose, unable to suppress a broad smile. 'Welcome aboard, Mr Craddock! Never more welcome, I'm bound to say.'

'My pleasure and honour, Captain.' He looked about him, clearly impressed. 'And into such august surroundings as I've never encountered before. A magnificent vessel of such size and circumstance, if I be allowed to remark it.'

'*Thunderer*? A smart enough man-o'-war I'd be obliged to agree. But she comes with more than my fair share of grief and trouble.' He caught himself. 'But I'm neglecting my guest. Do sit.'

'Your guest? I was rather hoping to appear in quite another capacity,' Craddock said meaningfully.

'Ah, yes. Your post as confidential secretary.' Kydd found some papers to riffle. 'Er, dear fellow. This I can heartily assure you is yours, should you wish it. But first my conscience demands I lay before you some . . . unavoidable inconveniences that will be encountered.'

If he'd ever had any doubts concerning Craddock's character and qualities they were rapidly disposed of. The notional post of ship's clerk as a device for securing both a cabin and access to his friend brought ready agreement, and the happy observation that, being on the ship's books, he was entitled to an official share of prize money. And after Kydd explained the domestic hierarchy, he quite saw the necessity of falling in with the society of the gunroom.

'Shall we see then your quarters?' Kydd enquired, finding the key.

The little cabin was as he expected, stripped of personal effects. Piles of books and packs of files were heaped untidily on the long desk that occupied the after side of the cabin. The rest was bare, pitilessly illuminated by a single window, picking out a diminutive bare cot folded against the forward bulkhead. 'We'll soon have it shipshape for you, dear fellow, never fear.' Even if he had to do it himself.

In his mind Kydd was already seeing how Craddock would have his existence. This would be his private place, for work or leisure. He would dine with Kydd for breakfast and most days for dinner. During the day, when Kydd desired his attendance, he was within easy call. If Craddock needed him he was readily available, and if others wanted to see their captain they'd have first to consult him. It would work out, just as it had with Dillon.

As for his relations with *Thunderer*'s crew, the age-old custom of the sea was that any oddity of manner or appearance would never be made subject of remark or humour unless deserved. That Craddock was patently a gentleman, highly unusual in a warlike company, and equally clearly Kydd's close confidant and friend, would in the course of things be accepted in much the same way as the captain's coxswain was not challenged on what he'd witnessed from his privileged situation.

Fortunately the purser, distracted by overwork, simply took the captain's word for it that his new confidential secretary had kindly agreed to discharge the function of ship's clerk until a new one had been provided. All that was required was his brightest writer to act the assistant to Mr Craddock, both to turn to the next morning. One was found, the sick Allen's bookkeeper, profoundly relieved that order was to be restored.

'I'll leave you to it, Mr Craddock,' Kydd said, smothering his deep sigh of relief. 'Send for your baggage and we'll square away your quarters before evening gun tonight.'

# Chapter 12

Adockyard hoy hailed with the news that their press-gang harvest was aboard. Kydd tried not to show eagerness and watched from his quarter-gallery, the round balcony projecting out from the corners of the sternwork. At sea it would conveniently allow him to peer up to the set of the sails.

He left it to Roscoe. Only a dozen or so and, judging from their appearance and clumsy attempts at the side-steps, all useless lubbers. He quietly despaired. It wasn't meant to be like this, the commanding of the most powerful class of ship in the navy, the glorious pinnacle of a sea career. If he—

'Come!' He could recognise Roscoe's knock now, firm and only two.

'Sir, to acquaint you we've eleven hands, now rated and sent below.'

'How many bounty men?' Theoretically these were volunteers.

'One.'

'Any seamen among 'em?' He tried to sound approachable, but the lieutenant remained inflexible and unsmiling.

'No.'

'So we're now north of six hundred complement.'

'Not so – we lost four waisters during the night sharing a pig's bladder to shore.'

'Oh, bad luck, Mr Roscoe,' he responded, determined not to be provoked. 'How's the storing?'

'Two days.'

Kydd was taken by surprise. 'Only two? Well done, Mr Roscoe. That includes watering?'

'Of course.'

He swallowed his anger. If this attitude continued it would infect all in the wardroom, and *Thunderer* would be near unmanageable at sea and against the enemy. 'Very well. Carry on, please.'

The marine corporal excused himself, hefting in more cabin stores, which he was temporarily stowing in the stateroom. As a manservant he was adequate, but his idea of caring and arranging was solid, square and military, and he was never about when Kydd wanted him. Kydd wished Tysoe, his previous man's man, all the best for his retirement but how he missed him at this moment.

But now with a date for sea it was possible to make plans for the cleansing and liberating feel of the open ocean where cares and worries took their rightful place.

Feeling brighter, he went to see how Craddock was getting along. The snug cabin was well on its way to rights, gear stowed tightly but handily and the desk with its proper complement of pen-rests and inkwells. Every nook and cranny was exploited, resulting in an effect of extreme order.

'A right handsome home, Mr Craddock,' Kydd said, leaning in carefully for there was room only for Craddock and his writer.

'And workplace, Captain.' Craddock held up a much-thumbed book. 'And my bedtime reading spoken for by this tome lent to me by my doughty assistant, William – that is to say, William Franks, writer.'

The lad touched his forehead nervously.

Kydd took the book – it had an interminable title ending with '. . . and complete instructions in the duty of a captain's clerk,' author one R. Liddel, late purser of *Monarch* 74 in His Majesty's Service. 'Fascinating,' he murmured, and looked up to catch Craddock's conspiratorial smile.

# Chapter 13

As he lay awake in his cot Kydd gave thought to the morrow. He'd always made it a practice on the first night outward bound to bring everyone together in fellowship at a dinner, to welcome new faces, to discover anew the particular brotherhood of the wardroom, of the sea. Why shouldn't he make it a day earlier, to mark the quitting of the land?

Lyell hadn't had the means to support his own chef and had shared the officers' cook. Was the man up to an appropriate meal? He couldn't enjoy his last night ashore with Persephone but here was a way of spending it with her and at the same time introducing her to his new command. She'd be invited – and Craddock, to allow the afterguard to make his acquaintance.

As it turned out, the officers' cook, Tyler, was much in favour of a banquet. It would stretch his professional skills and allow him to make the most of the steadiness of the harbour calms. What did the good captain have in mind?

Heartened, Kydd told him to conjure up what he felt able to provide, given the numbers, and to furnish him with a list of ingredients he required. He would send ashore for them in good time for their preparation. The list arrived promptly and he had it landed with Persephone's invitation.

Another five men were taken in, worthless landmen. The hold completed stowage, hatches were replaced, and one by one the gunner, then the boatswain and others reported their needs satisfied and stores aboard.

He dared to believe *Thunderer* would put to sea very shortly.

The Blue Peter made its way to the masthead, the flag of blue containing an inner white square indicating to the anchorage that the ship was about to sail.

Shortly before midday Persephone's acceptance came, along with her last gift to him. One Josiah Luscombe, a young, fresh-faced man of about twenty was ushered in with a letter of introduction. It informed Kydd that Luscombe had lately been in the employ of the squire of Cornwood. On hearing of Kydd's need for a valet he'd let it be known that he would be honoured if Sir Thomas would consider him for the post. Although he had no experience of life at sea he'd been in service in a distinguished estate since childhood.

Kydd didn't worry about details. Persephone wouldn't have put him forward unless he had the makings for the post and she knew how much he needed a manservant.

Luscombe was a serious young man, trying to hide his anxiety but holding himself with dignity. Soft-spoken, he moved gracefully and had a quiet presence with natural intelligence showing through. Kydd felt they'd get along.

'You must know that the sea life is hard for everyone,' Kydd began, and stopped. Luscombe would find it out for himself before long. 'You have your dunnage with you?'

At his blank look he added, 'That is, your sea baggage?'

He nodded and Kydd briskly welcomed him aboard. 'You've the rest of the day to find your way around.' He summoned two of the first-class volunteers. 'Stay with Mr Luscombe, take him around the ship and show him the important things he needs to know.'

They left and he got on with his work.

Later that afternoon he summoned the marine servant, gravely thanked him for his assistance and, handing him a small reward, released him.

When Luscombe and the volunteers returned, he asked, 'Well, young man, how do you like *Thunderer*?'

'A very big ship, Sir Thomas.' The eyes were round.

'What did you see, then?'

'Oh, you have three masts and many guns. And not forgetting the front one lying down with the statue underneath.'

'Our figurehead.'

'Yes, Sir Thomas. And the steering wheel and chicken coops and—'

'Where does the purser issue his provisions, pray?'

'P-purser?'

'And where is my dinner cooked?'

'Um . . .'

Kydd rounded on the volunteers. 'This is not what I asked, you scoundrels. Luscombe is to be shown what he needs to know, not what is grand or interesting. I suggest he visits where people mess, sleep and eat, and where gear is stowed. No tricks or pranks, take him away again and return him before four bells. Remember, at sea he's to be in charge of you and will give me due report on you both. Compree?'

After that he'd get his cabin stores properly packed away and his personal tackle in some sort of order.

Craddock joined him for the noonday meal and Kydd heard how much the naval system closely resembled shore-side clerking practices of earlier in the last century and how he felt quite at home with the arcane methods.

'The first sentence in Mr Liddel's volume, "The Duty of the Ship's Clerk is in the first Place, to keep all the Books necessary for passing the Captain's Accounts", is repeated above twenty times throughout. Your books will be passed, that I can solemnly assure you, Thomas.'

'I'm glad to hear it. Do you desire then to share in Queen Anne's gift?'

'Er . . .?'

'That's a sum of money awarded over and above the monthly twopence when my accounts are passed.'

'Oh – and if they're not?'

'Dire consequences that I will not dwell upon.'

With this Craddock rose to leave with a smile but Kydd waved him down. 'I need you, Harry. Tonight I'm to host a grand dinner for all the officers and a species of table plan will be required that satisfies honour and position. Will you . . .?'

The table had already been made ready, its cunning leaves manipulated to produce a twelve-place setting. But the seating arrangements took longer than expected as Kydd unburdened himself about each person as their cards were shuffled around the table – and then the purser's steward came demanding crockery, silver and his dining ornaments.

With a rush of warmth he saw Persephone's choice of green and gold service would make its first outing and it would be with her present. In the future he would always associate it with her, no matter the occasion. The pieces of silver he'd acquired over the years would do their duty now in a different ship, in loftier surroundings, but with their memories for him of a simpler, more carefree exist-ence.

Luscombe appeared, still dazed by his experiences, and was put to work on the decorations, while Kydd made himself available to the stream of those reporting ready for sea, Roscoe included.

'The tide will be right for tomorrow forenoon,' Kydd said neutrally. 'We'll weigh at eleven I believe, take advantage of this nor'-westerly while we can. Gives you time to lay along the gear without you need disturb the hands about their breakfast.'

'We're still short forty men.'

'And we're getting no more from the press or any other. This is your affair, Mr Roscoe. I need the ship manned in all respects even if we leave every other gun less one hand.'

It was hard on the fellow but to cover shortcomings in the manning, however grave, was one of the crosses the first lieutenant of any ship must bear. The eyes narrowed. Then he turned on his heel and left.

Kydd was not going to be dismayed. This evening he'd do his best to pull his officers together, talk to them, encourage them to enjoy themselves over a superb repast and possibly some jollity to conclude. If he couldn't, a future of endless sea-time in their company would be wretched.

Persephone came aboard an hour early, observed by a curious watch-on-deck who noticed her seaman-like mounting of the ship's side.

In the stateroom Kydd's full-dress uniform with its gold lace, star and sash, was being tugged into shape by Luscombe, who discreetly left when she entered.

She beamed. 'My darling! You do look so handsome. I'm sure there are quantities of ladies whose heads would be quite turned by your appearance.'

'A fine fellow, Luscombe,' Kydd told her. The young man was taking it very seriously and this evening he would wait at table in the naval manner, standing behind his captain to attend to his wants as the meal progressed.

She looked about, pleased with the changes that had been wrought in such a short time. Little touches that Kydd would not have thought of, pictures and hangings, the near Persian luxury of the cot and the now resplendent wash-place, fully equipped with masculine articles of toilet.

# Chapter 14

Craddock apologetically invited himself into Kydd's private quarters, the great cabin imminently to fill with guests. 'The first of many, I trust,' he murmured to Kydd. His dress was perfectly the gentleman's.

Luscombe entered nervously to announce that guests had begun arriving and Kydd went into the splendidly appointed great cabin to welcome them, accompanied by Persephone with the table plan.

'To the forrard end opposite me, Mr Mayne,' Kydd instructed his fourth lieutenant. 'You're Mr Vice tonight, in course.'

One by one the officers made their way in, efficiently placed by Lady Kydd. With all seated, Kydd took the other end before the stern-gallery. On his right hand was Persephone, next to her Roscoe. On his other side, he had placed Hare, the officious captain of marines, in his dramatic scarlet and gold full-dress. On Kydd's left sat Craddock, then the second and third lieutenants. The further end of the table was occupied on the right by the master and purser, and on the left by the lieutenant of marines and the surgeon.

The servants leaned forward to fill their glasses, a disconcertingly expensive Vouvray sec, dry, acidic, but sparkling with zest. 'Gentlemen, I'd be obliged for your opinion of this wine. It may be Gallic but should be fine enough for all that.'

It was a quiet, even sombre table that raised glasses and sipped cautiously. Was this a test by their captain, known among the highest society in the land?

No one spoke.

'Come, come, gentlemen! It's not, as who should say, an indifferent potion. Mr Vice?'

Being so addressed before every one of his seniors, Mayne jerked alert. 'Oh, well, in my taste it seems a mite tart for a champagne,' he attempted.

No one seemed inclined to contradict him as Kydd looked about the table hopefully. 'Is there nobody a judge of wine in *Thunderer*, then?' He turned to Roscoe, who had put his glass down, barely tasted. 'Sir?'

'I agree, but perhaps this is not a champagne.'

Every face turned to Kydd but before he could respond, Smale, the second lieutenant, held up his glass before the light. 'And if I'm not adrift in my bearings we're muzzling a rather fine Vouvray – and the Arbois grape, not your common chenin blanc?'

'Well said, Mr Smale,' Kydd told him. Next to him Craddock murmured something, and Smale smiled, a smug expression just under control. 'So we enjoy it as we may. Drink up, gentlemen, I believe our first course is on the way.'

Still the heavy silence, broken only occasionally by a soft exchange here and there.

'Rather a noble tipple, I vow,' Persephone said, rather more loudly than was indicated, and made much of sampling further. Kydd knew that she had chosen the bottles from the

Knowle Manor cellar, as were others to make their appearance later.

'Do you not feel so . . . Mr Roscoe, is it not?' she said sweetly, to the stiff-faced lieutenant on her right, laying her hand lightly on his arm.

'A fine wine, yes, m' lady.'

Kydd hid a smile. The polite address had been extracted from him by her patrician bearing and striking looks. 'Er, gentlemen, if I might have your attention? In derogation of my duty I have failed to introduce all of you to my guests.' He gave a mock apologetic grin. 'Here on my right hand is my charming wife, the Lady Kydd, who has importuned me shamefully to be here tonight, desiring so much to meet you all.'

She nodded shyly left and right.

'While here on my other hand is a gentleman you will come to know more in the future. He is my confidential secretary, Mr Lucius Craddock. He kindly stepped forward at the last moment to agree to discharge the function of ship's clerk until we are provided with another. I might point out that he has lately served with me in my previous ship, *Tyger*, so you may understand he is no stranger to war in all its forms.'

He paused, watching their faces. In the main it was a studied blankness but he knew the message had been passed. This was the captain's friend, an evident gentleman but, with the exception of the purser, he had no function aboard that intersected with theirs.

The first course of dishes was carried in. A veal fricandeau, chine of mutton, forced lamb's ears, more. The red wine, a silky smooth Margaux, had Luscombe hesitating as to whose glass he should fill first: the grand lady's or his fearsome captain's.

There were murmurs of appreciation but none of the whole-hearted acclaim that viands of this quality would have received in *Tyger*.

'Wine with you, Mr Roscoe,' Kydd urged, drawing the officer's glass to him. 'You're enjoying your meal?'

'Thank you, yes.' The eyes remained cold and distant, the sips at his glass careful, controlled.

Anger surged in Kydd once more. Was this the man who would stand by him on his quarterdeck in battle, whom he could trust to send on a cutting-out expedition?

'Tell me, Mr Roscoe,' Persephone cut in, 'what's your opinion of the state of the war as it stands?'

Kydd left them to it, hearing from Craddock how the nobs in Manchester set about entertaining themselves at a civic occasion, and then it was the second course: oyster patties, woodcock, pork griskins and others equally admirable in their presentation, yet still the gathering had not begun to warm. More wines appeared, but the low hum of guarded conversation was resolutely unchanging.

One thing he'd planned on doing when the affair had got more lively was to take advantage of their presence together and make some kind of commencement of commission address. This moment was probably as good as any.

'Gentlemen! Your attention, please.'

The talking stopped as if cut off with a knife. Faces turned to him, wary, cautious, blank.

'I shall be brief, the third course is still to come and there's brandy and cigars to follow.' He smiled winningly. 'But all I wished to say is how honoured I am to be given command of *Thunderer*, holder of above the ordinary number of honours of battle in her distinguished career.' He went on in similar vein and saw one or two expressions ease.

'I've spent nearly my whole time at sea in frigates, and by

that I mean in the service of the fleet as well as independent cruises. What I learned there I can say in one: that we could do our small part. But it is upon the battleships, the princes of the sea, that England depends as her true wooden walls. And I know to my cost what it is to face the outcome when, perhaps in unfortunate circumstances, the enemy gets past them to the open ocean. Where *Thunderer* is concerned this will never happen.'

There were frowns now, one or two raised eyebrows.

'*Thunderer* will do more than succeed at her purpose – she will excel!' He allowed his voice to harden. 'Different ships, different long-splices. Some captains are known for riding hard on sail-handling, others a smart appearance, more still for signals and manoeuvres. In fair warning you should know that for me it can only be . . . gunnery! A ship exists to prevail over another. She does this by virtue of her superior powers of destruction. I don't need to remind you that a reloading time half that of the enemy is precisely the same as possessing double the number of guns. HMS *Thunderer* of 148 guns! I like the sound of that, gentlemen.'

Expressions were set. So this was the flavour of what lay ahead. Gun drill at all hours.

'You'll know what to expect, then, so I bid you enjoy the rest of this fine repast while you may.' He sat down to a polite scatter of applause, which quickly relapsed into the same joyless reticence.

Kydd was aware of its cause. With perceived injustice done to Lyell, and as a wardroom serving together for years, they had closed ranks against him with Roscoe as their leader. No one was inclined to be the first to break.

And the expensive dinner he'd conjured had not had the effect he wanted: a thaw in relations. It was probably being seen as yet another courtly feast by one whose daily fare must always be something like this. It could even be possible that they believed he would lord it over them, that being his accustomed style of life.

The final course came and with it some choice dessert wines. Kydd sensed Persephone had caught the mood and was despairing. There was Roscoe with his monosyllabic replies and the captain of marines with ponderous anecdotes of times past. Craddock was being monopolised by Smale. Kydd, caught in the middle, was finding himself gazing about inanely without a conversational partner.

At an awkward break in the general conversation, Persephone challenged the first lieutenant. 'Sir, surely a big ship like *Thunderer* has a fiddler at its capstan.'

Taken aback, Roscoe hesitated. Briggs leaned across and mouthed, 'Watkins, fo'c'sle division.'

'Oh, yes. We do have one, m' lady.'

'Then would it be too much to ask the gentleman to oblige me by lending me his violin?'

After a dumbfounded marine returned with it, Persephone stood and took position behind Kydd. 'Not so many know that your captain – my husband – has a very fine singing voice.' Kydd looked up in embarrassment as she went on, 'And tonight you shall hear him!'

She plucked the strings and made one or two adjustments in the tuning, then addressed them: 'This is a piece with which I accompanied him when first we met at a country estate. Do forgive my playing as it's been a long time since I picked up an instrument. I shall feel well rewarded if you do join in, gentlemen.'

Tucking the violin under her chin, she played a few experimental notes and Kydd rose, his embarrassment falling away to be replaced by a special feeling of warmth towards her.

At his nod she launched into the piece, strongly and gaily.

His voice, now well accustomed to command, had deepened over the years from a pleasant baritone into something closer to a bass. To the astonishment of all they heard him launch into the salty, driving strains of the sailors' favourite, 'Spanish Ladies', letting its well-known cadences fill the cabin.

He gestured to the table, urging them to join in the full-throated refrain:

> *We'll rant and we'll roar like true British sailors,*
> *We'll rant and we'll rave across the salt seas;*
> *Till we strike soundings in the Channel of Old England,*
> *From Ushant to Scilly 'tis thirty-four leagues . . .*

One or two began mouthing the words but from most it was a discomfiting mumble, trying to avoid each other's eye. Kydd persevered, thundering out the verses, Persephone now adding lively embellishments that would do credit to any seasoned sea fiddler.

> *We hove our ship to, with the wind at sou' west, boys*
> *We hove our ship to, for to take soundings clear,*
> *In fifty-five fathoms with a fine sandy bottom,*
> *We filled our main tops'l, up Channel did we steer . . .*

The song progressed past the familiar sea-marks – the Deadman, Rame's Head, Start Point, Portland, right on to the Downs. Then it was the triumphant final stanza:

> *Now let every man take up his full bumper,*
> *Let every man take up his full bowl;*
> *For we will be jolly, and drown melancholy*
> *With a health to each jovial and true-hearted soul!*

At its conclusion there was a timid scatter of applause. Still standing, Kydd looked about. 'Do we have another who will entertain us? Anyone? Mr Roscoe, there must be a song in you!'

The man shook his head and calmly took another taste of his wine.

'You disappoint me, sir. How about you, Mr Smale?'

'Sir, after our storing ship I've a raw throat, I fear.'

'So *Thunderer* must be accounted a ship of Philistines.' Kydd snorted theatrically.

In his full-dress with its daunting amounts of gold lace and star of knighthood he knew he cut an imposing figure. Was it that they felt he had no right to act out of part, to confuse the issue? That his it was to sit back in regal splendour and himself be entertained – and, if this was his taste, by a jolly jack tar sent for to perform? And to have his impeccably well-brought-up and presumably aristocratic wife sawing away on the fiddle was surely demeaning.

It was going to be a hard beat to windward to reach an understanding with this crew, let alone gain their trust and loyalty.

And they put to sea tomorrow.

'If you'll excuse me, gentlemen.' The surgeon got to his feet and gave a jerky half-bow in Kydd's direction. 'I've a patient I must attend to.' He left awkwardly.

'Yes, Mr Gubb?'

The purser stood nervously and stuttered, 'The ship sails tomorrow. I have my reservations about the gunner's stores and . . . and . . .'

Did they think that this was just the beginning of some bacchanal, an evening of riot and song into the early hours like some frolic of high society?

Kydd's face set. The evening was effectively over – ruined

by a company whose idea of welcoming a new captain was to set their faces against him.

'Oh, my dear,' Persephone said loudly, 'I do really feel it time for me to retire. Is my boat ready?'

'Of course, my love.' He nodded to Briggs, who left to make it so, then turned to the silent gathering and said lightly, 'And if any so desire, there is an excellent cognac and cigars to be had.'

He shepherded her out and on to the deck, now shrouded in warm summer dusk. She looked up at him, her features wreathed in love and concern. 'My sweet darling, my love,' she began, her voice husky and troubled.

'Dearest,' he answered softly, caressing her hair – but he was forbidden to sleep out of his ship and found himself lost for words.

Seizing both his hands she gazed at him deeply. 'Thomas. I'm frightened. This ship . . . *Thunderer*. It – it's too big, too cold, a hostile stranger, you might say. And it doesn't like you or want you. I'm fearful. I worry it'll not rest until it's seen the end of you, my love.' Tears glistened and where she held him hurt with its intensity. 'You will take special care of yourself, darling? You're everything there is in this world that's sweet and true and . . . and . . .'

The tears began to flow, quite unlike any time previously when they'd parted before a foreign commission, however dire its prospects. Then, she'd always bravely seen him go without an unseemly display. Her farewell now affected him more than he cared to admit.

Briggs appeared quietly and waited.

Kydd crushed her to him, careless of the watch-on-deck. 'Goodbye, my love – and take heart. Remember, I'm the captain.'

She pulled herself together and, with a single wave, followed Briggs.

81

# Chapter 15

'Yes, Mr Roscoe, I do wish it.'

'For me to take the ship out?'

'That's what I said. Have you an objection?'

They stood together on the quarterdeck. Around them the bustle of preparations for putting to sea were well advanced: ropes and falls faked out and laid clear for running, boats stowed, the lower boom and its Jacob's ladder brought in.

'No objection.'

For Kydd it addressed two matters in one. He would get to see what stuff Roscoe was made of and also be relieved of the perils of taking charge of a strange ship in not particularly advantageous weather. The wind was light and fluky, the very worst for winning clear of the land. A robust, reliable breeze was much more to be desired and he had no wish to make a fool of himself before the entire ship's company.

'How else in the short term might I see demonstrated what my premier can do? To trust or not to trust in the future, that is my question.' He gazed directly at Roscoe and was gratified when he dropped his eyes, then moved off to stand alone some yards away.

'You have the ship, sir,' Kydd called over meaningfully.

It left him able to take his measure of proceedings on deck, which his experiences in a frigate left him well able to do. A ship-of-the-line and frigate, three-masted ship rig both, shared most of the operating procedures and gear, with differences only in scale and the speed with which things happened.

Most of the effort now would be out of sight on the lower deck. There, at the capstan, something like two hundred men and boys would be readying, flexing their bodies and standing by for the brutal task of bringing in the anchor. Cable nearly two feet around, weighing as much as a full-grown man every fathom or two and with a three-ton anchor hanging from its end made for a muscle-searing ordeal.

Roscoe had to know precisely the right moment to have sail set abroad. If too early, before the anchor was tripped from the ground, it would put intolerable strain on the cable and the men at the capstan. If left too late, the ship would be carried helpless on to the rock-strewn Rame.

Then, too, the arrangement and timing of making sail would be critical. To employ the staysails, all fore-and-aft rigged, to pay off to leeward before setting the square sails was easier, but needed more time and sea-room. On the other hand the more sure casting under square sail always began with a significant degree of sternway before a ship could take up on the appropriate tack and stretch out.

He would see.

The fo'c'sle party were closed up, tackles laid out, and at each mast topmen stood ready at the base, the sailing master waiting patiently near the group at the conn.

Time passed. In a frigate it was possible to sense slight shudders transmitted through the hull as the anchor came in, reassurance that the ground tackle was not caught up in any way. In *Thunderer* there was not the slightest sign and Roscoe stood rigid, his gaze clamped on the cluster of fo'c'slemen. A hand-flag continually showed the direction of the anchor cable while it gradually shortened as the slack came in. Several times he tore his gaze away to sniff at the wind, a light south-westerly. Then, lifting his speaking trumpet, he blared down the deck, 'Topmen aloft, prepare to cast to starb'd under tops'ls and courses.'

Kydd nodded. The ship was catching the breeze in her upperworks, considerably higher than in a frigate, and ignoring the other influence, the swirling current. Her bows pointed directly at the rocky heights of the headland and he could see that the inevitable sternway of a cast under square sail would prove the more useful.

The flag was nearly up and down, *Thunderer* was directly above her anchor. A particularly back-breaking effort at the capstan – the heavy heave – was now being called on below to release the giant hook from the seabed.

Roscoe leaned forward, tense. Then faintly, down the deck, came the triumphant cry, 'Thick and dry for weighing!' The anchor had been tripped and now hung freely down.

This point in unmooring, termed 'anchors a-weigh', was a decisive moment for it meant that *Thunderer* was now legally at sea. But it also signified that the ship was free to be driven by wind or tide, and sail had to be set without delay.

Orders volleyed out – fore topsail to be loosed and backed, main and mizzen topsails sheeted in to the opposite side and hands to clap on braces for some rapid work.

So far, so good.

The big ship imperceptibly gathered sternway, and as this strengthened, with doubled helmsmen struggling to hold her, she began a sheer to pass through the eye of the wind and at the same time put her head to seaward.

In a way Kydd would not have been sorry to see some kind of blunder, a human mistake on Roscoe's part, but when the fore had been braced around and courses were set, he could see he'd called it at precisely the right time. Their sternway lessened and, after a heart-stopping pause, a chuckle of water under her forefoot indicated that she was safely under sail and outward bound.

Forward, the dripping black of the anchor broke surface and the fo'c'slemen bent to cat and fish it before too much way was on the ship, while everywhere a hive of activity was securing the ship for sea.

*Thunderer* was on her way to war.

'A satisfactory evolution, Mr Roscoe,' Kydd told him.

The man merely glanced sideways once.

'As will allow you to set sea watches.'

His gaze locked with Kydd's for a heartbeat before he turned and went forward.

Taking a last sight of the safely approaching Penlee Point, beyond which was the massive Rame Head, Kydd could see nothing to stop him leaving the deck to the officer-of-the-watch, Briggs, and he retired to his cabin.

Luscombe helped him off with his coat and Kydd fumbled for his worn and comfortable sea-going one. He was about to return to the quarterdeck when his eye fell on the screen door. Impulsively he crossed to it and found himself on the holy ground of the stern gallery, the entire width of the ship, beautiful carvings on all sides and a fretworked rail at its after edge. He stood for a moment, held by the spectacle granted to him alone in the ship. It was of a gentle wake roiling astern and the peculiar sensation of the sea and land slipping back on either side, a perspective he'd never experienced before. It provoked a surge of emotion, the age-old elation of putting out into the vast wastes of ocean and the adventures lying in wait – but at the same time, all he held dear in this world was out of sight now and he was leaving it indefinitely for who knew what fate.

He took it in for a little while longer, then retreated into the great cabin.

'Hello, Harry.'

Craddock rose from his chair in embarrassment. 'Oh, the sentry said you were here but when I entered . . .'

'I was enjoying the view from my stern walk. Do join me.'

They stood together, wordless, as Penlee slid past and merged into anonymity with the Devon countryside, then into a blue-grey haze of land fading into the distance. Kydd's senses told him that Briggs was making directly south, close-hauled on the starboard tack with a slight Atlantic swell coming in abeam, and for the first time the distinctive symphony of creaks and groans that were *Thunderer*'s unique response to the sea were evident.

'Well, old fellow, how are you settling in?'

Craddock considered for a space, then answered, 'As no one knows me or where I've sprung from, shall we say tolerably well?'

'You're not sure.'

'The midshipmen generally leave me alone but the warrant officers I feel are wanting in common courtesy to a newcomer.'

'Oh?' Kydd growled.

'Nothing of an aggressive nature but rather more of a sniff and ignore. A trifle wounding in the circumstances.'

It would be hard going for an intelligent creature, little or no conversation except with the child-like midshipmen, and having one's social and bodily being in with the old, bold sea masters and their often narrow views.

'Let me think on it,' Kydd murmured.

Luscombe hovered, unsure what to do next.

'See the cook, if you please, and let him know I'd like to have my dinner at one bell after midday, as the men take theirs.' The officers generally came together for a meal at about two, but Kydd liked to have his at an hour when there'd be useful time left in the afternoon for work. 'You'll join me, Harry?'

'I will, with pleasure.'

They were interrupted by the firm double knock that announced the first lieutenant.

'Sea watches set, Mr Briggs and larbowlines closed up for the forenoon.' With a single side-glance at Craddock he went on with his recitation of the state of the ship.

'Thank you, Mr Roscoe.'

He turned to go but Kydd called him back. 'Mr Roscoe. Another matter, less connected with the ship, more concerning her citizens.'

At least it brought raised eyebrows.

'You being president of the wardroom mess. You'll know that Mr Craddock here as my confidential secretary is out of the goodness of his heart as well temporarily discharging the function of ship's clerk.'

'I'm aware of it.'

'And that he is a distinguished gentleman, not to be thought one comfortable with the company to be obtained in a gunroom mess. Might the wardroom consider him suitable for honorary membership, upon payment of a full subscription in course?'

87

'I rather doubt it,' Roscoe retorted.

'Oh? One would imagine Mr Craddock to be a valued member. Pray why not?'

'There are no precedents that I've heard that allow a ship's clerk and fore-mast hand be granted fellowship of the wardroom of a ship-of-the-line. Further, it would undoubtedly be viewed as a blatant attempt to secure for a favourite a greater prize-money share than he'd otherwise be entitled to.'

'Favourite? I resent the implication, sir!' Kydd said hotly. 'Friend, yes. Favoured above all others, no!'

'Nonetheless, I believe it not unknown in the sea service for gentlemen – no doubt for reasons of their own – to take anonymous refuge in a ship-of-war. It will be pointed out that as they must needs berth with the men, why not your, er, gentleman?'

'Mr Craddock? Sir, if you knew the one fourth of what he's gone through when—'

'Captain Kydd,' Craddock interrupted calmly. 'Sir, do not vex yourself on my account. I will mess in the gunroom – the nature's gentlemen there are pure in spirit if not in speech and I shall find my place.'

There was little Kydd could do and Roscoe knew it. He was president of the wardroom mess and held powers of moral and social discipline in addition to oversight of the catering and wine books. If he objected to Kydd's humane suggestion then Kydd was powerless, for the wardroom was their own to regulate and run without interference.

That in the past he'd been able to secure the privilege for his particular friend Renzi was only because a frigate's society was much smaller and tighter, which had allowed Renzi, somewhat illegally, to claim it as a captain's secretary. In a battleship's wardroom it was all big ships and regulations, and he couldn't ask it.

'Is that all, Captain?'

Kydd bit back a retort, then said, 'Mr Craddock will mess in the gunroom. Carry on, Mr Roscoe.'

# Chapter 16

A ship-of-the-line is a quite different beast from a frigate, Craddock mused, as he went below for his meal the following day, past strangers without count, rows of vast guns, expanses of deck that in other circumstances could do service as a ballroom. Above all there was a feeling of massive bulk, of indomitable strength, so different from the light and almost nervous movements of a frigate, with its emphasis on finer lines and speed. It would take a little getting used to.

He couldn't blame Kydd for not winning him a place in the wardroom against the immovable mass of crusted tradition, so valued in the Royal Navy. Still, he would see Kydd regularly to their mutual intellectual benefit, and in the meantime would keep up an appearance in the gunroom, with its concentration of sea elders.

It was midday and he joined those bellying up to the gunroom table for their meal, easing himself in beside one of the master's mates. The dining appointments were robust but plain, well scrubbed and neat: two gunroom servants to bring the mess-kids of stew and bread – in its barge still soft tommy so soon after leaving port.

A chipped crockery bowl and pewter spoon were provided and he tried to make light conversation with the master's mate while awaiting his turn. The gunner, the unsmiling Lawlor, sat in state at the end of the table, glowering until his serve of stew, with the best lumps of mutton, was dished out. On one side of him was the oaken bulk of Opie, the boatswain, on the other the wiry form of Upcot, the carpenter, who were in some kind of amiable disagreement. Further down sat three master's mates with a youngster at the opposite end allowed the privilege of eating with them in return for running errands.

Presumably the half-dozen midshipmen berthed in the orlop below would take their victuals when their betters had eaten.

'Free the slide then, y' idlers,' the carpenter threw down the table in ill-tempered impatience. The butter dish was obediently pushed up to Craddock and conversations resumed. The master's mate next to him seemed to have no larger vocabulary than grunted monosyllables and the one opposite refused to catch his eye. As he was seated at the furthest remove, there was only the ship's boy to talk to and his anxious attention was reserved for the seniors at the other end.

At last the mess-kid arrived at him and from its hollow depths a few wooden ladles' worth of stew and bones were scraped and slopped into his bowl, the penalty for being last. Craddock burned. It wasn't so much that his food portion was so miserly but that this was the third time it had happened. It would never have occurred if he was recognised as a full member of the mess and able to claim his fair whack. He was still waiting for his blackjack, the leather tankard used for beer. Everyone else had theirs in front of them.

He pushed away the bowl and stood up. 'Mr Lawlor, I feel

I must point out that I believe I'm hardly done by in the article of food and claim your intercession.' The rest of the table stopped eating in frank astonishment.

The gunner barely glanced up from the spooning of his gravy. 'It's talkin' again.' He glanced at the boatswain. 'Bull, tell him to siddown and get on with it. This'n is all he's goin' to get.'

Opie swivelled around to see Craddock with his one good eye and took in the miserable serving. 'An' he's got a case, Nobby,' he rumbled. 'The thin end o' the scran every time.'

'So? He's a clerk, ain't he? Does no work as a man would call it.' He put down his spoon. 'Hey, you, Pedro.'

Pedro? The Spanish beard, of course. 'Mr Lawlor?'

'Claim dismissed, mate.'

The table resumed its noise and chatter and Craddock hesitated then sat down. The master's mate opposite gave a sly smile and found something technical to engage his neighbour. He thought he detected a shadow of sympathy in Opie but it was a closed community and he was the despised outsider.

# Chapter 17

That evening Kydd was alone. It would not help Craddock just now for the captain in front of the others to invite him to dine, but he missed his company. In *Tyger* the first night at sea would be marked by noise and jollity but that was not to be in *Thunderer*. In palatial splendour he would take his victuals on his own, lord of all he surveyed but master of precious little. He could give orders as he liked but to direct men's minds and allegiance was not within his power, only his persuasion.

He tried to read an improving book on the possible developments the war could take but flung it aside in despair. He crossed to the stern walk and stood gazing out into the gathering dusk where the land was disappearing as the officer-of-the-watch made his offing and with it his last tenuous hold on the life he'd come to cherish.

Irritated with himself, he went back to the great cabin. Luscombe had lit the lamps in their sconces and he sat in his chair, awaiting supper. The pipe 'down hammocks' would turn the mess-deck into a dense sea of swaying canvas when the men had finished their grog and supper.

He would end with a nightcap and then he would be ready to turn in.

The pipe duly pealed, and Kydd heard the usual thunder of hundreds of feet as seamen took down their hammocks from the nettings on deck and flung themselves below. But after some minutes his supper had still not arrived. He waited, becoming more annoyed: he knew the officers would be well into their own with the cheer and joviality of old friends finishing their day.

Eventually Luscombe appeared, flustered and pale-faced, bearing a tray.

'Where have you been, pray?' Kydd asked, frowning.

'Oh, s-sir, the cook said as how you have yours after he's done for the officers. And as we're now at sea the galley fire is out . . .' He trailed off.

The captain to be served after the officers? Clearly they were taking advantage of the young innocent, and in any event the galley fire was always doused for the silent hours so a cold collation was all that was to be expected. If he made a fuss it would go hard on the lad and he would spare him that. 'Ah. Then what do we have tonight?'

The covers came off. Cheese and bread. Ship's issue cheese sliced into near transparent thinness, four slices of cask beef similarly treated, all garnished with an unidentifiable sprig of greenery. And a delicate silver goblet containing some kind of thin gruel.

He began to eat. It was no fault of his servant that the victuals were so poor. In the morning he would discipline the pranksters. Kydd was tempted to send for wine to take away the taste of the musty cheese but he did not feel like drinking. 'Well, young man, how are you taking to a life at sea?' he asked genially, finishing the humble repast.

Luscombe blinked and avoided his eye. 'Not as I'd fancied it afore,' he mumbled.

'Oh? Then what can this be?'

'Er . . .'

'Speak up, lad!'

'They . . . they jest and laugh at me for a Johnny Newcome and won't tell me how to do things. And make me do their washing as well as yours, and—'

'Laundry is not in your duty and they know it, the low shicers.' He stopped himself – he couldn't interfere here either. He was as powerless as ever. They were showing contempt for their captain by taking it out on the young man, and unless Kydd could deal with the larger issue it would go on.

'Well, never mind, Luscombe. This is the tradition of the sea, as I suffered it once. Turn in now and get your head down. It'll pass.'

The hunted expression eased at the extraordinary confession of his captain, and Kydd sent him away before his messmates could do much with his hammock.

That these petty fooleries must concern the captain of a mighty ship-of-the-line with far greater worries was aggravating. His primary duty was to the ship, to bring her to full fighting trim in the shortest possible time. Within three or four days he would be making his number with the commander-in-chief, then taking his place in the line-of-battle, no more to decide *Thunderer*'s day. With a rush of feeling he realised he had only this handful of time to bring her to a level of effectiveness that could see her a trustworthy part of the fleet.

He would start tomorrow. Sail, guns, evolutions.

It wouldn't be easy. He knew nothing about the ship he

was commanding, what was possible, what was asking too much – of *Thunderer* and his men. He had to know all the little foibles and eccentricities that his ship possessed so that he would not be caught out in the heat of battle. He had to make discovery of these in the few days left to him. Once he knew the weaknesses he could concentrate on them.

Feeling better, he turned in and dropped into a dreamless slumber.

# Chapter 18

In the pre-dawn half-light Kydd was jerked awake by a grating discord. A mournful ringing, the knell of hopes and dreams, a sepulchral reminder of mortality – for whom?

Struggling awake he shook his head to clear it and realised it was the bell forward tolling: the mariner's worst fear – fog. A glance from a window confirmed a milky blankness in every direction.

The ship was barely under way. His ornate hanging cabin compass was showing their course as west by south, set to round Ushant later but from now on there would be no certainty in their progress. It wasn't likely that they could end on rocks as they were well mid-channel by now but, in the busiest shipping lane in the world, they could find themselves in a collision course to a homeward-bound merchantman.

On deck Smale was hunched in his foul-weather gear, dewdrops of condensation forming runnels down it. He looked up in relief as Kydd approached. 'Came on just now after the wind veered. And out of soundings, hereabouts,' he added. The usual remedy, to anchor until the fog burned away in the morning sun, was thus not open to them. They must press ahead at some three knots or more merely to keep steerage way on, with the risks this would bring.

The morning-watchmen appeared, padding to their stations in the cold and damp, a savage contrast after their warm hammocks.

'Minute guns, if you please,' Kydd ordered. It would make it hard on the off-going middle-watchmen trying to snatch their rest, but the safety of the ship came first. After an interval the first fo'c'sle swivel barked into the blanketing softness.

The fog wouldn't last. Already, the high royals and topgallants were taking a breeze that, with the sun in an hour or two, would result in a clearing to brilliant sunshine.

Then, almost as a ghostly spectre high in the whiteness, Kydd saw the suggestion of a fore topgallant sail. And, from its perspective, it was ignorant of their presence and cutting across their bows.

'Hard up the helm!' Kydd roared. 'Hard up!'

Painfully slowly, *Thunderer* paid off to leeward, her bowsprit tracking away from the menace, but the unknown ship was under all plain sail and moving fast. Thinking quickly Kydd leaped over to the mizzen course sheets and began throwing off the turns to slacken the sail until relieved by startled seamen. Hopefully the crew on the fo'c'sle would think to flat out jibs and staysails to form a rotating lever to help her around faster. It seemed to work – they were going to make it!

But in the other ship the lookouts woke up and screamed their alarm aft. In a panic of fear the wheel was put hard over to the wrong side. The end was inevitable, a long drawn-out colliding bow to bow, thankfully at a fine angle but the noise and bedlam were overwhelming. A rending, cracking and splintering gave way to a visceral thumping and deep twanging as rigging caught.

*Thunderer* was close-hauled and had been struck on her weather side with sails and gear sagging to leeward. Mercifully, little damage was done but the nameless merchant jack was going large downwind: she had suffered more, her canvas ripped, ropes stranded and trailing.

*Thunderer* tore free from the assault and fell off to leeward. Kydd rapped out the orders to douse sail, then rounded on Smale. 'A boat in the water, with Mr Briggs and half a dozen marines. Now!' he barked at the flustered lieutenant.

'Sir, they won't need rescuing, they're—'

'Do it!' snarled Kydd.

The merchant ship was now dead in the water, drifting slowly ahead. It gave him plenty of time to do what he planned.

'I'll thank you to discover our hurts while I'm away, Mr Roscoe,' Kydd ordered the newly arrived first lieutenant.

'Away? You're thinking to board that merchantman?'

'I am.'

Kydd buckled on his sword, clapped on his gold-laced cocked hat and got aboard after Briggs. With his coxswain, Boxall, at the tiller they headed for the mutilated vessel.

Kydd snatched a glimpse of the outside of *Thunderer* as they passed. She looked half in ruin but he knew appearances could deceive. Small damage and disorder in the extraordinarily complex tracery of lines that was a square-rigger's gear might look calamitous but could quickly be put right by a skilled crew.

The merchantman, a fair-sized general cargo vessel with no flag to be seen, was in a worse state but her spars still held. Her name was *Success of Bristol* and there was little doubt of her nationality. Eventually a rope ladder unrolled and Kydd hauled himself up, seething with anger and resentment.

'The master?' he roared, unmoved by the disorder and ruin on deck.

A figure approached, picking his way through the tangle of debris. 'Youlden, barque *Success o' Bristol*, Tilbury in spices.' The man was sullen and defensive, desiccated by long tropic service.

'Captain Sir Thomas Kydd, His Majesty's Ship *Thunderer*.' He paused to let it sink in. 'Mr Youlden. You'll know why I've come,' Kydd said, his voice tight.

'You were athwart my bows as I couldn't do aught to stop it.'

'Under full sail in a fog? And helm orders all ahoo when we're sighted at last? I won't argue, let your owners do that. You'll sign a deposition as to events and times before I think to leave.' He was conscious that the Royal Marines sergeant in charge had paraded his men at attention in a line behind him.

Youlden mumbled something but Kydd guessed what had happened. Towards the end of his voyage the master had been cracking on into the fog competing for his freight first landing and his lookouts had been few or none. The affidavits from both sides would clear Kydd, and if *Thunderer* was fit to resume her passage, it could safely be left to the Admiralty lawyers to bring justice to the situation.

'The barky's in no danger, I see,' Kydd said, as he was ushered below. All damage was above the waterline and a group of men were beginning the long and disheartening process of hauling in and repairing the ravelled lines while others took in the rags of canvas and brought up more to bend on in their place.

Getting the deposition was not a protracted business, the facts speaking for themselves, and tucking away the signed papers in his coat, Kydd regained the deck.

He looked about, then declared loudly, 'And I'll take a score of your hands, if you please, Mr Youlden.'

There was a concerted rush to the hatchways but the wily sergeant had already posted his men well.

Youlden turned on Kydd in a fury. 'You're pressing men after all this and a six-month voyage from the Indies?'

Kydd nodded, a hard smile playing. After what had happened he had little compunction in stripping the merchantman. 'Mr Briggs?'

It was neatly done. At the collision every seaman had hurried on deck and since had been put to work clearing the raffle. With them prevented from hiding below, Briggs had his pick.

'Let 'em collect their dunnage while Mr Youlden writes me a note-of-hand on the owners for their back wages.'

# Chapter 19

*The gunroom,* Thunderer

'The kind o' guardo move you'd expect from a dandy-prat frigate-built bastard,' the gunner said, licking his burgoo spoon and looking around the mess table. The general consensus was that it was a crying shame on the poor beggars within hours of England after so long at sea and Kydd deserved nothing but scorn for his action.

Craddock kept his opinions to himself. If they hadn't the sense to see that getting the extra hands would make it easier for them he wouldn't be the one to bring it up. Kydd was on deck with the boatswain, who was at work with his mates bringing order to the chaos, and Craddock was taking breakfast in the gunroom with the seamen not in the boatswain's party.

*Thunderer* had not suffered overmuch in the incident and a morning's splicing and re-reeving, some timber repairs and paintwork fully restored would see them much as they had been.

With the brilliant morning sun came a veering and

strengthening of the wind into the north-west. Impatiently Kydd let them get on with their repairs, and when they were completed he sent the men to dinner an hour early and told Roscoe that he expected the officers on deck for sail-drill with the men. It would rouse their hostility but there was more at stake than their feelings.

He stood by the wheel as men tumbled up from below and took station – Briggs at the fore-mast with the experienced fo'c'slemen, Smale at the main and Mayne at the mizzen and under eye. The breeze was obligingly freshening, the seas were no more than playful and the Channel was opening up to the Atlantic with all the world ahead of them.

It was time to make the ship dance.

First the basics. 'Full and bye,' he ordered. As comfortably close to the wind as she would lie.

A dog-vane fluttered in the weather shrouds and Kydd could see that they were achieving a steady six points by the wind – not bad.

'Heave the log,' he rapped. The midshipmen went into action. One held the rotary log-reel over his head while the other prepared the log-ship, the wooden stop to be streamed. It was hurled into their wake and the shout 'Mark!' went out when the first knot on the line shot past. A sand-glass was turned and the log-line rattled away until the glass had run out. The number of knots that had gone over the taffrail was noted.

'Seven and a whisker,' the master's mate reported.

Kydd sniffed the wind and stowed the information in his memory. 'Luff 'n' touch her,' he called, ordering them to ease the helm until the weather leech of the main topsail began fluttering. *Thunderer* was as close as she could claw to the wind. He peered over the leeward side and saw that the lower-deck gun-ports were still a good four feet above the seething side-wake. So, they could fight to leeward when hard by the wind.

The slight swell and running seas were coming in on the bow. 'Lay over to starboard until the seas come in abeam,' he commanded. Obediently the helmsman eased the wheel until the slap and thump of the waves along their sides became constant. Kydd, balancing on the balls of his feet, sensed the change in the motion of the ship. She sailed on smoothly, not deigning to dip and wallow – she was therefore not crank, reacting with excessive lean and slow recovery to the swell of the waves under her. Neither was she stiff, jerking upright as soon as the swell passed beneath her keel. She would be a good gun platform.

'Put the ship about, if you please,' he told the sailing master. The old ship had docile manners and he was beginning to breathe easier.

Now to where the mettle of his seamen mattered. They moved mechanically, carefully, with none of the egoistic leaping of the frigate sailor.

The shouts rang out: 'Ease down the helm!'; 'Helm's a-lee!'; 'Rise tacks and sheets!' and then a satisfied 'Mainsail haul!' and finally 'Let go and haul' and on to the new tack.

Kydd timed it: twelve minutes in all. If the breeze had picked up there was every chance she could make it in ten and never a foot of sternboard. It was more than adequate and even compared favourably with *Tyger*. The drill, however, had been suspiciously faultless. Was it the result of so many empty exercises of a fleet on blockade?

'I'll have the courses taken in and tops'ls with two reefs.' This was more or less as would be needed when closing in on the enemy for a gun duel or desperately easing the strain on masts damaged by enemy fire. His timepiece still out, Kydd consulted it, glancing up every so often to see the men racing up the shrouds and crowding into the tops. He waited until the midshipmen messengers hurried to report their masts as completed. Suspiciously, they arrived within seconds of each other, and the times were woeful. Was this because the order was unusual in a fleet and therefore not practised?

'Not as I'd say a prize showing,' he muttered to Roscoe, who recoiled and looked away.

'Now let's get the reefs out and courses set in half the time,' Kydd said briskly. 'Carry on.'

This time he didn't concentrate his attention on the watch but kept his eyes on the men.

The fore topsail was handed and reef points let fly in a fine show, but then the men stayed where they were, out on the yard. The main topmen were slower and they, too, came to a stop. Then the mizzen – the least skilled in the ship and accordingly kept aft under eye. And when they had laboriously completed it was as if a starting gun had fired. On all three masts there was a disciplined scramble as the topmen laid into the tops and, as one, the shrouds became black with men as they made the deck together.

'What the . . . what the devil's this about?' Kydd exclaimed in amazement to Roscoe.

'I thought myself it was rather well done,' was the tight reply.

Kydd grimaced: the performance was just that, a pretty and spectacular circus trick designed to make the ship look smart and prove how it was working faultlessly together. 'Rubbish!' he snorted, consulting his watch. 'I've never seen slower times. What's the meaning of it, sir?'

Roscoe drew himself up. 'These men have done their best,' he ground out. 'And you're obliged to admit, they all touched deck again within seconds, first and last. Do you really expect—'

'I expect to loose sail under fire or stress of weather in the smallest possible time, not entertain the crowd.' Kydd was conscious their raised words were reaching many ears but didn't care. 'We do it again, but frigate-fashion.'

The features of his first lieutenant were pinched and dangerous. He was responsible to the captain for the manning and rating of the men aloft and Kydd's words were a condemnation.

'Be damned to it!' he burst out. 'You're going to cripple this ship with your small-ship ways. These men at least know exactly what's expected of them and do it. Now you're—'

'*L'tenant Roscoe!*' Kydd blared. 'Go to my cabin and wait on me there – *this instant, sir.*'

In the appalled silence he caught Smale's eye and rapped, 'You have the deck, Mr Smale. I won't be long.'

# Chapter 20

Roscoe stood in the centre of the cabin, his face white but resolute.

Kydd didn't waste time. 'Sir, what I heard on my own quarterdeck just now I might choose to consider an insult before witnesses. And prejudicial to the provisions of the Articles of War relating to the conduct of an officer to his superior. Pray give me reason why I shouldn't seek court-martial on you?'

Leaving no time for a reply he went on, 'I've suffered all the provocation I need to have you confined to your cabin until such times as we join the fleet, there to be removed. You'll be broke, sir.'

There was no change in the tense, defiant features.

Kydd felt a moment of hesitation: the man was in other ways a good officer, who cared for his men. 'Before I do, Mr Roscoe, I ask you one last time. Why in Hades do you behave towards me in this manner?'

For a long moment there was nothing. And then Roscoe looked away, clearly struggling. Something was riding him, a personal animus that went beyond his resentment of a frigate captain.

Kydd waited patiently but the defences remained up, the unyielding obstinacy still plain. He wavered, at the very edge of making the order.

'I must apologise to you, Sir Thomas, if it appears I'm wanting in conduct to your principles. I shall endeavour to improve my behaviour.' The voice was a monotone, under great self-control.

Kydd drew in a ragged breath. It was barely enough but could he take the gamble of keeping him, at the risk of his remaining a focus of disaffection in the ship?

He let out the breath slowly. 'You've just three days to renew my confidence in you as my first lieutenant. Fail me and you're finished, Mr Roscoe. Understood?'

'Sir.'

'Then we'll return and continue with our little exercise.'

'Sir.'

The first two marks of respect he could remember from him. Was this a turning point?

On deck no one had moved an inch. Men still clutched ropes, tailed on tackles and stood in orderly groups, stolidly waiting.

Kydd strode out and stopped by the helm. 'Hale aft all the mast officers and their warrant officers,' he demanded. He waited until they had presented themselves, then began, in a friendly voice, 'The first l'tenant has been good enough to explain to me how sail-handling has until now been conducted in *Thunderer*. As you know, I come from frigates and I'm used to a different way of doing things. A faster way.'

He could tell by their expressions that hackles had risen but gave a boyish grin and continued, 'But I can give you a smart turn-out all the same.'

What they wanted were the regimented movements that resulted in a synchronised mast-by-mast sequence ending with a mass return to the deck. They were achieving it, but by the device of taking their time from the mizzen. Consequently all three masts were held back by the speed of the slowest.

'Sir. The mizzen is going as quick as it may,' Mayne blurted. 'I don't think we can—'

'This is nothing to do with the mizzen, sir. We change our objectives. Frigate-fashion, we put times before appearances and in doing so retain our smartness.'

Briggs looked puzzled. 'How is this, Sir Thomas? I've served in single-deckers and never a care given to mast times or evolutions by the book.'

'Then do learn how it's done in a crack frigate. This will be carried through by *you*, gentlemen.'

He saw he had their attention now – and, out of the corner of his eye, Roscoe's.

'At the next drill each of you will observe along the yards to determine the most able topmen in action aloft. The object is to put them out at the yardarm for any manoeuvre. The slower go to the bunt. We shall do more than a few exercises and between each you'll refine your positioning on each yard until you have your fastest crew. Clear?'

There were slow nods, so he went on: 'And this is not all. Then we run the drills several more times and each yard is timed. At the end the first lieutenant, from these, will evenly distribute the best crews across all three masts. This way you'll get them naturally finishing and getting off the yard and on deck together. Compree?'

This time there were smiles of understanding.

He had lied: this was not how it was done in any crack frigate he had known. In a frigate an officer *knew* his men for he could be leading them, without much warning, into a boarding or stealthily on a hand-to-hand cutting-out expedition and needed to be aware of their qualities intimately. To distribute their seaman-like talents evenly was a trivial task.

'Oh – and allow to the people that their captain believes their hard labour is deserving of reward. It's to be a double grog at supper.'

'Knows his nauticals, then.'

The boatswain nodded in acknowledgement. 'None o' your strut-noddy fancy ways, Nobby.'

'Aye. An' I knows why.'

'What's that, then, Nobby?'

'Cos he's a foul-weather jack. Can see it in the cut o' his jib. He doesn't want t' be laid by the lee in a blow by a parcel of landmen.'

The carpenter slapped down his leather blackjack. 'Not as I sees it,' he said definitively.

'Tell us, why don't ye, Lofty?'

Craddock set aside his book to listen to the carpenter, a long-serving standing officer through several captains and years of service.

'You should know. Different ships, different long-splices – some owners come down hard on sail, others for gunnery. You're safe wi' yer iron, Nobby – he's a salt-horse sailin' man.'

Opie sank his drink and gave a satisfied smile. 'Um. Nice touch of him, the tots. Many wouldn't give a toss about what it takes to fist a sail.'

'Bribes.'

'No, Lofty, don't reckon on this one needin' to do that.'

'Doesn't have to. He's not goin' to be in *Thunderer* fer long, mates. He's in thick with the Prince o' Wales an' his crew who won't stand to see him out o' hail for long. Just putting in time for his admiral's flag.'

'Heard he's a fightin' seaman – Spain, the Med, Java, all over,' Opie said uneasily.

'O' course ye has,' the gunner replied forcefully. 'Any small powder gets burned, it's in all the papers, a proper noise. I'll believe it when m' peepers tell me.'

Craddock couldn't help it. 'In his last ship they called him "Tom Cutlass" and no doubts as to his mettle with a fat purse of prize money for all hands after the last voyage.'

'Bull, tell yon Pedro that we don't need 'im to put his oar in. We makes up our own mind.'

# Chapter 21

It must be all around the ship by now, Kydd mused. He and Roscoe were not getting along and there were no guesses as to who would be first to suffer. The first lieutenant was always strictly polite, still speaking few words but punctilious with at least one 'sir' in each utterance. After a while its near artificial expression grated on Kydd but he realised its purpose: evidence. In any future court-martial the question 'How did you address Sir Thomas?' would be answered with a factual reply that he'd rendered marks of respect always.

Whatever the state below decks, one thing was plain. At this time it would be disastrous to invite Craddock to share his cabin in companionship. It would be seen as the formation of factions with Craddock, as his man, in the midst of them all. Kydd would have to endure his solitude for now. He could only hope that the man would take care of himself in the meantime.

The trick with the sail-handling the previous day was easy enough with those not living daily at the edge of imminent action, but in a few minutes the bell would strike the forenoon watch when the entire ship's company would turn to for exercise at the great guns. There were no bluffs or short-cuts in gun-handling, and it would be a hard day for all.

Luscombe entered with Kydd's action rig – a near threadbare coat with the minimum of gold lace that would very soon be smeared with powder residue, and old-fashioned breeches but with fine silk stockings in stout shoes against wounding. And his fighting sword. He caught sight of the lad's features and his heart wrung. Dark pits around the eyes, listless movements and avoidance of Kydd's gaze.

'Are the beggars not leaving you alone, Josiah?' he asked kindly, deliberately choosing to use his forename. 'I'll have 'em keel-hauled!' But Kydd couldn't do a thing about it and the young man's tormentors would know it.

'It's not just the names, it's the jokes,' he said miserably. 'Y'see, I can't understand them and they fall about laughing.'

Common seamen were continually with their shipmates, their messmates, and very soon they'd get to know a raw new friend and take him in hand. Luscombe didn't have that asset: theirs was not his society of equals. Instead he was in with the idlers, the stewards, servants and suchlike, and his world was half theirs and half that of the potentate in his palace.

The firm double knock. 'Both watches of the hands mustered. Sir.'

'Thank you, Mr Roscoe. I shall be on deck presently.'

He had moments to detach himself from one distressing problem to concentrate on the larger issue at hand. Should he reach out to the crew, who would have to fight for him, in a stirring speech, trying to make himself heard to six-hundred-odd men on a blowing deck in a seaway, or limit it to the principals to pass on as they pleased? Or begin without ceremony or notice the savage and brutal ballet that was gun-play in a man-o'-war?

They'd had warning enough. He'd made plain his views on the primacy of gunnery in a warship at last night's dinner, but then only the officers had been present. It was the seamen at the guns he needed to inspire, smashing in the broadsides to fight the ship for him.

They were by their guns when he emerged on deck. In their hundreds, a battleship at quarters, but with expressions varying from boredom to glassy-eyed indifference.

Kydd was no stranger to thirty-two-pounders, the biggest great guns afloat, as carried by first-rates like *Victory*. He'd served his time at them as a young pressed man, and the drill he'd learned then was deeply ingrained.

'Officers at quarters, lay aft,' he ordered those who, during action, were stationed on the gun-decks fore and aft. Under them strove the lesser mortals, the master's mates, midshipmen, quarter-gunners.

In pithy, down-to-earth terms Kydd laid down what he wanted: two entire decks of guns working together to make a species of hell for the enemy such that *Thunderer* must inevitably prevail. Speed, coolness under fire, care and attention to the safety of the ship, with cross-training to ensure a gun would not be put out of action by a key member of the gun-crew made a casualty.

The first concern was to take measure of the gun-crews, their performance at standard gun drill.

He took out his watch and gave the order.

Harsh shouts rang out and the men bent to their task in a methodical flourish, but wielding their implements sloppily, rammers of one gun tangling with spongers of the adjacent. Consequently those on the gun-tackle of a 'fired' gun interfered with the neighbouring gun running out.

It was a dreadful display of incompetence. These men had

obviously not exercised together for some time. They were simply going through the motions.

'Cease fire.'

Almost lost for words, Kydd hesitated. All thought of timings was irrelevant – this performance was not even half decent. It had been sham firing, of course, imaginary round-shot and powder cartridges used. Would they do better in the din and blood of a genuine action?

'Mr Roscoe, when was the last gun practice?'

'Um, I believe the last Friday of the month previous. Sir.'

'And the last live firing exercise?'

'I – I cannot readily recall, sir. I can ask the gunner if you wish.'

Kydd bit his lip. 'The last engagement with the enemy at which *Thunderer* burned powder?'

'Oh, er, that must have been the hostility off Rochefort, in deterring a sortie putting to sea.'

'When was that, pray?'

'About two years ago, or was it nearer to three? Sir.'

No wonder it was such an abominable showing. In the same period *Tyger* had been in furious action more than half a dozen times at least.

It was no excuse, and Lyell should have countered it with imaginative exercising, competition and rewards. This was a mere grudging byplay, the main attention going to smart-ness and appearances.

'I shan't conceal it, sir,' Kydd told him sorrowfully, 'this greatly disappoints me. And we shall do something about it. I want the officers, assisted by their warrant officers, to observe closely the guns being served, to take particular written note of those of each crew who gets out of the way of others.'

He hoped he could bring about the same kind of even distribution of talent as in the sail-handling. It would be painful, breaking up gun-crews and their comfortable relationship with each other, but greater issues were at stake. And in both cases the priceless side benefit would be the officers' acquisition of a close familiarity with their men, their capabilities, weaknesses, peculiarities.

'Sir?'

'I'm interested in the ones spry enough to make good gun-handlers, ignoring the rest getting in the way.' It was obvious to him that this was a sign of superior agility and alertness. It seemed not to his first lieutenant.

'Quarter-gunners are now responsible for their gun-captains,' he continued. Those were the petty officers in close charge of every four guns and the most experienced gunners. 'Should they see any failing in their duty they're to rate the second gun-captain in his place without the necessity of consulting the officer of his division.'

Their duty would be read as not only competence at the gun-lock but, more importantly, power of command in their crew.

Once a quarter-gunner had a list of the better ones they would be put to the more skilled tasks: manipulating the rammer, the wad and cartridge, the shot. The remainder would be condemned to the brute labour of the tackle falls each side of the gun, which were used to run out the three tons of iron after reloading inboard.

And, finally, the timings would be used to show up the more successful gun-crews and those who were weaker, a continual process as crews were refined to a point at which Kydd was satisfied that an elite was emerging. To earn distinction and public incentives, these men would then be set to instruct the rest of the gun-deck on how it was done.

If only he had *Tyger*'s gunner's mate Toby Stirk aboard to take them by the scruff!

Impatient to be started, he set the larboard side guns to three firing cycles under the mocking eye of the starboard crews. It was a shambles as the quarter-gunners came down hard on the gun-captains, who in turn bullied their crews, but the process was beginning and Kydd left them to it. They would exercise all forenoon and again in the first dog-watch. By tomorrow he'd have his list and the laborious upward path to skill-at-arms with the great guns would begin.

# Chapter 22

*The gunroom*

Lawlor came below in a foul mood, throwing himself into his chair with a growl. 'He'll be the ruin of a good barky, that scrim-shanking knows-it-all,' he snarled.

'Nobby, he's got his ways, an' it's how they does it in frigates,' the boatswain soothed, ruefully inspecting the bread-barge, now with none of the soft tommy from shore. 'Younker, get us some more,' he snapped at the gunroom boy.

Craddock sighed and laid his book down. 'I'd advise you fall in with Sir Thomas's desires, er, Nobby. He's a habit of dealing harshly with those who cross him. Better for you in the long run.'

Lawlor ignored him and made much of screwing his chair around so his back was towards Craddock, who burned at the insult.

'Lofty, why does we have t' suffer a clerk in the gunroom? Why don't 'e sling his hook with his high-struttin' matey aft?'

'Yeah! Why doesn't ye, Pedro?' the carpenter grunted.

'Because this is my mess,' Craddock replied bluntly, and buried himself in his book.

'Fair enough, mates.' Opie chuckled then looked reflective. 'So we're back wi' the fleet tomorrow. Floggin' up and down until we rot with our ships. Ain't human. I'm missin' m' woman, don't mind tellin' ye.'

'Me as well,' the carpenter said, in a low voice. 'Lives up at Clydeside and I haven't seen m' Mary and the little 'uns in a dog's age. How's it fer you, Nobby?'

'Wife's dead 'n' buried these four years, mate. Lives with the family now.'

Opie glanced across at Craddock and said mildly, 'Y'r lady has t' get used to you bein' at sea for years now. How does she feel about that, Pedro?'

At first Craddock didn't respond, his gaze fixed on the page, then he paled, his grasp on the book near manic.

'Hey, Pedro,' the boatswain said, concerned. 'I didn't mean t' say—'

'I saw my wife and children some months ago burned alive by the French in the Adriatic,' he said quietly, but with an edge of madness. 'And I'm on the ship as the best way I know to afflict the monster Bonaparte. To torment the very coast of France seems a fine enough thing.'

The gunroom was shocked into stillness.

'I think . . . a little sea air is what I need at the moment.' The book fell to the deck as he rose carefully, dignified, and took his leave.

'Harry – how good to see you!' Kydd exclaimed. 'Sit down, old chap – a snorter?'

Craddock eased himself into an armchair with a wry smile. Solitude dure must take a toll on a fine mind like Kydd's. 'Just wanted to see if there's anything I can do for you.'

'Let's not worry about that,' Kydd said happily, then noticed something in Craddock's face. 'You're feeling well, Harry? Are they treating you with respect in the gunroom, the salty devils?'

'I have a question.'

'Fire away, old fellow.' The lines in Kydd's face were easing in the warmth of their meeting again.

'You said before your officers at dinner that I was acting as ship's clerk *in temporarius* only until another be found. Does this mean—'

'Dear chap, believe me when I say you shall have tenure for as long as you desire it,' Kydd answered fervently. 'It was only a device to explain your presence on board.'

Craddock loosened and smiled. 'Then I shall rest content.' The fingers twisted together unconsciously as he went on lightly, 'As I do confess that I find myself not yet ready to take my place among the shore creatures as you'll understand.'

'I do, Harry – I do. I can only apologise deeply for the condition of this ship. It's not what I'd want for my friend to endure.'

'Take no mind on my situation, Thomas. My messmates are a parcel of nature's children only and have no real apprehension of the wider world and its sorry tales of suffering *in extremis*. Or even the ineffable rapture of having one's being cradled in the deep while in the society of those of like mind and character, never to be plagued by the alien beasts of the land.'

Kydd looked at him in awe and affection. This was the friend he so desperately needed to see him through this time of trial. 'Talking of beasts . . .' He hesitated. What he was about to say went across all his years of sea service on the quarterdeck but at the same time it would tell him how far he could go with Craddock.

'Beasts, yes?'

'My precious first lieutenant . . . Harry, believe me when I tell you that a first lieutenant is a priceless fellow whom I must trust with my life and, even more importantly, the ship. It's a sad problem for me.'

Craddock heard him out then answered, 'I rather think that it's not your problem, more the sainted Roscoe's.'

'Yes, but—'

'The problem is his to solve. Inside, he's nursing a canker, a grievance or hatred, but unless he conquers it himself, his future is to be damned. His end in *Thunderer* is inevitable, and once removed under a cloud, his chances of either promotion or another ship are not to be entertained.'

'That's as may be, Harry but what's to do?'

'I believe you're right in the particulars – you're powerless to do anything. He must be the one to move. Your only course is to give him every chance to find a remedy or let Fate take him from the board.'

'He's at root a good hand,' Kydd admitted, 'and if it weren't for his infernals I'd welcome him as premier.' But the three days he had given him to prove himself worthy would soon be up . . .

The gunroom fell silent as Craddock returned. Without comment he saw his book had been carefully placed on the table and he picked it up. Finding his chair still available he settled to resume it.

'Feelin' better, shipmate?' Opie said quietly.

'Thank you, yes.'

'Um, I has a drop o' the right sort as'll cure y'r mullygrubs, Pedro.'

Surprisingly, it was the gunner, his voice now low and gruff. He fumbled in his ditty-bag and, looking about him suspiciously, came out with a bottle.

'That's kind in you, Nobby,' Craddock said politely. 'Just a small one, if you would.'

'Nasty blows topside, this time o' the year,' the carpenter said, with a rumbling sympathy. 'Watch y' don't catch a green sea as you're not expecting, mate.'

'I will.'

'Is there anything we can do fer you, cully?' Opie's compassion was transparent.

Craddock gave a smile of appreciation. 'That's well meant, Bull, and I thank you for it, but time will heal everything, I'm persuaded. For now I feel all a-taunto.'

This brought grins all round.

'Can I ask it, Pedro? How did youse and the captain get alongside each other in the first place?'

'Certainly you may, Lofty. In short, he was on a raiding party on the Balkan shore and . . . and did rescue me from the flames. Since, I flatter myself that I was in some measure of use to him in the article of intelligence as he roamed the Adriatic bringing disaster and ruin to the enemy.'

'In a frigate.'

'Yes, *Tyger* frigate as distinguished herself nobly at Lissa where I had the honour of being present.'

'So it's true, what we heard, that 'twas a right good drubbing?' On blockade, news filtered through slowly.

'It was. That I can assure you – and as well, that Tom Cutlass is your natural-born fighting captain as you'd be proud to own to.'

The gunner looked awkward. 'But – I humbly begs pardon – it doesn't sit s' good with us as he gets in thick with that scowbunkin' crew at the King's court just to get hisself a sail-o'-the-line.'

'Aye,' the carpenter said, his voice rising. 'Specially when it costs a man his own ship.'

'Hold, you ignorant swabs,' Craddock said, in his best seamanlike growl. 'He didn't even want a ship-of-the-line. I tell you, as I'm the nearest thing he's got to a friend, that when he heard he was to take *Thunderer* he nearly wept. You see, he once did a favour for the Prince of Wales who thought he'd be returning it by insisting he gets a bigger ship, more prizes, he thinks.'

'Than a frigate? The loon.'

'Just so, Lofty. Now can you imagine how Captain Kydd feels? All his honours and prize-tickets won in a frigate, to have it taken away, a fast, sweet-lined frigate, with independent cruises for blockading. But he's never going to be cast down. He's going to do his duty and bring *Thunderer* up to the mark as he sees it – frigate fashion.'

There were thoughtful looks before the gunner declared, 'Then we goes for it. Give 'im a chance. Right, mates?'

# Chapter 23

U shant could just be made out emerging from the grey murk of mist and drizzle to larboard. A long south-westerly swell from the opposite direction told of a wicked storm far out in the Atlantic. Here, however, winds were sullen and fluky and, given his concerns of his unknown crew, Kydd wasn't going to attempt stunsails to make a quicker passage. In any case the Channel Squadron was just around the corner.

'Stand down, starb'd gun-crews, close up larb'd.'

For the starbowlines there was panting, stretching and rueful flexing, but he noticed that the men had turned to more willing, giving it heart. Also, the larbowlines clapped on to their tackles with real purpose.

Kydd was not about to give away precious hours of practice simply because Admiral Keith's fleet was not far off and they would still be drilling when the flagship hove in sight.

Grimly, he paced the gun-decks, his splendid silver hunter on open display.

The miserable light rain didn't spare the nine-pounder

crews at individual practice on the quarterdeck and fo'c'sle, but where was it decreed that battles were fought only on a fine day?

Quite unexpectedly a man-o'-war slid into view from the lee side of Ushant. It flaunted the red ensign of the commander-in-chief and its challenge was replied to in the correct manner. Kydd ordered the signals master's mate to hoist 'Come within hail,' inwardly exulting in the power he now had to order about the grandest frigate.

Obediently the vessel swung about and glided into their lee, striking sail as she did so. He watched, knowing exactly what was going on – the languid movements deliberately designed to yield sea-room to the massive and less agile 74.

'*Jason*, Captain Everard, sir,' came a blare from a speaking trumpet held by a figure on her quarterdeck, no doubt curious to know who had relieved Lyell at such notice.

'*Thunderer*, Captain Sir Thomas Kydd. Any news?'

'None, the mongseers so shy. If it's news, do you have anything from England, Sir Thomas?'

'Send a boat and you shall have a newspaper or two, Captain. Where are Lord Keith and the fleet?'

'In this breeze? In the Iroise, somewhere between the Vieux Moines and Raz de Sein, Sir Thomas.' That was the age-old fair-weather station, clamped directly across the harbour like a rat trap and about thirty miles distant.

*Thunderer* would rejoin the fleet in the small hours.

Meanwhile the order went out, 'Hands turn to, part-of-ship, to clean.'

Admiral Keith, a dour Scot of unbending will and probity, would have seen *Thunderer* depart the trimmest and most cared-for ship in the squadron, and would expect her back in the same condition. If it cost Kydd his precious hours at the sails and guns so be it, in this his first appearance before the commander-in-chief.

The Western Squadron of the Channel Fleet was raised later in the afternoon, a straggling line hardly moving in the oily swell and peevish winds. The flagship was nearly hidden behind a slow-drifting curtain of light rain, but when she emerged, glistening and stark in colour, there was a hoist at her mizzen peak halliards.

'Our pennants, sir – "Captain to repair on board".'

There would be no gun salutes, for this would alert the French that the forces opposing them outside had increased, unwise when everything was being done to lure them out.

*Thunderer* lay off to leeward and Kydd took to his barge.

The 100-gun first-rate *Royal Sovereign* was one of the legendary ships of Trafalgar. She had flown the flag of Admiral Collingwood and had had the honour of being the first ship in action that fateful day. Kydd had vivid memories of seeing her from *L'Aurore*, his first ship as a post-captain. This day, however, he was boarding her a baronet, with fame and honours – and as the captain of a ship-of-the-line that had been at Trafalgar in that same line-of-battle with Collingwood.

He mounted the side-steps, hauling on the beautifully knotted man-rope to the entry-port. It was thrilling to be piped aboard by a full crew of side-boys and lieutenants, each in white gloves in honour of his august rank, only a step below an admiral.

He faced aft and doffed his hat, then acknowledged the group of officers inboard, who stood together while he was relieved of his dripping oilskins. And in the centre waited a slender, long-faced senior officer, with cold, flint-like eyes and hard features: the commander-in-chief, Lord Keith.

This was the admiral who had lifted him from the common

herd as a lieutenant and raised him to commander of his own ship, the brig-sloop *Teazer*. In those fearful days on the eve of invasion when the navy had stood alone against Napoleon, Kydd had served in the white-hot centre of the fight, Keith's Downs Squadron.

He snatched off his hat and bowed. 'Captain Sir Thomas Kydd joining your command, my lord.'

'With *Thunderer* in hand and fit for service?' That well-remembered Scots brogue and cold stare. 'Much the more important to me, sir.'

He followed the admiral aft to his day cabin and took the chair offered him. A long, appraising look and then, 'Ship in good order, ready for what must come?'

'She is, sir.'

'Then it's well with ye.' A tiny icy smile briefly appeared. 'As before you've proved yourself worthy o' my trust – when was it, the year aught one, a lieutenant running afoul of your captain? And turned y'sel' into a first-rank frigate man since.'

'Sir. I can only thank you again for—'

'Which is what I want to talk to ye about.'

'Sir.'

'I've no sense of why their lordships took you out of a crack frigate and pitchforked you into a sail-of-the-line. Some say it was the Prince of Wales interfering on your behalf, but I doubt it. You're a prime frigate driver, Kydd, and it doesn't have much meaning.'

'I can assure you, my lord, that it wasn't myself who—'

'Be that as it may, sir, my advice to you is that you must be prepared to change your ways. More to my sorrow, I've no place for a daring, bold and thrusting captain in my fleet. Before, you made a decision and acted on it to secure prizes by your own efforts. What I want and need is a captain I can rely on to a split yarn in carrying out my orders in the heat

127

of battle, who'll stay the course and suffer grievous enemy fire while stoutly remaining in the line, who'll keep the vessel fighting whatever its wounds.

'The age of Nelson quitting the line is over. We may well be summoned to our duty supreme at any moment and I want no heroes at my expense.'

'I understand you, my lord.'

'Then we shall get along. Now, have you seen service before in these waters?'

'Never at length, sir.'

'A pity for, as ye'd know, this is an iron-bound coast and among the worst to be found anywhere. La Rochelle and to the suth'ard?'

'With Captain Cochrane at the Basque Roads engagement and above the usual sea service off northern Spain.'

'That will do. I will attach you to the Rochefort squadron, Rear Admiral Houghton. At the moment all is quiet and you should not look to much entertainment from Boney but you'll no doubt be informed of the strategic situation by the admiral.'

'Thank you, my lord. It shall be my pleasure to serve under you.'

'Oh – so remiss of me. Before you quit the station for Rochefort do stay and take dinner with us. There's precious little diversion on blockade and I would have you meet your fellow captains.'

# Chapter 24

'Rochefort, La Rochelle?' Craddock said lazily, as he took his ease with Kydd in *Thunderer*'s great cabin. 'As I spent a glorious summer there in business before the Revolution. Rochefort and its cheeses, Bordeaux to the south with its claret and, should you need more, Cognac to the east for its *eau de vie*. That the Aquitainians should be caught up in this madness is none of their doing. By the way, how did the dinner go?' He hoisted his glass high and squinted through it in mock concern.

'Such a quantity of naval officers of the highest *éclat*, it would turn the head of the most jaded.' He didn't mention that for the most part the looks cast across the table had been ill-natured and sour, the conversations abrupt and barbed. It didn't take much to realise that the canard of his reaching for influence at court had reached even there.

*Thunderer* would depart at dawn the next day. Two days more of independence to bring his ship to a full fighting asset.

Kydd remembered a hard-countenanced Captain Houghton

in the old 64 *Tenacious* years ago. Was this the same man and, if so, how would he be as an admiral?

At some two hundred miles southward there were the same baffling breezes and sullen swell. *Thunderer* was not at her best in light airs and, with diminished wind force on her higher sails, she rolled badly with the swell coming abeam. Kydd sent Luscombe away, his seasickness wretched. Others fell into the same miserable existence: gunnery practice was a shadow of what it should have been and, with only a slight breathy wind, sail-handling would have little meaning.

The Rochefort Squadron was at neither of the two rendezvous, north of the Île de Ré and the estuary of the Gironde, and no cutter or frigate was posted to inform of their whereabouts. There was only one thing Kydd could do: sail up and down between the nominated points and hope to sight them or be spotted by scouting frigates. It was odd: a blockade required that a deterring force be seen to be effective, and there was not a warship in view.

The following day, passing the lighthouse at the tip of the Île de Ré, they came upon four battleships lying at anchor, several frigates and brigs moored further inshore. Challenges exchanged, Kydd brought *Thunderer* to anchor at the end of the line and prepared to make visit.

Houghton's flag was in the centre, in *Pembroke*, not a 100-gun first-rate but a 74, like *Thunderer*. To man and maintain such giant ships was an expensive and questionable act when a squadron was so small.

Kydd mounted the side-steps to be received with side-boys and pipes in the now accustomed ceremony. He was greeted by *Pembroke*'s captain, who explained that Admiral Houghton was caught up with much work but would nevertheless like to see him.

*Pembroke* was a newer ship, built and launched with the rise of Bonaparte. Plain and sparing in adornments, she was a creature of war, not peace, and her great cabin seemed a place of frowning rather than ease. Houghton was standing legs abrace, his heavy face tugged into grim lines, the same unsmiling, abrupt manner that had kept the officers of *Tenacious* in humble subjection. But now there was also a marked paunch and sagging jowls.

'Sir Thomas Kydd, *Thunderer* 74, to join, sir.'

There were no decorations or sashes on Houghton's uniform and Kydd had never heard of any action in which he'd distinguished himself.

'You took your time, sir.' There was no sign that Kydd had been remembered, but it had been a long while ago.

'I raised rendezvous in two days from the Brest station, sir. In both I could not make out your squadron.'

'Didn't it cross your mind that we might be just to seaward on an important occasion?' His face was flushed.

'I felt it more in keeping with my orders to remain at the rendezvous, sir.'

'A gross lacking in initiative, sir. I was under the impression that you frigate captains had more backbone, b' God. But, then, could it be that, having laid hands on your ship-of-the-line – by whatever means – you may be inclined to a quiet life?'

Kydd's heart sank. Here was another tainted by Prinny's unfortunate act, however well meant. When *would* he be able to shake it off? 'My elevation to a sail-of-the-line command was not my doing, sir. It was—'

'Damn it all, sir. I will not have the pickerooning style of a frigate in my fleet! You'll act the captain of a ship-of-the-line both in my presence and away. Should you not, I'll see you relieved of your command. Understand?'

Whether it was the assumption of an unfair influence at court or rank jealousy at his successes and fame as a frigate captain, Kydd saw that in Houghton he had a dangerous enemy. One who could bring about his professional ruin. It would only show up the difference between them to remind him that at one point he was a first ship junior officer under him. Kydd had risen swiftly, a knighthood and prize money, and through all the ranks bar Houghton's, while the other man had progressed, but that one step.

'I do, sir,' Kydd replied evenly.

'Then see Flags, sign my order book and get back to your ship. We sail as a squadron tomorrow for fleet exercises.' He regarded Kydd with pursed lips for a space and, with a muttered 'Carry on, Captain,' sat heavily at his desk.

The flag-lieutenant was garrulous but all sympathy. 'His Nibs only made flag earlier this year, and all the world knows it'll be his last appointment, only in post because Essington at the Admiralty owes him a service.'

'I see.'

'Likes to think he's a Nelson but this translates into bullying his squadron when at his copious exercises. Here's your orders, Fighting Instructions and signal codes. Could I suggest, Sir Thomas, you ensure your signal crew gets it by heart?'

'So, not a fighting admiral.'

'You burn powder, you account for it in five ways or you'll be held to the expense.'

'Sociable?'

'In a word – no. Just between we two he's plenty of friends he keeps in his quarter gallery, and every so often he invites one out to make merry, not forgetting to remove the cork first.'

'The other captains?'

'They seem content enough with ship-visiting each other when at anchor. You'll get to know them soon enough.'

He rattled off the names. *Malabar*, *Resolution*, *Asia* and, of course, *Pembroke*. All 74s and a mix of new and old. The captains' names meant nothing but they were the ones he would join in the line-of-battle, placing *Thunderer* where it may, trusting their courage and seamanship to keep the line unbroken.

So, a crabbed and envious admiral, a quiet station and no prospect of action or distinction in these times of stalemate. It was the worst situation for any officer trying to catch the eye of the highest. On the other side of the scale was the certainty that if he stumbled in his command of a ship-of-the-line it would be seized on by his enemies to bring about his public downfall.

The evening gun thumped out from *Pembroke* at the point when Kydd's barge was halfway back. A scurvy move by Houghton: the practice was for each ship to follow this with guard and band of marines paraded as the ensign was lowered. All officers would solemnly face aft and remove their hats in respect. What was he expected to do, being at neither one place nor another?

'Oars!' he growled. The boat glided to a stop and Kydd stood up, faced *Pembroke* and slowly removed his hat, remaining in position until the last faint strains of the band had drifted over the still waters. He would not be found lacking in respect for his superior.

His spirits were low when he returned to *Thunderer*. Under Houghton, all thoughts of a chance at independence, of a personal hammer blow at the enemy, were derisory. He could look forward only to a future in this backwater of animosity and futility, even with his own officers and ship's company.

Craddock was waiting for him and picked up on his mood. 'Not a joyous meeting, I'm sanguine.'

'No.' Kydd looked around for Luscombe. 'Where's that youngster now?' he muttered. 'Had enough time to learn the ropes and so forth, surely.'

'Ah. I meant to see you about that.'

'Why?'

'Because the lad came to me in some misery and distress and asked me for advice he couldn't get from you.'

'Oh?'

'Recollect, Thomas, he comes from a different world, the genteel society of the Devon countryside. His head was no doubt filled with dreams of adventure and prize money with a legendary local sea fighter. Now he's finding that the rations are vile, the company worse and seasickness thrown in free of charge. And no prospects for advancement that the meanest pressed man can hope for. He's bright and well-mannered, holds himself proud and doesn't indulge in profanity. Dear fellow, he doesn't belong in a ship of war.'

Kydd slumped back in his chair. In effect Luscombe was enduring *Thunderer* in much the same way as he was, but without the benison of being able to do something about it, however slight in effect. 'So what should I do for the poor wight?'

Craddock gave a lengthy sigh. 'I cannot conceive of any act you might take that will relieve what ails him. Like your Roscoe, his salvation lies within himself.'

# Chapter 25

'Prep, "unmoor", sir,' Mayne, the signals lieutenant, called out smartly. He'd been warned off by Kydd that any slackness in responding to the flagship's hoists due to unfamiliarity with the signal book would have serious consequences.

'Very good. Messenger, let the fo'c'sle know.'

Kydd had their hastily scrawled orders from *Pembroke* to proceed to sea by a cast to larboard when all anchors were signalled a-weigh, leading to a forming up in Order of Sailing on a line of bearing west by north.

Anchors were won more or less together, but *Thunderer* and *Malabar* took more of the cheerful breeze on their beam and, when their anchors broke ground, began drifting to leeward. *Thunderer* was dangerously overlapping and bearing down on the other ship.

All ships had not yet hoisted their 'anchors a-weigh' and therefore no sail could be set without orders. Kydd felt a paralysing inevitability. But then, galvanised, he roared forward, 'Let fly jibs and headsails!' and spinning about ordered, 'Sheet in the driver!'

It gradually stopped the frightful sight of their spearing bowsprit aimed into the belly of *Malabar* but at the cost of setting his ship aback. The only solution was to bring the wind on the opposite side. This sent *Thunderer* back through the forming line, mercifully missing *Asia* and ending up well to weather of the ragged line.

The 'Form order of sailing' hoist was thrown out and jerked down in the 'execute', and the remaining two ships scrabbled to obey. Almost immediately the signal was hoisted again, and with it *Thunderer*'s pennants, and the flat thud of a gun to draw attention of the delinquent to it. Kydd's ship was being held up before the world as laggardly and incompetent.

Inwardly raging he began the difficult and dangerous manoeuvre of taking up parallel with the line before insinuating himself under full sail between *Resolution* and *Asia* in accordance with the Order of Sailing. Before he could complete it, in a maliciously timed act, Houghton required the squadron to execute a 'wear squadron in line', the order for all ships to turn as one off the wind and around to take up on the opposite tack.

It threw out Kydd's meticulous calculations but he saw a way through. To wear a ship needed plenty of searoom in their wide wheel-about but Kydd had *Thunderer* at a sharper angle in his attempt to regain the line and, able to cut across the turning circle, he eased in astern of *Asia* and settled on course as before.

Taking up on the new track, Kydd absorbed the arresting sight of a fleet of ships from the inside. Foaming along in *Asia*'s wake, the ships ahead were all but out of sight, occasionally visible when sagging to leeward but for the most part his view was dominated by the ship ahead's stern of martial plainness.

Further on, *Pembroke* was completely obscured but that was what the repeating frigate *Hyperion* was for, standing well out to windward to read the flagship's signals and hoisting them for all to see. Kydd had more than once performed this office and knew that from the moment battle was joined the flagship would be near hidden in a double measure of rolling gun-smoke and the frigate's purpose gone.

The line-of-battle was a completely different experience and gave meaning to much of what he'd seen from the outside in the several fleet engagements he'd been at in a frigate. He realised what it meant to be part of a fully formed-up fleet. Bucketing along at twice the speed of a running man, he was expected to keep a steady two hundred yards from the ship ahead – a bare three ships' lengths, or forty seconds of travel, with all the inertia of several thousand tons of battleship.

'*Hyperion* from Flag. Squadron, take station line-ahead, one cable.'

When a ponderous ship-of-the-line took whole minutes to bring in sail, the equivalent of the brake on a carriage, this was a fearful demand on seamanship. At first Kydd burned with resentment until a calmer voice told him that not only was the reigning admiral perfectly entitled to order this, to close the line for an impact from an enemy trying to pierce it, but this was precisely what he himself had ordered at Lissa.

'Mr Hobbs,' he called to the sailing master. 'A cable apart. Can we do it?'

'Sir.'

'Carry on, if you please.'

He'd never been in a fleet manoeuvring in such close order, except the informal succession of eager men-o'-war entering the bay at the Nile. But then he'd been a junior signal lieutenant in an old 64 and had had little interest in the technical details of the manoeuvre. Now it was completely different: he was a captain. He watched an elaborate positioning of men on all three masts, tailing on to the braces, the weather tack and sheet of every large sail.

Crisp orders from Hobbs had sails trimmed from forward, coming aft one after the other until he was satisfied. *Thunderer*'s bowsprit unerringly tracked *Asia*'s stern walk as it advanced slowly by yards. No need for sextant angles between mast height and waterline, a single cable's distance was easy enough to judge by eye.

'One cable, sir,' Hobbs said impassively, his seamed countenance immovably fixed on the ship ahead.

It was intimidating, the continual stream of trimming orders forward to aft that kept them in place, and the large number of men involved, but this was how it was done apparently. Why so many? It seemed it was believed that a precise distance apart could be achieved better by many small adjustments, and therefore most of the watch-on-deck would be standing by a line, ready to trim.

Kydd turned and raised his pocket telescope to check on *Malabar*, next astern of them. As far as he could make out she had the same arrangement, and all three ships were scrupulously at their correct distance.

But something in him rebelled. The object was achieved, but was that all? If a desperate encounter was looming, a clash of fleets in a grand way, with nearly all of the ship's company employed at sail-trimming to keep an admiral satisfied, they could not be manning guns or readying weapons. Admittedly the close order of sailing was necessary in certain circumstances but there must be a better way.

In frigates there were occasions without number when a convoy was escorted. Some, like the Baltic convoys, included hundreds of ships by column and row. He'd taken it for granted when as escort he'd closed with them to demand better station-keeping but how actually had they done it? With the whole crew constantly stationed at the lines? No. With crew numbers cut to the bone they all used the same method: a chosen sail, usually a topsail, with one corner led up on the lee side to the tops by a strong purchase. The idea was to spill wind in a controlled manner simply by this one tackle and a small number of men on it.

His mind saw how he could rig *Thunderer*'s fore topsail, leaving all its gear in place so when battle was joined it could readily be cast off. Meanwhile a small party would be all that was necessary to spill wind to the master's order to scrub off speed or ease out to spread more canvas, more speed, in just the same way as the merchant jacks.

Inelegant but effective. He'd do it!

By now he knew Houghton's intention was to make life as difficult as possible for him so, without doubt, he would spring a new manoeuvre shortly. The most complex and intricate had to be setting the squadron to sail large, the winds from directly astern. At this point of sailing there were no weather tacks and sheets because they'd be on neither a larboard nor a starboard tack but in effect both. By the usual method employed he had no other option but to man both sides of every sail, every hand he could find on the end of a line. In his way of doing it, they'd simply rig a similar purchase on the other side of the sail as well.

But that wasn't the worst of it: each ship, apart from the last in line, would be blanketing the next ahead, stealing her wind. It would make for a nightmare of orders rattling out to deal with the fluky wind currents swirling up the line, and the chances of a collision, through inability to manage speed, were that much greater.

By his method, adjustments could be made far more rapidly

– again not so prettily, viewed from outside, but much more safely.

'Mr Hobbs. A word with you, if I may.'

The master didn't argue, simply saying neutrally, 'This then is frigate fashion, sir?'

'No,' Kydd said shortly. 'As they do it in a merchantman.'

At Hobbs's suggestion, in view of the blanketing effect of their own sails, the mizzen topsail would be handed and the main topsail was put to taking the purchases.

As he'd suspected, within the hour *Hyperion* threw out the signal for the squadron to run large.

It worked immediately. Moving forward to the quarterdeck rail to stand by the men at the purchases, Hobbs could see as well their side wake and their next ahead, and quickly developed a system of hand signals to control their wind-spilling and hauling.

And for the first time in a long while Kydd gave a long, slow smile.

Hardly had the squadron come to moor at the end of the day than 'all captains' was demanded from the flagship.

'A fair day's work,' Houghton said gruffly, 'were it not for the abominable display of attempted station-keeping by one of you.' His pompous and carefully enunciated speech spoke of his having visited his friends not very long before.

'I won't name the ship concerned but you all will have seen her lubberly exhibition of man-hauling her canvas about in an ungainly and grossly unprofessional manner. Such ignorance of elementary fleet manoeuvres has no place in the Rochefort Squadron, I must with pain point out.'

No one caught Kydd's eye. In career terms it was better to fall in with the admiral than stand with Kydd, no matter the justice of the cause.

'As a consequence we shall repeat the manoeuvres tomorrow. I trust I shall see a marked improvement or I shall be compelled to take strong measures in the case of any unable to stay with the squadron in its motions.'

There was little more to discuss. Houghton had had his petty triumphs and the captains left the great cabin, visibly relieved.

# Chapter 26

They congregated on *Pembroke*'s quarterdeck while they waited for their boats, chatting amiably about everything except the day's events.

The urbane and polished Devenish of *Malabar* came over to Kydd, the only one of them to do so, and murmured something he couldn't catch, then paused and said more loudly, 'And I'd consider it an honour to entertain the victor of Lissa tonight, Sir Thomas.'

Kydd was still boiling with rage and knew he'd be a poor guest. 'Thank you, no,' he said unsteadily. 'Too much work.'

Devenish looked at him curiously then courteously took his leave when *Thunderer*'s boat was announced.

The pull back was conducted in silence, the boat's crew quailing under Kydd's black expression. When back aboard he strode viciously to his cabin and flopped into his chair. He needed a whisky badly and roared for Luscombe. There was no response and Kydd swore under his breath. Where's that useless galley skulker?' he spluttered. Something would have to be done, no matter the lad was having a hard time settling in.

Then he noticed one of the doors to the stern walk ajar. And on a small table near it a piece of paper. Crossly Kydd got up and retrieved it.

*To Captain Sir Thomas Kydd, Bart.*

*Sir. I am truely sorry for my actions of this day. It is not becuse of you, dear Sir Thomas. It is that i made my own mistak to go on a ship. I haite and lothe the sea and some of the saylers who think it funy to tawnt me so. This is why i leave Thunderer for a beter place. Dont worry of me, wherevr I go will be a happier lyfe for me. I pray, do give my humbal presnts to Lady Kydd and it is my last wish that you shuld prosper and be victorius alwyas.*
*Josiah Luscombe*
*Capts servant, HMS* Thunderer.

*ps — yr breeches for tomorow are wanting a press but are lade out on yr bed.*

Kydd froze. If the tormented soul had done away with himself then the blame was largely his for taking on a young-ster rather than a mature man able to care for himself below decks. His heart wrung with pity.

The door opened noiselessly. 'Dear fellow, I thought you were . . .' Craddock tailed off at Kydd's obvious distress. 'Something has happened?'

'Luscombe. He's gone over the side.'

'What?'

'He's drowned himself out of loathing of his situation.' He handed over the paper.

'Not necessarily. By these words he could have equally, um, left for the land in some way,' he finished lamely.

'The stern walk,' Kydd said abruptly and made for the screen door. On the gallery outside he saw a thin rope tied to the rail that led down to the water. 'You see?'

Craddock peered over. 'Ah. Then from this I deduce that, far from doing away with himself, he had the intention and means to flee the ship. A body bent on self-slaughter would plunge without complications into the deep, and here . . .'

Kydd returned to the cabin. 'Pass the word for the purser's steward,' he snapped.

After some minutes he appeared, puzzled and apprehensive.

'Luscombe is absent from place of duty. Do you and your men search for him – and report to me the state of his berth. Whether his clothing is still in his chest and so forth.'

In a short while the man returned to report there was no sign of Luscombe and his shared chest was empty of his gear.

'You see?' Craddock said, relieved. 'No suicide takes a change of clothes and his small valuables in his last plunge. He's headed for the land, sure enough. He's safe, but this makes him a common deserter, does it not?'

'Hold hard, Harry. He didn't have a boat,' Kydd said, with rising feeling.

Hurrying out on the stern walk he looked again and could picture it all happening. The lad had bundled up his clothes and lowered himself over the side. In the water he had struck out for the nearest land, Île de Ré, only a few hundred yards away. It would seem so close, but it was something no seaman would dare to attempt. The young landman had not realised that the island was off the estuary of the tidal Charente river. Fierce offshore currents were at play whenever the tide was on the make or ebb, and ran parallel to the coast, not directly into the shore.

He would panic, not knowing what was happening. The slight chop Kydd remembered from earlier had seemed to Luscombe like the waves of a storm. His bundle of clothes would become waterlogged, a dead weight, and in his terror he would let them go, splashing out in a muscle-sapping frenzy for the passing shoreline. His maniac efforts would rob him of his strength and the cold remorselessly seize him through his outer layers, insidiously penetrating until only a tiny core of warmth remained.

Somewhere out in the inner estuary he had known his last moments on earth.

Kydd gulped then ran through the cabin to the watch-on-deck. 'Man the cutter, hoist "Man overboard", and alert the first lieutenant.'

He ignored the curious glances and forced his mind to concentrate. The tide was on the flood at the time, and *Thunderer* was still at anchor in the same spot. A free-floating object from here would be carried in a giant spiral even further into the seven-mile width of the Pertuis d'Antioche.

'Boat ahoy! Search on a line of bearing sou'-east b' south.'

Roscoe appeared. 'Man overboard, sir?'

'My servant. Fell when priddying the stern walk. I sent away the cutter.'

Roscoe said nothing and fell back, awaiting events with the others.

In the gathering dusk the cutter was soon lost to sight but ominously reappeared some twenty minutes later. Closer to, Kydd's glass picked out a still shape under a tarpaulin. It brought with it a flood of despair that threatened to choke him.

'No, it's nothin' to do with the younker,' Kydd slurred, slapping down his whisky tumbler, annoyed that Craddock was taking it all so calmly. 'I mean, o' course it has, but why I'm s' down on the world is that it's as if his life was wasted in

145

the same w-way as 'most everything else is wasted in this accursed barky.' He took another pull, taking a fierce glee in the fiery path of the liquor down to his belly.

'Thomas, my dear friend. Do allow that I'm no simkin. I've been witness to all your travails, no matter that I can neither appreciate to the full their foolishness nor do anything about it.'

'Damn r-right you don't know the all of it . . . That's t' say, Harry ol' fish, there's much 'twould not be seemly for you t' know.'

'And at the same time I've seen you take full on each stab of malice, every idiocy – and win. I'm persuaded you've only to stay with it to prevail, dear fellow.'

'B-balderdash! In a sail-o'-the-line on blockade there's nothin' to give me hope I'll e-ever be noticed. Kydd o' the *Tyger* is no more. He's faded from the public eye an' will finish a sad figure nobody remembers.' He hiccuped, staring morosely at his glass.

'Of course not!' Craddock came back strongly. 'This is only a short period before you get an admiral's flag, and then—'

'With Houghton riding me all the time?' Kydd sneered. 'He's going to make damn sure I don't get anywhere near a fair report, an' admirals get made b' seniority an' old age, not even a rousing good battle.'

'Dear chap, you can't just—'

'Can't what? I've done main well in the article of prize cobbs, m' name's still known all over the country. Why not take t' my estate an' my most excellen' wife?'

'This is not what I heard before.'

'Well, you're hearing it now,' Kydd growled. 'I don't fancy t' spend the rest of my life witherin' my soul in pleasing that precious bastard, years o' nothing but—' He broke off, taking a long swig, wiping his mouth afterwards. 'Y' see, I don't need the navy any more. I've run m' course an' I'm ready t' cast anchor ashore.' He chortled as if in memory of something. 'Who was it said, "I'll leave the sea an' carry an oar into the land, an' the first man that asks, 'What's that thing you're carrying?' that's where I'll set up hearth an' home"?'

'That would be Odysseus, I think you'll find.'

'Yes. Him.'

It didn't seem to satisfy.

'Why not—'

Kydd's face crumpled. 'I own before you, m' dear friend, this'n is the worst, the lowest as I've ever been. No e-escape! Even my first luff hates me, an' the ship's company, why, they may be f-fine fellows for all I know, but they're not frigate man-o'-war's men, an' if it comes to a mill with the mongseers where'll they be?'

'At your side!'

Kydd seemed not to hear. 'I had m' dreams before, even as a green l'tenant, thinking about what it'd be, right up there as cap'n of a ship-of-the-line. Now I know an' I don't want it any more.'

'Not want the glorious elevation to the god-hood of captain of a battleship?'

'Don't mock me, Harry.'

'I'm not, dear fellow. But simple observation tells me there's still more you can give to your country. Much more and . . .'

But from the armchair there came only snores.

# Chapter 27

'Thick and dry for weighing.'

Kydd glowered. His wounded head did nothing for his mental acuity and he cravenly left the unmooring to Roscoe.

'Flagship – "Proceed in order of sailing",' Mayne called.

It was going to be a repeat exercise of before, as threatened by Houghton, and Kydd was faced with the decision of whether to do it the admiral's way or his own. In a wave of desolation he decided to let them do it any way they wanted to. He was finished with the navy.

After an interminable fussing they stood out for the open sea, back past the shoreline of the Île de Ré, young Luscombe's last sight of land.

The island was set out from the land at an angle, one side Pertuis d'Antioche and La Rochelle, the other Pertuis Breton and shelter against Biscay storms from the southwest. Any sail on one side would be hidden from vessels on the other.

The squadron reached the tip of the island in impeccable line – and were met with a shocking sight. A cloud of French ships not a mile distant was emerging from the other side on the same course and same larboard tack.

Kydd's bitter thoughts fled in an instant. He whipped up his pocket telescope, a beautiful three-draw model finished in mahogany and brass that Persephone had given him.

Concentrating on their manoeuvre the British squadron was slower to respond. The French, under the goading of their flagship, soon manoeuvred themselves into line – four ships-of-the-line and two outer frigates, standing out to sea in the freshening breeze.

Kydd didn't wait for Houghton's order. Cutting through the ecstatic jabber on the upper deck, the marine trumpeter and the pipes of the boatswain's mates sounded together the 'Clear for action'.

'Flag to squadron. "Form line-of-battle, west-nor'-west, distance two cables".'

The shuffling and commotion of the two-cable spacing seemed interminable before *Thunderer* could set about going to quarters and Kydd swore roundly. He was immovably locked into position in the line and could do nothing to alter the outcome. In the meantime the French were making good sailing while their opponents were sorting themselves out. They had not opened fire – at near a mile off they were now pulling ahead.

Kydd's mind took on an icy focus. What were the French doing? Most likely they had sheltered in the Pertuis Breton before the last leg to Rochefort past the Île de Ré, and with the short distance to go had neglected to send out a reconnaissance before leaving. It was their bad luck to choose the same time as the British. Or was it?

It was the greatest wish of a French admiral to successfully break out of blockade to the open sea, to stalk the sea lanes or join with others in ports closer to England to overwhelm the forces there and make invasion a reality. Houghton's foolish insistence on meaningless exercises instead of a blockade with patrols in depth had provided their chance. These four battleships – a very respectable force – were now ignoring the invitation to close action of the English forming up in line-of-battle and were on their way to freedom.

By now it was obvious to all on deck what was going on and the exultation and cheering died away, replaced by resentful looks at the ships streaming ahead.

Houghton, no doubt realising with horror that he would be held accountable for the release of these predators on the world, made an urgent signal.

'Sir – "General chase"!' whooped Mayne, as the order came to abandon the formal line-of-battle and make full-tilt for the enemy by any means.

Kydd seized the moment. 'Luff 'n' touch her!' he bawled. The move to windward took him out of the line at the cost of some way lost. But he'd craftily avoided the fate of the others who had all instinctively put their helm over to the easier leeward and now were trying to avoid each other and the balky winds.

The French would not give up their chance just to oblige the English with a general battle. Their intent was to disappear into the limitless wastes of the Atlantic, lose their pursuers and be free to do as they wished. There was little likelihood that they would turn back on their pursuers.

'Mr Hobbs – I want bowlines on the fore and main course and topsails.' These were lines led from forward that, by means of a bridle, stretched the forward edge of the sail to offer the tightest surface for working to windward.

'Sir, I'll do my best for you, but we never use 'em in the squadron. Y' see—'

'I can guess. You go at the speed of the slowest. Then do

what you can.' Kydd paused, then asked, 'How's her trim this morning?'

'Er, by the stern five inches.' It was the sailing master's job when at anchor to take note of the attitude of the ship in water as stores were consumed. Trimmed by the bow, her deeper forefoot would bite higher to the wind at the cost of delay in putting about; trimmed by the stern gave more manoeuvrability but meant pointing less high into the wind.

There were various devices he could put in train in a frigate to bring about a more bows-down trim, from moving guns forward over the deck to re-stowing the hold. But this was a massive ship-of-the-line and needed *all* the tricks he could think of that he'd used in the long years of running down his prey.

Soon *Thunderer* was foaming along, every sinew taut and straining, well out in front of the rest of the squadron. Hour by hour they drew further ahead and were hauling in on the French.

It was decision time for Kydd: join action when within range to delay the Frenchies' escape, with the risk that they could turn on him? Or track and follow them to discover their destination?

*Thunderer* was showing her mettle. Ropes thrumming with eagerness, sails flat and hard, the elderly battleship was thrusting forward like a cavalry horse in a charge, bursting through the waves on her weather bow. Eruptions of white sent the spray back aft in stinging, exhilarating succession.

At this rate they would be well up with the French before midday – burning powder before the sun reached its height. Kydd felt the age-old excitement build, now with the added zest that he commanded a ship of real force. He paced up and down with an impatience that was difficult to control after the recent heaviness of his heart.

'May I know what you intend, sir?' Roscoe stood by his side. He was wearing his fighting sword, a plain blued-steel weapon with a standard lion-headed pommel.

'What would you do, sir?' Kydd challenged.

'Fall in astern and follow,' he answered, in a level voice, without hesitation.

'And wait while our friends catch up?' Kydd came back ironically, flicking a glance astern. Houghton's squadron would be out of sight below the horizon in another hour.

'You'll offer combat, then.'

'We'll see. Pipe the men to quarters when the enemy's one mile distant and I'll make inspection. I may tell you that there's every reason to suppose we'll suffer grievously if there's an engagement. All attention should be directed to get the ship in the stoutest possible condition.'

'Aye aye, sir.' Was Roscoe showing spirit, animation, even?

At two bells, with the British squadron now completely out of sight, *Thunderer* went to quarters. In *Tyger* they'd appreciated a pre-battle rousing talk but in this ship, with him days only as her captain, it would be received in suspicion and possibly with contempt. Besides, it wasn't at all certain that there would be a battle, for what could be achieved? On her own *Thunderer* could inflict some damage to one or two ships of the enemy but the rest would plunge scornfully on, the prize of the open sea too alluring.

An hour later, as *Thunderer* closed from astern on the close-knit group of enemy ships the decision was taken out of his hands.

A string of flags mounted the signal halliards of the foremost, larger vessel. Taking Kydd by surprise it was answered by the rearmost two ships-of-the-line, which fell away from their close-hauled line and continued to turn in a wide arc, effectively splitting the line into two. The first continued their dash to seaward but the others were making as if to go after the now disappeared British ships.

What was happening? There was no meaning in the action and Kydd felt the first stirrings of foreboding.

There was not long to wait for the rear two were continuing around in what amounted to a circle and soon they would be as firmly in Kydd's rear as he was with the first division ahead.

Neatly done!

*Thunderer* was now in the jaws of a professionally sprung trap with no way out.

Kydd forced his mind to an icy calm. The logical thing now was for the foremost French to throw over their helm together to present their starboard broadsides and begin the execution. After their cannonade the rear division would lay out to smash their larboard broadside into *Thunderer*'s unprotected stern, as the first reloaded to continue the pounding.

But Kydd was about to do the unexpected: take the extraordinary risk of putting about to the starboard tack and away in the opposite direction. This was their only chance.

With a crew barely understanding his frigate-fashion methods he had to loose his own broadside. Then force the men in the smoke to abandon their guns and take to the lines to put the ship about while under cruel fire. Something he'd hesitate to do even with the Tygers. At four to one the odds were ridiculous but if this worked . . .

Kydd sent midshipman messengers racing down the deck to the guns with his orders and the strictest instructions for speed when the time came.

The French rear division had nearly completed their circle. Ahead, the first two threw over the wheel and began to heel as they fell off before the wind, in the process bringing their broadside to bear.

Getting in first, Kydd threw *Thunderer* up into the wind and, true to her name, she slammed out a full starboard broadside, the first time he had heard his ship shout in anger. Instantly he roared, 'Hands to 'bout ship!'

Pale-faced seamen leaped to obey the routine orders as the big ship began to turn, so incongruous in the bedlam of combat.

The smoke from *Thunderer*'s two decks of guns was tremendous, towering down on the first two preparing to open up with their own broadside. The barely trained conscript crew was near blinded of their target and their shot went wild, but *Thunderer*'s guns, crashing out their tons' weight of roundshot, lent their assistance to propel her around in the act of putting about.

When the rear division finished their circle they found the previously flying *Thunderer* stopped across their path, daring a collision. Their only recourse was to keep helm on to take them around again, but their guns were manned on the wrong side. Before the crews could cross the deck, Kydd loosed his own larboard broadside into the helplessly careering vessel.

It was breathtaking, only minutes from a doomed encounter to taking up on the new tack and putting distance between them.

A storm of cheering erupted in *Thunderer*, hoarse and unbelieving – but it was not over yet. The quandary still remained: to follow or delay? It was critical for Houghton to put an end to the foray. If Kydd wore around to resume position, without question the French commander would envelop him with his superior numbers.

Out of nothing came a glorious, battle-winning thought. 'Mr Mayne,' Kydd growled.

The signals lieutenant hurried up. 'Make – "Request shore provisions include treacle for thirty men".'

'S-sir?'

'Instantly – at the main, and with the priority pennant.'

'B-but—'

'Now!' Kydd said dangerously.

*Thunderer* threw out her urgent signal, followed by another at the mizzen – 'Permission for hands to bathe'. There were more but *Thunderer* was now shaping course to sail ahead of the French as they regrouped.

The dilemma had passed from Kydd to the French admiral. Could the whole thing, the absurdly handled main squadron and the remarkably speedy 74, be a larger trap to lure them seaward, to be set upon front and rear by a pair of squadrons acting together, as urgently summoned at that moment by this daring ship?

Napoleon Bonaparte would never forgive the admiral who gave the Royal Navy yet another victory, and that risk was not worth taking simply for a taste of freedom. Without further delay the French hauled their wind and scuttled back in the direction of Rochefort, leaving HMS *Thunderer* victor of the field.

# Chapter 28

*Aboard* Pembroke

'A near thing indeed, sir,' Devenish of *Malabar* said, with feeling. The admiral looked up with an ill-natured frown but Devenish went on strongly, 'As deserves our approbation and respect of Captain Kydd's action, I believe.'

'Rubbish,' growled Houghton. 'It's nonsense to believe four sail-of-the-line would in any wise take flight before a single. Without doubt the enemy saw our advance as the main force and decided on a retreat rather than risk an engagement.'

'But, still, when Sir Thomas—'

'Sir. Know that I take Captain Kydd's action as impulsive and ill-considered, not as befitting the command of a ship-of-the-line, more that of a buccaneer.'

Around the table the senior captains stiffened. They were not fooled by this bluster, and its public airing was in bad taste.

Kydd said nothing. He knew what had been achieved.

The transformation in his ship's company was almost palpable, and to hear the happy buzz from the mess-deck at grog and later the gleeful singing on the fore-deck told of a much different relationship developing. Roscoe had not shared in it, though, keeping out of Kydd's way and excusing himself from the evening's celebratory dinner.

'However, we're not here to debate a brush with the enemy, albeit well intentioned,' Houghton continued. 'It is to take note of a change of my plan for the blockade of Rochefort. Given that the French are daring to sortie in numbers, we shall no longer act as an offshore fleet in deterrent. We will disperse our effort among all their ports, patrols in depth to ensure it cannot happen again.'

His impressive tone did nothing to spark enthusiasm and he continued in evident pique. 'The following ports will be invested by one 74 and attendant sloop. La Rochelle, Rochefort, Bordeaux and Les Sables d'Olonne by *Resolution*, *Malabar*, *Asia* and *Thunderer* respectively. Your orders will detail how the squadron will gather and form line in the event a species of sortie is reported from any one of the above. Questions?'

It was only what was normally done at other blockaded ports and the region was quiet, no longer the powerful naval base it had once been. And the recent break-out attempt had been an unplanned, impromptu sally but it had alarmed Houghton enough to have his futile exercising dropped for the more usual and effective method.

No one had questions, and even if they had, they would not have been answered so they left for their ships.

Kydd knew the area well. With Cochrane he'd been with fireships at the battle of Basque Roads some years ago and remembered the shoals, currents and island forts that infested the coastline. He couldn't put a reason to why his port – Les Sables d'Olonne – was to be noticed. A medieval dried-fish port, tidal and cramped, it was never going to be the lair for a powerful battle squadron. Was this a move by Houghton to keep him from gaining any kind of win?

At least he was, for the moment, independent, and he had the quaint but reliable brig-sloop *Daphne* as his gun-dog to sniff out the game close inshore.

They headed north together, the sloop demurely in *Thunderer*'s wake, until towards evening they made out the low sandy coast of the Vendée and the sheltering headland of La Chaume.

Innocently continuing, Kydd waited until they'd passed out of sight from the shore, then hove to, signalling *Daphne* for a conference.

'Hoskyns, commander.'

The man was elderly but in keeping with his no-doubt foreign-built sloop had character and dignity.

'Welcome to the coast, Commander,' Kydd said easily, aware from his own experiences in the past that his exalted station and decorations might be intimidating.

The older man kept his composure. 'Ah, well, as I've been here nigh on four years, sir.'

'Then you're just the man I need. Our orders are to patrol and invest Les Sables d'Olonne.'

'Sir – why? It's rare good for stockfish and it has an inner harbour, but . . .'

'That these are our orders is all the reason both you and I will get. First I must have a reconnaissance. Is there anything of consequence within? It may be Admiral Houghton has intelligence that he's unwilling to share and inside there's a vessel of significance. The game is all yours, Mr Hoskyns. You have until this time tomorrow to take a peek.' It would be his decision whether to make it by day or night.

Even if he was on detached service, if this was going to

be the pattern for the weeks and months that followed it would be a tedious endurance, in effect like the Brest blockade, which had its inshore and offshore divisions with all the excitement belonging to the former. At least he was granted time to get his ship in order.

*Daphne* returned in due course, her commander somewhat downcast. 'In fine, nothing, Sir Thomas. And fired on for my pains by the heaviest metal they could offer.'

'Nothing?'

'A midshipman with a glass at the main-mast truck saw not a sign of anything three-masted within.' No sail beyond a brig or lugger.

'Then I've no alternative but to send you back, this time on patrol. La Chaume to Pointe de Tanchette until relieved. *Thunderer* will be in the offing at all times. Let me know should you spy anything interesting.'

'Sir. Oh, I did take note o' the guns, where they're sited an' such.' Diffidently, he handed over a folded piece of paper. It was a neatly executed plan of the small bay of d'Olonne with careful notations of the batteries and estimated size of the pieces, with their fields of fire.

'Thank you, Mr Hoskyns. Well spotted, and you're a caution to us all.'

# Chapter 29

The sloop leaned to the wind and was away, Kydd shading his eyes as he watched her go. In many ways these were the real heroes of blockade, not the lumbering line-of-battle ships, he reflected. Taking all the dangerous inshore work among the fringing reefs in brutish conditions of endless heaving seas and gales, prey for the men-o'-war that lurked safe in harbour, their endurance and skills were never going to be recognised by the public. Nor would they at any time be crowned with distinction.

*Thunderer* turned about for a three-mile run north, there to take up her night position. In the morning, under easy sail, she would put about and run down the coast for twelve miles before going about for the return, her passage in accordance with the table of rendezvous drawn up by the sailing master and given to *Daphne*.

The evening breeze was chilly and he went back to his cabin to call for a hot negus and warm togs, then remembered that he didn't have a manservant and therefore neither would supper be waiting. It would have to be the old marine of before and reluctantly he sent for Hare, captain of marines, to require him back. He picked up a copy of the *Gentleman's Magazine* but its earnest articles and long-winded opinion pieces didn't suit his mood and he laid it down.

A small procession arrived: the purser's steward, the marine and Craddock, each bearing some morsel for his supper.

'Harry, old fellow! How thoughtful.'

Kydd opened the wine and they settled back companionably.

The cabin with its discreet sconce lights and Persephone's feminine touches was turning into a snug retreat. But the thought of what was looking more and more likely, the prospect of years of inaction and an undistinguished conclusion to his career, nagged at him.

His dark mood returned.

The morning was equally depressing. Night had turned to a grey, cheerless day, chill and wet with a clamping mist. The wind had backed northerly with a sulky lop to the seas. Kydd knew that this was probably the beginning of a period of dispiriting weather but without the vicious squalls common to these parts.

Hands stood down from their customary dawn quarters but Kydd delayed going to his cabin: there'd probably be no breakfast waiting for him and Craddock was unavailable. The sodden atmosphere of mist and rain was beginning slowly to lift, the leaden curtain receding grudgingly.

He went below and his mind turned to the bad feeling that had developed between the marine, the purser's steward and the nameless cadre of servants, stewards and idlers who had made Luscombe's existence so unbearable. There was little he could do about it.

Disbelieving shouts came from the upper deck, joined by others. Kydd didn't need telling what it was. He raced on deck to see sailors excitedly pointing to starboard at the edge of the wall of mist.

161

'Oh, sir, I was going to call you, but I wasn't sure.' Briggs was uncharacteristically nervous.

A glimpsed grey shape had appeared shrouded in the mizzle long enough to catch the eye of a lookout. It had three masts, was headed south and as quickly had disappeared.

'We'll go to quarters, Mr Briggs,' Kydd said crisply. 'Let the first lieutenant know – and without drum or trumpet.' If there was something there, no need to announce themselves.

With Britain's command of the sea it was more than likely to be friendly, especially this far out, when the fearful French always clung to the land to move coastwise. Nevertheless, there was no harm in preparing, and it made a good exercise for the ship's company.

*Thunderer* was closed up well before the white curtains of drizzle finally lifted and a French corvette firmed out of a ghostly silhouette. It sighted them at the same time, not a mile to starboard, shocked, no doubt, to see a British ship-of-the-line appearing, like a nightmare, so close. Within moments, its helm went over, whether to hide in the fast-vanishing grey-white murk or reach for the embrace of the land was not clear.

An exultant roar came from every quarter of the ship. This was surely fitting meat for their Tom Cutlass!

Inconveniently, *Thunderer* was close-hauled to the north and the stranger was going with the wind to the south. Kydd gave the order to wear around and fall in astern of the chase. But the winds were not only in the wrong direction, they were light and fitful. Their sails hung limply wet and disconsolate, and *Thunderer*'s wear about was anything but swift and masterly. In the time it took to reverse course the corvette forged ahead, the gentle winds suiting its finer lines and lighter build.

Cursing under his breath, Kydd knew all eyes were on him to pull something from the same bag of tricks that had earlier seen them leave the squadron behind.

Why was the corvette so far to seaward? Was it making its way to the south by passing outside the blockade cruisers clustered around the ports? By its new course to the east-south-east it was almost certainly going to the nearest sanctuary port – under the guns of Les Sables d'Olonne.

They had to lay it by the tail before it reached its destination: thirty-six-pounders were mounted ashore, which greatly outgunned even a ship-of-the-line. But at this rate they weren't going to overhaul the corvette. It was no use spreading stunsails and the like, for in the fluky breeze the additional speed would be minuscule. Their only hope was for a change in the weather and even then it would chancy.

If they fell in with *Daphne* Kydd could send the smaller sloop to throw herself across the path of the corvette to delay it until he could deal with it but he couldn't find it in him to order such a sacrifice.

Arriving off the small port they found the corvette methodically settling to two anchors off the broad beach. At *Thunderer*'s appearance guns opened up from the shore. The heavy round-shot smashed out, skipping each side of the Frenchman in a show of spite and demonstration that any move against their visitor would be met with a righteous fury.

The corvette was safe and Kydd had to think again. As he considered the options, one thing became clear: he couldn't let it go. For the sake of British shipping at sea on the coast, this dangerous predator must be put down. The victuallers, powder hoys, dispatch cutters, lesser craft, even *Daphne* herself were menaced.

Also, if he left it in peace he would be handing Houghton

a perfect excuse to accuse him of lack of martial spirit, afraid to send his ship-of-the-line even against a paltry corvette. What could he do? Take *Thunderer* in and blow the corvette to flinders? In these light airs she would probably take hours in the approach and by that time would suffer unmercifully from the shore guns, the spoils not worth the bloodshed.

If they waited offshore until a brisk wind blew up, then stormed in under full sail, that would reduce the time exposed to the batteries to an acceptable level. Even if they spent days waiting, were they not ordered to clamp a hold on this very port?

As if on cue, *Daphne* came in sight from the south and together they retired out to sea to plot the future.

'Begging your pardon, Sir Thomas, but it won't do.'

'Mr Hoskyns?' Kydd said in surprise, not used to having his plans dismissed in a manner so out of hand.

'He's only waiting for the tide as will take him through the channel by warp and capstan to the inner harbour.'

'When's high water?'

'Just missed it, sir. I think he'll want to move in at some point tomorrow morning.'

That would give the corvette complete security where it could wait for months, if necessary, and at the first opportunity resume its voyage of destruction.

# Chapter 30

Kydd's duty was to clear the seas of these vermin and throttle all movement in and out of his designated blockade port. He was doing that by his presence but every fibre in his being cried out to do something active, a daring frigate-style stroke that would settle it once and for all.

In a ship-of-the-line? With this blashy weather slowing them to a crawl before the massed guns ashore?

The corvette was safe and they knew it. There was no doubt of the eventual outcome: an increasing number of boats were leisurely making their way to shore and into the channel. The colourful coats of officers could be seen plainly, doubtless to set up for a long stay at the town's expense.

Kydd had not much more than hours to make a decision. A cutting-out expedition? As soon as the thought came he dismissed it. Any attempt would be at night, but a half-competent captain would have a welcome of flares and pitiless illumination ready that would give the gunners ashore unmissable targets.

If not a strike by boats, then what? There was no answer

and Kydd stared gloomily into space under the sympathetic gaze of the sloop commander.

In a sudden flash of inspiration he snatched the paper out of his pocket that the officer had so carefully made of the battery sitings. Yes!

'Mr Hoskyns, how reliable are your observations here?' he said urgently.

'Sir. I was with Captain Hurd in the survey of Brest Roads.'

Hurd was the near mythical surveyor of the most challenging coastline to be found anywhere, later hydrographer to the Admiralty.

Kydd thought furiously. 'Commander – I do believe you've just solved our little problem.'

The four boats lay off under oars in the outer darkness, thankful that the moon had not yet risen and the blackness was near complete. On shore the lights of the town twinkled along the seafront, providing an impeccable navigational aid. At one place they were blotted out by the silhouette of the corvette, an even better fix.

They couldn't make a move yet. Hidden somewhere in the black of night, a French row-guard waited to give warning of any hostile approach. They could be anywhere but they'd have to keep within hail of the ship, a hundred yards off or so at most. Meanwhile their duty was to stay quiet and out of sight.

The boats were in two pairs, one to board at the bows, the other at the main-chains, the second of the pair to stand off and fire at the defenders as the first scrambled up. Who should command the assault had been a hard decision. By rights the first lieutenant had claim to the honour but Kydd couldn't allow it. He still had his doubts about Roscoe and especially his qualities of leadership and courage under the most severe conditions of all: mortal combat.

Roscoe had made his demand to lead in the most strenuous terms but Kydd bluntly pointed out that it was not only *his* plan but, without proof of battle reliability on all sides, he must take the responsibility for and leadership of the expedition. Only after Roscoe's near-begging pleas did Kydd realise there was more to it than simple honour and agreed they would share the charge. He would take the main-chains thrust while Roscoe would go over the bows.

In the boats, men crouched, faces and weapons blackened, each one a warrior as attested by his divisional officer. They engaged in the usual pre-combat banter in low whispers. Mayne was beside Kydd on the stern sheets of the long-boat, silent and rigid. The tension was snapping: there was no hiding the fact that in a short time each would be facing the enemy in a fight to the death.

The waiting was hard. Kydd had had his share of desperate occasions but he felt for the younger seamen who'd never had the chance to match themselves against a foe in this way.

'Sir!' hissed Mayne, his voice a croak. 'Beyond the point – to starboard.'

The lights in a farmstead blinked out then on again. A shadowy presence was moving about close inshore.

Kydd tensed. A gun-flash leaped out in the blackness, the heavy concussion carrying clearly in the night air.

It was *Daphne*, right on time. More savage gunfire erupted, with no response from the shore. She was using the night-time offshore breeze to slash past between the corvette and the beach, firing on the batteries as she went. With no lights showing from the land she was near invisible against the blackness out to sea.

'Ship oars – give way together,' Kydd rasped, 'and stretch out for your lives!'

The sloop was nearing the corvette, now firing furiously on both sides at the shore and enemy ship together.

All hostile eyes were on the sudden irruption – what did it mean? That the batteries were being pounded to give the ship-of-the-line a clear run against the corvette in the morning? Or was it a direct strike against the anchored ship itself? But if the shore batteries turned their guns on *Daphne* they'd lose their carefully sighted-in aiming set up by daylight and be much less of a threat to the boats.

The Thunderers had a chance – the corvette's guard boats would race back to join the defence and their approach would be discovered that much later.

As they neared, the men were beginning to pant and tire, even as they put everything into their strokes. Kydd knew this was because they were out of condition for such extremity of effort. Would they be exhausted at the supreme moment when they must clamber up on deck and face a waiting enemy?

Roscoe would be out there with the same doubts and fears. How would he respond? There was no way of knowing. They would both be on their own as they swarmed aboard, but if he failed, Kydd's party at the other end of the ship would be overwhelmed. Now was not the time for corrosive doubts.

Then the tables were comprehensively turned. The corvette was barely a quarter-mile distant when all along its seaward length flickers of flame appeared, quickly flaring from a suspended incendiary carcass that illuminated the sea for hundreds of yards around.

They'd been discovered and could expect prompt attention from the shore guns.

'Forrard there!' Kydd threw at the midshipman in the foresheets, an indistinct shape in the darkness. Would his other trick answer?

A splutter of sparks and a small lanthorn took life. Enough to read the eight-inch boat compass the youngster held.

'Le Remblai,' Kydd called impatiently.

A quick squint at a paper, then the compass and a young voice piped up, 'Starb'd!'

A boat under oars was an agile creature and quickly laid over to the right, the midshipman industriously noting the angle. 'Well!' he rapped.

The boat resumed its onward rush towards the corvette. Ashore, the sweating gunners slewing their cannon around saw the boat merge with the line of bearing of the corvette. The painstaking observations of *Daphne* were now paying off handsomely. Knowing the exact location of the batteries ashore, Kydd could make his deadly approach along that line of bearing with the target itself in the line of their fire.

Now also rudely illuminated by the carcass, level with them, and using the same trick, was Roscoe's launch. A standing figure in plain sight aft was wildly urging the boat's crew on, aimed unerringly for the beakhead.

As Kydd had guessed, the French officers heading ashore had left the corvette weakly led. No one was there to urge the gunners firing on *Daphne* to cross the deck to attend to the far deadlier threat.

The Thunderers closed in, past the point where the guns ashore could intervene, nearer still. A thin sputter of musketry played fitfully along the line of deck, a waste of powder and shot, given the blackness of the outer gloom.

The carcass flared and sparked, then died to a glow and Kydd's heart leaped. They had a chance!

Cast now in shadows, the seaward side of the corvette,

close to, towered up. The midshipman, at the risk of his life, had tied the lanthorn with its shutters wide open high up the long-boat's mast. In its light the boat thumped into the ship's side below the main-chains. Conscious of the cutter taking position behind them and peering up at the dark figures along the deck-line, Kydd thrust his way towards the bow. When it came within reach he leaped for the little platform that was the chains with its profusion of handholds. He paused, allowing another two seamen to vault up beside him – and for the marines in the cutter to realise what was wanted: ferocious fire upwards, a roar of English cheering, a bedlam of confusion!

Kydd reached for the lower shrouds, then wrenched himself upwards and around the lanyards to land on the enemy deck, his hand scrabbling for his cutlass, grateful for the fighting lanterns the French had provided.

A pike-head stabbed murderously at his face but he was ready and ducked. Grabbing the crude spike, he lunged forward to allow his blade to do its lethal work.

There was a concerted rush towards him but he let his cutlass drop and yanked out his pistols, thrusting them into the faces of his attackers and firing. One flopped down without a sound, the other clutched at his face, falling to his knees, blood spurting between his fingers.

'Thunderers with me!' he roared. With a frantic cheer others crowded on to the deck to stand by him, faced by a wavering line of defenders. This was the climax and finality of the boarding: if they were repulsed it was all over but if the French broke . . .

'At 'em!' he bawled, brandishing his bloodied cutlass and hurling himself forward.

He was not betrayed: in an ear-splitting screech every

man-jack of the boarders threw themselves after him – and the French broke and ran.

'Avast there, the boarders. With me – lay aft!' To the quarterdeck. To haul down the flag. At night the colours could not be seen but the significance of taking control of their display was undeniable.

He raced aft to the diminutive poop deck. By the halliards in the light of a rising moon was a bull of a man, clearly ready to sell his life in defence of his country's flag.

'*À bas le pavillon!*' Kydd bellowed.

The matelot replied immediately with a snarl and flourish at Kydd's face with a heavy, old-fashioned hanger.

It was pathetically noble. The man could be cut down in an instant by a boarding pistol and there was no shame in yielding to a superior enemy, but this fierce-eyed sea-dog was going down fighting.

Kydd gestured to his boarders to lower their weapons. There was no response, the man turned this way and that, threatening, taunting.

'*Laisse tomber ton arme, mon brave*,' Kydd said quietly, which provoked a torrent of execration.

'Drop him, sir?' The Royal Marine corporal with a musket made ready.

'No.' Kydd hadn't the heart to cease the existence of the brave man.

'Jimmy Rounds, sir?' The lower deck 'translation' of *je me rendre* – I surrender.

'Er, not until . . .' Kydd couldn't finish.

'Royal Marines – present!' A dozen muskets rose to settle on the man's breast. Fearlessly he tore open his jacket.

'Hold!' Kydd ordered.

'Go the bastard!' The corporal threw aside his musket and

flung himself bodily at the man, quickly followed by others, pinioning him with the weight of numbers.

Then Roscoe appeared out of the dark, with the rest of the boarders from forward, his sword not yet sheathed and visibly bloodied. He gave a bleak smile. 'You have the ship, sir. And my congratulations upon it.'

## Chapter 31

In the wan morning light the three made a satisfying picture. A sleek line-of-battle ship at anchor dwarfing the brig-sloop and the trim corvette that lay between them, not one scarred by war but preparing to set sail in triumph for the squadron and its admiral. Houghton might grind his teeth in frustration but Kydd had shown what a ship-of-the-line under a frigate captain could achieve.

*Thunderer* was a different vessel. Men swaggered about, now having a tale to tell of desperate doings the next time they were ashore and in company with men of the fleet. How Fighting Tom Cutlass himself had led them in to snatch a live corvette from under the guns of the mongseers without so much as a by-your-leave.

Kydd sat back, musing, as he paused in his dispatch. The men had more than earned his respect, crowding behind him as he hurled himself aboard, fighting like demons but showing mercy where it was deserved. Roscoe had acted in the best traditions of the service, leading his men to victory over the voluted beakhead in the darkness and he now had no doubts about his professional fitness to be his second.

Were it not for the first lieutenant's moody antagonism he would be happy to have him remain in the post. Even so, he wouldn't let this affect the natural justice of what he was saying. He wrote on.

*. . . he at all times manifested that zeal which is so indispensable in the character of a British officer and—*

A firm double knock interrupted him.

'Come.'

Roscoe stood on the threshold for a moment, as if reluctant to enter. Face set, he collected himself and approached Kydd at his desk. 'Might we talk, sir?'

'By all means,' Kydd said, sensing a moment had come. When Roscoe had returned on board he'd gone straight to his cabin, which he'd put down to the man's reaction after the one-to-one savagery and bloodshed.

'Sir, I desire to express my regret – my repentance, for my attitude towards you since you took command.' The voice was unnaturally low and constrained.

'Oh?'

'There was a reason, a compelling excuse, if you will, for it.'

'Go on.'

'My family . . . is related to Viscount Carlisle.'

'Yes?' It meant nothing to Kydd.

'Who, some small years ago, we heard was cruelly deprived of the object of his affections by one who deployed despicable means involving the Prince of Wales to gain an ascendancy over her. The name mentioned . . . was yours, Sir Thomas.'

'Charles Pountney.'

'As was before his elevation. You will conceive my feelings then, sir, to be confronted by that very one as our new captain

174

who had achieved his command by the same method, at the cost of a fine man's career and the advancement prospects of all aboard.'

'Mr Roscoe, I've told you before that—'

'Sir. This is to allow before you that my views are changed. These past few days I've been privileged to see not only a master seaman at his craft, but a fighting sailor and true-blooded hero. This has been enough to persuade me that your promotion into *Thunderer* was well considered and entirely upon merit. I cannot believe there are any other reasons for it.'

'Ah, thank you, Mr Roscoe.'

'Therefore I'm obliged to suppose that those who hold otherwise can only be impelled by motives of a more sinister cast.'

'Um, possibly.'

The stiffness fell away and an unexpectedly shy, warm smile spread. 'Which obliges me to say as well that I must acknowledge that Miss Lockwood ended with the right man, Sir Thomas.'

Kydd felt a blush rising.

'Sir, I would that we could reset the clocks and begin our association anew. Would you . . .?'

He held out his hand hesitantly and Kydd hurried around the desk to grasp it in both of his. 'Dear fellow, you had good enough reasons. Consider it so!'

'Oh, and I may have omitted to mention, sir. The wardroom in its collective wisdom have reflected and do conclude that Mr Craddock would indeed prove a worthy and interesting messmate and, for the usual subscription, do invite him to join them.'

'He would be delighted, I'm sure.'

'Just so. Then I must on deck. We've the corvette to fettle for her voyage of prize. Her name's *Volage*, by the way.'

'Do carry on, Mr Roscoe.'

He turned to go, then remembered something. 'Oh, and there's one of the prisoners insisting to see you. A most importunate fellow, making a nuisance of himself and not saying why. Do you wish to indulge him?'

'Send him. It may be important intelligence. And shall we take a brimmer together before supper?'

'I'd like that, sir.'

After Roscoe left, Kydd settled in a chair to marvel at the turn of events. He'd had the feeling that, for an intelligent man like Roscoe, there had to be a deeper reason for his hostility. And now he knew, and there would be a cheerful postscript in his ongoing letter to Persephone.

But before he could begin, a curious Craddock made his appearance. 'Did I see what I saw?' he said, in something like awe. 'Your Mr Roscoe, and he—'

'You did, Harry. And you'll never fathom why.'

Detailed explanations were made and Craddock shook his head in amazement.

'So as of now you're a wardroom-mess member, old fellow. Felicitations on your translation.'

With a knock at the door Briggs looked in apologetically. 'You asked to see the prisoner, sir.'

Raised voices outside tailed off and a slender individual with a sensitive face was escorted in, manacled.

'Won't tell his name or business with you, sir.'

'Very well. Escorts to leave us – and does he really need the irons?'

'Master-at-arms insists on it, sir.'

'Remove them.' Kydd resumed his place at the desk and waited until the man stood free.

'You have some information for me, perhaps?' he prompted.

176

'You are ze *capitaine de vaisseau*?' he said quietly, in a peculiarly well-modulated tone, the English not at all native.

'I am he,' Kydd said, 'Captain Sir Thomas Kydd.'

'Then I 'ave something to offer you, *mon capitaine*, as will be of much advantage to us both.'

'Carry on.'

'Not wiz zis gentleman. It is private, *n'est-ce pas*?'

Craddock got up to leave but Kydd motioned him down. 'This is my confidential secretary. He will stay to listen to you, sir.'

The man hesitated, glancing once at Craddock then resumed: 'Ees it to occur that I will be *prisonnier de guerre* – ze prisoner of war?'

The man's refined nature was unlike that of any French *matelot* Kydd could bring to mind. 'Your ship was fairly captured. The laws of war must take their course.'

'So I shall be sent to *les pontons*, you say, er, ze hulks.'

'It would seem so. I'm sorry.'

The man's well-kept hands twitched spasmodically. 'Sir. Then I make offer. On board of ze *Volage* I was ze *maître de navire* to Capitaine Delvaille. If you will spare me ze hulks I vill glory to be the same for you, sir.'

'*Maître de navire* – sailing master?' Kydd hazarded.

He looked pained. 'No, sir. You know ze *maître d'hôtel*? Well, *maître de navire* for ze ship. I take care for you in all things.'

'I already have a manservant,' Kydd said abruptly.

'Before ze revolution my family serve an English wine merchant in Bordeaux. We keep ze standards of the *ancien régime*, very 'appy together. I know your English ways an' for your distinguished banquet I can make a gran' affair.'

'I'm sure you could. But a Frenchman aboard an English ship, that's another matter. How can I know you are not an agent of the state, a saboteur who will take any opportunity to harm the ship?'

'In Bordeaux we 'ate Napoleon, we 'ate ze Revolution. It bring us nothin' but ruin and *dépourvu*, um, the bankrupt. We long for zis miserable war to end, the British to come back to their wine houses, an' the good times, they return.'

If this man was who he said he was, a professional in the duties of service, then Kydd would be prepared to take him on even if it meant posting a sentry to follow him every hour of the day.

Craddock leaned forward to speak. 'Dear fellow, may I make contribution?'

'Do so, please.'

'M'sieur, I have done business in your fair town in the old days,' Craddock opened easily. 'I'd be interested to know the name of your English employer. I may remember him.'

'Sir, it was Monseiur Frank Douglas. At La Maison Bleu. His château, of course, in Mérignac, a very fine—'

'The colour of Madame's hair?'

'Ah, I cannot know. She die before I come. Monsieur take comfort with Madame Arnaud. Her hair change all the time but if you want . . .'

Craddock glanced at Kydd and gave a slow nod.

'Then what is your family name, if you please?'

'Sir, ze secret police are everywhere in Bordeaux. If I am discovered to serve an English, zen my family, they will be arrest.'

'This is not a problem,' Kydd said briskly. 'In the Royal Navy we have the custom that those who volunteer, but don't want their name known, are given instead a "purser's name" for the ship's books. No one will ever learn you've been on an English ship.'

In something near a whisper the Frenchman told Craddock his name. Craddock gave a satisfied smile. 'Captain, the name is honourable and has given long service to the English community. If he were known to have betrayed us he would bring shame and disgrace on his family. I believe you may trust him.'

In a gleeful rush of hope Kydd pretended to consider. That he'd already performed duty in the corvette meant that he was no stranger to sea service and needed no coddling. His distinguished bearing would go far in insulating him against the petty vanities of the lower orders aboard – there was no reason he couldn't make a start. Why not at once?

'Very well. A purser's name for our latest volunteer, Mr Craddock?'

It penetrated that the tide had turned in his favour and the man struggled to keep his features composed.

'Er, perhaps Binard? René Binard? An ancient and well-known name in the Vendée, I believe.'

'So how do you like that, M'sieur, er, Binard?'

'*Merci, merci, mille fois merci, mon seigneur!*'

'Then to the details. Mr Craddock here will instruct you in your duties, which will begin immediately. Have you any questions?'

'None, m'lord. Oh – an' when will I meet my staff?'

'Staff?' Kydd asked in astonishment.

'Your pastry chef, *coiffeur, valet de chambre? Les domestiques?*'

'Mr Craddock. Do ensure M'sieur Binard makes acquaintance with the ship's boys and, for now, the officers' cook, who will be told that he might well learn much if he takes on board M'sieur Binard's wise advice.'

After they'd left he resumed his musings in his armchair,

trying to get over his astonishment at the change of fortune that had seen him plucked from the depths of misery to the heights of felicity. Service in a ship-of-the-line from this time forward might well be very different.

# Chapter 32

*The House of Commons, London*

'Order! Order! The witness will be heard,' Speaker Babington bellowed, above the raucous catcalls that filled the hallowed chamber.

The hearing was not proceeding well, the fractious displays of temper doing little to clarify the issue. Yet it was one of the utmost importance: an examination into the effects of the Orders-in-Council that had set the Royal Navy into wholesale blockade of the Continent and Bonaparte into inflicting his Continental System in retaliation.

'I call Robert Hamilton.' The eminent barrister James Stephen, who had famously steered through the anti-slave-trade bill, waited patiently for the uproar to subside to begin his cross-examination.

'Order! I will have order in the house!' Babington repeated, but a cry rang out abruptly from the back-benches, demanding why the prime minister was not in attendance to justify the Orders-in-Council that he himself had authored.

It was an extraordinary request but these were extraordinary times. After a whispered discussion it was decided that a messenger would be sent to Downing Street desiring the presence of the honourable Mr Spencer Perceval at the hearing.

In the crowded lobby the news was received with resignation. Many had congregated outside the chamber in these frenetic times and Peregrine Fookes MP, as a master lobbyist, was used to it.

'You'll know there'll be no answer today, old man,' he replied, an irate Lancashire ironmaster.

The messenger pushed through urgently and disappeared into the evening throng outside.

'His Nibs will be along shortly, you'll find,' Fookes muttered, to a colleague.

A tall figure in brown and yellow appeared at his elbow, his hair dark and curly, his serene blue eyes seeming never to rest on anyone in particular. It was the fellow who'd asked him earlier that day to point out Perceval for him. 'Sir, is it that the prime minister will be coming?'

'Er, yes, Mr, um, Bellingham. He'll have to come through here and you'll get a good view of the fellow, don't worry.'

The man's hand strayed inside his coat as though to scratch at a flea. Fookes shuddered and looked away. Bellingham had some sort of grievance following a failed business venture in Archangel, Russia, of all places, but he'd get no satisfaction from Perceval, who was only holding together the finances of the realm with prodigies of invention.

The ironmaster was having no nonsense, though. There had to be a reckoning – these Orders-in-Council of blockade might be the sharpest blade in the armoury but they cut both ways: there was real hardship in the industrial north, with unsold goods lying about and workers laid off to the mercies of parish relief.

There were raised voices outside. At the door a short, plain-looking gentleman came into view, a distracted frown on his pale, boyish features. His appearance was so nondescript and private that those not knowing him would have been forgiven for failing to recognise the revered yet notorious Spencer Perceval, prime minister and chancellor of the exchequer of the kingdom of Great Britain and Ireland.

The press of lobbyists fell back respectfully to make a lane.

'He's in a hurry, old fellow. You'd be better off catching him as he leaves,' Fookes murmured, annoyed that Bellingham had stepped out to intercept him.

'Are you the prime minister?' he asked calmly.

'I am, but do let me pass, sir. I'm in haste to be done.'

Bellingham pulled his hand from the coat's breast pocket and came out with a short, ugly pistol, which he thrust hard against Perceval's chest and pulled the trigger. There was a sharp flash and blast and Perceval recoiled with a strangled gasp. He dropped to the floor, blood gouting. In a spasm of agony he cried out, then lay still.

Pandemonium erupted. Fookes and others hurried to the fallen man, the sightless eyes paralysing them with horror. Screams and shrieks filled the air as men began running aimlessly, some shouting for meaning of the helplessness they felt. And the man who had done the deed, with the same serenity as before, turned, crossed to a bench and sat down, his smoking pistol still in his hand.

He it was who had assassinated the prime minister of Great Britain.

Spencer Perceval was lifted tenderly by two bystanders, Fookes trailing in the throes of shock, and they took him into the nearby room of the speaker's clerk and laid him on the table.

A passing surgeon was brought in and took less than a minute to pronounce life extinct. All present fell back in frozen horror.

Hammering at Fookes's reason was the overwhelming realisation that at this moment Great Britain's parliament had been decapitated, its leader and figurehead taken, to leave it rudderless, unable to function – or even to exist. He took a long, quavering breath, and made the first contribution to the scrabble for sanity in a world gone mad. 'G-gentlemen, the cabinet must m-meet.'

Outside the news spread wildly, and within the hour Parliament Square was filled with an excited, seething crowd, hundreds swelling to thousands, screaming and hurling insults, lunatic, out of control.

The doors were slammed and a cry rose, 'Cabinet! Cabinet! In the committee room.'

As members of Perceval's cabinet stumbled up they were shown into the room until enough were present and the door locked. The home secretary, Ryder, was Perceval's closest friend, but he was plunged into a paroxysm of helpless weeping, as were several others. Even Lord Eldon, the High Tory lord chancellor and senior minister, was too shocked to continue, and for some time in the stunned atmosphere all were unable to speak.

Then the first tentative conclusions came. In Perceval they had lost not only a prime minister but the chancellor of the exchequer and of the Duchy of Lancaster, as well as leader of the House of Commons, all of whom had to be replaced without delay. Yet no one could conceive of anyone who was constitutionally able to perform this and, with the home secretary still prostrated in grief, none to take it further.

By now the menacing tumult and bedlam outside were

tearing at nerves on edge and grieving turned to fear. What if this was the first act in a Jacobin uprising, paralysing the country until the conspiracy was complete? A link-up with murderous Revolutionaries, deranged Republicans and Levellers? Was a wider plot signalled by the assassination? Were others involved? Given the situation, the under-secretary to the Home Office should be empowered to call out the militia, the volunteers, nothing less.

A breathless Treasury clerk broke in to announce that an attempt to smuggle Bellingham out to Newgate prison had been thwarted by the mob, who showed every inclination to free their hero as a liberator from Tory tyranny. His escorts were still fighting to keep the hostile rabble at bay.

The men about the table stared at each other in dismay. Then at the door appeared the patrician form of the secretary of state for war, the second Earl of Liverpool.

'R-Robert – you're here,' gasped Ryder, through his sobs.

Liverpool took in the hapless sight with a glance and found himself a chair. 'Mr Perceval has been taken from us, this much I've heard. What else do you know?'

In a chorus he was told of the rioting crowds outside, the threat of an imminent uprising and—

'We must have a prime minister – a head of government. To take charge before the mob does.'

'My lord, we know this, but there's no precedent, no constitutional path without we have a general election,' the lord chancellor pontificated.

'There is.'

'Pray do enlighten us.'

'We are the cabinet, the king's ministers. We choose one of our number and desire the Prince Regent to empower him with office.'

*　　*　　*

'Prime Minister. Might I be among the first to felicitate you on your elevation?' purred Nicholas Vansittart, the new chancellor of the exchequer, as the cabinet sat for the first time.

'As meet and right as it turned out to be,' the home secretary, Viscount Sidmouth, harrumphed.

It had taken three weeks of chaos and confusion, and four others rejected before him, but finally, in despair, the Prince Regent had made his choice and Great Britain now possessed a prime minister.

'Your kind sentiments are noted and now this cabinet is in session,' Lord Liverpool snapped. 'We've a devil of a lot to deal with and not a lot of time to do it in. The first is to secure the kingdom.'

The Horse Guards were ordered from their barracks and the Foot Guards set to clearing the streets. Ringleaders of the mob would face justices of the peace, parish beadles made into special constables and the militia turned out, the watch doubled.

'What is perhaps even graver is the wider issue of foreign involvement,' Liverpool continued. 'For instance, a revolt of the disaffected harnessed by those desiring a revolution.' He stopped, looking suddenly grave and tired. 'Gentlemen, I've had a passing chance to read Mr Perceval's secret papers and what I've seen frightens me.'

'Concerning the external situation of this country?' Castlereagh, foreign secretary, wanted to know.

'I would think so.' Liverpool sighed. 'Much beyond a mere affair of hay-forks and rick-burning, I'd believe.'

'May we know the contents of what you saw?'

'Until I've digested its import, no, you may not.'

'If we are to move on this, my lord, then we—'

'I've already decided the action, sir.'

'Might we understand which?'

186

'As any other sane prime minister will think it with the country *in extremis*.' He looked down the table to the still figure of Melville, the newly appointed first lord of the Admiralty. 'I desire you, sir, to strip the nearer blockading squadrons of any available battleships and concentrate them at Portsmouth where they may best be disposed as the threat develops.'

'Immediately, my lord.'

There was a rustle of relief about the table.

They were in the best possible hands. The navy was being brought home to defend them.

# Chapter 33

It made no sense. After a successful action that was going to add to his laurels as the reigning admiral, Houghton had abruptly sent Kydd to report to the commander-in-chief off Brest. Then the mystery deepened. Boarding *Royal Sovereign* in full dress, he'd found that Keith had already quit his flagship for the Admiralty and had left instructions that Kydd would, without a moment's delay, press on to Portsmouth and the Spithead anchorage for orders, no reason given.

*Thunderer* leaned to the stiff north-westerly, the gunmetal sea moody and restless, but not so far ahead lay the grey headland of St Catherine's Point with its medieval lighthouse. Beyond was the dog-leg past the Isle of Wight and then the great naval anchorage athwart the entrance to Portsmouth.

In the early afternoon Kydd spotted a fleet at anchor, a line of eight 74s that could neither be the Channel Squadron, which was on its station off Brest, nor the Western Squadron, which was at the ready in its home port, Plymouth. What in Heaven's name did all this mean?

His pulse quickened at the obvious explanation: that a

special expedition was being mounted and secrecy was key. But where were the army transports, the victuallers, the necessary frigate escorts? Only 74s?

Just as soon as their anchor had rumbled out, he was in his barge making for the dockyard and the port admiral. As they passed Portsmouth Point the rollicking old town was curiously subdued, no uproarious taverns spilling rioting customers into the narrow alleys. With a fleet manning of many thousands, this was odd.

Disturbed, he landed at the dockyard steps and hurried to the port admiral's office. When he appeared at the anteroom there was more astonishment: neither the admiral nor his flag lieutenant was present, apparently on their way to London. Orders for *Thunderer* were waiting but they instructed him only to come to a twelve-hour notice for sea. No liberty for the hands was to be granted and row-guard and nettings were to be deployed to prevent desertions. No indication as to how long the situation would obtain.

Baffled and annoyed, Kydd returned to his ship and went to his cabin to shift back to sea rig. A pleasant-looking fellow in the comfortable uniform of a post-captain rose from a chair at his appearance.

'*Montagu* 74, Dick Moubray. I do apologise for this intrusion, old chap. Kydd, is it not? Heard much of you in these home waters but didn't know you'd deserted frigates for a battler.'

'It is and I have so. Er, do you have business with me as will throw a bit of light on this ragabash situation?'

Binard noiselessly appeared, a starched napkin over his arm.

'Ah. And I was hoping *you* might.'

'*Thunderer*? We've been on blockade until untimely snatched away and sent here. A snort of sherry?' He nodded to Binard who gave a short bow and left, returning suspiciously quickly with a silver tray and two glasses.

'So you haven't heard.'

'I've only cast anchor this hour, sir.'

'The prime minister is . . . no more.'

'What did you say?' Kydd was incredulous.

'In the lobby of the House of Commons. A pistol shot to the heart by one many rate as a common lunatic. Others shout that it's the work of revolutionaries or such. Whatever the right of it, we're now without a premier and line of authority from the Admiralty.'

It was stunning. Kydd's mind reeled at the implications. The ship of state without a rudder: no decisions could be made, no precautions taken. The future was a bleak unknown.

'So what are we doing here?'

'No idea. Intelligence of a rising by the Irish? Boney up to his scurvy tricks? A break-out from Antwerp or ports east of it?'

They were interrupted by the mate-of-the-watch who reported that the admiral's flag had broken at the dockyard signal tower, signifying his arrival back and this had been quickly followed by an 'All captains'. Kydd could not remember that this signal had ever been made in Portsmouth before.

The nine captains filed into the upper meeting room and sat in a loose gathering. The admiral, Strickland, stood waiting, grim-faced but patient. There were no rolled maps, blackboards, piles of operational orders. This was not a council-of-war.

'You will all have heard of the much-lamented loss of our noble leader, Mr Spencer Perceval. It's thrown the kingdom into an uproar and made all our plans moot.'

After the rustle of comment died away he continued: 'I'm

able to tell you now that we have a new prime minister – and, in fact, a new cabinet who are meeting as I speak.'

'Sir, who—'

'Our new man at the helm is my lord Liverpool, who before was our secretary of state for war. I won't bore you with all the details of his administration but one you'll take notice of. It's Melville – not Nelson's man but his son, the second Viscount Melville. A steady hand on the tiller, you'll grant.'

The group remained silent, watchful.

'So what are we doing here? I will tell you. From various sources on the Continent of Europe we've heard rumours of a shocking and disturbing development. A move by the French to break the stalemate there by amassing an army of colossal and unstoppable size. What it's for and where it's aimed nobody knows, possibly at this stage not even Bonaparte himself, but it's increasingly obvious that it's of serious intent to do us harm. The reason we're summoned here is that, in this time of immense threat, the prime minister has acted instinctively. With an invasion army some twenty times that of the one poised before Trafalgar threatening, he remembered what the Earl St Vincent said at the time and acted accordingly.'

Standing in Parliament, the crusty admiral had intoned grimly, 'This only am I sure upon: I do not say, my lords, that the French will not come. I say only they will not come by sea.'

Strickland continued. 'Yes. When it's clear what mischief Boney is up to we sail instantly to deal with it, which is to say why we lie at Spithead in the highest degree of readiness.'

So that was the reason. Without knowing where the blow was aimed, a significant force was now assembled at Portsmouth, a point halfway along the Channel from where they could proceed either east or west as necessary.

'How long should we expect to be at readiness, sir?' Moubray queried. It was asking a lot – sail bent on in all weathers, seamen at sea watches, keeping up on victuals and water as they were consumed, routine maintenance without entering a dockyard.

'As long as Boney keeps shaking his fist at the world.'

'Sir, it could be considered unreasonable to deny men their liberty ashore,' Kydd said carefully. 'Might we—'

'Captain, you're at twelve hours' readiness. If you can assure me your ship will be fully manned and ready to face the enemy within that time I don't give a fig about your liberty arrangements.'

The older Davis of *Blake* asked, 'Should we sail as a fleet, whose flag will we be under?'

'If you sail it will be as a squadron, part of the Channel Fleet and therefore under the flag of Admiral Keith, who will in any event be leading in *Royal Sovereign*. He will be arriving here presently and will no doubt be plainer in his requirements. Any other questions?'

At first the unusual routine and tension kept *Thunderer* alert and braced but as the days passed so did the feeling that they were a first-rank fighting force about to save England. With only a small number of exercises possible at anchor, no firing drill or mock landings to keep up an edge, and means ashore all spent, it was the dreaded tedium of any lengthy harbour stay.

Kydd was delighted when Persephone arrived. She made herself comfortable in the George, which Kydd pointed out was where Nelson had stayed for his last night before sailing to destiny.

Over a sturdy roast of beef and a decent claret, she told him breathlessly of the riotous chaos breaking out in the street she'd seen with her friend when the news of Perceval's assassination reached Plymouth. With no coaches running, they'd had to take rooms but the drunken revels and boisterous marches had kept them awake the whole night.

No revolution had taken place and the disorder was apparently over now. Kydd feared, however, that this was the beginning of a much worse phase, with Britain stretched to the utmost in a world-spanning war that had reached colossal proportions. He made light of the reason *Thunderer* was in port, telling Persephone of the changes aboard, especially in the first lieutenant. Not wishing to upset her, he mentioned that young Luscombe had swum to shore on realising that he wasn't fitted for a life at sea but that he'd been able to find a replacement in a Monsieur Binard.

'Other ladies of fashion boast a French cook but my fine husband has a French *homme de chambre*,' she noted happily.

He smugly presented her with a conversational bauble by telling her that, after reading the newspaper accounts of Perceval's end, he'd remembered the name Bellingham. A somewhat unhinged Englishman in a Russian gaol when *Tyger* had first visited, Kydd had spoken at length with him, more out of pity than anything else. With female eagerness she demanded he describe the encounter in detail.


The wardroom found no shortage of questions to chew over in their leisurely dinners, the most raised being just what Napoleon Bonaparte was going to do next.

Attack Russia? An outrageous suggestion, Russia being, first, his ally and, second, having done nothing to cause even the voracious Bonaparte, at insane expense, to mount an invasion.

Flood his great army westwards to put down the rebellious Spaniards and their small but impudent English ally in one overwhelming stroke? Possible, but unlikely, for the prize was hardly worth the effort.

It was generally conceded that the most credible was to right the wrong of Trafalgar by throwing the entire gigantic horde in a never-ceasing flood into the south of England, then march on London. That would end the war once and for all and, with Great Britain in chains, the world would be Napoleon's by right of conquest.

This was usually the signal to raise a bumper in a brave and defiant toast of damnation to the Corsican tyrant, which was inevitably followed by a lull of introspective silence.

One evening Briggs changed the subject, reflecting that the recent noisy accusations and calumnies coming from the United States might develop into war. This brought on much merriment at the thought of a vast army of Red Indians falling on the green fields and forests of ancient England to march on the Tower of London.

And what did Briggs think was worth risking their great merchant fleet that carried so much of the world's trade to their very considerable profit? And inviting the ire of a nation with the biggest navy at sea at this time, which was quite capable of landing whole armies? No: however loud their demands, the Americans were not a nation of lunatics.

In the fog of rumour and fear there was only one thing that was to be done: stay where they were and wait.

# Chapter 34

The tedium fell away abruptly for Kydd when a note was handed in to the officer-of-the-watch. It was short and to the point, from a Mr Johnstone, who begged an interview with him ashore at the Swan and Compass, concerning a matter of grave importance. There was no indication of the subject but a postscript added that, were it not so urgent a matter, he would have enclosed a covering from one Nicholas Renzi attesting to his bona fides. The mention of his dearest friend was enough for Kydd and he hurried ashore, some instinct telling him to go in plain clothes.

He knew the inn, not far off in Southsea, and soon he was being shown into the snug by a respectful maid.

A man rose noiselessly. His appearance – perfectly anonymous clerkly black, dark eyes a-glitter, like a crow's, in a pallid face, a spare frame almost ascetic – was arresting.

'Charles Johnstone. You may understand I represent the secretary of state for foreign affairs.' The voice was low but dry and elegant.

'You mentioned Mr Renzi.'

'Lord Farndon. He's been so good as to work for us in the past on several concerns of a vexatious nature.'

'Is he in any kind of danger?' Kydd wanted to know.

'No. This meeting is on quite another matter, which I must tell you is of the gravest moment and considerable urgency.'

'We may be interrupted, Mr Johnstone.'

'I don't believe so, Sir Thomas. I have hired the snug for the nonce. Shall we sit by the fire?'

No convivial glasses were summoned, and Kydd felt the stirrings of unease. The man was of the government but not in the public eye or an elected official. Who was he?

'What I have to tell you is to be reckoned secret, not to be discussed with any.'

'Not even my officers? I find that a hard thing for an active captain of a 74.'

'None. Sir, there is a service you may render the Crown for which you are particularly well suited, so much so that your name was put forward as the first I might try.'

'Sir. I'm captain of HMS *Thunderer*, a ship-of-the-line under twelve hours' notice for sea. I cannot see how—'

'Arrangements at the highest level will be made. Do, sir, hear what I have to say.'

'Very well. Fire away, Mr Johnstone.'

'You will have a fair idea of the forces by sea that Bonaparte commands.'

'That he keeps in idleness in port, never to sail against us.'

'There have been developments we've been made aware of that throw your conceiving into considerable doubt.'

'With all due respect I hardly think you in a position to make comment on strategic naval dispositions, sir.'

'Captain, what I can say is that Bonaparte's idleness is a deliberate policy. They are in effect being husbanded against a great enterprise. We in government think it unwise to allow the scale of this accession to strength be known to the general public, and therefore have reported fewer than there actually are.'

'Oh?'

'Let me give you an example. Toulon and lesser ports comprehended by the name. How many ships of what weight of metal do you believe to lie there within?'

'Eighteen – seven of the line and eleven frigates have been sighted. Possibly more we haven't heard about.'

'It will certainly shock you to discover that, from deserters and other sources, we find that there are now one hundred and twenty-one men-o'-war massed in Toulon of which twenty-two are sail-of-the-line. Eleven of these are of 80 guns and above.'

'Above an 80?' That would mean a sore fight for *Thunderer* with her 74.

'As it happens, yes. And even three of 120 guns.' The first-rate *Victory* was only of 100 guns. Remorselessly he concluded, 'And no less than five of 130 guns.' Far bigger than anything the Royal Navy possessed, a truly staggering imbalance and in only one of the ports ringing France.

'Why do we not . . .?' But Kydd couldn't finish, the thought of such menace freezing his words.

'The Admiralty in its anxiety has sent for Admiral Pellew to take command of the Mediterranean fleet and increased the number of his ships as much as they are able, but we're greatly outnumbered.'

Pellew was a renowned fighter but it was a dismaying situation.

'You said husbanded for a great enterprise?'

'Less than one month ago, Bonaparte demanded the expenditure of two millions in the furbishing of a fleet. Sir Thomas, this is no less than the invasion fleet of England, which, since Trafalgar, has not only been kept at the ready but subjected to a continuous building programme.'

'Sir, if you intend to frighten me, you're succeeding.'

'With this we must observe that an army of unknown but vast size is assembling under Bonaparte's personal command. It is of such huge dimensions that it must be employed soon or cause a ruinous drain on his treasury. The collective belief in Lord Liverpool's administration is that its destination cannot be other than England.'

Kydd swallowed. The months before Trafalgar in *Teazer* when he'd been part of the last line of defence against invasion had scarred his memory: at every dawn the last act always poised to occur, the continual near-suicidal attempts on a swarming enemy. Now it was all about to burst on them once more. 'You asked a service.'

'I did. In all this there may be a flaw in the reasoning. Napoleon Bonaparte is an arch deceiver. That we know. If his object is not England but some other, then he may desire to create fear and confusion among us such that we draw in our defences to guard these islands and abandon all else.'

'I see.'

'We need to know, sir. The cabinet has to make terrible decisions bearing on the safety of this realm and must have the truth of the matter. In short, if the invasion fleet is an invention, a cheap mockery made up of imitation craft or such, then we may suspect the last. If it is credible, a seagoing armada truly capable of conveying an army, we must then look to our defences as a dire necessity.'

'Mr Johnstone, have you not spies or their ilk available to do this?'

'Spies are rarely knowledgeable in the maritime arts and cannot be expected to recognise the soundness of a vessel or its equipment for the task. More to the point is the enormity of the decisions to be made. Only if the report stems from an absolutely unimpeachable source will the prime minister feel able to act upon it.'

'Myself.'

'Your name will ensure your intelligence will be received with due reverence, I can assure you, sir.'

In growing horror Kydd realised the implications. 'You wish me to land on the coast of France and satisfy myself as to the particulars? Like a common spy?'

'Not at all.'

Kydd let out his breath in relief.

'The coast before Antwerp instead will be satisfactory for the purpose. If two or three shipyards are sampled it will be enough to tell us if the rest of Bonaparte's invasion fleet is a sham or a deadly threat, for there's no point in producing the actual article in one place and its counterfeit in another.'

'Antwerp, Calais – it's all the same to me, sir. Enemy territory as requires me to act the phantom, the footpad. This is not within my power, sir.'

'Sir Thomas. Your role does not demand you do. You'll be landed privily to be met by the agent who alerted us to the threat. Your only duty is under direction to sight what you're shown to make report later, the entire business to be concluded within a very few days.'

Kydd was under no illusions as to what would happen should he fall into French hands, but a mischievous voice pointed out what a splendid opportunity it would be later to mention casually to Renzi that he'd been involved in just the same kind of furtive mission as he'd undertaken in the past.

'Very well, Mr Johnstone, I'll do it – supposing only that I'm to be satisfied with the details.'

# Chapter 35

The smuggling craft bobbed and splashed as it made its way through the short and choppy seas of the Channel, Kydd's instincts in the chill darkness telling him they were coming up with the land, the low, dune-fronted flatlands of Zeeland. There was no other in the lugger beside the man at the tiller and two hands at the sheets. They kept their silence, peering intently ahead into the clamping murk of night.

The choice of a smuggler was inspired: he would know to an inch the coast so they were assured a safe passage. The *douaniers* of the Batavian Republic were as anxious to let past English goods into the Continent as those making the crossing were to supply, and no strict examination of the crew was expected. Kydd was not in uniform: he wore a frayed jacket and wide trousers with a kerchief, the traditional clothing of a common seaman.

He smiled wryly. This was a stretch of coast he knew well: it had figured several times in his past, the first as a lowly master's mate before the ferocious battle of Camperdown, during the long years of blockade and in the first war cruise of *Tyger*.

A quarter-moon dared peep out from beyond the scud, and reluctantly the shoreline was revealed, anonymous, level and fringed with a pale beach. In the minutes before the light died as the moon was obscured again, he noticed a tell-tale well-remembered seamark: some two miles inland a fat church with a spindly, out-of-proportion steeple, Koudekerke. It told him they were up the coast from Flushing, the ancient medieval port set right at the mouth of the Scheldt.

A man forward raised a device like a watering can, a spout lantern, and held it steadily. From high on the Koudekerke steeple a light glimmered in return, on and off, on and off. Kydd knew the routine and felt the boat heel slightly, then head inshore. He scanned the pale beach for sign of movement and saw none but his pulse quickened as the shore neared. It was so different from casually scrutinising on the deck of a heavily armed man-o'-war. The agent had better be waiting or he'd be away again very smartly.

He spotted a twist in the smooth line of beach, hardly noticeable. A small stream ran into the sea from behind a hillock and, sails doused, the craft nosed in and came to a stop by a dilapidated jetty with figures waiting. It was swiftly and economically done, the boat held by a painter forward and rotated to face out to sea again before being hauled in. Low voices sounded in the night and Kydd was gestured impatiently to get out: these men had work to do, passing contraband ashore and into the ruined house beyond.

The tiller-man whispered to him. He was to make his way inland a hundred yards, and behind the dunes he'd find a fisherman's hut where his agent was waiting. Feeling half naked without arms of any kind, he set off and, after trudging across the sand for a short while, he saw the hut, showing a soft light within.

He knocked gently and heard a scraping movement inside.

Then the door slowly opened. An old lady sitting in a chair by the fire, knitting, looked up at him, bemused.

'Um, good evening, Madame,' was all Kydd could think to say, in English.

'*Kom binnen, mijnheer*,' she replied, gesturing inwards.

The door closed behind Kydd, and he swung around to see another woman standing with a large military pistol trained on him.

'Are the oranges yet ripe?' she asked evenly and in perfect English, her eyes never once straying from his.

The part of his mind that had remained cool noted that she was remarkably attractive, with dark looks reminding him of his sister Cecilia. But if he was to avoid an ignominious end the correct response was needed straight away. 'Oh. No, they're not, but, um, the raspberries are.'

She paused fractionally, then lowered the weapon. 'You may call me Anneke.'

'And I am—'

'I need no name. I will call you Piet.'

'Anneke.'

'Listen carefully, Piet. You will do exactly as I tell you, however stupid it seems to you. There are those who long for freedom and there are those who lust for gold, but there is no telling the difference.'

'I understand.'

'Do you? I've been told that you are an adept on ships, not on secret work.' Her tone hid a brittle tremor, which, in a perverse way, comforted Kydd, with its hint of humanity.

'I will do what you ask, Anneke,' Kydd said quietly. 'What is first?'

'The Van Beek shipyard. Now.'

She eased outside, carefully checking, then beckoned him to follow.

Once in the night air she walked briskly along a path until it was crossed by a road. A small calèche was drawn up there, its driver nodding in sleep. They clambered aboard. At Anneke's sharp Dutch he came to and snapped a whip over the patient horse.

There was no talk as they made off down the road but Kydd was uncomfortably aware of her thigh pressing into his in the narrow seating. After an infinity of turns he was relieved to see the glitter of water ahead and the gaunt ribs of a vessel on the stocks against the night sky. Anneke had timed their visit to the hours of darkness when no workmen would be on the site.

'Wait,' she hissed imperiously, jumped down and disappeared into the blackness. She returned with a man and a lantern. 'He says be quick – the *veldwachteren* are out.'

The elderly man clucked in alarm at a strange noise in a field and Kydd's heart jumped. This creeping and dread were not to his liking. Anneke snapped something contemptuous and went to the side door of a large shed, let them in and set a lantern going.

In its ghostly light Kydd saw the outlines of two craft and recognised them immediately from his experiences off Calais. The nearer was a *chaloupe canonnière*, this one sizeable, quite able to mount a twenty-four-pounder on a slide and pound to ruins anything smaller than a frigate. The other, by its Scandinavian lines, was a *crache feu*, the kind of gunboat that had made life so galling for the Royal Navy after the Copenhagen action.

He went up to the slip, managing in the gloom to trip over some loose timbers, which tumbled about with a wooden clatter. The hull was half straked and he bent to smell the new work. It was fir, Baltic pine probably, as far as he could see, straight-grained and prime timber deals. He put his ear to the topmost and tapped sharply. It rang sound and true, not the dull clunk of deadwork.

He called for the lantern and inspected the line of fastenings along its edge. Copper, flush on the outer side and properly secured with roves on the inner. At the bow of the craft, much as he expected, the fay of the planking to the stem was neat and workmanlike.

He drew back and considered. This was no mockery or sham: it was a well turned-out article of the shipwright's art and of new construction.

Outside again, stray light caught shapes in the background. Three, five: these were completed craft lying in a creek, masted and with standing rigging rove. He reached one and looked at it carefully. A Dutch *schuyt*, two-masted, shallow draught and strong, ideal for landing either troops or artillery in quantity on a shingle beach. It, too, was sound and clean-lined, an occasional pale streak revealing recent repair or refurbishment. The rigging was taut, well tarred and, as far as he could tell in the dimness, ready for immediate use.

Bonaparte was not bluffing: if others along the coast were like this then the invasion fleet was a reality and once again England was under threat.

'We can go,' he said. Anneke turned sharply at the tone of his voice.

The older man scuttled away and they returned to the calèche. Anneke urged on the driver and, as her gaze fixed pointedly ahead, the vehicle ground off sharply.

Kydd needed to think. How much evidence should he find before breaking it to Johnstone that a genuine invasion fleet was poised? Was the sample method sufficient? Setting a fleet to sea was much more than the sum of the ships involved. There had to be storehouses crammed with supplies – powder, shot, rations. Should he be looking for these as well to prove the enterprise was on a credible footing?

His thoughts were interrupted when Anneke asked, 'Can you tell me what you think, Piet?'

They were grinding down a featureless, straight road with nothing in sight but Kydd kept his voice low. 'Those are true sea-going craft, well able to do duty in an invasion. If there are others like it, I fear for England.'

She looked at him intently, then patted his knee. 'You English have friends, do not fear.' The hand stayed where it was as the vehicle slewed sharply to the right, down a smaller track and to another shed among others nearby. It came to a stop by the deep shadow of an overhang.

Leaning across her to open the door politely, he was taken by surprise when she threw herself at him, her arms around his neck, her dress wrenched high to reveal a pale flash of her upper thigh in the moonlight. 'Kiss me! Now, you fool!'

Kydd was shocked rigid. She redoubled her passion, writhing in ecstasy and mumbling something between a smother of kisses.

Then he saw what had caused it. A figure materialising from the shadows came to a halt uncertainly, unslinging a musket.

She hastily smoothed down her dress, screaming curses and waving her hands in anger.

Sheepishly, the man resumed his sentry-go in the shadows, but she hurled more insults until he gave a grin and shuffled off into the night.

'I – I . . .' Kydd was lost for words, aware his gentlemanly instincts were at war with the baser ones.

'I believe it safe to enter,' she said primly, adjusting her clothing. 'The time of darkness is passing. We've more to do.'

Let in by another older man, Kydd took his lantern and advanced on the vessel on the stocks. In the dark and confined space it seemed massive. It, too, he recognised: a *praam*, the most dangerous of all. Three-masted, full-rigged and armed like a miniature frigate, it drew so little water that it could go in with the boats and slaughter any opposition. This one was nearly completed and, from the whiff of Baltic resin, he knew it, too, was the genuine article.

He withdrew quickly – he'd seen enough. That she'd been so keen-eyed to spot the *veldwachter* and had known instantly what to do left him in admiration of her.

'Anneke, we must go to another place, not near here. See if they too are building.'

'There is shipbuilding of all kinds along the Scheldt. We are famous for it, Piet.'

'Well, perhaps—'

'I shall find one. There are many in Flushing but it is running in those French bastards.' Kydd flinched to hear her language but it was she who was suffering the occupation.

'The other direction. Six, seven miles north. Westkapelle.'

The calèche turned inland and found the road up the coast, the noise of its passage through villages echoing from quaint Dutch houses looming out of the darkness. Occasionally a splutter of a light showed at a window and a face appeared. Several times a dog barked witlessly. It was not wise to be making a fast run through the night at a time when no one had business to be out, but it was unlikely that any curfew would extend so far into the country.

An argument with the driver appeared to be under way and Kydd asked if there was a problem.

Anneke bit her lip. 'This is not part of the arrangement and he worries that there will be trouble. I have to pay him more.'

There was tension in the air as they swung off the road and took a track out to the seaward line of dunes. Kydd's senses detected the barest lifting of the darkness, the quarter-moon beginning to pale. 'We have to go faster,' he said, trying to keep the nervousness out of his voice.

'Not so far, Piet,' she said reassuringly.

They passed through the dunes to a seafront dominated by a line of sheds and slipways behind a high fence. She told the driver to stop where the fence was closest to the sheds, and in the chill of the pre-dawn darkness she got out and ran to the fence. Kydd loped after her.

'This is the biggest boatyard in Westkapelle, but I haven't made agreement with Mr Heemskerk or his brother to come in the night. We have to find our own way in.'

Break into a shipyard?

'Here,' she commanded, pointing to a loose paling. 'Make it bigger.'

Kydd pulled it from the top. It gave, with an appalling *screeeak* into the calm of the night. He did the same with the one next to it, leaving a vertical hole just large enough to squeeze through.

They ran to the shed to find the door unlocked and went hastily inside. They didn't have a lantern and she cast about in the disordered gloom for one. Kydd didn't wait, feeling his way forward until he came up with the bulk of a hull. He didn't care what it was: all he needed to know was if it was ever going to be seaworthy.

The smell was right, the timbers of the outer side of the frames planed smooth. It was a good professional job and he moved towards the bow further inside.

Suddenly he heard her whisper an alarm. Her grip on his arm tightened. A figure at the door held a lantern high and called out a querulous demand. Kydd held still, her grasp fierce.

The figure entered the shed. By now the early light had begun to steal in and there was an angry shout and a determined advance towards them through the work debris.

'Go!' Anneke said, and stumbled away in the opposite direction. Kydd hesitated, then followed. Intelligently, she was making for the bow and as soon as she reached it she hurried down the other side to the open door.

There was a shrieking challenge but they reached it first and ran outside. Frantically searching, Kydd spotted salvation: a gig of sorts drawn up to a dilapidated jetty, probably the watchman's.

The man emerged, screeching incomprehensibly.

'Quick – he's calling the gendarmes!'

A muffled trumpet call came from behind the dunes and distant return shouts. Kydd pushed Anneke into the boat. There were oars and it was the matter of moments to untie the painter and shove off into the creek just as a squad of men burst into view. An officer with them gestured to half of his men who doubled off along the bank.

'He's told them to get another boat and intercept us,' she said, her fears under tight control.

Even with their start, that boat with at least double the men at its oars would outrun them.

Kydd put all he had into pulling and, unused to it after all his years as an officer, was soon panting, his muscles burning. All the while the detachment loped along the bank, effortlessly keeping up in the grey light of daybreak. The end couldn't be far off. To be captured not from the deck of a man-o'-war but a workman's gig would make splendid copy for Boney's newspapers, Kydd grimly reflected.

As he strained to the limits Anneke got to her feet and clambered awkwardly over his oars. Through runnels of sweat and a universe of pain he looked up and saw a *schuyt* putting out to sea past them, its sails lazily sheeting in. Anneke stood erect, shouting and waving the end of a rope.

Answering calls came back. 'To the *schuyt*!' she screamed in excitement to Kydd. 'He's going to tow us to sea!'

# Chapter 36

*Downing Street, London*

A light still shone in the upper rooms of Number Ten, the thin rain giving it a somewhat melancholic cast – or was it the pressing news that Henry Bathurst, the third earl of that ilk, minister of state for war and the colonies, was bringing to the prime minister? He gave a nod to his assistant and they hurried in, their capes and hoods imperturbably taken by the major-domo.

The head footman preceded them up the portrait-hung staircase to the Cabinet Room, his footsteps echoing in the late-night stillness. Bathurst knew that it was always Lord Liverpool's practice diligently to prepare the night before a planned division in the House.

'Oh, it's you, Henry.' Liverpool yawned, pushing away the papers in front of him. 'Now why do I sigh at your appearance, old fellow?'

'Prime Minister. We've word back from Antwerp as you required.'

'The invasion fleet? That was quick work – perhaps too quick? Did your man spend enough time to be sure?'

'Sir. We took the precaution of employing a serving officer of distinction whose judgement in the matter may certainly be relied upon.'

'Oh? Who is that, pray?'

'At his particular request I beg to be excused mentioning his name but I do allow he is a post-captain and bears the honour both of a knighthood and baronetcy.'

'I see. Then what are his conclusions?' Tension had crept into his voice as he waited unblinkingly for the answer.

'It's genuine. By means of random selections he's established that the boat and shipyards between Flushing and Westkapelle are actively building all manner of invasion craft and harbouring the completed articles. Sir, we must accept it as a verity that the invasion fleet exists and is in a condition to put to sea.'

Liverpool slumped back, his expression bleak.

'Not only that, Prime Minister, but it was determined from local sources that the entire Scheldt river is crowded by slipyards that at the moment are engaged in swelling Bonaparte's battle fleets. The number of twenty-four line-of-battleships as nearing completion was mentioned. And there is no reason to suppose it's any different in the Batavian Republic or certainly in France itself.'

'Good God. So it isn't a species of bluff. They really mean it.'

'Or in truth they actually want us to discover the extent of the fleet and its quality in order to oblige us to withdraw our blockade squadrons and other in the defence of the kingdom, giving them a free hand in Russia or to indulge in mischief anywhere. Cheap at the price, I'd say.'

'You're a cynic, Henry. We've always known they never discarded the invasion flotillas after Trafalgar. Why should we be frightened now?'

'Because for the seven years since then they've been steadily building and building. Two million francs laid out this year alone. It must be of an astonishing size by now, Prime Minister.'

'And so you leave me with the choice of whether or not to call an invasion alarm along the lines of what we did in the year five.'

'Yes, Prime Minister.'

Liverpool groaned, holding his head in his hands.

'It truly grieves me to add to your burden, sir.'

'Heaven preserve us. What now?'

'I'm in receipt of hard evidence of the size of Bonaparte's latest army. Sir, I must warn you it greatly exceeds what rumour holds.'

'Well?'

'In excess of some six hundred thousand under arms. Past half a million men from a dozen nations in full marching order. The greatest military horde seen on earth since the time of the ancient Persians, a vast, seething mass of—'

'Yes, yes.' The premier's voice dropped almost to a whisper. 'How sure are you of this? Rumour and hearsay are no substitute for hard intelligence and—'

'The Russians have a man well placed in Paris. He's passed back to his masters copies of the orders-of-battle of the entire army, courtesy their foolish notions of seniority among their field commanders, which demand they have knowledge of what their rivals command. Our man in St Petersburg has, for a suitable fee, passed them on. Do you . . .?'

'No, I leave that kind of thing to you,' Liverpool said, staring down at the table as if it had answers for him.

'It means—'

'I know what it means. A host of such terrifying size can have but one purpose – to crush and extirpate. The question must be – is it to be unleashed on the Russians or Napoleon's greatest foe, England?'

# Chapter 37

*Boulogne*

The skies above were deep blue and almost cloudless, as if they were obeying the wishes of the all-puissant Emperor of the French, Napoleon Bonaparte, for perfect weather on the occasion of a grand review before the massed splendour of his Grande Armée. For miles on either side a horde of eighty thousands was encamped on the high ground overlooking the seaport.

This day a marine pageant was to be mounted in honour of the most powerful man on earth, a parade of the countless craft of the invasion flotilla dedicated to the destruction of Great Britain, displaying their might and numbers before their emperor.

Placed prominently on the heights was the splendid panoply of Bonaparte's campaign headquarters, transported from Paris for the occasion. Princes, grand marshals, the imperial gendarmerie, all summoned to a spectacle of the pomp and majesty at the Emperor's command.

In the largest, most sumptuous tent, the glittering few were gathered, those who rode to war at his side in the army general headquarters, called from all corners of the empire, in a near-blinding display of gold lace, swords of great beauty, cockades and gleaming gold-spurred boots. It was a show, too, of hauteur, pomposity and arrogance, as duke and viscount, baron and marquis paraded their wealth and finery before the military.

On the edge of the throng stood a no longer youthful colonel of engineers, Jean-Baptiste Moreau, summoned imperiously from his post with the eighth division in Prussia to be adjutant commandant in the Imperial General Staff of the greatly swollen Grande Armée. He sipped his champagne, not to his taste so early in the morning but it was essential to appear ardent in the service of the Emperor at this level or risk the ignominy of recall to his old brigade. It was, of course, a heady, glorious sensation to be plucked from the common run of the army and called to service with the Emperor himself. To this very hour he still had no idea why he'd been chosen – was it that lucky bridge-sapping operation at Wagram? He'd never even seen Bonaparte but shortly he would appear before him.

If only Angélique could see him now! His wife had not had an easy time during his progression through the ranks. He'd not gone in for the vainglorious strutting or shameless plundering that got one ahead in these times but she'd always taken pride in him, and his two sons, now at the prestigious St-Cyr military academy, also rejoiced at his promotion.

But he had to admit to unease. The Emperor had carried the nation before him, with his promises of honour and glory for all in a war of conquest and liberation. He'd made good on those, but at the cost of nearly twenty years' continuous warfare that had led to victorious Frenchmen under arms across Europe but also to unknown graves in far-off lands. Why could they not cease the eternal blood-letting, settle down with the spoils of their conquests, and discuss the limits of empire, with England their only remaining opponent?

If the rumours held true, a grand enterprise was afoot, for which an immense army was being brought into being. It could be anything: the Ottomans, the Russians, even the British. Were they extending themselves too far? For any one of those it was not just a matter of conquering but of imposing Gallic civilisation, with laws and taxation that would require a different army: a civil administration watched over by garrisons without number.

A small voice within asked a simple question: Was this aggrandisement for the cause of France or that of yet more *gloire* for Emperor Napoleon Bonaparte?

'*Eh, bien, je n'ai jamais!* If it isn't the little cockerel!'

Moreau swung round and saw, to his delight, his old friend of the years before Austerlitz, Rochambeau. He was in the high-collared blue and silver of an *ingénieur géographe*, a staff officer concerned with maps and topographical advisories.

'Bertrand! How are you? I haven't seen your hide since . . . well, a long time ago. Are you on staff to the Emperor?'

'As of a month ago, brother. And you?'

'New called from Berlin and the corps of engineers – I drink to our reacquaintance.' The champagne tasted better already.

Rochambeau eyed him steadily. 'Have you heard anything of why we're here? A junket called by His Nibs is all very well, and on this scale, but I'd like to know why, if you see what I mean.'

'No idea. I'm still finding my feet.' It was his old friend but he wasn't about to open his mind in these surroundings.

'We'll learn soon enough, I suspect.'

An aide announced that all who were going aboard the Emperor's state barge should now make their way to the quay.

'Isn't that Murat?' Rochambeau surreptitiously indicated a gorgeously apparelled, exquisitely tonsured officer ahead.

'Um, I've never met him.' He had, in earlier times, but never as the King of Naples as he now was. 'Over there – it's got to be Duroc, grand equerry.'

'No, that's Berthier.' Moreau's chief of general staff.

'There's Junot – I know him from the Lisbon folly. And next to him Savary. He's your new Fouché.' Minister of police and a very dangerous man.

It occupied them until, in an easy promenade before the good citizens of Boulogne, they reached the richly decorated barge. It was a large galley of eighty oars, its long deck with raised dais in the stern designed for spectacle with pennons, ornate flags and every kind of ornamentation. On the quay the galaxy of nobles and officers jostled for position: not to be the first to board but the last in order to make an ever grander entrance than the previous. It enabled them both to select an unobtrusive position below the Emperor's throne on its dais, where they settled to wait.

A distant baying of trumpets sounded nearer and the crowds grew frenzied, then, as the Emperor's entourage was glimpsed, subsided into awed whispers. Moreau couldn't see over the enormous tasselled cocked hats of the notables but knew that he'd soon be getting a close view of the man who held the fate of nations in his hands.

With a spreading rustle of bowing, scraping and subdued conversation, he heard the Emperor approach. Suddenly those in front of him parted and drew back. And there, unmistakable in his tricorn worn across, white breeches, a plain dark-green tunic, with a single star, and a grey overcoat against the sea breeze, was Napoleon Bonaparte.

The recognition was like an electric shock, followed by another equally unsettling impression – of fallibility. Moreau saw past the trappings and noted the thinning hair with forelocks curled forward theatrically, the massive head carried low between hunched shoulders and a well-concealed flabbiness. At the same time there was a feral quality about the man – the pale grey eyes piercing mercilessly, the smile with the lips only, the rest a brooding mask – and he was shorter than nearly all of his followers. This was not the heroic Greek god of the painter David, or the majestic figure of his coronation, but a creature of restless energy, his undoubted air of genius and terrifying presence conveying a message of destiny and conviction.

'Get going,' Bonaparte snapped, as soon as he'd finished receiving the inevitable ovations from his throne.

A naval officer in splendid garb coldly shouldered past Moreau to take position at Bonaparte's right hand. 'Rear Admiral Baste, Your Imperial Majesty,' he pronounced. 'Fleet commander of the Boulogne Flotilla.'

Napoleon gave a cursory acknowledgement and impatiently stared ahead at the lines of anchored craft, his lips moving as he counted. 'Two hundred? Where's the rest for which all year I've been shovelling francs into your hands?'

'This is the outer harbour, sire. The inner harbour is resident to twice their number,' the admiral said complacently. 'Safe from storm and tempest – and the impertinence of the English pirates.'

'Take care of them, Baste. I may have need of them very soon.'

'I will, Majesty.'

They reached the first line of invasion craft, moored parallel with the shore in an immaculate line. Bonaparte stood up, his pose haughty and imperious. One hand inside his coat, his gaze far-seeing and commanding, he nodded slowly as they passed the array of might.

'All is well, Baste. They parade like the Old Guard. I like it. But who is that out of line?' His finger pointed impatiently at a vessel at anchor further out to seaward. 'Tell the wretch to fall in with the rest or I'll know the reason why.'

'I beg Your Imperial Majesty's pardon, but . . . but it is not to be commanded, sire. It's a vessel of the Royal Navy that visits on occasion to be awed and intimidated by our great fleet.'

'Comes visiting? Sails in and drops anchor to – to come visiting?' exploded Bonaparte, in a choking rage. '*Merde!* It's not to be borne by any Frenchman and certainly not by me! Get rid of it, Baste! I'll not be gawped at by English sailors!'

'Yes, sire.' Baste bowed low and, snarling under his breath, pushed past. Summoning his boat, he departed hurriedly.

It didn't take long. From the inner harbour sailed a line of the biggest invasion escort vessels: *prames*, three-masted, full-rigged and armed like frigates, seven of them.

'That'll settle the beggar,' Rochambeau chuckled.

Bonaparte drew out his campaign telescope and watched developments grimly.

It soon became clear that the British commander knew his business. As the line of *prames* emerged from the harbour it was into a stiff breeze that was foul for leaving, obliging them to take the same track out. And his chosen anchoring spot just happened to be precisely opposite. Not even bothering to raise anchor, the unknown frigate opened a crushing fire on them, a spring passed to her mooring cable enabling her guns to bear with devastating accuracy.

More French ships were sent out, a bomb vessel and no

less than an additional ten brigs that threw themselves into the fight, knowing all the time their emperor was looking on.

The ominous sound of the guns reached the shore. Through the roiling gun-smoke the sea-fight was visible, a single ship surrounded and blazing away – but still confidently at anchor. For hours into the afternoon it went on until a wounded flotilla made its way back into Boulogne, leaving the frigate still at anchor, apparently without a scratch.

In an unforgiving fury of indignation and frustration, Bonaparte called off the grand review until such time as Rear Admiral Baste saw fit to put down the impudent frigate.

But the next day it was still there. And it now had re-inforcements, if only two small brigs and a cutter, together mustering a fire-power barely that of one or two of those ranged against them.

But Admiral Baste, now at sea with *Ville de Lyon* to take personal command, knew his standing with the Emperor was at stake. He had with him another fifteen of all classes of warship, making up an overwhelming twenty-seven men-o'-war sailing to obliterate the impudent English vessel.

Battle was joined early. Napoleon Bonaparte observed from the heights as the bay before him, crowded with sail, erupted into violence. The English frigate, however, gave no ground in its position before him and it soon became clear that Baste's flagship was in trouble. *Ville de Lyon* closed to help it but the game little English brigs snapped at its heels and brought it to a standstill. Almost immediately boats from the frigate put off and, with Bonaparte a helpless and enraged witness, boarded and captured the vessel. Its colours were struck and in minutes the intolerable sight was witnessed of it being unceremoniously taken out to sea and away.

Bonaparte lowered his telescope and for a long and awful space, he gazed after it and at the scene of shattered, still smoking wrecks drifting in with the tide. No-one dared a comment as he turned on his heel and stalked away, his face like stone.

# Chapter 38

*Paris*

The City of Light in springtime was a delight – it was what she had been born for – but Moreau was unable to take joy in her. Bonaparte had stormed back from Boulogne in a foul temper and had not been seen for some days. Today he'd called a conclave of the Army General Staff, implying that decisions had been made.

In the ornamented anteroom Moreau took position, his duty as an adjutant commandant to escort the Emperor into the inner military council at ten thirty precisely. Standing by the door were two others, Grand Marshal Montand of Mecklenburg and his deputy, talking animatedly, clearly excited to meet Bonaparte face to face. Another three stood gravely nearby, cavalry brigadiers and adjutants, too junior to attend the council.

They ignored Moreau with his blue-white engineer signifier. He drew out his watch and consulted it. Another twenty minutes before the Emperor was expected into the chamber – and suddenly he was striding into the anteroom, looking as though to assure himself of an audience.

Snapping to attention all five murmured greeting, but Bonaparte took no notice, a black scowl on his face. He snatched off his hat and thwacked it at his side, irritated, distracted.

'Sire,' said the grand marshal, lightly, 'do we see our chieftain cast down?'

Gazing moodily into space, Bonaparte made no reply.

'As it's not granted to mere mortals to command the Fates—'

'Cease your babbling, Montand. If you knew the worries of state I have on my back you'd spare me an hour of peace.'

'My most earnest sympathies, Majesty. The English?' he finished delicately.

'Of course, cretin. While they cowardly hide behind their precious wooden walls instead of fighting it out man-to-man on the good land, like any other self-respecting and honourable nation, we're deprived of the opportunity of uniting the affairs of the world under the one fair polity. Thus I fear we'll be driven to stern measures as will inconvenience if they persist in their intransigence.'

'Should we land on their shores with the Grande Armée they will sing a different tune, I'm persuaded.'

'At a cost!' Bonaparte snarled. 'Which I'm not prepared to pay. There is another course in bringing them to their knees upon which I'm tempted to embark.'

'Sir?'

'To humble the Tsar of Russia before his people and thus isolate Great Britain, who shall be obliged to treat on my terms.'

'Invade Russia?' gobbled Montand. 'Not as if—'

'As if it were not justified?' Bonaparte roared. 'An ally of France, sharing in all the spoils of war that French bayonets have won, and now has broken her sacred oath of alliance which we have faithfully kept? I have every excuse for a chastising, but in this I stay my hand!'

'May we know—'

'My Continental System. The only sure way of bringing the foe to his knees, and they seek to spurn it for the sake of sordid profits! To allow neutrals free access to Russian ports – with false papers. This is the same as inviting British ships to trade openly with the Continent! Above two thousand made port last year alone, an intolerable insult when but a dozen honest French vessels docked.'

'Unforgivable, Majesty,' quavered the grand marshal. Bonaparte, when angry, intimidated, like a lion out of its cage.

'And I will not forgive! Of that you may be assured.'

'Sire?'

'Ah. You would know the mind of an emperor.' He glanced imperiously at them all, one by one, then grunted, 'So. I like what I see. Loyal and true, serving only the state and the people.'

Legs astride and eyes piercing, he went on, 'And you will here learn how a master attends to his trade. I will tell you.'

Moreau kept well out of the circle of admirers, as befitted a senior officer of the Army General Staff shortly to be under Bonaparte's direct orders. But what was happening? Why were these nonentities being brought into secrets of state?

'On the one hand I sweeten the alliance for Tsar Alexander. Should he stay staunch at our side in this matter, he shall have a free hand in recovering the ancient sovereign lands of Russia in Poland and Prussia.' This was greeted by wise nods of understanding.

'And on the other I allow him a glimpse of my golden horde of half a million under arms, the guns, the horses, the powder stockpiles. This I bring within a short distance of the Niemen, the Russian border. It presents Alexander with a conundrum. Should he cast in his lot with the English, suffering beyond endurance the rigours of our trade blockade and the last nation in the civilised world still standing against us? Or receive from us a guarantee of peace, with rich pickings in old Prussia and a withdrawal of our terrifying host, displayed before him, for the trifling act of maintaining the existing alliance in all its provisions?'

'Will he listen, sire?'

'He'd better,' Bonaparte said grimly, seemingly mollified by this recitation of his plans. 'As my demands in this tenor have very lately been sent to him for his prompt and earnest reply.'

A breathless silence fell.

'Alexander, brought within our empire so securely, and consequently being thus humbled, will be of no further use to the English who, exhausted, must sue for terms. And, as you may perceive, my object is gained with no blood spilled in any wise.'

Then in quite another tone he resumed: 'Naturally this privileged information is not to be divulged to any outside this room. I'm sanguine you'll agree the next month will be interesting indeed, citizens.'

Moreau held his breath. He'd been in Headquarters long enough to know that the ways of a Caesar were above those of mere mortals. He clearly wanted these five to know his plans, even in the almost certain knowledge that they'd

225

let them slip in a bragging to their juniors or even to their families.

Why? To put pressure on the players? It mattered little to England that he was making gestures to Alexander. As far as the English were concerned, France and Russia were in an alliance already and maintaining that was no alarming news. To the Tsar, Bonaparte's wishes and intent had always been clear. This was only a pointed reminder. So why . . .?

In a creeping chill he realised the shocking, terrifying reason. It was Bonaparte's secret plan to fall without warning upon Russia with his colossal Grande Armée.

His intention? To eliminate any distraction from the greater objective of putting down his last rival, Great Britain. And to add lustre and glory to the sum of the conquests in his name by conquering the biggest country in the world.

To this end, in the guise of pressuring Alexander with the proximity of his host, he could work up his legions and stores close to the border without triggering a panicked response. And bring on a cataclysm of opposing forces such as the world had never seen.

'Sire, if the Tsar refuses?'

'He won't,' Bonaparte said cuttingly. 'His own people won't allow him to take the wrong side. They've too much to lose.'

Discreetly, Moreau eased out his watch. 'Your Majesty? Time for your conference.'

The council was already in session. In the modest room it was like a busy campaign headquarters. A vast table in the centre was scattered with maps and diagrams, and over-hung with bright lamps, aides and equerries stepping aside in favour of generals, brigadiers and fighting soldiers of every stripe.

Bonaparte entered briskly, acknowledging this one and that, considerately answering the murmured enquiries after his health. This was quite another creature again and Moreau was fascinated: there was no denying that he dominated the room, a focus of all the energy that whirled about him.

'If the grey wolf can find it in him to save his shaggy stories for later, *hein*, Pelleton?' It brought a ripple of laughter about the table, for Napoleon Bonaparte missed nothing and the grey-whiskered major general chortled. It was this intimate knowledge of his men and the camp-fire camaraderie that had made him a leader to follow anywhere.

'So. Our priorities have altered, gentlemen. Lack of time and naval preparation force me to reorder the options before us.' The expressionless faces left no doubt that the real reason for putting aside the employment of the Grande Armée in an invasion of Great Britain was well taken.

His voice dropped to a commanding dictation. 'I've been assembling my host these last weeks for one object and only one object. You'll mark well what it is and act upon it.'

Moreau held his breath.

'This being the mustering of an overwhelming force next to the Russian border in an open display of might, that the Tsar will see what a broken oath will cost him.' He drew himself up, his expression stony. 'To that end I've instructed my ambassador to deliver a note to the Tsar, requiring he stand by the terms of our alliance in return for attractive territorial concessions, a soft demand. I do believe that will be enough.'

Letting the moment hang, he swept his gaze about the room, but in the stillness Moreau heard himself ask steadily, 'Sire, but what if he refuses?'

'Who's that?' Bonaparte asked sharply.

'Jean-Baptiste Moreau, adjutant commandant in the Imperial General Staff engineers.'

'Well asked, *mon brave*. You shall have a rapid answer. And it is that if I get no satisfactory reply, a second note will be given. The hard demand. This will specify that unless the alliance is publicly reaffirmed I shall consider it breached and Russia subject to retaliatory measures.'

'An invasion.'

'Sir, hear again this one word I uttered. *Unless.*' His frown cleared. 'I shall accompany this with a massing of my Grande Armée along his borders to demonstrate to the most ignorant just what it is that's being risked – and, above all, what the empire can do if spurned. The stubborn clique next to Tsar Alexander will realise by this that their bluff is called. No longer can they practise delay in pursuit of sordid profit. They must preserve themselves and their holdings in the only way possible: by resuming the provisions of Tilsit and that directly.' Without waiting for comment he added, 'The strategy needs every one of you to play his part.'

He went to the table and smoothed out the map of Central Europe, then looked up as they crowded around.

'The entire conceit of my note is rendered useless if it's concluded that this is naught but a threatening troop movement. To be credible it must appear to be in earnest. Guns, stores, baggage, supplies for a deep thrust beyond. Therefore I desire that as of this date we act as if an invasion is truly planned. Grand Marshal Berthier has been working hard on this appearance and he has the order of march for each of you. Our focus for the accumulating of war stores is Danzig, the assembly area Prussia and the Duchy of Warsaw.

'The soft demand has been dispatched. Gentlemen, before the hard demand is delivered I want the border from end to end lined with imperial bayonets and artillery, baggage trains and field-kitchens. All to show to the meanest peasant that without question Napoleon Bonaparte stands true to his word.'

# Chapter 39

*London*

'Darling?' Cecilia called softly to her husband, Nicholas Renzi, Lord Farndon. He was in their town-house drawing room appreciatively taking in a clever but scurrilous article in the *Morning Chronicle*. 'I am sorry to disturb you, my love, but there's a messenger boy outside desires to deliver his note into your hands directly.' The curiosity in her voice was barely disguised.

'Oh? Then I'll come.'

It was a single folded note, sealed with a wafer he recognised at once. He tore it open, pulse racing. If this was what he thought it was, the future could be much more interesting very quickly. *My club, if it does not inconvenience, my lord.* Yes! It was signed Congalton and this was a request from the high-ranking member of the British secret service to see him in his discreet Whitehall office as soon as possible.

'That's sixpence, m' lord,' the youngster piped, holding out his hand.

Cecilia supplied the coin but he remained standing there. 'Off you go, then,' she scolded.

'A reply is begged, an' that'll be another sixpence.'

Renzi dashed *Directly* underneath Congalton's scribble and the lad darted off.

'You'll go,' Cecilia said, in a small voice. 'Even after Vienna? You've done enough, Nicholas.'

It was always amazing to Renzi how women with some kind of sixth sense could so easily penetrate the thoughts of their menfolk. 'I'll see what's to do only, my dear.'

Congalton rose respectfully at his desk, a wintry smile playing. 'You are most kind to visit, my lord. Refreshment?'

Renzi politely refused. Not the re-corked civil service dry sherry so early. He took the single visitor's chair and waited.

'Your success in Vienna was much remarked, my lord. In fact, I have it as a surety that the prime minister was well impressed.'

'And I'm persuaded wishes me to repeat the exercise?' Renzi said, with a raised eyebrow.

'Most insistent it is your good self that is employed in the venture, my lord.'

'Shall you now tell me what is contemplated, Mr Congalton?'

'You will have heard the noise occasioned by the discovery of Bonaparte's assembling of a great army on the Continent.'

'Indeed, as with a vast invasion fleet bound for these shores.'

'Yes. Well, we've since received indisputable information that leads us to conclude that the invasion of these islands is no longer Bonaparte's first objective.'

'Russia.'

'Quite.'

An unspeakably vast country ruled by a tiny elite and, in

particular, an autocratic tsar of mystical persuasion and child-like impulses.

'Then do I understand you wish me to call upon the person of the Tsar?'

'I do, my lord.'

Russia – a nation in alliance with Bonaparte, an enemy of Great Britain and with an unreadable complexity of rivalries and interests connected with its bid to be recognised as European. And now threatened by the greatest military power in the world, both reigned over by a despot.

'The government is greatly desirous that the mind of Alexander is known, whether or no he intends to stand against Boney if he invades.'

'Not as if that is a difficult task, in course.'

'As usual, His Majesty's Government has its sources, all of whom are either diplomats or inferior paid intelligence, neither being well placed in the article of trust or insight.'

'It will be gratifying to hear of your scheme to find me on easy terms with the Tsar of all the Russias, that I shall have the honour of achieving where they have signally failed.'

'Then if I satisfy you in the particulars you will agree?'

'Should it prove . . . conceivable. Do share it with me, sir.'

'I have naught to share, my lord. I rather felt that you should create your own situation as it were . . .' Before Renzi could respond Congalton was reaching for his hat and coat. '. . . in the presence of one who should know. A short walk only, my lord. The gentleman concerned may be considered most reliable in matters of discretion and you may speak freely before him.'

The mansion in Belgravia was large and secluded, well away from the din and odours of London. When Congalton showed his card he and Renzi were admitted to be greeted by a genial figure in a colourful crimson velvet jacket and tasselled cap.

'Velcome, my friend!' he exclaimed in a startling bass, advancing to bestow a hug on Congalton, his eyes coolly taking in Renzi as he did so.

'Dimitry, this is Renzi, come to seek your advice upon the usual terms, and this is Count Dimitry Vonskoy, late of Moscow.'

'Honoured,' murmured Vonskoy, with an English handshake. 'Shall we fin' somewhere quiet?' He padded along the hall and entered a drawing room, dismissing the two footmen with an irritable wave. A samovar stood on a side dresser. 'Tea?'

'Kind in you,' Renzi said.

'To what I owe your wisit?' Vonskoy asked, passing him a glass in an ornate silver holder.

'Count Vonskoy is, shall we say, a broker, and lately a gentleman of consequence at the court of the Romanovs,' Congalton explained.

'Until I dismissed the presence,' he said darkly. 'Of zat, nothing more said.'

'Then he is precisely the one who might advise me.'

Vonskoy bowed shortly and listened.

'Should one desire to be close to the Tsar, upon friendly speaking terms as it were, how best to achieve this?'

The eyes opened wide in surprise, followed by a bellow of laughter. 'No one achieves it! Around his person contend not one or ten, but a hundred who seek his favours. An' protection, lands – his gold. Why, is zis what you want?' he said in a fruity chortle.

With a snatched glance at the imperturbable Congalton, Renzi gave a polite smile. 'Yes, it is.'

The laughter ceased as though cut off with a knife. 'Vy?'

'To learn as much as I may about him.' Even to his ears it sounded a thin and unconvincing purpose.

To his surprise, after a keen glance, Vonskoy nodded. 'I accepts that. Come, let us talk together.'

They settled in a pair of huge chintz Oriental armchairs, Congalton nearby.

'You are Englishman. Is not difficult, there are many in Moscow, more in Petersburg. Merchants, money-men, those who make it their business, we Russian do not lack your English baubles.'

Renzi inclined his head attentively.

'But none at court among the boyars.'

'You're saying it is not possible.'

'Not that, Sir Renzi. More difficult. A pity you no scholard – Alexander worship learning, most particular of Europe. An' he will want to quiz you, to discuss and acquire wisdom.'

Congalton harrumphed firmly. 'Ah, but he is, Dimitry. He corresponds with Count Rumford upon the vexing questions of the age in natural philosophy and notably the study of ethnicals in their economic striving related to their culture.'

'Oh, bravo, Sir Renzi. Zis study is much applauded. Ve much desire to know whether our origin the Kievan Rus or is to be a more antique Slavic peoples.' He broke into a smile. 'Which give me idea. You shall go to Moscow, or better, Petersburg, to consult an academician. Lebedev – he will glory in your attention – and that will be your starting point.

'No difficulty about a passport, you may be sure,' he added.

Renzi shifted uncomfortably. It had been years since last he'd done serious work on his opus on the subject. His horizons had immeasurably widened since he'd acceded to the earldom of Farndon and soon afterwards adopted his clandestine lifestyle in service to Congalton and his mysterious masters. But his interest in the field remained and he'd met

234

Rumford several times at the Royal Institution, the proximity of a fecund mind always stimulating.

'The idea has merit, I agree, Count Vonskoy.'

'You shall go to Petersburg an' take lodgings with Lebedev. Write now, Sir Renzi! I will see it get to him the fastest way. Desire you shall visit him to discuss the serfs of Russia, perhaps.'

'Is there not a danger Napoleon will invade?'

'Not a chance,' Vonskoy replied impatiently. 'Even the Corsican tyrant know better than to march against a country of such vastness of size an' uncounted millions. He will make noise but never to go too far.'

Later, as he and Congalton strode back to Whitehall it all seemed possible. A Baltic trader at this time of the year could receive a reply very quickly, and in that time he could immerse himself in his studies again and learn from Vonskoy about life in the Romanov court.

# Chapter 40

*St Petersburg*

What had been a noisome swamp just a single century before was now Russia's proud capital, the seat of the Tsar, with palaces and parks, ornamentation, and grand buildings without number, as part of a sanguinary and enigmatic history of enormous complexity.

As the trading barque eased sheets for the final approach to the docks, Renzi looked out over the low and flat Vasilyevsky Island where his voyage would end. As with all docklands it was a dingy, drab prospect with no promise of the wonders that he knew lay within this Venice of the North. Despite himself, his heart beat faster in anticipation of the compelling aesthetics to be found in a city that had brought the barbarians of Tartary face to face with the civilisation of Europe.

Lines were thrown ashore for warping alongside and Renzi felt in his waistcoat for his precious documents. He was the only passenger on board and he hoped to be dealt with promptly.

The customs officer wordlessly accepted his administration fee and handed him a letter. It was from Lebedev and urged him as soon as he landed to take a *fiacre* to the address shown. Very soon the carriage had left the dock area and was bowling along a fine embankment that looked out on the broad river he knew to be the Neva, with the frontages of imposing buildings along the way. Before the straight road took a sharp curve he was deposited in the inner courtyard of a classically styled but oddly different establishment. It was the Imperial Academy of Sciences, the affable doorman assured him, and, yes, Academician Lebedev was in and expecting him.

Renzi was met by a short, bearded man of mature years with fierce grey eyes. He greeted him fussily in meticulous French and an awkward bear hug. '*Mon cher collègue!*' he cried, holding him at arm's length the better to regard him. 'We are honoured in the extreme by your visit. Come, I will show you to your rooms.'

They were along the hall from Lebedev's own quarters and were comfortable, if somewhat monastic in appointments. Renzi left the servants to arrange them to his requirements while he was welcomed into Lebedev's apartment.

Clearly the domestics of a bachelor, it was snug and warm, dominated by a huge writing desk flanked by ceiling-high bookshelves. A silver bell tinkled, prompting the appearance of a servant.

Lebedev looked at him respectfully. 'A restorative, my lord?'

'Thank you, yes.' Renzi knew what was meant, and when the vodka arrived he downed it in one. 'A fine drop, sir.'

'Pertsovka, my particular favourite, which is with honey and pepper and bison grass.' He leaned forward with intensity and said, 'Tell me, my lord, for I do crave to know, what is your interest in us?'

With a light smile Renzi answered with as much gravity as he could muster. 'My study is in the production of a hypothesis of economic response to stress on resources, as mediated by culture.' He sat back and pondered. 'I've been fortunate in the matter of means and have travelled far in pursuit of my object. As an Englishman the oceans of the world are an open highway to me and the Great South Seas, Constantinople, darkest Africa, all these have furnished me with much material, but I'm persuaded there's a great deal to be learned in Russia, an ancient and oft overlooked land.'

'I fear this is an unfortunate time for you to arrive here. Bonaparte threatens us and has caused much mischief in our ranks, but the Tsar holds staunch and you will be safe in St Petersburg, I believe.'

'Yes, very tiresome. I had hoped to—'

'You shall – you shall!' Lebedev exclaimed earnestly. 'In the morning we will meet my associates and others most curious to see an English lord and member of the great Royal Institution to hear of your travels in far places unknown to them. It will be a distinguished occasion. And then we shall go forth to explore our famed Imperial Library on the Nevsky Prospekt. After that—'

'Academician, pray allow me to make occupation of my quarters and we shall meet at breakfast?'

The man was insatiable. Renzi was accustomed to the frowning silence and defensive flourishing of newspapers in an English gentleman's club at breakfast but Lebedev had found a corner of the academy refectory and was badgering him with questions and opinions even before the day had begun. Only the need for a hurried change into morning dress before the reception was enough to part them.

Who would come? If it was a handful of desiccated scholars only, his mission would be near inconceivable – but just one notable with access to the Tsar would be enough.

The occasion was not formal: if Renzi, Lord Farndon, was not of value or interest the higher-placed could slip away, while if he was, then the same could meet him to take his measure. Thankfully, it meant that probably he was not expected to address the learned throng and therefore could direct conversations as he pleased.

In the large chamber, hung with portraits and with a minstrel's gallery at one end, above a hundred were assembled. Conversations stilled and heads turned curiously as he entered by Lebedev's side. In the middle of the floor the academician proudly stepped forward and declaimed in Russian something that evoked a round of polite applause and an expectant hush.

'Honoured colleagues – peers and associates all,' Renzi replied urbanely, in courtly French. 'It is indeed an honour . . .'

It was received well, his frequent and deliberate references to Count Rumford, the Royal Institution, and his travels provoking admiring looks from some, stony-faced envy from others.

Afterwards there was a press of people towards him. A stiff bow and click of the heels from the president of the Academy of Sciences, a fulsome greeting from the professor of humanities and a brace of enthusiastic young men introduced as student *doktorskaya*. They, and the crush of unnamed others, were not whom he was interested in. It was those who stayed back, biding their time until they could get his undivided attention.

A ridiculously ornamented military officer waited with heavy patience, his hand on his sword, glowering. Next to him, occupied with a scruffy, beady-eyed figure in dress more seen in a past age, a tall, well-dressed individual, whose friendly looks were betrayed by thin lips, gazed at Renzi with disconcerting precision.

Renzi freed himself from his admirers and strolled over to them, by now supplied with the inevitable refreshments. Above the hubbub he learned that the officer was one General Arakcheyev, who needed to know his views on whether the British, not a race of soldiers or known for Continental ambition, would face up to Bonaparte's half-million-strong army. He stalked off at Renzi's innocent ignorance and left him with the dishevelled but intense man, still in conversation with the taller, who broke off when he saw Renzi was free.

'Mikhail Speransky, administrator,' he said, with an elegant bow. 'An honour to meet you, Graf Farndon.'

'Er, yes. Thank you.' This was the powerful and feared courtier that Vonskoy had spoken about, who had the one quality he needed above all others. He was personal assistant to the Tsar.

'You are a scholar about to make exploration of the Russian soul, I've heard.'

Renzi inclined his head politely. 'Fortune has been kind to me as providing for my travels and studies even as I sustain my duties as the Earl of Farndon.' The potted version of his study did not appear to satisfy and he launched into a more rarefied account, which caused the intelligent features to wrinkle in concentration.

'Graf Farndon, I believe your hypothesis has both merit and application in the Russia of these times. I would wish to debate it with you at a more opportune time.'

'It would be my pleasure, Mr Speransky.' He bowed. 'As I can be parted from Academician Lebedev.' It couldn't have been more fortuitous. In fact, it was more than his pathway to the Tsar: it was the chance to wrangle his logic and thesis with a worthy disputant.

It brought a fleeting smile. 'Then perhaps tea when you're free?' He turned and left.

'The most dangerous man in all Tsardom.' It was the untidy individual still remaining.

'I beg your pardon?'

'Karamzin. A historian you won't have heard of, yet not without influence. Yes, there's a devil in Speransky that drives him to an elevation of confidence by the Tsar, and yet at the same time to outlandish and exotic theories of governance of the Russian peoples that betrays this same confidence.'

So. Factions and enemies. As must be the case anywhere. All the more reason to act the disinterested savant.

Lebedev took possession of him once again and in the afternoon they visited Catherine the Great's Imperial Library. This was not among the buildings along the embankment but on the other side of the Neva, in the centre of St Petersburg, not very far from the squares and palaces of the Romanovs. Although it was not yet officially open, he was an honoured guest and given a research alcove of his own in the huge edifice, which he was told contained more than a hundred thousand works of scholarship and learning.

It was a pleasant and stimulating visit but time was pressing. Speransky was the key, and it was with marked relief that he boarded the carriage for his estate and the promised tea. It was out in the country, giving Renzi a chance to take his fill of the sights, even if his mind was racing with both possibilities and dangers.

Would he be credible enough to gain admittance to the person of the Tsar? Inevitably he would be seen as cleaving to the Speransky faction, whom Lebedev had dismissed as trouble-makers of reformist liberals and therefore in the conspicuous minority in this deeply conservative country.

Would it matter? Possibly – but he had to reach the Tsar. And this was his only chance. Without question Speransky was testing him against his reputation for evidence of value and would decide whether or not to take things further with him. It had to be done in this way, and by the time he entered the stately villa he was prepared to fall in with any opinions of Speransky that would help the situation.

'Welcome, Graf Farndon, welcome,' Speransky said heartily, standing in front of the fire in the well-appointed sitting room. 'I do feel gratified at your visit, my lord. If there's anything I might get for you after your journey, do pray let me know.'

He was in a comfortable wine-coloured coat with velvet lapels in the new Romantic fashion taking hold in London. Renzi had taken care with his appearance: as a harmless scholar, his dress was modest, understated, dark, but as an earl the material was costly and elegant.

'Tea?'

After Count Vonskoy's tuition he knew what to do. When Speransky had filled his glass with an intense black brew from the samovar, he reached for a sugar cube, put it between his teeth and drank through it. With a gracious inclination of the head in acknowledgement, Speransky produced a platter of dainty biscuits thick with jam and heavy cream.

Renzi took one and pronounced it good, even if his palate was unused to the assault of sweetness.

'Named after Suvorov, our imperial marshal who put down the Kościuszko uprising,' Speransky mentioned smoothly.

'Oh, do forgive me – I find military matters so tedious in the detail,' Renzi murmured, secretly pleased to have his harmlessness confirmed so early.

'Of course, dear fellow.'

Lebedev had been free with his insights and opinions, and Renzi had already formed his ideas about what drove Speransky. The man was some form of reformer in a liberal mould. In a state so autocratic and diehard traditional, he would find himself very much on the defensive – but Speransky had the Tsar's ear and could keep them at bay indefinitely. Apparently he was a logician and took well to arguments so presented, even if opposed to his.

If he was to get further, Renzi had a single overriding objective: to win over the man by showing he had personal value.

'So your studies have brought you here?' Speransky continued pleasantly.

'Indeed. Would you wish to hear them?'

'Very much indeed, sir.'

As warmly as he could Renzi set out his thesis that common underlying strands of human striving lay beneath the daily challenges of life, hidden by distracting cultural layers. Only by comparing in detail these responses could the strands be made to reveal themselves for use by the governing class.

'You have made progress, Graf Farndon? I'm much taken by the vision of your comparing the natives of the South Seas and the serfs that toil in the fields of Russia. Do tell.'

The interest was genuine but tinged with an element of cynicism. He would have to try harder.

243

'Sir, much of what I discovered is claimed by politicking animals whose desire is to appear scholarly in their views. Without a reigning hypothesis and data to support it, they tread upon treacherous sands and cannot prove their position. Take, for example, the role of human bondage in the getting of food . . .'

He had the man's interest now and, with persuasive conviction, went on to examine on the one side crucial economic factors and on the other the irrational, affective motivations involved – and how bondage as a method of extracting labour must inevitably fail.

Before he'd finished he could see that he'd succeeded. Possibly because in his heart he believed in what he was saying.

Speransky's eyes glowed and, in his rapt attention, he still held his empty tea-glass. 'Bravo!' he said huskily. 'As I'd give much to be at the address to the academy that will no doubt be asked of you.'

'Then should I now take my leave, Count Speransky?'

'No!' Speransky said hastily. 'No. That is, I rather feel that Alexander – the Tsar, I mean – would be much seized by your work. If I introduced you to him, would you be so good as to attend on His Majesty to discuss it? I can assure you of an intelligent audience.'

Renzi felt a leap of exultation. He'd done it! Speransky had seized on what he had to offer. That which gave him special value. He was going to be flourished before the Tsar as a scholar of distinction who would publicly declare the rightness, grounded in science, of his liberal reforms.

'The Tsar!' Renzi breathed, overcome. 'B-but this is . . .'

'Come, sir. This is only your due in bringing to us the fruits of your enlightened position. I have His Imperial Majesty's particular trust and affection and you may be sure of an audience on my account. He takes a keen concern in the practices of other polities, and to couple this with the rigours of natural philosophy will be most engaging to him, I assure you.'

# Chapter 41

It was just a short passage by ferry across the Neva to the South Bank, the heart of St Petersburg. In keeping with his vision of a Venice of the North, Peter the Great had ordained that there would be no bridges, only boats, and in winter, sleighs over the ice. The crossing gave a stunning view of the principal splendours of Russia, but Renzi was distracted.

To have gained the attention of the Tsar at this early stage was miraculous but so much was riding on this first encounter. Every instinct urged that time was running out, that there would be an eruption into war very soon. It was of crucial importance that he let London know his best estimate of Alexander's intentions in that event. Any judgement of the autocrat as a military leader, however, was a task for another.

If he could provoke the Tsar's curiosity he had a chance – but if Vonskoy and Speransky were wrong about his thirst for learning, he'd be ignored and would have no alternative but to return to England empty-handed.

He was jerked back to the present by the spectacle of magnificence the avenues of imperial buildings made: the gold-finished onion-shaped domes of churches, the regular symmetry of the architecture, the simplicity yet grandeur of the stately monuments to one man's purpose. Truly a city of princes. And none was more majestic than the residence of the Tsar, the Winter Palace. Renzi's intellects told him it was in style late Baroque, but in its white and turquoise finished in gold, and contrasting stately yellow stucco walls, there was an alluring emotional component that was purely Russian. Within, it was a glory of the most exquisite ornamentation on walls of every colour conceivable, each room furnished in carved elaborature and red velvet. There was nothing remotely like it in the England of George III that Renzi knew of, a sumptuous and exotic feast for the senses.

'My friend,' Speransky murmured, 'at this notice even I cannot command an audience. We shall join others who wait on His Majesty's appearance and I shall then introduce you to him.'

Flanked by bewigged footmen they passed down a passage and entered a day-room resplendent with mirrors, paintings and ormolu. Inside, ladies in the height of fashion, jewelled, with romantic head-dressings, were accompanied by officers in elaborate uniforms and swords. Faces turned in surprise at their entry.

Near the window a lady of splendid maturity was holding court, and at Renzi's appearance conversations fell away. He gave an elegant bow as Speransky introduced him in French. There were disdainful and even hostile expressions on the men, but from several ladies there were bold, appraising looks, languid fluttering of fans doing nothing to hide their naked interest.

'An Englishman?' one of the officers said, in a bored tone. 'Come to tell us how to beat Napoleon?'

Through scattered titters Renzi gave a beatific smile and

in the flowery French of the old regime replied, 'As came to Russia to see whether to admire or merely pity. Lord Farndon, at your service, sir.'

Speransky touched his arm. 'The son of Grand Duke Nikolai, and a soldier of brave heart – in the salons.'

The sound of voices approaching brought tension to the gathering and two guards entered, taking position each side of the door.

Then into the room came the unmistakable form of Alexander, Tsar of Russia.

Instantly everyone made obeisance, ladies held in a deep curtsey, the gentlemen dropping to one knee. Renzi compromised with an elaborate bow as might be expected at the Court of St James.

'Do rise, my people,' the Tsar said, his voice carrying, high-pitched and light. A tall, even boyish figure in pearl-grey plain military uniform with sash and decorations, he carried himself well, statuesque yet delicate, his golden hair slightly balding. He approached the elderly woman, wearing a fortune in pearls, who made to rise from her chair, but Alexander quickly went to her and gently kissed her, exchanging soft words. Renzi was touched at the tenderness he saw in him, unaccountable in a suzerain of Tartary.

He greeted each group politely, exchanging quiet words with this one and that until he arrived before Renzi.

Speransky's bow was familiar, and in return Alexander reached out and patted his arm. 'Well, old fellow, you're bearing up after your fever?' he asked and, without waiting for a reply, his gaze alighted on Renzi.

'Sire, it's with pleasure I'm able to introduce the Earl of Farndon of Great Britain who's journeyed here to make study of our ways.'

'Goodness me, whatever for?' Alexander said, in a benevolent but curious tone. 'In an Englishman I find that singular indeed!'

'He is a well-regarded scholar, Majesty, whose interests do not include the practice of war. At the moment he's engaged in a monumental work of natural philosophy that I would be failing Your Majesty if it were not brought to your attention.'

The Tsar turned to Renzi, who had a fleeting impression of cloudless blue eyes and a soft, near-luminous presence. 'Would you explain it to me, sir?'

Renzi had practised his words until he could deliver their essence in short, pithy phrases leading inexorably from the general to the particular and then a conclusion.

'Fascinating.' Alexander's gaze rested on him for a moment longer. Then he smiled briefly and walked on, leaving Renzi holding his breath in suspense, but it was over, Speransky silently motioning him to remain.

After the Tsar had left, the room burst into excited chatter.

'Well, did I—'

'I cannot say,' replied Speransky, and held his silence.

Before long an imperial functionary entered. The chatter died as he crossed to Speransky, who bent to catch the whispered message.

'I may say that it seems you have succeeded, Lord Farndon. Tsar Alexander begs that if you are at leisure this afternoon you will attend on him to further discuss your hypothesis.'

Accompanied by Speransky, Renzi was ushered into the Tsar's presence, this time in the sanctity and quiet of a private imperial withdrawing room, set about with crimson damask, gilt bronzes and malachite, a fire blazing comfortably. The refreshments were more to Renzi's taste: a brandy of the first rank.

With only the three together, the threads of Renzi's thesis were explored and Renzi found himself warming to the Tsar, his transparent desire for answers, for reasons and causes. If he was guided by a worldly but progressive statesman such as Speransky, who knew what Russia could aspire to?

At one point Speransky excused himself for a short while, leaving them alone together. Almost immediately Alexander turned anxiously to Renzi. 'Tell me, Nikolai, Speransky is a vastly able thinker but he frowns on some of my theorising. For instance, do you not believe the ancients have much to teach us?'

'I do, sire.' What was going on? This was an autocrat of immense powers keeping at bay both the patriciate factions and the peasantry: what need had he of ancient Grecian politicking? And any reasonably educated person could have no quarrel with the precepts of Pythagoras, Hipparchus and the rest.

'You do? Then if we accept their precepts and propositions we do so in full acceptance of their circumstances and conditions?'

'Er, it would seem wise to do so.'

'Yes!' exulted the Tsar. 'As I do! That Achilles dwelled in his tent has deeper meaning, as does Ulysses upon the rock of despair. If we are to aspire to rule in all unassailable logic, then surely we must invoke the same conditions as then.'

Turn Russia into a three-thousand-year-old throwback? He was saved from answer by Speransky's return, but he'd seen what Vonskoy had hinted at – the Tsar's mystic nature, which ruled his thoughts.

Speransky effortlessly took charge of the conversation. 'Ah, yes. We were discussing the role of the land-owning power in the choices facing the tenant?'

The offer, when it came, was both flattering and dangerous. 'It has been most interesting, Nikolai. Regrettably I've a state dinner tonight that Elizabeth accounts important I must attend. I have it in mind to grant you a state apartment here in the Winter Palace for the length of your stay in Russia. For selfish reasons only – that we might spend more time together.'

# Chapter 42

Thunderer, *at sea*

At last! The brisk south-westerly, a fine, quartering breeze with the clean tang of brine in it, purged away all the gross humours of the land, carrying Kydd's ship on with a will up-Channel.

The new administration had concluded that the vast host gathering on the Continent was not intended for the invasion of Britain whatever else Bonaparte had in view, and the hastily assembled fleet of defence at Portsmouth was released to go its separate ways.

The situation, however, was grave, unstable and unknowable. The great horde was intended for a purpose that would probably be set in motion very shortly. It was thus considered prudent to strengthen what was now Britain's most vulnerable preserve, the Baltic, and *Thunderer*, with two other ships-of-the-line, was on her way to Admiral Saumarez to reinforce his command. Ahead, *Montagu* was taking the seas spectacularly on the bow. Tucked in astern, the elderly *Blake* made best speed to keep with them as they passed the familiar coastal sea marks.

Kydd and Craddock took their ease for a space in the stern gallery, hearing the swash and roar of the ship's wake below and admiring the soft green of the English countryside as it slipped by. They passed the mass of ships anchored in the Downs waiting for a fair wind, held up by the same south-westerly that was making their own passage so lively. Then it was around the North Foreland, to Sheppey and the Nore.

They didn't linger and, after passing over dispatches and mail to Flag, they made the most of the bracing wind to stand off for the Yarmouth Roads and the convoy assembling for the Baltic. Kydd knew that to land there to replenish cabin stores for himself and the wardroom would be to compete with the hundreds of vessels preparing to sail. Instead he sent away a cutter under sail south to Lowestoft with Binard and a good-sized purse, to be back before sunset.

The convoy-escort commander in his brig-sloop, with responsibility for near six hundred ships, was gratified to have an unchallengeable addition to his force with the three sail-of-the-line. In the Navy way of things, they would be under his command.

It was an uneventful few days across the North Sea and to the dispersal point, Wingo Sound, discreetly to the west of Gothenburg. Kydd saw to his pleasure the noble bulk of *Victory* at the naval anchorage, the flagship of Admiral Saumarez whom he'd known as a young commander in his first ship. 'Mr Roscoe, call away my barge. I'm to make my number, I believe.' He didn't return for some time and that night was invited to a wardroom dinner.

'The admiral was delayed, sir?' enquired Smale, filling Kydd's glass.

'Not as if he meant to,' Kydd came back mildly, raising his glass to admire its lustre. The low evening sun's glitter on the water reflected prettily on the deckhead and was picked up in flares by the mess silverware. 'He was flag when I was a raw commander of my first ship. Caught up in an affair alongshore in Guernsey for which he turned me out of my ship and I went a-privateering.'

It brought gasps of astonishment.

'The occasion not being any culpability of mine, I was able to prove my innocence and was restored. Today he was moved to remark my elevation in the service since, is all.'

'We'd be obliged for details, if you'd confide them, Sir Thomas.' Roscoe could clearly smell a good dit. Sailors told these yarns among themselves in the leisure sea-time together allowed.

'On another occasion, perhaps,' Kydd said, preferring to let it rest until he knew them better.

Briggs murmured politely, 'You've served in the Baltic before, I understand, sir.'

'Yes, and not so long ago.' This was when *Tyger* was part of the urgent need to preserve the critical Baltic trade, closed off by Bonaparte's recent Continental System of economic blockade. In those desperate times the threat to Britain's supply of naval stores alone could have brought down the country. A third major fleet, after the Channel Fleet and Advanced Squadron, was set up to defend it from, among other menaces, the Russian battle fleet lying in Kronstadt ready to pounce on the foreigners to the Baltic.

Kydd had been delayed in his return because he wanted to know from Admiral Saumarez where they stood these days.

The answer had been chilling. At this moment every single nation bordering the Baltic was an enemy, an ally of Napoleon

Bonaparte and therefore must support his Continental System. If together they willed it, England would be on her knees in weeks and out of the war. Or, if Bonaparte exerted his maritime strength, put to sea even some of his many sail-of-the-line, the handful of ships Saumarez commanded would be quickly overcome and the result would be the same.

And was his massing of a colossal army not so far to the south a prelude to an occupation of the Baltic coast end-to-end, designed to bring about the collapse of Britain's presence and trade as Kydd knew it, again with war-losing consequences?

Kydd had come to appreciate that Saumarez was an undisputed master at manipulating, cajoling and threatening in a bizarre conjuring of diplomatic moves that had the Baltic – for now – open and free.

It was extraordinary: Sweden was at war with Great Britain but Saumarez had privately conceded to him that not a shot would be fired in what amounted to a friendly war. Furthermore, they would not be watching as big convoys assembled off Gothenburg and Hanö to convey, like a mill-race, the products of Britain's industrial might into the very heartland of the Continent. In the many trading ports customs officials were bribed, hidden caches of goods were auctioned off, smugglers alerted – in a wholesale circumventing of the Emperor's will.

Other wildly irregular means were found to make the Baltic the fatal wound in the Continental System. At an early stage Saumarez had let it be known that neutral shipping would be afforded a place in the convoys for their protection, on production of their papers. They were forged on a massive scale, but escort commanders and shore authorities alike accepted them with straight faces. Bonaparte's subjects had a taste for the tin pots, cheap lace, crockery, fine linen, machinery and robust clothing that poured out of England's factories and furtively into homes under his subjection. In return, precious supplies of grain, timber, iron ore and hemp made their way back. Even Lloyds of London was hesitant about insuring a vessel for a voyage to the Baltic unless it carried 'simulated papers'.

But the entire system hung on a ramshackle framework that could so easily be upset. If there was a concerted move to stand by obligations under the Continental System – under threat or otherwise – it would all come undone for Saumarez and his conjuring. But at this point there was only one nation in active opposition to the British, faithfully supporting Bonaparte with its geographical situation at the entrance to the Baltic, the Sound, which it had traditionally commanded with passage dues and strict regulation. Since the British Navy had robbed it of the entirety of its navy, Denmark had gamely fallen back on home-built gunboats and brigs to enforce them. They used the craft as best they could, rowing boats against frigates, brigs before ships-of-the-line, in a courageous but doomed fight for honour.

'I do not in the slightest underestimate the Danes. They of all have reason to hate us,' Saumarez had murmured.

Now, glass in hand, Kydd had to make clear to his officers their purpose in these waters, what they faced in coming to the support of the Baltic Fleet and what was the best guess for Bonaparte's next move.

'Where shall we be doing duty do you think, sir?' Roscoe asked.

Saumarez and the majority of his fleet were stationed at the mouth of the Baltic where they could move with dispatch to counter threats either within or outside the landlocked sea. But a substantial number of his ships, including sail-of-the-line, were far inside, keeping unblinking watch on the major naval base of Kronstadt at the other end of the Baltic where Russia maintained its fleet. Leave and diversion were easily found in Gothenburg, a handful of miles under their lee, but not for those on vigil far in.

'I've been led to believe we shall shortly be relieving the Kronstadt guard.'

Long faces appeared around the table. This was no better than the blockade they'd left, with the added disadvantage of the weather as the year moved into autumn and then the winter ice.

The next few days saw *Thunderer* storing for the hostile station she was about to take up but matters were interrupted by a sudden summons from *Victory*.

'Sir Thomas. I fear your joining Admiral Byam Martin off Kronstadt will have to be delayed.'

'Sir?'

'On account of word I've received from Denmark.' Saumarez had a first-class intelligence network and it could be relied upon. 'Which is most disturbing.'

Kydd waited patiently.

'You were at the bombardment of Copenhagen.'

'I was.'

'Where we removed their navy and stores, leaving them nothing.'

'Sir.'

'This makes it near impossible for them to achieve what they most need to do – choke off the Sound to us on the one hand and look to their dependency, Norway, on the other.'

'Dependency?' Kydd asked.

'Union, if you must. All matters such as foreign affairs, trade and so forth are centralised in Copenhagen, and they have a common monarchy – a Danish king. This war with

Bonaparte has been ruinous to the Danes and nothing more so than to their Norwegian brethren, who are now cut off from their governors and trade partner.'

'You mentioned intelligence, sir?'

'Yes. What single thing do you think could, in one, restore the situation for the Danes?'

'Er, an alliance?'

'They already have one – with Napoleon Bonaparte. No, sir. Consider a frigate – a heavy frigate of 42 guns loose on the sea-lanes. Coming upon one of our prodigious convoys guarded only by a gaggle of sloops, they'd be cut to pieces at immense loss in treasure to us. And the opposite – an enemy convoy of military contraband with an untouchable escort that can cross to Norway and plant an unstoppable insurrection in our rear.'

'And there is such a one?'

'There is. The cunning and resourceful Danes have scraped together all the timbers that remain from when we destroyed any of their ships-of-the-line we couldn't take in prize and from it have built a formidable frigate. And it has just left the shipyards, bound for Norway, fully armed and stored for a cruise of plunder and ravage. It must be stopped. Sir Thomas, I want you to hunt it down and destroy it.'

# Chapter 43

Kydd knew why Saumarez had chosen him: as a proven frigate warrior he was best able to fathom the reasoning of another of the breed. The choice of *Thunderer*, a ship-of-the-line, was another matter. If he was to run a frigate to earth it wasn't so much a matter of speed or gun-power but the fact that Norway's coast opposite Denmark was a frightful chaos of skerried reefs, inner leads and craggy, rocky islands. They ranged in size from puny to substantial and numbered in the thousands. Not the place for a deep-draught battleship but a measure of how consequential Saumarez believed the frigate's destruction to be.

Their charts were old and unreliable but he'd been given a brig-sloop, *Calypso*, and two unrated gun-brigs, *Podargus* and *Flamer*. They would have less trouble with the shoals, but if they came upon the Dane they'd be comprehensively outclassed.

His information from the flag-lieutenant was clear and concise as far as it went. The frigate's name was *Najaden*. Captained by one Hans Peter Holm, it was manned mostly with Norwegians and was said to be a flyer. It was now heading for the capital of Norway, Christiansand, the base for their privateers and gunboats, which were the only weapons left to the Danes. Accompanied by three brig-sloops it could call on up to twenty-five gunboats, each armed with at least a twenty-four-pounder long gun.

Kydd knew the best outcome of the hunt was a meeting in the open sea where his much larger armament would tell decisively. But Holm would be too astute for that, plying the inner leads among the treacherous reefs and islands between strikes.

Saumarez couldn't afford to keep one of his precious sail-of-the-line out of the fleet indefinitely in a fruitless flogging up and down the hundreds of miles of coast: the way ahead had to be information.

*Thunderer* raised the untidy scatter of forested islets off Christiansand in an easy westerly and almost immediately sighted sail, two merchant brigs outward bound from the capital.

'Heave 'em to, Mr Roscoe.'

They were a pair of Swedish Pomeranian fish traders lightly disguised as Estonians. Kydd didn't pry too deeply for he wanted something of them far more precious than their prize value.

'Sir,' his first lieutenant reported, 'they said that the Danish frigate arrived three days ago and left again for the north yesterday with three brigs-of-war in company.'

'Where bound?' Kydd asked hopefully.

'Rumour has it that it's gone to join with the gunboats in Arendal.'

A notorious nest of the vermin some forty miles to the north-east. It made a good deal of sense for Holm to keep away from Christiansand, a well-watched seaport. And from Arendal he would be central to the length of Norway's eastern seaboard, an intolerable threat.

'Clap on all sail! I want to be smelling powder before sunset, Mr Hobbs.'

To be on the scent before even they'd arrived – was this too good to be true? Nevertheless the little squadron shaped course resolutely for the north.

Kydd paced impatiently up and down the quarterdeck. He had *Calypso* in the lead, a brig-sloop smaller even than *Teazer*, his first command, but more sizeable than *Podargus* and *Flamer*, the little brigs out on either beam. These were of the same class as the legendary Cochrane's *Speedy*: the admiral had famously said he could walk his quarterdeck with her whole broadside in his pockets. They wouldn't have a chance against *Najaden* but they didn't have to face the big frigate, just keep *Thunderer* informed.

*Flamer* lagged, taking seas on the bow that others could shoulder aside. *Thunderer* had to bring in sail to compensate, but Kydd did not believe that Holm would be taking the direct route by sea: he'd be threading his way up by the tortuous inner leads and losing time because of it.

They had a chance.

As a lazy evening began to draw in they were at the seaward approaches to Arendal. Two islands loomed, the larger to the right, Merdø, under a mile long of ugly bone-grey rock. Beyond them was an obscure channel barely a couple of hundred yards wide, presumably leading to the inner leads and the harbour.

'We can't enter there,' the sailing master pronounced, with finality. 'Give 'em best, sir.'

Kydd took in the reality of the iron-bound coastline and knew he was right. But as he pondered *Podargus* hauled its wind to come within hail.

'Sir Thomas? I've a man aboard knows these parts. I submit we're best suited to lead us in.'

'Are you sure he can act the pilot?' It was an immense responsibility, and if he was some kind of lower-deck braggart, disaster would be complete. And saying 'lead us in' – it was foolish in the extreme to contemplate taking in a ship-of-the-line.

'He says he's certain, having been this way many times before.'

'Very well,' Kydd said reluctantly. 'But *Calypso* and I will wait for your reconnaissance.'

He'd only met Lieutenant-in-Command Robillard once but had been impressed. With growing concern he watched as the young man eased sheets and brought his ship around and into the narrowing passage. The little sloop had only just cleared Merdø when she sheered violently to one side. A signal jerked excitedly up – 'Enemy in sight'!

At the same time a lookout in *Thunderer*'s foretop shrieked down, '*Deck hoooo!* There's ships a-lying t'other side of the island! I just seen their masts!'

The object of the mission lay out of sight behind the island, a shrewd move by Holm. He was protected by the horrors of rock and shoal that would deter outsiders from entry while leaving him within minutes of putting out, able to fall on a convoy.

What Holm hadn't reckoned on was that the hunters would have a pilot to show the way.

The crump and slam of firing sounded from beyond Merdø. Columns of gun-smoke rose into the air and shot-strike tore the water viciously around the hapless *Podargus*. Ominously, from the island opposite, shore batteries sighted in to cover *Najaden*'s anchorage began to speak.

Kydd knew he couldn't simply give up and sail away, the deadly threat nearly in his hands. Neither could he lie off to wait for it to emerge: an infinity of inner hidden inlets and passages would allow it to make off unseen. 'We go in,' he snapped. 'Take station on *Podargus* – she'll be in the deeper water. As soon as *Najaden* is in sight, give it a starb'd broadside.'

'Sir? There's no room to manoeuvre in there!'

'Get under weigh this minute, sir!'

*Thunderer* took up ponderously in the fjord-like calm and slid past Merdø, her guns run out, but instead of a clear field of fire they found the enemy frigate near encircled by another three islets.

And *Podargus* was stopped with a very definite list, gone aground in going about to warn *Thunderer*.

'Sir! I see one – no, three – five gunboats to the nor'ard!' From out of the eye of the Arendal passage and almost certainly with more on their way.

And then came a barely perceptible shudder, then another, sharper, and a significant slowing. 'Hard a larb'd!' the master shouted, but it was too late. *Thunderer* was brought up all standing, herself victim of a hidden skerry outcrop.

'Get the sail off her!' Kydd roared, in desperate frustration. Not yet within striking range of *Najaden*, they were motionless, unable to either move forward or retreat. *Flamer* sailed past gamely on her way in to stand by *Podargus*, now under fire from the first gunboats. As long as she could keep clear of the reefs she was a mortal threat to them, moving faster and with carronades and grape-shot. But *Najaden* thundered out her spite on them both.

Furiously Kydd forced his mind to concentrate. Shadows were lengthening as the evening drew to a close but night would bring no relief. Unless he could come up with a plan they stood to be battered to pieces or brought to an inevitable surrender.

Then he had it: as long as Holm thought *Thunderer* was at

his mercy, *Najaden* would take her time to warp out and take position on the big ship's bow to hammer *Thunderer* into oblivion. If he saw that she wasn't helpless under his guns, he'd wish he were somewhere else.

'Mr Roscoe, I want every boat in the water with a line to our bow.'

'We're going to tow off the reef?' the first lieutenant came back incredulously.

'Yes – and no. Go to it, sir!'

In the last of the light, watchers from *Najaden* saw furious activity in the fore-part of *Thunderer*, then boats with towing lines clawing the water directly towards the frigate. It seemed the massive ship-of-the-line was only lightly aground and in a short time would be in position to bring a storming rage of shot to destroy them.

Sometime during the night the frigate slipped away into one of the many inlets or sounds to the inner reaches of the jagged Norwegian coastline, leaving *Thunderer* to ease free on the tide in the early hours of the morning.

Re-grouping in the slop and hurry of the blessed open sea Kydd had much to think on.

Among these craggy archipelagos it was going to be next to impossible to force a conclusion with a man-o'-war that had all the advantages of local knowledge. Unless Robillard's seaman pilot . . . Could this tip the balance back?

'I'll trouble you for your man,' Kydd hailed *Podargus*.

He watched as the seaman warily came over the bulwark, his bag thrown expertly ahead of him.

'Todd, sir. Quartermaster,' he said, touching his hat.

Kydd noted the lines of maturity in his open face, the well-kept sailor's rig that was the mark of the born mariner. 'Come below and tell me something of the coast,' he invited. 'You'll be given a mess but no duties while you're aboard.'

It was a revealing talk. Todd had been a merchant seaman earlier, unusually in the coastal trade in a Danish-flag brig that needed to pass through the appropriate leads and inlets in accordance with the weather at the time, a perfect qualification.

Questioned about where Holm would most likely go now, he had no doubts. 'He'll not want to return t' Christiansand with you in the offing and agin this westerly, sir. So he has to go up the coast, taking the inner sound. Once he's in there, he can't get out to sea until he's passed right through – and there with brisker winds offshore you'll be waiting for him.'

This was something like Kydd needed.

With the westerly holding they made good time to seaward of the Hasteinsundet sound and, with sails backed, waited.

Later in the afternoon sail was spotted about to round the end of the outer island. It was *Najaden*.

'You see, sir, he's well aggrieved,' Todd said quietly, next to Kydd on the quarterdeck.

'Yes, well done,' Kydd replied.

'Oh, not that, sir. I meant as it's not what he wanted. He sees us but, in this westerly, can't go back down his bolt-hole. He has to stay out t' sea, and sailing north there's no channel to the inner leads for a dozen or more miles.'

The frigate was doomed.

As it emerged Kydd saw three more warships keeping close company, brig-sloops mounting full-calibre carriage guns, but none that could deter *Thunderer*'s unanswerable might.

The ship was already at quarters, and as they closed in for the kill, a mighty cheer broke out. After so long on dreary blockade they were going to be blooded!

But the canny Danish captain had not finished. The only advantage of a following wind was the ability to select his course with precision and he chose well. To his left were the impassable dour heights of a long island, but all along its outer seaboard was a near continuous necklace of islets. Jagged rock tips protruded from white sea-scars, an ugly roiling of sub-sea menaces all along the sea-cliffs.

Holm could be seen next to the helm, conning his ship directly towards them, not slackening the pace in the slightest. Then, in a masterly show of seamanship, he began threading his way through them, close in up the coast and safe from *Thunderer*.

Kydd looked at Todd who gave a wry smile. 'Can't follow, sir. Not in this'n. What does she draw?'

'Say twenty feet aft.'

A sorrowful shake of the head in response.

All afternoon the English squadron paralleled the Danish a mile or more out to sea. Sooner or later, when the coast cleared of hazard they would have a chance to pounce, but at four, conditions changed.

From astern, with the wind, a white curtain of rain advanced slowly, enveloping the ship in a cold deluge, hissing loudly in the sea and bringing misery to all on deck, but, worse, cutting visibility to yards until they lost sight of *Najaden* and her consorts.

What would Holm do? Would he take in sail and reduce speed in prudence, leaving *Thunderer* to forge ahead and lose him? Or would he take the opportunity to dog-leg to sea for a rapid advance to the next channel inshore? Possibly he'd merely go to anchor, knowing *Thunderer* was standing north and making away.

It was an old saying: 'Long foretold, long past – short notice, soon past.' The rain squall would not go away for some hours.

'Get *Podargus* alongside,' Kydd ordered.

Briefly he told her to remain in the vicinity and, when the

squall lifted, look out for *Najaden*. He ordered *Calypso* to stretch out ahead to do the same. *Thunderer* and *Flamer* would go on at best guess for the north.

The rain lasted for another two hours before it thinned and cleared.

*Najaden* was nowhere in sight.

Kydd had half hoped that the frigate in its hubris would appear wrecked and broken on some craggy reef, but it seemed that Holm was too good a seaman to let that happen. From Todd he discovered that there were channels bearing off each islet, which, while leading to a seaport of sorts, would be a trap for him, a dead-end. With no word from *Podargus* Holm had to be somewhere ahead.

*Calypso* appeared but with no sighting signal flying. 'Spotted, sir. Three miles south of here, but since vanished.'

'Mr Todd?'

'Can't think why . . . Yes, I can! He's gone to ground, and I know where.'

'Say on.'

'A snug little anchorage, sheltered on all sides an' not seeable from the sea.'

'Go on,' Kydd encouraged.

'We used it to make Vinterstø in the winter and—'

'Show me on the chart.'

It was an insignificant cove off an impossibly narrow waterway to the larger coastwise sound.

In his bones Kydd could feel Holm gloating that no Englishman would know of this hideaway, with its convenient access to the open sea and passing convoys, as he lay low there.

Send in *Calypso* and the others? Against a heavy frigate at rest – they wouldn't last more than minutes. But *Thunderer* . . .

'Todd, draw me a chart – a diagram. Show me everything.'

His heart sank as he studied it closely. A perfect maze, a warren of paths and inlets, sounds and fjords. And basically an impossible situation: *Najaden* and her consorts lay concealed in the tiny harbour of Lyngør to one side of a narrow channel through which *Thunderer* might pass but could never turn and go back. Or manoeuvre to bring guns to bear or any other motions against the enemy.

Kydd looked again. If this was what Holm was able to do every time he was sighted and chased, the hunt could last for ever.

How could he conceivably turn it to advantage, having the knowledge but not the ability to do anything?

He racked his brain. 'What's the depth of water?'

'Main north–south passage near bottomless. Off Lyngør it shallows.'

'And *Najaden* lies there.'

'Sir.'

What he was thinking of was a desperate, even lunatic act but, given the stakes, he'd do it – he'd have to.

'Mr Hobbs,' he told the sailing master. 'I'm going in. Mr Roscoe, gun-crews to their guns, sail trimmers to stand by tacks and sheets.'

'Sir, would it not be better—'

'No, Mr Roscoe.' If it failed he wanted it laid entirely to his account. 'As well, I want a well-secured kedge anchor over the stern.'

When all was ready Kydd took a deep breath. 'Ease her away, if you please.'

The deck fell silent as the rocky grey coast pressed in on them as they slid by, close enough to see the splash of orange lichen and individual details of the dark green northern scrub. And then a quarter-mile past the steep bulk of the final island the Danish frigate and its three brigs burst into view.

'Hard a' starb'd!' Kydd roared. Then, to the tense sail-handlers, 'Let loose and throw off the lines!'

*Najaden* was taken by surprise, and *Thunderer* was left to complete her manoeuvre.

The sailing master, appalled at where they were going, gripped the rail in despair. 'Sir – we're . . . we're . . .'

The bowsprit of the great ship-of-the-line continued to track around to point accusingly at the frigate.

But it didn't stop there. With loose sail banging and slatting, she continued the turn as though wearing about, her yards seemingly within feet of the rugged stone of the shore.

'Slip the after kedge and stand by!' Kydd bawled, and spun about again for the crowning move.

Roscoe turned to him, his face pale and set but holding back as *Thunderer* completed her turn – and ran her bow ashore in a grinding thud and long drawn-out squeal.

'You . . . you've—'

'Hold your peace, Mr Roscoe,' Kydd said, gazing intently at the angles, for what happened next would either make or break his wild plan.

And it was working! Pinioned by her forefoot, the inertia of the turn kept her stern swinging until she was at right angles to the rocky coastline.

'Kedge – hold her at that!' he bellowed, his voice breaking with the intensity of his feeling. The seamen out of sight below threw on turns and hauled taut, the line thrumming dangerously, but the swing was caught. *Thunderer* eased and stopped. It left her broadside facing precisely the awkwardly placed *Najaden* not two hundred yards distant. Two whole decks of guns, including thirty-two-pounders, the armament of the biggest battleship, was now aimed at the frigate which was helpless and bottled up before them.

They were close enough to see every detail as Kydd stared at its quarterdeck, at the figures who seemed to stand waiting for death. Under such menace surely it would be understandable to strike colours now.

There was no movement but then foolishly, heroically, came a thin cry and the frigate's guns threw out their defiance, knowing full well what the awful response would be.

'Open fire,' Kydd said woodenly. Such courage deserved better than what had to happen now.

*Thunderer*'s guns erupted in a blast of sound that echoed off the rocks, magnifying their rage and making all the more brutish the savagery of the ruin brought on the frigate. Battering to death the sleek creature, destroying the proud command of Holm, the seaman Kydd had come to admire, and leaving in its place a broken, shattered and flame-devoured wreck.

# Chapter 44

*St Petersburg*

Outside the Winter Palace a soft wind rustled leaves and set a loosely fastened window shutter creaking. The profound darkness couldn't have made better conditions for the two figures on the balcony. Quietly cursing, the smaller tried yet another key on the ring but this time, with an oily click, the lock obeyed.

Noiselessly they dropped inside on to the deep carpet and eased the window shut behind them.

'Light!' hissed the smaller. A small dark-lantern was passed and one of its shutters was opened, shedding a dim glow in the large room. Their eyes darted about. It was richly appointed – even in the shadows the glitter of gold took the eye, as did the intricate carved giltwork and mantelpiece ornaments. But these men were not interested in costly gew-gaws; theirs was a stealthy quest for something of far more value: the rumoured evidence of the grossest act of treachery against the Tsar of Russia.

'Here!' one said, crossing quickly to a large ornate writing desk. It was locked but these men were professionals and it took little to force it open. He began swiftly rummaging, glancing at each article by the light of the lantern resting close by, and discarding them as quickly for they knew what they were looking for.

The other went from chair to table, carefully feeling beneath them for concealed packets or clipped papers. Behind pictures and hangings, under porcelain, heavy urns.

'*Chert voz'mi*,' the one at the desk muttered, under his breath. 'If it's not here, where the devil can it be?'

He straightened, catching an ornate vase on a nearby table. It fell, shattering noisily on one of the extended legs.

Both men froze for a long minute.

'Nothing.'

But then a shrill, agitated female voice sounded from the top of the stairs outside. 'Grigor! Grigor! There's someone inside – come quick!'

'We have to get out,' the smaller intruder snapped, slamming shut the desk leaf and making for the window.

'Wait!' the other said, bending to the wastepaper basket under the desk and feeling about in it.

'Leave it – he's no fool, he'd never make that stupid mistake. Drop it – let's go!'

The window opened out but then the door handle began rattling. 'Grigor, here!' the voice on the other side demanded loudly. 'Come here, bring help, you oaf!'

'Get out! Now!'

'Not yet – what's this? Take a look, Vladimir.'

He clutched several crumpled pieces of paper showing without doubt that ciphers had recently been worked on in that room.

'Thank God! We have it.'

# Chapter 45

*Renzi's apartment the following day*

'But, dear fellow, if you do allow that the serfs go free to bestow their vote on any they deem worthy, you'll replace one set of problems with another.'

'To be dealt with in due time.'

'Unhappily that is not a quantity you can command.' Renzi was enjoying a cosy debate with Speransky, an intelligent and cool analyst. 'Without they understand the principles and facts, their choice is worthless. I rather feel a vast programme of education is called for to yield an informed vote, else—'

A thunderous tattoo at the door interrupted him. Before Speransky could answer, it burst open and half a dozen burly uniformed men flooded in, a sneering officer taking position in the centre.

'What's this, Balashov? You dare to—'

'Gosudárstvennyy Ministr Speransky. You have been arrested for crimes of treason and the betrayal of His Imperial Majesty's trust for which you will now answer – if you can.'

'You're insane, Balashov. This is the apartment of our distinguished English guest—'

It was the French of the Imperial Court that was being spoken and Renzi could understand all of what was being said but not its meaning. As far as it made sense, it was something of a coup by one of the many factions opposed to Speransky's reforms that threatened the age-old ancestral power structure. If so, he was caught up in as dangerous a plot as any he'd survived. And Renzi's fate was unconditionally bound up with Speransky's: he was the foreign savant who was giving the legitimacy of learning and natural philosophy to the man's visions.

'What are you trying to say, you idiot?'

The man's face darkened but he went on doggedly: 'You omitted to destroy these.'

He held up the pages of code, snatching them away when Speransky reached for them.

'So, you broke into my study, a flagrant criminal act.'

Renzi saw, however, that his face had gone white, and his voice was unsteady.

'These talk of high things, Speransky, and they're coded to "Toad", an address in Paris we've been watching and believe to be that of the traitorous Talleyrand. What do you say to that?'

'It's not as it appears. Take me to the Tsar. I'll explain only to him.'

'You're a cold-blooded criminal, Speransky. I can't allow that.'

'If you do not, my evil friend, you'll have to explain why you've removed his chief minister from his side without leave from him. You fancy standing before his wrath then, Balashov?'

\*    \*    \*

The closed carriage rattled through the empty streets and out into the black and somnolent countryside as the cavalcade clattered on to Tsarskoe Selo, the retreat of the Tsar of Russia. So early in the morning the blustering Balashov was refused admission, Alexander said to be at his morning prayers, so the prisoner and escort, along with Renzi and the others, were left in a small room until after ten.

'Well, Balashov, what is so urgent it demands I abandon my presence before the Almighty?' Alexander snapped, at the chief of police on his knee before him.

'Grave and treasonous charges to be laid against Gosudárstvennyy Ministr Speransky, Your Imperial Majesty.'

Evidence was produced and allegations made, but Speransky remained stubbornly mute until Alexander cut through the stream of spite. 'Speransky, you shall account for it to me personally. Not you, Balashov.'

The two went into the stateroom together, the door firmly shut in the face of the chief of police and his entourage.

Renzi's fears retreated. For as long as Speransky held the Tsar's favour he was safe.

It was more than two hours of tension and boredom before there was movement and then they reappeared. Speransky emerged first, white and shaking. Behind him, Tsar Alexander had tears in his eyes. He called softly, brokenly, 'Mikhailo Mikhailovitch – this is our farewell!'

Speransky stopped and looked back. Impulsively Alexander went to him, embraced him warmly, and sobbed, 'Once again, farewell!'

They parted and the Tsar fled back into the stateroom.

As if under a spell, the onlookers moved aside as Speransky walked through them, like a condemned man. As he passed Renzi he looked at him and murmured, 'Siberia.'

Balashov rounded genially on his followers. 'Thus do perish all tyrants. Let's drink on that, comrades!'

Departing noisily they disappeared, leaving Renzi alone. He was no longer a threat, just another doddering intellectual who'd lost his audience. With his access to the Tsar now cut short, there was little advantage and much danger if he stayed in Russia. He'd apply for his passport and quit the realm as quickly as he could.

Returning to his apartment he began sorting his belongings ready for the journey, reflecting on the near-criminal carelessness of Speransky in not destroying his workings. And if he had indeed been in correspondence with the wily Talleyrand it could only be for the purpose of undermining Bonaparte and now that was finished. It was a disastrous end to a promising beginning.

A reply to his request for papers to leave arrived within forty-eight hours but not in the form he expected.

'Graf Farndon, His Imperial Majesty desires you should attend him, if you will.' Renzi followed the chamberlain down the passages to the withdrawing room and was ushered in.

Tsar Alexander turned and straightened, clearly distraught.

'Dear Sir Farndon, so good in you to come.' He advanced with both hands outstretched to take Renzi's. 'I do so need a clear and honest mind to join with mine in finding a course through this quagmire of . . . of . . .'

'I understand, Majesty,' Renzi said, with a polite bow.

'Do know that it has been a practice in Russia since the esteemed and revered Pyotr Velikiy – that is to say, the Great – to seek counsel and philosophies from those in eminence in western lands. Should I beg it of you, sir, you will not deny me?'

Renzi held down a leaping exultation: this was more than

276

he had dared hope. 'I shall, sire, with my most sincere endeavours. I pray, however, I might stand excused from discussing matters military or even of diplomacy, in neither of which can I claim a sufficient degree of comprehension in their complexities.'

'You desire to avoid the unreason, the mischances and ill-fortune that follow in their study. That I can understand, my friend.'

'Sir.'

'Then do consider my plight, sir. I'm autocrat and ruler of all the Russias, yet must part with my most trusted adviser. Is this what it must cost me?'

There was nothing Renzi could do for Speransky: the Russian's foolish mistake had brought about his downfall. 'I fear so, Majesty.'

'It was I who told him to make contact with Talleyrand. He is innocent of treason.'

Renzi was momentarily at a loss for words but knew everything now hung on his response. 'Neither are you to blame for your action. A statesman is ruled by his reason, not his emotions, Majesty. You correctly saw that if you continued to lay your trust in one revealed as in communication with a hostile power it would be seen as the act of a weak-minded ruler. For the sake of all Russia, he must be offered up to martyrdom.'

Alexander's eyes glistened. 'You are right. Sir, you are undoubtedly right.'

'And I dare to say you will make his time of exile as comfortable as shall match his past status?'

'Yes, yes. That I can do for him.'

'Then you will have done all that is expected of you, Majesty.'

'Not all. I have no adviser and am presented with a

277

perplexity no man on earth can support without divine aid. I wish to share it with you, Nikolai.'

'Sire.'

'Not so long ago I made visit to Moscow. There the Patriarch himself stirred me to the bottom of my heart. He pronounced before all in the cathedral that I was the living icon of Russia and the instrument of God on earth. Into my hands was placed the destiny not only of Russia but of creation itself, to be the Almighty's shield and sword. Nikolai, when I stood before the tombs of great men in the Kremlin I was transfigured in heart and soul and for the first time saw this destiny before me.'

He drew himself up, a rosy flush mounting to his cheeks, and in a sublimely expressive gesture, he mimed opening a holy book. 'And that night I read in the Book of Revelation, "And I saw, and beheld a white horse: and he that sat on him had a bow; and a crown was given unto him: and he went forth conquering, and to conquer." My dear friend, I knew those words were meant for me alone. I'd had a dream of setting forth on such a white horse, but only to be set upon by another clad in black and intent on a duel to the death.'

The Tsar paused, his child-like blue eyes lifted in ecstasy. Then he dropped his gaze and, looking directly at Renzi, said gravely, 'Nikolai, by this I know that I'm fated to lead the world on a crusade against the Antichrist who is even now on earth, incarnate.'

Renzi managed to say, 'And you have identified the Antichrist?'

A slight frown passed quickly. Then Alexander replied, without hesitation, 'Of course. It's the Emperor of the French, Napoleon Bonaparte.'

'Yes, sire. But, er, where is your perplexity, pray?'

Just as rapidly the mood of ecstasy passed and the Tsar's

expression turned wooden. 'If I'm to lead the world, will the peasants fight for me?'

'I beg your pardon?'

'Russia is a country of millions. Against such a number none can resist. But only if they follow me. Will they?'

Entirely out of his depth, Renzi was floundering. 'I cannot know that, sire. But it is written that whosoever is of brave heart will never lack for followers.'

'My army commanders – Bagration, Barclay de Tolly, Rostopchin – bicker among themselves for honour and advantage. Some desire peace at any cost to save Russia from the greatest army the world has seen, led by its most victorious general. Others clamour for a surprise first attack on the French to deflect their purpose. What is your view, Nikolai?'

This was far past what Renzi should have been doing, but to retain any kind of presence he had to prove supportive. After all, he reasoned, the Tsar didn't have to take his counsel.

'Majesty. You yourself have said you are to be the Almighty's shield and sword. Not your subordinate generals. You shall be the one to appear at their head to inspire and lead. You shall assume the post of supreme commander and bear the honour and responsibility for the destiny of Russia in accordance with your vision and all shall obey.'

It was without question that if it came to war the autocratic Tsar would in any event trust no one but himself and seize the reins of military power. This provided only a gloss for the move.

Alexander's eyes glowed. 'This is how it must be. You are wise and understanding, Nikolai.'

'Therefore—'

'Therefore my decision is made.'

'May I—'

'Certainly.'

Renzi held his breath. In the next moments he would be getting precisely what he needed.

'I shall not move against Napoleon Bonaparte.'

Then it was not going to be war.

'Russia will be defended by the moral rightness of her cause.'

'And if Bonaparte attacks?'

'It will be a fatal mistake. But know that while I shall not be the first to draw the sword, I shall be the last to return it to the scabbard.'

The uneasy peace could yet endure. Without an ill-considered flourish by Russia to provoke war, Bonaparte was not in any position to keep his colossal army in existence indefinitely and must retire for the foreseeable future.

'A wise and thoughtful decision, sire,' Renzi said encouragingly, for with it the world would be spared the appalling spectacle of the slaughter of hordes that would follow any other course.

'You think so? I'm glad, Nikolai. Now, if you'll excuse me, I have an important journey to make. I hope you will be able to accompany me.'

'Of course, Majesty. Er, where will this be?'

'To Vilna,' Alexander said briskly. 'As my forebears have done before me, to seek aid and guidance from the Black Virgin at the Gate of Dawn.'

Renzi sat alone in his apartment. He had no illusions. At the moment he was of use to the Tsar, possibly even a genuine friend. If for any reason he failed him, he would be cast out by the eccentric autocrat as speedily as he'd been taken up. Yet at the moment Renzi was as close to his decision processes as any.

It was time to let London know. But what would he tell

them? That Tsar Alexander was anything but a ferocious barbarian Tartar lord, ready to summon up the unknown millions in Russia's vast interior to fall in a frenzied madness on Bonaparte's army? That instead he had to be reckoned an arch mystic, convinced his holy mission on earth was to rid it of the Antichrist Bonaparte – but not yet?

In answer to his quest to discover whether he would fight or no, there could only be one answer: it depended.

The Tsar would not declare war, that Renzi believed. At the head of an untrained peasant army and facing Napoleon Bonaparte, who had beaten him twice before, all that could be said was that if Bonaparte provoked an aggression he would respond.

The auguries were bleak, and he couldn't see how Great Britain could justify sending troops and wealth into such an apocalyptic unknown future. Now it was his duty to lay out his findings.

He sighed deeply and reached for the materials that would begin the procedure of activating Congalton's network to get out his vital message.

# Chapter 46

*The border at the Niemen river*

The fire crackled and spat as the mess-pot was lifted off and taken away for doling out the contents to the soldiers, leaving the officers to their evening conviviality.

Adjutant Commandant Moreau enjoyed this time of the day, even though he disliked the crudity of mess arrangements while on campaign. Although they were not on the march, this was as much a campaign as any. The Grande Armée, encamped so close to the Russian border, was there to put the fear of God, or more precisely that of Napoleon Bonaparte, into the heart of the Tsar, his army and his people. Its purpose was to bring about a submission before even a shot was fired.

It was something Moreau greatly wished for as he knew the Emperor would not rest until the Tsar and his realm were his. He went along with the posturing, gestures and deceit for that very reason, knowing it was bringing ever more pressure to bear to this end.

The parading of a hundred thousands along this side of

the Niemen river border, drums thundering, bayonets glittering, all the panoply and raw colour of war, was a daily occurrence. Only today the Emperor had made another of his inspections for his strict instructions were that appearances must be as realistic as possible. With spies everywhere it had to be seen that the Grande Armée was ready in every particular or it would be put down as a grand charade, the vast, expensive assembling all for nothing. Any makeshift, and not only the men involved but their commanders would face harsh penalties.

Moreau had taken appropriate steps in his engineering corps to meet the demand, the whole a unit that was war-ready to move out at once. His speciality was the building of bridges, or pontoons as the army liked to call them. His meticulousness was well known: the long carts with the pre-drilled timber lengths also carried bolts and brackets, each keyed to a single position in the finished article, and strictly matched against a check-off list. Each man had an assigned function in the bridge-building, was responsible for his specialised tools and could be challenged for them.

'How much do you reckon this is costing the Emperor?' His friend, Ingénieur Géographe Rochambeau mused, sipping his wine. An unconventional, warm-hearted fellow, he'd done well to reach where he had and was at his best when about him things were at their worst.

'Does it matter? He'll screw it all back from Alexander after our eccentric Tsar comes to his senses.' It didn't escape Moreau's attention that it had been 'costing the Emperor' rather than 'costing the public purse'. His friend took it for granted, just as he did, that the Republic's treasury was in fact the Emperor's property.

'Hmm. Sooner this is over and done with the better I'd

like it. A dash of leave, say six weeks in dear Cavaillon with Marie, and I'm set up for the year. You?'

'I tell you confidentially, Bertrand,' Moreau said, looking over his shoulder, 'this marching back and forth the whole length of the civilised world for near twenty years on end leaves me tired and sick of it. And how we're to show enthusiasm for a crack now at the barbarian world is beyond me.'

'Don't worry, *mon ami*. I heard that Bonaparte sent an emissary to Alexander demanding final satisfaction in the strongest terms. It'll all be over shortly, you'll see.'

The evening drew in, supper was taken and moodily Moreau wandered to where the camp ended above the river and stared over into Russian territory, which was quickly shading into darkness. There were one or two pinpricks of light, but no acres of campfires stretching into the distance as there were on their side where a great army crouched. The population of the Grande Armée exceeded that of most cities in Christendom. It contrasted ominously with his view across the banks where an unearthly stillness spread from the interior of a continent that ranged many thousands of miles into the savage, unknowable east.

He shuddered and turned to go back before the darkness became complete.

There seemed to be some kind of activity, movement – lanterns, torches, raised voices.

'Where have you been, Moreau?' a high aide-de-camp snapped. 'Never mind. Join them in the General Staff pavilion.'

There was an almost palpable tension in the air. Senior officers in every degree of splendour occupied the chairs in front, and the rest, including Moreau and Rochambeau, stood.

'Marshal of the Empire Berthier.'

There was a small delay as the slight figure of Napoleon's

famed chief-of-staff took his place on an improvised dais. Significantly, he was arrayed not in imperial court regalia but in plain campaign dress and appeared ill at ease.

'Gentlemen. This is to acquaint you with the fact that the Imperial Grand Council has met in session with the Emperor.'

An announcement of sorts so soon afterwards implied a momentous outcome, and the assembly settled into watchfulness.

'At which it was decided what must be done to resolve our differences with the Russian Tsar following an unsatisfactory reply to our latest offer of peace.

'For reasons of state – I say again, for reasons of state – it was concluded that we have no other alternative than to make good on our final warning . . . and to launch a punitive strike into Russia.'

For long moments there was utter stillness. Then pandemonium broke out. Shouts punctuated it from all parts while Berthier waited, visibly distressed. He held up his hands for quiet.

A red-faced general in the front row stood up and shouted, 'Whose decision was this, sir, that plunges us into—'

Berthier cut him off coldly: 'Sir, it was the Grand Council in its collective wisdom that reluctantly took judgement so.'

'Madness!'

'His Imperial Majesty has declared that any who refuse to follow the eagles against the enemy will answer for it before the people. Those who do their duty, on the other hand, will share to the full in the plunder from the greatest adventure the Empire of the French has yet seen.'

'When shall we be called to arms?'

'Immediately, sir. While the enemy has not yet thought to bring up his legions to resist us. In short, sir, we launch our enterprise this very night.'

'You cannot mean it, sir!'

'The engineers are to throw up bridges in accordance with their current plans within the hour. The army will step off at four, no later.'

'What is our first objective?'

'A good question. And I will tell you that it is Vilna, in central Courland, where at this moment Tsar Alexander is undergoing a religious ritual of some nature. Our advance will be rapid and devastating, and should an army be thrown out to meet us or the Tsar be encircled, our business will then be concluded.'

'And Vilna is on the road to Moscow.'

Marshal Berthier stayed silent.

In an electrifying pause the news was taken in.

'Gentlemen. Your orders are being prepared at this very moment. Go to your duties and I wish you well for the future . . . whatever it may bring.'

Stunned, Moreau turned to his friend but found words wouldn't come. It seemed Rochambeau had the same difficulty and instead he gripped Moreau's hands wordlessly, then disappeared into the crowd.

The planning, the practice, now it was the reality.

Moreau hurried to his own staff marquee and was besieged by so many he had to take refuge inside.

One by one campfires were doused for night-time rest but under cover of darkness troops were now moving up to the border, concealing themselves in the fringing forest. Their marching packs were stuffed with twenty days' emergency rations of rice, flour and biscuits, as well as the usual campaign impedimenta.

For Moreau it was straightforward enough: pull out the operational order book and detail off the units in sequence as laid down – transports, escorts, stores. A colonel presented himself as the authority who would show him where the crossings were required, and another from a horse artillery regiment announced he was ready to site guns to cover proceedings.

All around there was a ferment of commotion and excitement, hurrying troops and equipment dragged along.

The places had been carefully chosen by Bonaparte himself, an artilleryman by training. One was at the nearer bend in the river, narrowed by the curve. Moreau's experienced eye noted higher ground suitable for mounting the guns to oversee their activity, and access roads existed ready to be extended to serve the crossing. He also saw that where the bend constricted the river flow the water was running faster and a central sandbank would cause trouble. He would take charge there and send a less experienced junior colonel to attend to the existing bridge at Kovno, a small medieval town several miles downstream.

'Well, get on with it!' he roared, at a dithering officer at the pontoons. In hours, tens, hundreds of thousands had to be tramping across their bridges.

He lost no time in taking boat with the *voltigeurs* who would secure the opposite bank, and soon found himself standing in wonder that this dark and still land under his feet was Russia. Where would it all end?

The *vedettes* returned from their reconnaissance with the astonishing news that no Russians opposed them whatsoever: they had achieved the surprise necessary to get the army across and assembled for their march. Moreau whipped his engineers into action and, with the benefit of their weeks of practice and no interference from the enemy, they were able to throw across four bridges before day dawned.

First over was Davout's light cavalry, which spread without pause over the country in a protective shield. Columns of infantry followed and, once across, their bands burst into heart-thumping martial music, their welcome on to Russian soil. In the early hours the figure of the Emperor, in his green redingote and unmistakable plain cocked hat, was seen making the crossing to full-throated roars of '*Vive l'empéreur!*' from the stolidly marching horde.

The endless tramping of his host into Russia had begun.

# Chapter 47

The sun, from a tentative appearance at daybreak, strengthened through the morning, beating down on the snaking lines of humanity that led to the horizon. A pall of dust hung over them, choking and blinding, the merciless heat making the march a harsh trial.

Moreau rode at the head of his corps and was soon joined by Rochambeau falling back to be with him, head bowed and unspeaking. The Grande Armée's orders were brutally clear: the Tsar was in Vilna and the deciding battle would take place before it. A lightning forced march, of the kind that had won battles and that the Emperor had made famous, had been commanded.

The punishing pace was telling but those falling out of the line of march were treated mercilessly as an example while the columns trudged on, endlessly. Dutch, Polish, Bosnians, Italians – soldiers from a score or more of nations marching together at the will of one man and with one objective. The pitiless sun picked out the breastplates of the cuirassiers, the fierce helmets of the dragoons, the colours of the lancers and the red, gold and blue of infantrymen.

On and on, ever deeper into the country, days more before they would sight the spires and churches of Vilna, ever marching, ever hungry and ever thirsty.

'It's too quiet. I don't like it,' Rochambeau said uneasily. They had just passed through a village but there were no sullen inhabitants standing by their doors watching their conquerors march arrogantly by. There was no-one, just a dreary desolation.

'They're terrified by us,' Moreau replied. This was not how it had been on every other occasion he'd been with Bonaparte's advancing armies. It was an uneasy, inexplicable bleakness.

'I heard that we crossed successfully.' There was no joy in his voice.

'Yes. At Tilsit, then two bridges for infantry, supplies and artillery at Grodno, all on their way to join us.' There didn't seem to be much more to say in the face of what was happening – half a million men, a hundred thousand horses, flooding onto the plains of eastern Europe and on into the barbarian east, a colossal movement of humanity.

'Didn't you notice, old fellow?'

'Notice what?'

'All this and we haven't troubled the Tsar by declaring war on him. This is entirely illegal. Should we not go back until we do?'

Once they passed an open field with a scatter of anonymous, untidy bundles – corpses. Who were they? Nameless victims, perhaps hiding in a barn and resisting French foraging parties? A forlorn band who thought to attack the fast-moving column? Even a Russian post flushed out and killed by their dragoons?

At another small township furtive figures darted among the streets but Moreau knew they were looters whose officers had let them loose in return for a cut of the plunder. His lip curled in contempt. By the time the first ten thousand had passed this way they would leave the sad little town picked to the bone, like a carcass left to the buzzards.

The evening bivouac saw little laughter or jollity. Men slept where they fell, and when morning came it was all the sergeants could do to get them on their feet again, to work tortured muscles, to heft knapsacks swollen with plunder, and move out. Relief came when clouds gathered to shroud the sun but this turned into yet more suffering. The distant rumble of thunder developed into a late-summer storm, the sultry heat displaced by squalls. Before long, amid vicious lightning and claps of thunder, a heavy deluge whipped in.

Quickly the dust was laid but in its place the road was turned into a quagmire under the churning from uncountable legions of feet. Supply wagons, guns, baggage trains, all struggled to move forward in the treacherous mud. Disciplined columns became fragmented – and the Grande Armée came to a halt.

The rains continued into the night, guaranteeing miserable sleep, but in the morning the weather improved and once again the marching columns formed up. The sun started to dry the road and, in its fitful appearances, spirits rose. Still the savage, horse-killing pace went on.

Another sprawl of corpses could be seen at the edge of a forest.

'They're ours, Bertrand. How . . .?'

'It's bad, my friend. It means Ivan has finally woken up. Austrians by the look of them. One of our patrols taken by surprise, and I dare say we'll be facing an army very soon. The only question everyone asks is, how many bayonets can they put up?'

That evening, word got around that the Cossacks had been sent to harry and delay them, presumably while the Tsar mustered his army. They were the worst of enemies. Born horsemen from beyond the Don and the Volga, they were hardy, ferocious and knew no fear as they swept in with lances, sabres and carbines to cut off stragglers, working parties and patrols. They used tactics honed by centuries of Tartar warfare on the plains and in the forests, intricate manoeuvres intended to trick and baffle, tire and threaten. A formally constituted military had no ready defence against them.

That night fearful sentries and pickets took position, knowing that out in the darkness those merciless riders were circling, waiting their chance.

And the next day they struck, once, twice and again. Always against detached units, and once, as the Grande Armée passed a sprawl of farmhouse buildings, they recoiled in shock at the sight of the body parts of looters from a Polish regiment hung brazenly on a fence.

Still the punishing advance.

A little before noon the marching columns were brought to a halt. Riders galloped up and down and they were passed by the imperial cavalcade of carriages and escorts. At the lead was the Emperor's legendary six-horse yellow campaign carriage with its turbaned Mameluke bodyguard by the driver; inside Bonaparte was in deep consultation with some general. It pressed on urgently leaving speculation in its wake.

Within the hour orders had been sent back that had Moreau standing at the edge of a river, looking at the smoking ruin of a bridge destroyed by the Russians to delay the advance to Vilna.

He knew what he had to do and waited for the *ingénieur*

*géographe* to report the best place for a new crossing to be put in place. The Grande Armée was at a standstill until the pontoons were ready, and Bonaparte would be furious at any delay.

Rochambeau had thrashed his horse unmercifully to reach him. 'Upriver, a mile and a half. Bit exposed but I'd think Himself won't thank you to wait for artillery cover.'

Moreau didn't waste time. '*Pontonniers – en avant!*' he bellowed and the ungainly carts left the road one by one for the spot nominated.

It was exposed – flat and with a fast-flowing river but agreeably narrow. Rochambeau was right: he could span it in small hours.

There was no sign of the enemy on the far bank and he sent across boats with their watch-guard, who reported it clear.

In a fever of haste, Moreau dispatched further parties to either side to secure two more crossing points with what escorts he could contrive: it was vital that the Grande Armée faced no bottleneck at the crossing. It left them with little protection for themselves but he'd assurance there was nothing to fear on the other side, and in any case, the covering horse artillery would arrive soon.

The first pontoons were floated and secured. Cross-planking was prepared, doubled in view of the swiftness of the current.

'Dear fellow, do you mind much if I observe at all? I've never really seen a bridge magicked out of thin air,' Rochambeau asked.

'By all means, Bertrand. But do stand aside, dear fellow. These beams can cause a fearful bruise if encountered untoward.'

The pontoon bridge quickly began to take shape.

Then musket shots sounded in a flurry, close, but the danger was on the opposite bank. This was coming from the wrong side.

An ominous drumming of hoof-beats to the left revealed its deadly source: a band of horsemen with swirling scarlet pantaloons and exotic astrakhan busbies, lances lowered in battle position. The fierce glee on their swarthy faces told of one thing. These were Cossacks and their murderous charge was directed squarely at the bridge builders, in particular the loose gathering of officers overseeing them.

They burst through the outer defenders, heavy sabres swinging mercilessly, a bloody swathe leading straight towards Moreau and his group. God knew what Cossacks were doing on this side of the river, and there was nowhere to run, to hide on the flat, cleared area.

Moreau struggled to free his sword toggle to snatch it from its scabbard. The Cossacks thundered nearer, swinging around a small square of infantry in an almost poetic swaying motion that took them past and then, in a tight body, straight for the doomed party. He could see his death in the eyes of the hulking rider of the leading horse who, with a triumphant grimace, lined up his lance for the kill.

Out of nowhere Moreau was struck and sent sprawling to the side. Disoriented, his sword knocked from his hand, he was aware that the light had been briefly interrupted by the great bulk of a galloping animal passing over him. He scrabbled to all-fours and tried to make sense of things.

The horsemen had ridden on, slashing and skewering as they pounded off – but a few feet away an arched body shuddered and dropped to a final stillness. It was Rochambeau. His friend had cannoned him aside and taken the lance in his own body.

Seized by an extremity of grief Moreau fell on the lifeless

body, its mortal warmth not yet faded. He shrieked the unfairness of it all to the uncaring heavens until the tears came to rack him and leave him in an inconsolable huddle. How many more would there be before it ended?

# Chapter 48

*The Zakret Palace, Vilna*

The sentry slowly paced along the ornate gates of the palace, enviously eyeing the bright light of a dozen chandeliers in the ballroom. The gay strains of a Viennese waltz wafted out on the warm night air. The Tsar was in town with his entourage and military council in their splendid uniforms, an irresistible chance for Vilna society to strut its finery and forget the hulking beast that lay across the border.

At this hour, honest citizens had long retired to their beds, but these would see in the dawn. There were worse duties for a private soldier to endure than sentry-go while being entertained by the gaiety of the highest in the land coming and going.

He reached the end of his beat, twirled about in an elaborate turn and began a leisurely return. Suddenly echoing in the empty streets came the strident clatter of a horse being thrashed to its limit. Out from the darkness burst a rider in the uniform of an imperial courier, pulling up at the gate with a crash and a perilous slither on the cobblestones.

'His Imperial Majesty is still here?' he demanded breathlessly, his horse in a lather and trembling.

'He is.'

'Well, open the gate! I've dispatches of the utmost importance for him.'

'Oh? What's to do, then?'

'Get that gate open, you fool!'

The glittering ballroom was alive with colour and noise, animation and spectacle, and when the courier dramatically appeared at the door, travel-worn and wild-eyed, demanding the Tsar, it dissolved into uproar.

Alexander disappeared into an anteroom with the messenger. A little later he hurried to his carriage, pale-faced and flanked by grim military figures, leaving behind a seething frenzy of speculation.

'For those of you not yet aware of it, I'm to tell you that the French tyrant has, without declaring war, launched an attack on Russia.' The Tsar was visibly shaken, pale and emotional, as he faced the army commanders in his headquarters.

'Across the Niemen at Kovno, Grodno, other places. An impossible host thrown into the motherland, which flies like a spear towards us here, Vilna.'

'So . . .'

'He broke his word to me, the sacred word he swore at Tilsit when we—'

'Sire. We must resist. For the sake of our honour, the honour of our country,' Arakcheyev, the hard-featured destroyer of Speransky, declared.

'Yes. Yes. But how?'

'We stand before Vilna with every man and beast that glories in his Russian birthright.'

'No. We do not,' came in the minister of war, Prince

Michael, Barclay de Tolly, known as an intelligent, cunning and forthright field marshal. 'We retire with our army intact.'

'Retreat?

'We fall back. The advantages are so obvious I refrain from mentioning them.'

'Sir, do so,' the Tsar insisted.

'Sire, at the moment we cannot in any wise stand against the numbers against us. Six hundred thousands, not counting support troops.'

'Two hundred and thirty thousand only, and that from Marshal Bagration himself,' offered another.

'Let us agree to disagree. The numbers are still over-whelming. If we face them in the open we will be defeated, just as at Austerlitz, Eylau, Friedland.'

Alexander winced. 'Agreed. Go on, sir.'

'We're not yet ready to face him – but we will be! We need time to call upon the inexhaustible resources of Russia from far parts to swell our army to a million or more, then fall upon the foul beast.'

Arakcheyev snorted in derision. 'So while we run and hide, Bonaparte will stop his onslaught and wait for us? Never! At the moment he's afoot with his invasion and moving at a cruel pace. What's to stop him if we do not?'

'De Tolly?' Alexander prompted.

'The Corsican would like nothing better than he meets us in battle with our inferior force, enabling him to destroy us piece by piece, army by army. If we waste our being on the battlefield like this, he's won the war and nothing will prevent him becoming conqueror of all Russia. No, Majesty, we must husband our forces until we are ready to face the Antichrist.'

'And meanwhile let him devour us at the speed of a marching army!' Arakcheyev sneered.

De Tolly coolly let him finish. Then, as if delivering

a lecture at a military academy, he went on, 'There are other advantages. Bonaparte is even now in extended order, his supply lines hundreds of miles long over bad roads. The further he penetrates, the longer and more vulnerable these become. He has to garrison towns along his route to safeguard them, and this will be at the cost of his numbers. If he goes much further this becomes a serious problem.'

'Since when did Napoleon Bonaparte worry about feeding his troops? He takes what he needs, makes his enemy pay for its own destruction.'

'He does, but in Russia it will be different. We make orderly plans to fall back ahead of him – and when we do, we take all the food, the animals and feedstock with us. What we can't carry off we destroy by fire. By this, every mouthful his army consumes must be brought up over the long weeks by wagon, while we will have all the fresh supplies we could ever need.'

'Are you mad? You want to turn the motherland into one vast wasteland as a deliberate act of war in place of a battle of courage and honour?'

Tsar Alexander held up his hand to speak and they turned to listen to his pronouncement. 'If we offer battle now we will be defeated. This is sure. If we lure the tyrant ever deeper into Russia then I shall have time to raise the nation to defend Holy Mother Russia's sacred soil against him. I have had a vision and this has been told to me as my sacred mission to rid the world of the beast of Revelation and this I shall do, to the very gates of Paris and beyond.'

'Yes, Your Imperial Majesty. Er, the French are advancing on Vilna. What is to be done?'

'Did you not hear me, Marshal Arakcheyev? We fall back. Yield the town to Bonaparte but not its foodstuffs and military stores, its farm animals, grain and so forth.'

'And the people?' a younger general intervened quietly.

'They fall back with us, the sacrifice of their lands and crops a contribution that will rank in honour along with death on the battlefield. This shall include all levels of society, even the nobility, and for time out of mind will stand to their glory.'

Renzi had declined an invitation to the ball, missing Cecilia's presence. In his quarters he woke to the sudden irruption of chaos and disorder and knew instinctively what it was.

He dressed, expecting to be called, and shortly was summoned to the imperial suite.

The Tsar was pacing about his study. Clearly in a tense but elevated mood, he received him absently. There was a sense of disorder, of untidiness that indicated a meeting of many had taken place recently in the room.

'Dear Graf Farndon, you won't have heard the news – I will tell it.'

Renzi was not surprised, the wonder being that the Tsar was. He listened politely, chilled at the speed and ferocity of Bonaparte's advance, however sketchy the details, and knew that the scale, the magnitude of the events, was far beyond his ability to render into some distilled package of wisdom. Yet as he listened he became aware that Alexander had achieved a form of serene dignity, a confidence it seemed was rooted in his sacred calling to deliver his people from the terror falling on them.

Humbly he agreed that, as far as he was concerned, the measures he heard were the only ones possible in the circumstances and that the Tsar should have no fear that he'd chosen the wrong path.

Alexander melted, a beatific smile transforming him. 'And I was greatly troubled that I was being swayed by the arguments of this one or that – but you, standing outside these self-centred cliques, will always tell me true.'

'I will do my best, sire.'

The Tsar, in his exalted mood, looked at him kindly. 'I know you will. A refreshment?'

Renzi agreed. The civilised Alexander would not be offering him vodka.

'When this unpleasantness is at last over, we shall discuss further your thesis on economics relating to national experiences.' Alexander looked sadly at his glass and murmured, 'It's what I'm sure Speransky was fumbling for in all his talk of manumitting the serfs. Poor fellow.'

He finished the cognac reflectively and the moment hung. Then, as though it was just dawning on him, an expression of anxiety turned into one of dread. 'You don't think that . . . My friend, tell me – will they still love me, the common people, I mean, after their only land and possessions are made an ashen wilderness?'

In a frenzy of haste Renzi found his chamber and reached for his concealed materials to begin a message to Congalton. The whole world had changed out of recognition, Alexander with it, so his mission to plumb the Tsar's intentions had to alter. Ironically his task was that much easier. The autocrat's mystic leanings had resulted in a firming of his resolve under the shock of the onslaught and he could safely say that the Tsar of Russia would fight – but only on his own terms, which would not necessarily be those recognisable by Whitehall.

Whether this would answer their need to know if they should come to the support of Russia in any material way, or even with battalions, was another matter, and he wouldn't wish to be the British functionary with the responsibility of deciding. Would this 'wasteland' strategy work against the greatest conqueror seen in centuries?

He finished the cipher in a frantic scribble. Was the chain leading all the way to Congalton still functioning? He forced the tiny roll of paper into the base of the oil-lamp and placed it next to the clock. The Tsar was going to leave Vilna under cover of darkness before dawn on the long journey to St Petersburg, and he had little time to be ready to accompany him.

After five hundred miles or more, through the archaic lands of Courland, Livonia and Estonia, they emerged on the banks of the Neva and went on to the inexpressibly civilised outlines of the Winter Palace and their rest. The Tsar was spirited away by anxious courtiers, and Renzi was left alone to contemplate.

There would be no doubt that, in the time of their slow progress needed to keep the Tsar's flight from Vilna hidden from his subjects, Bonaparte could have changed his objective. He had lost the chance to trap and capture the Tsar so what was his intention now? The news waiting for them in St Petersburg would be of the utmost importance for it could well signal the end – a threat so grave Alexander had no alternative than to treat for peace.

It didn't take long to find out. Bonaparte had not paused for more than days in Vilna and had now moved on, driving a massive column in a swathe a hundred miles wide directly east in a straight line for the border and Holy Mother Russia herself. Could nothing stop the monster?

It was time for Renzi to consider his position. He'd done remarkably well to get so close to the Tsar, a fortunate coincidence of the man's need and the success of his 'scholar' conceit. He had used his position to arrive at conclusions impossible for an outside observer but, with the question he was here to answer rendered moot by events, should he leave, job completed?

Alexander liked him, even needed him for his reassurances. Was now the time to abandon him?

His logic took firm hold. The likelihood of the Tsar's probable fate in the extraordinarily adverse circumstances closing in on him was assassination, exactly what had happened to the three previous tsars in far less menacing contexts. That being so, there was every prospect that Renzi would share that fate, being of the hated tribe of foreigners Alexander openly trusted more than his own. Even if he survived it would be quite impossible to build the same relationship with whoever emerged at the head of the power struggle.

'Graf Farndon?' It was a chamberlain with a message on a silver tray.

Renzi was not surprised to find it was an invitation from Alexander to take tea with him. He knew enough of the Tsar to realise that, if he'd seen fit to make time for him in this whirling chaos of beseeching military and petrified citizens, it implied a crisis had thrown up the need for a hard and immediate decision.

'Ah, my friend,' Alexander opened, readying the samovar and tea-dishes. 'So kind of you to attend on me so directly. Tea?'

'As always, sire, at your service at all times.' The bow was returned formally but it was distracted and traces of exhaustion were not hard to perceive. Slow movements, red-rimmed eyes, a slight slur in the speech.

'Have you heard the news?' the Tsar asked, with false lightness.

'I'm sorry to say I've been resting after our journey, Majesty.' He'd been told for his own safety not under any circumstance to leave his quarters, and without a soul to speak with, the reason for the angry shouts and urgent footsteps in the passages outside had been left to his imagination.

'Of course. Well, the news is not at all good. The beast is pressing on at a ferocious rate, which we can only assume is aimed at nothing less than a violation of the soil of Holy Mother Russia itself. We fall back daily, unable to delay it in any wise.'

Renzi murmured sympathetically and Alexander went on calmly, 'And now we have a new threat, one that I fear will prove final.'

'Sire?'

'The French have Danzig into which they pour their supplies but this is now far in their rear and their lines are sorely extended as they advance. Because of this Bonaparte has detached an entire division under Marshal Macdonald to divert from the order-of-march to make for Riga and the Baltic shore. His orders are to take the port and make it a new bridgehead for supplying the armies as they plunge into Russia. You will understand that—'

'I do, Majesty.'

It was a shrewd and devastating move. In one stroke Napoleon's line of supply would be shortened to just a few days: a flooding river of powder and shot, victuals and clothing, artillery and all the impedimenta of war would reach the invaders wherever they chose to head – St Petersburg or Moscow.

And it made a pathetic mockery of Russia's sacrificial wasteland retreat.

'Riga is under siege at this moment. If not relieved, it will fall and bring catastrophe. I must not allow this to happen but without fighting men I cannot prevent it.'

There was nothing Renzi could say in reply.

'Not two hours ago there was put to me a suggestion that I'd be beholden if you'd hear and make comment.'

'Insofar as my limited abilities allow, sire.'

'Then I shall tell you. In Finland I have men, there in occupation these last two years since I took the country from the Swedes. They are many and in idleness. The suggestion is that should I compound with the Swedish so in some way I can recover these men for defence of their mother country. Except that the Swedes, under Prince Bernadotte, still burn for their humiliation at losing their Finnish territory so recently, and to win their compliance will be hard indeed. But a way has been proposed. If they see fit to comply, we shall not stand in the way of their detaching Norway for themselves from the Danish Crown, the Danes, having their fleet taken by the British, being in no position to defend it.'

'Sir, this—'

'To avoid possible prejudice, I will not tell whose initiative this was, but my desire is for you to tell me if you see any evidence that other motives less than honourable are at play.'

The worst of all worlds. Renzi was expected to make judgement on a strategy of state and a military question. He couldn't for any number of reasons.

'Your Imperial Majesty. I'm but a humble scholar, more comfortable with postulates and hypotheses. Should I make comment, without learning in the field, it would be valueless. I do apologise, but as I told you—'

Alexander held up his hand. 'You did say as much, Nikolai, I do remember.' He sighed, but it was not in despair. 'Yet I'm minded to proceed with it.' He gave a wry smile. 'Just how I'm able to stir those idle diplomats to open negotiations with Sweden in the time we have left to us will be difficult in the extreme. Do go to your rest, my friend, and leave these matters to me.'

'Sire, there is . . .' A tiny thought was taking shape as he spoke.

'Yes, Nikolai?'

'Time is of the essence in this case. I beg you will forgive my bold speaking but it crosses my mind that we have a sovereign solution. Your Majesty, you must meet Bernadotte personally and settle the matter face to face. Immediately.'

'You mean . . .?'

'Sire. Time is to be measured in days. If you go to a town near Sweden and invite the prince to a meeting, I'm certain he will see it in his best interests to come. Is there not a city of consequence in Finland close to Sweden? I seem to recollect—'

'A meeting of princes! A fine notion, Nikolai, and you're thinking of Åbo, directly opposite Stockholm.' The impulsive animation quickly died. 'But then what are we contemplating? From Petersburg to Åbo will take all of three weeks, given the shocking roads, and it will then be too late.'

'Not by road, I beg. By sea a brace of days only.'

'Not possible,' Alexander said sadly. 'The Baltic is alive with privateers and other vermin who would spare nothing to secure the body of the Tsar of Russia. I cannot take the risk.'

Renzi thought quickly. 'Then your conveyance shall be an English man-o'-war. The admiral will see the importance of the mission and will, I'm sure, make provision accordingly. I myself will make the request, sire.'

As soon as it came out, he knew it was asking a lot – possibly too much. His own service in the navy told him that a fleet and its admiral were never at the disposition of any casual outsider, however eminent. He could see a crusty old admiral snorting at the impertinence and reaching for a pen to protest at the gall of it all, then requiring the request be directed to the Admiralty itself.

But if it was spelled out in good round naval phrases, with solid cogent reasons, common sense might well prevail.

A smile tugged at his lips. It might well be that, shortly, some unknown captain would receive orders to transform his vessel from a roving warship into an imperial carriage for the convenience of the Tsar of Russia. Providing, of course, that the Royal Navy still maintained a fleet at this far end of the Baltic and that its patrolling craft were not too distant.

# Chapter 49

A shabby *kibitka* waited behind a line of warehouses, its curtains drawn. The patient coachmen kept the horses in check while inside two passengers held themselves in tense readiness.

Renzi's answer had not been long in coming. A report had been made of a British warship coming to anchor out of sight in the St Petersburg roads. Given the state of war that still existed between them it could only be on an official mission and a boat was expected at any moment. If it proved to be what they were hoping for they would be away without delay.

In the feverish atmosphere it was essential that the Tsar left St Petersburg secretively. Onlookers might take the view that he was abandoning the city to its fate and an ugly riot could erupt.

Renzi stepped cautiously out of the carriage to make his way the short distance to the waterfront. A flash of pale sail to the westward resolved by degrees into the familiar lines of a Royal Navy ship's launch under sail, a white ensign and patch of colour in the stern sheets token that an officer was aboard. It was escorted by a pair of harbour craft for the final approach.

At the jetty Renzi waited as the officer in cocked hat and sword mounted the steps and looked about, no doubt expecting a guard and band turned out.

Renzi approached him and, with a bow, introduced himself. 'Lord Farndon in advance of the Tsar of Russia, sir.' The officer looked at him suspiciously for his dress was that of a humble Russian dominie and he was flanked by a pair of hard-faced Slavic keepers. 'And here are my credentials.'

They were taken and studied as the boat's crew looked on with interest.

'Very well, my lord. We are instructed to make known to you that our ship lies ready to convey the Tsar to a destination to be disclosed at a later time. Shall we make arrangements for the imperial progress now?'

'Not at all. His Imperial Majesty is travelling incognito and is anxious to board without delay.' The boat's bowman was still hooked on, watching curiously. 'Do bring the boat close alongside. His Imperial Majesty is no sailor and desires no notice be made of his departure, so I bid you stand fast salutes and piping.'

The lieutenant, a young but hard-eyed individual turned to go but Renzi couldn't help asking, 'What ship, sir?'

'Ah, I do beg your pardon, my lord,' he said, removing his hat. 'My name is Roscoe and I'm first of *Thunderer*, 74.'

*Thunderer*? A ship he had no knowledge of other than that she'd fought at Trafalgar, but a ship-of-the-line – this was gratifying.

Roscoe gave his orders quietly to the boat's crew as the Tsar, muffled in a cloak, was hustled to the steps and into the boat. 'You will be coming too, Nikolai?'

It wasn't what Renzi had in mind but he followed without protest and the boat put off.

'When the Tsar is safely away his retinue will follow,' Renzi informed the lieutenant. Another thirty-odd to victual and accommodate would not please the ship's captain but this was not his concern.

HMS *Thunderer*, a mighty vessel of arrogance and beauty, dominated the anchorage, a towering symbol of Britain's sea power. As they neared her Renzi was struck by her fine appearance: the old-fashioned carvings and stern-gallery well gilded and varnished, the brightwork between the awesome lines of guns, the precisely squared spars. Whoever her captain was, he was running a taut ship and had to be admired for the state of his command.

'Please convey to His, um, Majesty that we will sway him aboard by bosun's chair and I will take a turn around the ship to give them time to rig it.' Apparently Lieutenant Roscoe did not have French enough to explain it.

Renzi passed this on to the Tsar but Alexander was rapt, staring up at the spectacle of this great lion of the seas.

The manoeuvre went well, the all-puissant Romanov Emperor sitting nervously as he was gently hauled up and away. Renzi didn't want to wait for it to return and instead leaped to the side-steps with its man-rope and clambered up just as he had those years before as a naval officer.

He arrived at the bulwark in time to catch the diverting sight of a hastily assembled side-party and the vessel's captain bowing low before the Tsar. A sharp-eyed petty officer saw Renzi come in over the bulwarks and the side-party moved smartly to reassemble in his honour, the captain hesitating before hurrying across to stand at the head of the double line to bow to yet another Russian dignitary.

Kydd straightened – and looked directly into the eyes of his dearest friend. 'Nicholas!' he gasped. 'You – you . . .'

'Dear fellow,' Renzi said, taken quite aback, but with the presence of mind to speak in courtly French in front of the curious side-party. 'Pray do not enquire,' he said rapidly. 'But allow that I present as someone you once knew but find you are mistaken.'

'Oh. Well, welcome aboard *Thunderer*, Mr . . . er, sir.' Kydd spoke in English. 'If you'll accompany me below shall we discuss the Tsar's accommodation arrangements?'

They left the deck and, out of sight, enthusiastically greeted each other.

'Dear fellow—'

'Nicholas, old horse, what—'

Kydd drew up a chair and took in the sight of his friend, obviously in some sort of guise. 'It's as well there's no one aboard from dear old *Tyger* as knows you. May I be told . . .?'

A soft knock and Craddock leaned in. 'Did you wish me to—'

'Come in, old fellow. I think you should hear this. Oh – this is Lord Farndon, whom I've known for many years by the name of Renzi. Nicholas, this is Mr Craddock, my confidential secretary, whom I acquired in the Adriatic in adventurous circumstances. Carry on, please, Nicholas.'

Renzi acknowledged Craddock with a slight bow and continued: 'For my sins I'm a confidant of Tsar Alexander and hated by every right-thinking denizen of the Romanov court. Pray do not enquire of this further – we shall have time enough to talk of it later. For now, I cannot help but remark you have a rattling fine ship in *Thunderer*! It does have to be said, however, that this cabin appears a little less grand than I'd suppose for the captain of a sail-of-the-line.'

'This is the first lieutenant's cabin, Nicholas. Mine is given over to the Tsar while all officers are turned out to have their existence at the after end of the gun-deck behind canvas in favour of his more important followers – such as you, who is now rated gentleman counsellor to the Grand Panjandrum.'

'After the sybaritics of the Winter Palace I would be more than satisfied with a gunroom hammock, if truth be told.'

Kydd grinned and went on, 'I understand this voyage is in some degree one of urgency. I haven't yet a destination and—'

'Äbo to the west, and haste would be welcomed. Just as soon as His Majesty's baggage is aboard.'

During the night *Thunderer* slipped to sea without ceremony or escort, laying course down the Baltic for Äbo a bare two days or so away. With a mountain of baggage struck down in the cable tiers and a dozen Russian nobles endeavouring to deal with their outlandish quarters she leaned to a useful north-easterly and made good time.

Renzi was able to acquaint Kydd of the mission and its reasons, and also give him an idea of how disastrous the campaign was for the Russians. It was hard to credit, but probably by the time they returned to St Petersburg Bonaparte's savage thrust east would have advanced half a thousand miles in just short weeks with no sign of any serious resistance. It was galling to Kydd, for like all the Continental wars of conquest there was little the Navy could do to engage the enemy directly, especially in this case where the immense column marched along, now hundreds of miles inland and ever deeper.

The Tsar was enchanted by his sea venturing and, at his request, strolled about the ship freely, attended by a lieutenant to explain its wonders. When they raised the densely scattered archipelago guarding Äbo from seaward, he seemed sincerely regretful.

It was a charming and at the same time imposing city. Discovering that they were to be blessed with a visit by the Tsar it became a time of festival and celebration, fireworks and gun salutes lighting the sky. The imperial party made their way ashore without lingering but Renzi returned in only an hour. 'Banquets and balls without end. I leave the joys to those who do appreciate such occasions. Should we take our victuals together, brother?'

In years past Kydd had come across Bernadotte as a marshal of the French Empire in command of the army ranged along the border of Denmark during the British bombardment of Copenhagen. In a drama involving the exiled Bourbon king, he had had reason to believe that Bernadotte held no burning loyalty to Bonaparte and he told Renzi so.

'It's as I understand it. You are, of course, referring to the head of state, who should more properly be addressed as Charles John, Crown Prince of Sweden. One who holds honour dear but even more the advancing of his realm I've heard.'

On the following day Bernadotte arrived in his royal yacht to a warm reception from the populace, who had been Swedes until two years before.

It was made clear that Renzi, as a foreigner, was not welcome at the table of the greats in the days to follow so he took to cultivating the confidences of others for his information. Then, on the pretext that he felt the mark of assassins, he declared that while the imperial envoys made much of their lavish and opulent lodgings he himself would sleep aboard ship.

'So how is it progressing, Nicholas? Are they talking together or . . .?'

'Satisfactory indeed. The first words from Bernadotte were

"If Russia falls then Sweden will follow. Therefore we have common cause, do we not?" They thereupon embraced. A pretty scene, you'll agree.'

'And the Norway bait?'

'Do not be so precipitate, old fellow. Bernadotte is a crafty fox and does not want to appear too hungry. We shall see.'

The next night Renzi brought the news that, despite the humiliation of the loss of Finland, Bernadotte might be persuaded to relinquish all claim to the country, allowing Alexander to withdraw his garrisons. It was the 'might be' that brought up short all satisfaction. 'The Norway ploy is too blatant,' Renzi pronounced.

It needed one final push and this was provided by the Tsar – an offer to Bernadotte that should he make attempt to recover Swedish Pomerania, shamefully taken by Bonaparte in a coup, Russia would assist with troops and supplies. There was no prospect at this time that Sweden would attempt to cross the Baltic and confront Bonaparte, but it would serve as a token gesture to rally the waverers behind him.

'So, all is settled, the garrisons released to go to the aid of Riga and a unity of purpose declared. I do believe we may expect to return tomorrow.'

# Chapter 50

*St Petersburg*

Impatiently Alexander stood by Kydd on the quarterdeck as *Thunderer* went to her moorings off the great city. He could not leave until the situation ashore was known. A boat took away an envoy but, by degrees, it became evident that something was not right. When the pinnace returned, it was accompanied ominously by an imperial barge carrying armed soldiers.

The envoy hauled himself aboard and, face set, hurried to the Tsar. 'Your Majesty,' he blurted, 'grave news has been received from your generals. A battle – at Smolensk. It did not necessarily end to our advantage and there are terror and disorder on the streets, which it would be wise to avoid. I cannot give more details in front of the foreigners but if you would return speedily with us it may calm the anxious.'

Renzi shivered but it had nothing to do with the chill of the autumn breeze. Was this a sign of a crumbling of the Russian will to resist? The beginning of the end?

Kydd pulled him aside. 'Nicholas,' he said, his voice thick

with concern, 'you must get away from this madness. Stay aboard and I can give you safe passage out.'

'Nothing would please me more, you may believe.' He glanced across at the Tsar, now to one side and in worried conversation with the envoy. If something serious had taken place he had to know what it was and, crucially, how this affected Alexander in his judgements. Anything less would betray his mission. 'But I have to tell you that I must remain.'

'Then . . . then I can wait no more than a day,' Kydd said, 'as I must have the ship squared away after that scrovy crew leaves. But if you can find out what you have to in that time, I'll be here for you, never fear.'

The Tsar and his retinue were bundled ashore, where carriages were waiting, and a squadron of cavalry to go ahead and clear the way, the fine boulevards and avenues choked with aimless crowds and occasional groups fighting.

At the Winter Palace Alexander disappeared in a throng of gesticulating supplicants. Renzi turned away. He had to discover the situation, but not in this bedlam, and he walked rapidly towards his chambers.

Passing a familiar painting, a painstakingly detailed and florid oil of some past battle a good twelve feet across, he was jerked to a stop. An imposing hulk of a man in elaborate courtly regalia, a magnificent black beard and commanding eyes clutched at his arm. He vaguely recognised him as Count Aleksey Denisov, an ardent patriot.

'Stay, my friend!' he said unsteadily, in a bear-like growl. 'I demand you toast with me to the glories of Russia as must never be forgotten!' The intensity of his words was not affected by a stray hiccup, and he fished a bottle out of his coat with two small glasses and proceeded to fill them.

'Za nas,' he commanded, lifting his glass in admiration to

the painting, giving Renzi the chance surreptitiously to get rid of the contents of his.

'I would cheerfully drink to Russia in her time of need,' Renzi said softly. 'But why at this moment?'

'Smolensk!' roared Denisov, glaring at him as if he were demented.

'Um, I've been out of the country. What is the news, pray?'

'Hmmph. You'll learn soon enough but I'll tell you.'

First Renzi had to hear of how Smolensk had stood firm against the Mongols and later the Lithuanians, and in the days of the Swedish and Polish wars the city was a byword for staunch loyalty. It was squarely on the road into the heart of Russia and as a result the Tartar Tsar Boris Godunov had made certain the strongest fortress in Russia was built there. Consequently the much-venerated icon of St Luke was safeguarded within its walls.

How, then, was it possible to yield up the saintly city to the overwhelming forces of Napoleon Bonaparte in accordance with the strategy of wasteland retreat?

It wasn't, and Alexander's two army commanders, Barclay de Tolly and Bagration, were told to join together and make a stand.

Within just two days Bonaparte had put both to flight at the cost of some twenty-thousand casualties, an appalling loss. He was now in possession of the proud city, which lay at his feet utterly devastated, bombarded into submission, its inhabitants a mound of corpses, any still alive streaming away in misery and desolation.

There were tears as Denisov explained that Bonaparte's intentions were now open to all. The tyrant had crossed into Russia to defeat the noblest in the land and the highway was wide open to the biggest prize of all – Moscow. What did the future hold for this ancient land of the Rus?

Renzi left the man to his maudlin sorrowing and hurried on. He needed to think.

Outside his rooms a stiff-faced military officer waited. 'Graf Farndon, I'm to tell you that His Imperial Majesty in council desires your attendance. This way, if you please.'

No polite greetings or requesting. What did he expect from him, the academic, after this horrific event? And before his council?

He was ushered into a room very different from the Tsar's personal chambers. This was a military headquarters packed with officers, most gathered around a central table covered with maps. At his entrance, they looked up, hostility and resentment on their faces.

Alexander came out from behind them to meet him. Renzi made an elegant bow, but before he could straighten the Tsar spoke. 'Graf Farndon, you will have heard of the . . . adverse circumstance in which we are now placed.'

No one moved.

'Sire, I have,' Renzi said carefully, 'and can only deplore the situation in which Russia finds herself.'

'Yes. May I say before my commanders here assembled that your assistance in the matter of releasing my idle troops in Finland to go to the relief of Riga is handsomely appreciated.'

'Thank you, Your Majesty.'

'Regrettably I've been told that even with these reinforcements the French are pouring in additional divisions. It's considered that Riga cannot hold out for much longer in the face of such numbers.'

Surely they didn't expect him to think of some stratagem to counter the looming disaster, which if it happened would count on the same level as Smolensk.

'Sire, in matters of a military nature I cannot—'

318

'The council understands that, Graf Farndon.' He looked about significantly. 'It understands too that you are in a unique position to help us.'

Renzi kept silent – however they thought to use him he had to resist. He could not be drawn in, snared in some desperate plan.

'Riga will fall. This is certain, for we've learned in Danzig that a heavy siege train is being prepared that will bring our resistance to an end in a very short time.'

The room was still, every eye on him. What was happening? What did they want, for God's sake?

'Sire. I cannot see how—'

'Your success in obtaining a ship of the British Navy to go to Äbo at such notice is evidence of your authority. We desire you speak with the captain of this great vessel with a view to catching and sinking the armament before it can reach Riga.'

'Majesty,' Renzi stuttered, his breath taken away by the effrontery of the demand. 'For actions of a military nature he does not have the freedom to act. He must have his admiral's approval.'

The Tsar's voice tightened. 'It would go hard for the captain to be seen to refuse a request by the Tsar of Russia, and even harder should it be known that Riga fell for want of his resolve. Do you understand me, Graf Farndon?'

# Chapter 51

'Nicholas!' Kydd spluttered, as Renzi came over the bulwark. 'You've come to your senses! You're just in time – but where's your baggage?'

'Brother. We must speak. Your cabin?'

The essence was conveyed in a very few sentences. 'I couldn't argue. They fervently believe I have a mystical power within the sacred Royal Navy and if I don't exercise it it must be from want of respect for the person of the Tsar.'

'I see,' Kydd said, rubbing his chin thoughtfully. 'But if there's so little time I can't make petition to the admiral for a formal sally upon the enemy. If it's to be done, *Thunderer* must do it herself.'

'Dear fellow, I can't ask it of you. To proceed on an act of war without orders will damn you for ever.'

Kydd smiled at his dismay. 'If I did not, on the other hand, I'd be damned equally. Recollect, old horse, we're still at war with Russia, for in these few weeks the politicking is not yet done that will result in an alliance. If the Ruskies desire our help and it's refused, what will this do to the negotiations? As no motion against Bonaparte can ever be deplored by a right-thinking naval officer, a species of distraction is quite in order, I would have thought.'

Renzi gave a lop-sided grin. 'In this I'm only an untutored messenger. Should I return to Alexander to say you will, therefore?'

'You may. The good admiral Byam Martin will understand. He always did prefer the company of captains of active and zealous persuasion and will not suffer blame to attach to my actions.'

'Then do sail on and may good fortune attend always, dear fellow.'

'Thank you, Nicholas. And . . . and do recollect that whatever's to happen in this world gone lunatic,' he said softly, '*Thunderer* will be somewhere in the offing to deliver you.'

After he'd seen Renzi over the side Kydd needed to take a bracing turn around the deck. His breezy assurance that Byam Martin would approve of his unauthorised action now rang a little false in his ears.

An admiral needed to know what was happening in his own domain. If *he* were an admiral he'd be outraged if one of his ship-of-the-line captains took it upon himself to indulge in an act of war on his own initiative, like any common frigate captain on a cruise. This would be depriving the fleet of one of its few heavyweight assets and potentially blocking any higher purpose he had in mind. Kydd's only excuse was the pressing lack of time he had left to intercept the siege train. His only chance to escape a career-finishing censure was to succeed. But how?

Danzig was the point of entry of near the entirety of French war stores and was heavily defended. On the face of it, the only way to get at the quarry was to cruise off the port and intercept the transports on the way to Riga. They would, no doubt, be well escorted, but in a 74-gun ship-of-the-line he could expect to take on several frigates and more. Such an encounter, however, would allow the transports to escape. And, in any case, if the convoy commander was wise, he'd leave at night and they might miss it entirely.

He had to be certain of its destruction. This was too chancy, too uncertain. But what else was there?

He called the first lieutenant to his cabin.

'Come in, Mr Roscoe,' he invited. 'Do sit. I have a difficulty, a challenge, which I'd like to talk over with you. The watering near complete?'

'It is, sir, and . . . and thank you for your confiding in me.'

It took Kydd by surprise, and then he remembered that in *Tyger* he'd thought nothing of chewing over possibilities with his first lieutenant, Bowden. In the navy this was unusual, and he couldn't imagine the previous captain of *Thunderer* unbending to such a degree. Was it that his long relationship with the younger man had allowed him to unburden before him?

To be the sort of first lieutenant Kydd wanted, Roscoe would need to recognise his way and, in so doing, would benefit professionally, like Bowden, as he learned the reasons for decisions, the possibilities, the risks.

'Certainly I shall confide, old fellow. Are you not a prime hand, as we must say, that might be heard?'

'I shall do my best, sir.'

Kydd sat back, considering. 'I'm sure you will. But I'd think it better should we be on, who might say, friendlier terms. I desire you might speak your mind, be plain with me in your views.'

It was asking a lot of the mere lieutenant sitting upright before him, opposite a knighted and famous frigate captain, proven sea predator and known familiarly at the royal court. On the other hand, until he'd lately won Roscoe's respect the man had not been particularly intimidated by his rank and stature, and he suspected that a strong character lay not far beneath. Perhaps it was only necessary to provide a channel of informality and ease of approach to release it.

'Sir.'

'While we're on our own, shall we leave aside the "sirs"?'

'Very well, um, yes.'

'You're Christopher, I believe. What are you to your friends, pray?'

'They call me Kit, actually.'

'So.' Kydd lifted his little silver bell and rang it.

'*Mon capitaine*?' Binard didn't blink an eye but Kydd saw that he'd instantly taken in the relaxed scene.

'What can you suggest as will recruit the strength and sharpen the intellects?'

'Ah. Perhaps *un eau de vie*?'

'Do find us a brace, there's a good fellow. Now, Kit, this is the essence of what's exercising me.'

It was easy enough told: the grave, near catastrophic situation ashore and what hung on their intercepting the siege engines before Riga fell. The touching faith that the Royal Navy would naturally prevail in any contest. The urgency of the whole affair.

'Show me the chart,' was Roscoe's immediate response.

A large-scale Danzig approaches was found, with two merchant rutters in German, while the master looked out some sketches of the harbour made by Sanders, a Royal Navy officer present at the siege of 1807.

They pored over them carefully.

'Forts at the entrance, both sides, sir,' Roscoe murmured, remembering too late his dispensation.

'And a brute of a fortress well inside,' Kydd observed. 'I see that Danzig must be accounted an inland city, served only by the one waterway to the sea. And the town itself sits behind marshland on the coast and high ground all round further in.'

Even then it was obvious that if the siege train was being loaded at the town docks safely within the city walls it would take an entire army to reach it. No wonder Bonaparte had chosen Danzig as the route of his supply train into the interior.

Roscoe shook his head sadly. 'We might only conclude that their siege guns are safe from us while they're inside.'

'So we must take them at sea.'

'As is not at all certain,' Roscoe said quietly. 'They could slip out past us at night, or in mizzling weather, or . . .'

'Yes, Kit. Now you see my dilemma.'

But Roscoe's eyes were on the city plan, his eyes bright, searching. 'There may be . . .'

'Oh? Say on, old fellow.'

'I'd swear this is a canal, at least the stretch downstream from the big fortress to the Baltic itself.'

'And . . .?'

'We can't get at them where they lie, it's too chancy to rely on intercepting at sea, so why not stop 'em here, before they get to sea?'

'Kit, you mean—'

'I do. A ship across the canal, put a stopper on 'em!'

A blockship preventing the siege train ever getting out – it was as good as destruction at sea, and far more certain.

'Hmm. I like it. Let's see if we can come up with something. A canal – this implies it has warping piles. And an even bed – with a limited breadth of passage.'

Animated, Roscoe took it up. 'So – our blockship. We

secure the after end to one warping post, let the current take the forrard end out and, when athwart, secure to the other side, blocking navigation.'

'I rather fancy the French will have it free *tout de suite*, dear chap. More permanent would be—'

'Ha! Blow the bottom out of her. No tides in the Baltic, they'll have to get divers down from somewhere.'

'To break it up – this is a job of months. Riga is saved, I believe.'

Kydd inwardly exulted. It seemed he had the kind of first lieutenant he wanted – intelligent, imaginative and one who spoke his mind. What could the future not bring? 'To the details,' he cautioned. 'This ship, how do we get her past the forts and into the channel?'

The bones of the plot quickly took shape. A suitable ship, her hold packed with gunpowder. A small, picked crew. Appearing out of the blue, chased by a bully ship-of-the-line into the protecting arms of the forts, flustered but thankful to have made port. The rest was straightforward enough, the question only remaining of how her crew would be returned safely.

'You'll agree that I shall take the ship in,' Roscoe said firmly.

'In normal circumstances this would be the case,' Kydd replied, equally firmly.

'By the custom of the service a first lieutenant is offered the chance of distinction in these affairs. Do I understand you wish to reserve this to yourself?' The voice had grown tense and obstinate.

'Not at all. I shall be in charge for quite another reason.'

'You haven't trust in me.'

'This is not in question, Kit. The reason is that the matter is dire and, of us both, only I have the experience.'

'Experience?'

'Of touching off a fuse and making away. You see, I was at the Basque Roads leading the fireships.'

The younger man looked dogged. 'As was a great business. This is a trifling task by compare, the mere lighting of some slow-match and retiring. I believe my competence is sufficient for the task.'

Kydd sighed. He saw where this was going. Roscoe knew where honour and repute were to be won, and while service in an active 74 was all very well, the only opportunity for his individuality to come to notice was on very rare occasions. And he probably felt that Kydd had all the acclaim and renown he needed.

If Kydd gave him his chance, how much could he be relied upon?

'Very well, you shall lead.'

There was a flash of feeling – was it triumph? And then Roscoe announced calmly, 'As commander of the ship, and that in full measure.'

'Commander? You shall take her in at the right time, see the fuse is lit and your men leave in good order is all, Kit.'

'If I take charge and responsibility, the ship must be mine. To outfit, man and direct as I see fit for the needs of the operation.'

Kydd paused then responded, 'Agreed. Always providing the overall command stays with me.'

It was an almost unheard-of thing to demand of one's superior. But Kydd could appreciate his motive: that in the heat of the action he wanted to be free to make decisions not bound by the need to consult a superior. Once they got to know more of each other it would be taken as said.

'Shall we then find ourselves a ship to sacrifice?'

They had their pick from the scores of ships lying idle beyond Kronstadt, their trading patterns thrown into confusion by the rapid advance of the French. Roscoe's choice was *Azov*, a stoutly built Archangel trader of about 250 tons, barque-rigged and sound, her ice-strengthened hull not easily taken apart.

As the powder barrels were taken aboard, her manning was addressed. True to his word, Kydd stepped back as Roscoe found his volunteers, midshipmen to topmen, each without resort to coercion or vague promises. Before the day was done he had them aboard *Azov* laying along the gear necessary to turn her into a floating bomb.

And within a very short time the pair of ships had put to sea, bound for Danzig.

# Chapter 52

To Roscoe, the time seemed to pass interminably. He was fighting down by turns a fierce need to prove himself before the most prominent and inspiring figure in his life – and the challenge of the fearsome trial that lay ahead.

If he was truthful he'd have to admit that his cool confidence lay in the knowledge that in his entire career he'd never failed, never felt deficient. He'd always succeeded in whatever had been thrown up against him. Yet could this be because he'd never really been tried in the fires? His had been a big-ship calling, and until now he'd always been under eye and never had to act alone.

This time he was in personal charge of the assault and all responsibility lay on his shoulders. And, far from being a matter-of-course cutting-out expedition, this was unorthodox, against great odds, and its significance to the wider war went far beyond its immediate goal.

He was not prey to fears and anxieties but the wait was trying as the flat grey of the north Polish coast made its appearance to the south – or should that be the Duchy of Warsaw, Poland under Bonaparte having ceased to exist?

At ten miles offshore *Azov* came alongside *Thunderer* and all but the skeleton crew transferred to the bigger ship. It had begun!

Sail was spread and the chase started, *Thunderer* giving *Azov* a good start as the gallant little ship made for the safety not so far ahead.

Danzig lay deep into the self-named bay. The charts showed it with a narrow entrance flanked by forts. A south-south-easterly fairway led in that, within half a mile, made a sweeping curve to meet the canal at the main fortress.

Roscoe paced up and down in his borrowed merchant-service rig, the cramped deck space and utilitarian fittings so at odds with a proud man-o'-war. He flicked a glance astern at *Thunderer* and again was struck by the picture of warlike grace and lethal beauty the big 74 made, crowding on sail in her pursuit. Her staysails were cunningly led to spill wind and keep her speed down, not something a soldier in the forts would notice, with her battle ensign brazenly streaming out that would catch every eye.

The low shore firmed, the shadowed presence of wood-land over marshes, a few scattered hamlets. Off to the left, the dumpy grey and red of two forts straddled a narrow entryway, the larger with a lofty flagstaff and a signal tower.

A faint thud and rising powder smoke indicated they'd been noticed – there would be formalities on arrival, from customs to quarantine, and *Azov* was being invited to lie to while the authorities sent a boat. She took no notice, the fierce sight of her pursuer good enough reason to flee on.

A hoist of flags soared up the staff, undoubtedly a demand to reveal her colours, which Roscoe was damned sure he wasn't going to do. His terrified crew had other things to worry about, had they not?

There were buoys, then a series of posts, the beginning of the warping progression.

A flurry of thuds came. The forts were opening up – on the big warship. These were not warning shots: plumes of shot-strike leaped up close by.

The north-westerly was near perfect for Roscoe: they could carry sail right inside, before the fairway curved into the straight reaches of the canal.

More firing erupted, sharper now but aimed at their pursuing menace. It was working!

'Lay along the warp springs, fore 'n' aft!' Roscoe bellowed, the exhilaration of the moment keying him up while he fought for coolness and rationality. Eyeing the first warping stakes ahead, he set in train the 'panic' crew, who raced meaninglessly up into the rigging. Others hurried along the deck to the fo'c'sle where they excitedly waved on the fort gunners to greater efforts.

Under every rag of canvas they could hang out *Azov* plunged forward into the enfolding embrace of the forts, seething by them as they valiantly drove off the disappointed Englishman, which in a wide sweep made for the open sea and away.

Thankfully, *Azov* doused sail and settled to a more sedate pace, readying to bring up to the warping piles. It would be understood that she would secure to one to yield to a boarding for the formalities but also to spell the crew after their frenzy of deliverance.

For Roscoe it was now critical. The ship should be far enough in that there was no possibility that the wider last section of the fairway would allow the siege train transports to slip past to sea. At the same time they must not be so far in that their final flight could be headed off.

As they slowed his eyes picked out a place – at the beginning of the curve to the left, the waterway at its narrowest.

Alerting the after warp spring party, he concentrated on the approach, then tensed. From the opposite direction a heavily laden Dutchman under bare poles was hauling itself along, warping out the last few hundred yards to the sea. The convention in England was for the craft under sail to stand on, the other to haul in to the bank and pause until it was past. Was that how it was done on the Continent? If it wasn't, they would stand revealed at best as a trespasser.

Well before the chosen spot the fat Dutchman stopped and heaved itself in. They were safe but, with a wry grin, Roscoe realised that the unfortunate captain, by correctly observing nautical custom, had just condemned himself to a month or more trapped in the canal.

They eased off as sail came in, gliding in precisely to the correct spot. It was imperative to get the timing right and Roscoe himself took the wheel to nudge the stern quarters against the piles.

'Go!' he hissed. The line was looped over a pile and brought back inboard to the bitts. With a perceptible tug, *Azov* came to rest.

Everything depended on the next few seconds. Roscoe picked an argument with the fo'c'sle crew, who responded with angry shouts and waving arms. A fist flew out and in the next instant the deck was alive with fighting bodies. Imperceptibly at first but with increasing speed the current crowded into the space between ship and bank and *Azov*'s bow swung slowly out.

The Dutchman's crew saw what had happened and bawled out angrily at the lubberly sailors. In their mindless scuffling they took no notice until the ship was well across the waterway grounding with a soft bump against the opposite bank, comprehensively blocking the channel.

Now for the final, deadly stroke. The two boats were in

the water on the outward side, out of sight of the Dutch craft. One filled quickly with seamen and put off rapidly, the other lay hooked on while Roscoe raced below. In the gloom of the hold the stacked powder barrels, their copper bands glinting dully, waited patiently to do their work.

A lanthorn hung ready and Roscoe shoved the end of the match hose through the pane until it caught. He blew on it and a reassuring flare came in response. Laying it down carefully, he sprinted for the open air and hurtled into the boat. 'Give way, for your lives!' he panted.

The boat pushed off and the four men pulled like maniacs. On the shore they had seen that something was amiss and several figures gathered, shouting and gesticulating. Roscoe ignored them but first one, then several musket shots were heard, sending up warning splashes ahead of the two boats.

'Stretch out, damn it!' he urged, but a betraying thought tugged at him, becoming more insistent by the minute. By this time the charge should have gone off.

What was going on? How long should he give it? Must he go back and check at the risk of their being caught, unable to get away?

Common self-preservation led one way, duty another. If he left without ensuring *Azov* was sunk in place it could be cleared away quickly and the entire mission would fail.

'The charge hasn't exploded. We have to go back. Hold water larb'd, heavy up starb'd.'

There were disbelieving cries and his hand dropped to his sword. The boat reluctantly swung around and retraced its way back, but not before one of the crew muttered, 'An' if it goes off when we's a-looking?'

All it needed to bring the match to a fizzling stop was a chance imperfection in its composition. And all that was required to bring it to life was a remaining red ember to burn its way slowly past and burst into flame the other side, bringing on a delayed detonation. It could happen in the very next second.

Heart hammering Roscoe swung aboard and treading softly made his way down into the hold. Holding the lanthorn he stared at the deadly grey length of slow-match. Its course could be seen by the canvas tube rendered to ash as the burning fuse crept forward but in the dimness it was hard to see more.

He bent closer, a vision of an imminent explosion beating at him – and then he saw it. The fuse had led past a stanchion, and when laying it down after lighting, he'd not taken this into account. The cord had kinked as it went around.

He knew what he had to do and fumbled for his pocket knife. If he picked the match up it might catch again but he had to take the risk. There was no sudden blaze so with quick, hard slashes he cut it a few inches beyond the kink and threw the remnant nervously behind him, jamming the end of the match into the lanthorn, noting as he did that already the fuse was now near half its length.

It flared and caught. Letting it drop, Roscoe scrambled for fresh air but the boat had pushed off to keep at a safe distance if the worst happened.

Teetering at the edge of the deck for a heartbeat he neatly dived in and as he struck out for the boat the blast and visceral blow of a detonation took him painfully in his stomach, disorienting him. When his wits returned he saw that wreckage blown into the air was small and ragged. The detonation had vented upwards as it had punched its ship-killing spite into the vessel's bottom.

Taken short by the shocking development the firing ashore died away. Now, with their real purpose exposed, they could expect no mercy from the forts between the boats and the sea. They would slew their guns around and, at point-blank range, blast them to flinders.

It was hopeless but the oarsmen threw themselves at their task as the first of the big guns crashed out, narrowly missing them.

Roscoe felt a strange peace. It would be over very soon but at least in his last moments he would know that he'd succeeded in the mission.

Then a heavy rumble sounded out at sea and past the forts. Wonderfully, gloriously close, and under full sail, the over-looked *Thunderer* was blazing out broadsides that took the forts squarely, smashing and splintering stonework in a hell on earth for the gunners, who had the choice of fleeing or being torn apart.

The seamen pulling like lunatics, the boats won clear, and in the blessed freedom of the ocean they were reunited.

'Mr Roscoe,' Kydd said loudly, as he came over the side, 'well done! You and your Thunderers both.'

But then, without a pause, he turned to the sailing master. 'Mr Hobbs, clap on every stitch of canvas we have – I want to make St Petersburg before it falls!'

# Chapter 53

*St Petersburg*

On his way back to the shore Renzi glanced at the diminishing bulk of *Thunderer*. In her was his closest friend in this world and he was about to put out into the madness that was the despairing attempt to save Riga by destroying the siege train at sea. A near hopeless venture – all brought about by the end working of his own mission.

By the time he reached his quarters in the Winter Palace his desolate mood had deepened.

In a stab of harsh reality he began to question what he was doing there. His purpose was coldly to appraise whether Alexander would fight or seek peace with a conqueror – in effect whether Great Britain should trust him enough to commit troops and gold in the defence of Russia.

He'd achieved the priceless first step of winning Alexander's confidence and faith, but two things had conspired to make it near impossible to reach a usable conclusion. The first was the character of the man: he was a mystic, naïve, distant from the actuality of what was happening around him.

Nothing could be logically deduced, for he was not logical. Neither could he be relied upon in the article of consistency, often swayed by the arguments of the last he'd spoken to. The future of Russia was in his hands but how he would react was at the moment unfathomable.

The second was the nature of the peril. Bonaparte had confounded all by the speed and savagery of his movements, thrusting with unparalleled fury into the heart of Russia, in days and weeks overturning all notions of conventional war.

After the usual precautions Renzi found his materials and began to prepare a communication to England but failed at the first hurdle. What could he report that wouldn't be affected by the colossal events that even now were rapidly unfolding into uncharted regions? Could he say anything about Alexander that might reliably guide the British government to a course of action? No: therefore not to write anything was better than to offer guesses that could only mislead.

Days passed while, some hundreds of miles to the south, Bonaparte's army raged onward. In the feverish atmosphere of St Petersburg each scrap of news was seized avidly, then interpreted in different ways, but one thing was certain: its course after Smolensk was now undeniably straight as an arrow for the great prize – Moscow.

The Tsar did not call for Renzi. It was known that he'd caused the Black Virgin to be paraded through the streets and had attended the Patriarch's rambling services at the Kazan Cathedral but mostly he hid himself away at Tsarskoe Selo, his private palace in the country. Renzi found his time increasingly taken by Denisov, who inevitably ended his visits with impassioned accounts of the glory days of Russia, the Swedish wars and earlier.

He tried not to think of his dear friend Kydd throwing himself, his ship and his men at his vital objective. What if the transport was escorted by a powerful squadron? Without hesitation Kydd wouldn't flinch and would join battle whatever the odds.

On one afternoon, the same as so many before, Denisov suddenly paused in his story, his eyes wide. There were running footsteps and the door burst open. 'Aleksey – news!' It was a noble Renzi didn't recognise, dishevelled, his tunic unbuttoned as if carelessly thrown on.

Ignoring Renzi, Denisov leaped to his feet. 'Tell!' he demanded.

'A mighty battle as the world has never yet seen! Bagration and de Tolly both made a stand before Moscow!'

'Well, what happened, Pyotr? For God's sake, what happened, man?'

'I – I don't rightly know, but we've a battlefield messenger in the Imperial General Staff telling his story. Shall we go and hear?'

The room was crowded, its calm, lofty splendour out of keeping with the excitement and febrile atmosphere.

'The lieutenant is sore wounded and in with His Imperial Majesty,' was all the news they could get.

Frustration built until someone shouted, 'The stables! A survivor!'

The room emptied quickly as everyone hastened below. In the courtyard by a well a bandaged sergeant stood with a crowd about him. He looked up, startled by the rush of nobly dressed gentlemen.

'You were there?'

'Who won?'

'What was it like, at all?'

They were savagely shouted down by Denisov. 'Let the

creature speak, you fools.' When it was quiet he asked the man, 'Where was this battle?'

Forgetting himself, the sergeant answered in Russian, but then went on in crude French, 'Ah, near Borodino, twenty leagues afore Moscow, as please ye, sir.'

'Prince Bagration and Commander-in-chief de Tolly, no?' If it were both, then in and around the little village that day no less than a quarter of a million men had met in murderous combat.

'Yes, sir. Under Field Marshal Kutuzov. They forms up in the morning . . . when was it? On the twenty-sixth.'

'Well, what happened, damn it?'

'Can't rightly say, sir. I'se with L'tenant Borodinsky, galloper to General Ushakov, an' didn't have time to look around, like.' With an injured look the sergeant continued: 'Well, all hell breaks loose on us. Guns s' many it splits the air, fighting so fierce the ground's soaked in blood.'

The listening crowd fell silent as a harrowing tale unfolded in all its terrifying detail. The cruel cold of the pre-dawn when every man slept in the open with his musket, fearing what the day would bring, but with nothing to prepare him for the desperate actuality. A gigantic canvas portraying the hideous sight of line and column hacked into bloody corpses even as they screamed, '*Vive l'empéreur!*' Russian peasantry with pitchforks slaughtered to the last man in desperate, hopeless stands against Bonaparte's veterans. And always the dust and gun-smoke swirling about them in acrid clouds that threw every man into a world of isolation where only the imperative of kill or be killed had any meaning.

As the day went on and ammunition was spent, the fighting descending into animal savagery – screeching soldiers falling on each other with teeth and fists, piteous scenes of heroism and terror, blood and death until darkness came to shroud the scene from the eyes of men. And with the night came the looting – not for the usual pelf but precious food and water, for no supplies had crossed the hell on earth that was Borodino.

And then, mortally tired, their desperate ride for St Petersburg across square miles of corpses.

'Who won, damn you?' Denisov ground.

The sergeant looked pained. 'As I don't rightly know, sir. Difficult t' make out what's going on, all them guns a-roaring together, an' the lieutenant, he won't tell me.'

'We'll get no sense out of this ninny,' Denisov growled derisively. 'Let's wait for this messenger lieutenant.'

But the man stayed with the Tsar and the crowd dispersed. Renzi left Denisov in a frustrated pacing and went back to his quarters – almost an insult of comfort after what he'd heard.

Renzi was under no illusions: the de Tolly strategy of retreat and destruction had worked. That it had been thrown aside in favour of an out-and-out confrontation with Bonaparte was disastrous and he wouldn't be surprised to hear that the carefully hoarded Russian armies had been crushed and scattered, leaving nothing to stand between the Emperor and the soft body of Russia.

For a time St Petersburg was plunged into a nervous ferment, waiting for reliable tidings and then, as Renzi pored over yet another turgid exposition from the Imperial Library, there was an interruption that chilled him to the core.

Gunfire.

Flat thuds that came from the north-west. He jerked upright, straining to hear. Oddly it seemed to be single guns – and sounding at measured intervals. Then the bells began, first one, then a bedlam of sound as every cathedral and church joined in, a frenzy of joy that spread across the city.

Bemused, he sat back. This was a victory celebration. Sometime later, the streets below erupted in cheering and shouts that redoubled in commotion as if something momentous was approaching.

He rang for his servant who appeared, animated with excitement. 'Do pray open the window,' Renzi told him.

Renzi went to the balcony and looked down. It was some kind of military parade with an open carriage bearing a splendidly dressed officer. 'Do you know who that is?' he asked.

'That, sir, is the Field Marshal Kutuzov, victor of Borodino!'

The carriage turned off the street and into the gates of the Winter Palace where it was lost to view. The boulevard was quickly filling with people, wild with jubilation but held back by a line of grenadiers.

Victor? In a fury of impatience Renzi hurried to the Imperial General Staff. The room was in an uproar, packed with the military, the highest in the land, all talking animatedly. It wasn't hard to spot Denisov, loudly arguing with a hard-faced general, and he thrust through to him.

'What's the news?' he asked.

'A victory! We're in possession of a monstrous great victory!'

'Of course you are, but—'

'We have Kutuzov here, as he's left the field o' battle to tell us.'

'Yes, but what news does he bring, Aleksey?'

'When he departed Borodino he left the Russian Army standing proud, still in possession of the field. In the whole day never did he hear a single word of retreat, of yielding. Nikolai, we fought Bonaparte to a standstill. A famous victory that will resound down the centuries!'

'I see.'

'No, you don't, Nikolai! What this means is Bonaparte has been brought to a stand, he can't go further.'

'So—'

'So the devil is stopped in his tracks. He sees he can't get past us. Riga has been preserved to us, so he hasn't easy supplies, and there's only one thing he can do.'

'Yes?'

'He must give up, go home. Russia is saved, Nikolai!' He seized Renzi by the shoulders and hugged him. 'Glory be, and we're saved!'

If indeed Bonaparte's horde had been brought to a bloody halt, the Russians had good reason to be proud.

'My sincerest and deep-felt congratulations,' Renzi said formally, with a respectful bow. 'Shall you be celebrating at all?'

'Ha! Already His Imperial Majesty has decreed three days of official celebrations, beginning with an address to be read out in the Alexander Nevsky Cathedral. We shall not forget this day – ever!'

Renzi left him to his adulation of the victor Kutuzov and, in a daze of impressions and unsatisfied suppositions, he tried to return to his books, but the noise outside did not allow it. Again, there was no call from Alexander and he wondered why, in these momentous times, he hadn't been asked to make comment or pronouncement.

Denisov briefly visited with more details and in the evening Renzi went into the streets to take in the atmosphere.

It was an intoxicating, unforgettable and deeply moving sight as the Russian people gave vent to their feelings. Seething, happy crowds thronged the long avenues, trumpets blaring discordantly, drums thumping boisterously and fireworks swooshing and banging on all sides. Strings of multi-coloured lanterns and illuminations hung in windows for as far as he could see.

And then, by the edge of the water, glittering with reflections and alive with craft hurrying in every direction, he heard his name, faintly but clearly against the laughter and din of crowds. It came from a boat touching at the small sea-wall landing. To his intense pleasure he saw it was a British naval launch, which had to have come from *Thunderer*.

He waved an acknowledgement and hurried over.

'Lord Farndon, sir?' The lieutenant looked greatly relieved. 'It is.'

'The captain has given me instructions that we should without fail convey you this instant to the ship.'

On the way Renzi learned that Kydd's venture had been entirely successful and that no casualties had been sustained.

A beaming Kydd met him as he came aboard and they hastened to the privacy of his cabin.

'A cognac in a bumper, at seeing you spared!' Kydd declared warmly, taking a glass from Binard.

Their tales were exchanged, then Kydd leaned across seriously. 'Nicholas, know that I've to go now to Byam Martin to report myself and I cannot return. You will be coming with me, I beg.'

Renzi sighed, putting down his glass. 'Dear brother, there's nothing I crave more than to leave this madness, but unhappily the business is not yet concluded. Until I can see the tide irrevocably turning, I must not quit this benighted land.'

Kydd slumped back. 'There's nothing I can persuade you to that will see you on the way back to England and Cecilia?'

'No.'

'Then I must depart shortly, Nicholas. After storing and watering. And then . . .'

'I understand. Do not concern yourself on my account, my dear friend. I shall find ways to make my exit, I assure you.'

# Chapter 54

In the Winter Palace the celebrations were unending, a vast dinner given in honour of the Tsar, a magnificent ball, parades and salutes without number.

But then, without warning, it turned to ashes. Denisov burst into Renzi's rooms, his eyes wild. 'News – dispatches. I fear it's a calamity!'

Renzi felt a grim foreboding. 'A disaster? What's this, my friend?'

'All I know is that the news is bad, Nikolai – I must go and find out more.'

He was not away long, returning with an expression that told of all that Renzi had feared.

'Nikolai. Prepare yourself. The most terrible thing. That devil on earth has flung us aside. He's secretly outflanked our positions at Borodino and forced us to fall back in disorder. Our hero Prince Bagration has died of his wounds. Nikolai . . . Nikolai . . . it means the road to Moscow is wide open! We're lost! We're lost!' He gulped, his eyes filling.

It was a catastrophe of the first order. Moscow taken and Alexander reduced to treating for terms, Bonaparte dictating the future of the world from the Kremlin, a realignment of interests that left England firmly out in the cold to find peace as she could.

'Stay here, Nikolai. I'll see what further news there is.'

Renzi was left alone with his thoughts. One thing was sure: now he had no choice but to stay and see how the Tsar would handle the end game for his nation. It could all be for nothing: the most likely outcome was an assassination. His duty to the mission, though, was to see it through to the end. Kydd and *Thunderer* would have to leave without him.

A sinister quiet lay over St Petersburg. Renzi stole a peek at the street below. It was deserted, the decorations sadly askew. As dusk drew in, a light drizzle centred each in a soft, sad halo of light.

He couldn't concentrate. Even with the melancholic silence that had descended on St Petersburg the philosophic ruminations of scholars of the last age held no fascination for him. The present times now were too chaotic, leading nowhere.

He heard disturbances below in the wet boulevard, shouts and excitement. And, with growing insistence, a low, haunting chant from powerful masculine voices in unison. He hurried to the window and drew back the heavy curtain carefully. A sizeable crowd had gathered but this was not a dangerous mob. They carried icons, banners, images, and were looking up reverentially, some with hands in a prayerful position, others making the sign of the Cross, still more with candles illuminating their rapt faces. This was no religious parade of the sort he'd seen before. It was a loose, spontaneous expression of some kind.

He rang for his servant. 'What's this below, pray?'

The man turned to him slowly and spoke in a strange hushed tone. 'Sir, the Little Father has spoken to his people and they hear him. They come to offer up their lives to him and to Mother Russia in her time of need.'

Even as he gazed down on them, the multitudes of people outside the Winter Palace were increasing in number, now spilling into the roadway. The chant swelled and broadened, and he watched, captivated. This was the Russian masses, those whom Napoleon Bonaparte was bent on conquering, subduing. It suddenly didn't seem quite so certain. He turned back but was startled by the two figures arrayed in the livery of the Imperial Household who loomed impassively in the doorway.

They said nothing but Renzi knew why they'd come and followed them.

Tsar Alexander was not in the Imperial General Staff, or even in his private drawing room. Renzi was led along a plain, barely lit hallway to a pair of massive doors, embellished with the holy significations of the Russian Orthodox creed. The doors were opened soundlessly and he was ushered inside.

The chapel was illuminated only by a pair of candles, the soft gold touching the churchly objects with an unearthly magnificence, revealing figures kneeling before one standing motionless in what resembled a penitent's robe. It was the Tsar.

To one side Renzi could make out another, clad in costly vestments and wearing a jewel-encrusted ecclesiastical crown, murmuring continuously some beatitude. Nearby an acolyte swung a censer of incense.

'Be welcome, our loyal English companion.' Alexander's voice was low, soft and infinitely serene.

Renzi knelt, like the others.

'I have bid you come that you might hear the words I have to say from my own lips.'

'Sire.'

'Know that in this, our greatest hour of trial, I shall not rest my burdens until Bonaparte, the very sceptre of the Antichrist, is driven from Holy Mother Russia.' His voice had strengthened, risen in spiritual ecstasy. 'In the name of our sacred ancestors I shall stand before him. I shall fight to the last breath of my body and inch of my realm. Know, too, that with my people and nation rising in arms together against the usurping tyrant we shall remain in the forefront of battle until he is hounded from our land and then – as God is my witness – I will keep faith with the crushed and conquered of this world to rid the earth of this foul violator of mankind.'

His eyes, lifted in saintly rapture, dropped to look down on Renzi. 'Is it in your thoughts, my companion and counsellor, to remain by my side while my crusade is done?'

Taken by surprise, Renzi found himself saying into the stillness, 'I shall, if this be Your Majesty's desire.'

For a long moment he thought Alexander had not heard. Then the Tsar said, with a rising intensity, a vehemence that was almost fierce, 'It is not my desire. My wish and my prayer is that, now you have heard my words, noble lord, you will reverently take them to my brother, King George of Great Britain, the only remaining foe to the tyrant left in the field, as witness that Russia will never be vanquished, never yield to the oppressor of humankind. This is the greatest service you can do for Russia, dear friend. Will you swear it?'

'I so swear!' Renzi said, realising as he said it that his sincerity was genuine.

He rose from his knees and, with a profound bow, backed out of the presence.

Outside a bear-like figure took his arm. 'Alexsey,' Renzi murmured.

The man was clearly in thrall to the moment.

'Nikolai. The Little Father has spoken. When you bow before your king and convey his words, do know that they are being retold in the cathedrals, the market-squares, the lowest taverns. They will shout from the pages of newspapers and be written on banners and borne into battle by the common soldier. Nikolai, tell your king that it is not the Tsar only who stands alone before Bonaparte but the soul of Mother Russia – her people!'

'I know, my friend. I can hear them. And therefore I will truthfully say that I myself heard the soul of Russia cry aloud to be avenged.'

In bare hours Renzi was standing on the finely carved stern gallery of *Thunderer*, watching her wake dissipate in the cold grey waters while the coastline of Russia slipped away into the distance. The searing experiences of the last month were slowly rendering into memories that he knew he would take into the remainder of his life.

Russia – a monstrous conundrum. Congalton had said that France was a civilised country ruled by a barbarian, Russia a barbarian land ruled by a monk. So true – but he'd seen only part of the whole and knew there were unfathomable depths to which he'd never been witness. And now it was all over. The climax to this clash of Titans was imminent but its outcome was denied him. He didn't know whether to be thankful or melancholic, but in any event his part was complete. He had enough to state that Tsar Alexander would stand against Bonaparte and that the people of Russia were with him. Whether that led to

Continental-scale slaughter or a grave setback for Bonaparte could not be known at this time.

Kydd moved to his side. 'Nicholas, it would gratify me extremely were I to hear something of your adventures. I have a fine Madeira going a-begging in the telling.'

# Chapter 55

The grey bulk of *Aboukir* firmed out of the rain mist at last. With the entire length of the Baltic shore now in thrall to Napoleon Bonaparte, any fleet rendezvous was meaningless and Byam Martin's flagship could have been anywhere along its length. *Thunderer* knew better than to make the traditional thirteen-gun salute. As long ago as Cornwallis, most blockading admirals had seen it as not only a waste of powder but an alert to the enemy of big-ship movements.

Three other sail-of-the-line were in sight, all four under lazy sail, vaguely standing across the Gulf of Finland to some purpose that was not clear to Kydd.

He mounted the side-steps of the flagship to be met by a genial Admiral Byam Martin, who nevertheless seemed grey and drawn beneath his greeting. 'A welcome to ye, Kydd,' he rumbled warmly. 'As I've been desirous of making your acquaintance these weeks past.'

'I do apologise, sir. Delayed in joining by events in Russia – it's all in my report.'

'Let's below an' you can tell me about it.'

Below was really further aft on the same deck, similar to *Thunderer*, but long habit of using the term more appropriate to a single gun-deck marked him out, like Kydd, as a frigate man at heart.

It didn't take long to tell of the Danzig exploit and to receive full support for his action in falling in with the Tsar's call. 'As I'd hope an enterprising officer would behave, you receiving my blessing on your previous conveying of His Russian Nibs to Äbo.'

'Sir, there's a person aboard *Thunderer* of much importance. The Lord Farndon, who's been in clandestine service with the Tsar since before the descent on his country. He fervently desires to return to England and lay before the Foreign Office certain intelligence he's since acquired.'

'I see.' He reflected for a short space. 'Then we can do something about that. After Riga there's nothing of note that I need any kind of fleet for and I've lately a mind to send back some of my sail-of-the-line to Admiral Saumarez as dispensable, he having more of a need, I believe. Can't see why you shan't join 'em as well. No doubt Sir James will then find an aviso cutter on regular visit to England as will convey your man.'

'Thank you, sir.'

'It might be in order to pay a call on Admiral Reynolds at Hanö. He has a hard enough situation.'

'Our convoy collection point.'

'Just so. Well, off you go, dear fellow. No point in moping about.'

With much satisfaction Kydd laid *Thunderer*'s bows to the west and, in the increasingly chill autumn easterlies, made good time to Hanö Bay, flanked by two other sail-of-the-line. Without a naval or other base in the Baltic, this was where convoys from England were escorted, then to disperse under false colours and papers to the many ports within Bonaparte's Continental System. It was also where merchant ships with their vital Baltic cargoes would make their way to assemble into the regular convoys back to various ports in Britain.

With his several ships-of-the-line, the admiral's task was to watch over the immense gathering of wealth that was a several-hundred-ship convoy, as well as to see it on its way through the Great Belt passage and out of the Baltic. A glittering prize for any determined marauding enemy.

But Kydd saw that the two sail-of-the-line at anchor were old and worn out, assigned the station as deterrents, never to storm into line-of-battle as a fleet or even meet an equal on the high seas. The flagship, *St George*, was a 98-gun second rate dating back to before the war. The other, *Defence*, had already aged forty-odd years in her brave fight at Trafalgar.

Admiral Reynolds was affable and clearly felt honoured at Kydd's visit. 'Kind in you, old fellow. You should know, o' course, that the season's over in these parts.'

'Sir?'

'Sir James agrees a date for clearing the Baltic of our shipping well in advance of the winter icing over, since we once lost an entire convoy frozen in by leaving it too late. This is the last of 'em for this year.' He had kindly features, distinguished grey hair adding to a figure of some presence. Kydd recalled that, as the notable frigate captain of *Amazon* at the beginning of the wars, he'd been with Pellew in the celebrated action in the midst of a fierce storm that had ended with a French ship-of-the-line destroyed in the breakers.

'We sail shortly. Care to take passage with us?'

'I'd be honoured,' Kydd murmured. The two that had accompanied him could choose for themselves. Renzi would agree that a day or two's delay in exchange for undoubted security for his intelligence would be acceptable in the circumstances.

After his previous service in the Baltic, Kydd was no stranger to the arcane rituals of convoys. This one was of some hundred and fifty sail, which, while middling in size, at one or two cables spacing, covered the sea from horizon to horizon. Falling in at the rear with the others, *Thunderer* picked up speed and the entire company of ships put to sea. They emerged from behind Hanö island for the run along the south coast of Sweden. Almost immediately they were caught in an ugly cross-sea, the onrush of a powerful swell from the north-east contradicted by an increasing wind-driven bluster from the west-south-west.

Uncomfortably the convoy pressed on, smaller merchantmen falling astern with loss in speed after taking in sail to withstand the blow.

'Can't say as how it's looking so good for us, is my opinion, sir.'

Kydd trusted Hobbs, the sailing master, a steady hand and not given to undue alarm. 'How so?'

The man looked into the eye of the wind and bared his teeth, as though tasting its quality. 'Doesn't do to miscalculate in the Baltic. This snorter comes over from the North Sea t' bully us right enough, where's born some o' the worst seas on the planet. This time o' the year – autumn, like – we can expect evil weather any time.'

Kydd could remember some hard blows in his own service here. The fortunates in massive line-of-battle ships wouldn't find themselves threatened but the hundreds of merchant ships, each effectively on its own in the midst of many, didn't have that comfort and would be battening down and rigging lifelines.

They passed the southern entry to the Sound by

dead-reckoning, the air misty and storm-racked. Then it was tack and tack again to round Gedser Point and relief from the bruising cross-sea, before the last day's run to the enfolding peace of the Great Belt passage.

The final staying about was with Gedser Odde in plain view, the sullen roar of the wind's blast redoubling once around to its weather side, seething seas racing across offshore shoals with no sign of life ashore. And to the south, away from Denmark and not more than twenty-odd miles down-wind, was Rostock and the entire length of Bonaparte's hostile Baltic coast.

By now the convoy was losing any semblance of an organised body. Some ships fell off the wind to turn tail for the safety of whence they'd come. Others were in difficulties with torn canvas or splintered spars. Kydd wasn't surprised to see *St George* signal a run for shelter northwards, presumably deep into Nystad Bay.

As if in sympathy the winds eased and, at last able to shed oilskins, Kydd watched the motions of the flagship, determined to moor within easy sight for orders when they came. The bay, though, was shoal-ridden and dangerous. Hobbs shook his head at the sight of whitened humping waters betraying reefs and sandbars not far below the surface.

*St George* had her best bower anchor run out to its full scope, allowing her to swing and face into the wind's eye and Kydd did likewise at a safe distance off, the two other sail-of-the-line taking position on the side. All round them the convoy loosed their anchors and settled down to ride out the gale, a vast mass of ships in the sweep of the bay, each one bobbing and jibbing uncomfortably to their anchors.

Kydd had endured such before, but never for more than a day or two, and his sympathies were for Renzi, with urgent and vital intelligence locked in his breast, held to a standstill by the run for shelter. Then again, if he'd gone on in a dispatch cutter, he would have been no better off, balked by the same storm.

The day faded into a bleak dusk while the hurts of the ship were taken in hand, and the ship's company given a hot meal. Further off, *St George* hoisted three lanthorns into her maintop for all to be reassured. All around them lights appeared as the convoy waited out the night, but as the last dog-watchmen handed over to the first-watchmen Kydd, in his cabin at supper with Renzi and Craddock, felt a subtle but noticeable change in the ship's heave and snub at her anchor.

Within ten minutes a soaked and red-eyed midshipman-of-the-watch brought a message. 'Mr Briggs's respects an' the wind's backed into the sou'-west an' strengthening.'

In this short time, backing a whole quadrant and from that quarter was bad news, in a trice turning the whole bay into a lee shore. Kydd excused himself and, pulling on his foul-weather gear, hurried out on deck. It was now a flat, streaming blast and a glance at the compass told him it was indeed from the south-west.

'Don't like it, sir. With a bigger fetch it could turn ugly. Clear away second bower?'

Kydd hesitated but only for a moment. 'Compliments to Mr Hobbs and I'd be happy to see him on deck.'

The master had no doubts. 'A change so quick – we're going to a fresh gale afore long.' He sniffed at the wind distrustfully. 'An' anchors aren't all we'll need.'

'Mr Hobbs?'

'We're like to be embayed if this blow shapes more southerly. I'd advise we lay along sail ready to cut 'n' run, sir.'

'Thank you. We'll see how the breeze does in the next hour.'

Over on their bow the three lanthorns in *St George* were a beacon of calm in the gathering darkness. The big three-decker seemed hardly to notice the blow, but the merchant ships pitched and rolled, fretfully brought up to their anchors and simply enduring. *St George* serenely rode it out.

As far as the eye could see the convoy had been transformed into so many lights in the darkness, blinking as their low-slung navigation lamps were obscured by the short steep waves being kicked up. It would be an uncomfortable night, even in *Thunderer*, where the smash and judder of waves were beginning to make themselves felt. Kydd took a last look around before returning to finish his supper.

Craddock's face was a study in seriousness as he cradled his toddy. 'Mr Renzi warns it's as likely to get worse as better.'

'And he'd be right,' Kydd said, allowing Binard to whisk away his dripping oilskin. 'I'd pass a lashing over your cot if I were you.' He would be turning in all-standing, fully dressed to be ready if urgently called on deck, which was looking increasingly likely.

The gale increased remarkably rapidly, the motions of the ship-of-the-line less ponderous, now convulsive, the weighty sequence of creaks and groans along the length of the vessel louder and more insistent. The wind's whistle in the rigging turned into a continuous dull drone and then, quite audible even in the great cabin, rose to a demented organ pitch that clutched at the heart.

It was time to return on deck. It was all Kydd could do to stand upright against the savage blast, made all the more unnerving by the pitch-black darkness and the stinging spray. Briggs appeared out of nowhere, his foul-weather gear streaming and his face red with endurance. 'Barometer dropped three-quarters of an inch this last hour. Can't go on like this,' he shouted into Kydd's ear.

'I've seen worse in the Caribbee,' Kydd yelled back. 'Count on it, it will.'

'Flagship in sight, no signals,' Briggs added formally, as was required of him at the appearance of his captain on deck. He gestured mutely into the murk to leeward. *St George*'s three lights could just be glimpsed through the wild night, but there was little sign of the convoy lights, a few occasional pinpricks appearing and disappearing. The wind-driven spume stung Kydd's eyes as he took it all in.

'Carpenter reports two feet in the well, bosun says anchor holding,' Briggs added. Kydd knew that would be the stolid Opie right forward in the bows, his foot resting on the bar-taut cable to the hawse, feeling for dreaded irregular vibrations and twitches indicating that the three-ton bower anchor was ploughing a furrow in the seabed.

If it did fail he had to decide whether to let go more anchors at the cost of losing them if things got worse and they had to cut them free to make a break under sail to seaward. It would be certain destruction to face any other crisis with empty cables.

The watch on deck was nowhere to be seen. Kydd was not annoyed, for it showed the consideration Briggs had for his men, sending them to shelter in the deck below, on call.

Kydd shuddered in the cold. How long should he keep Briggs company on this awful night?

From somewhere far forward a faint cry cut through the hammering wind blast, the fore-deck lookout loyally singing out hazards. Kydd leaned into the bluster, shielding his eyes and gazed into the wind-torn welter of seas. At first he saw nothing. The three lights in the maintop of *St George* were still there but they had been visible as a threesome spaced along the after end of the top. Now they blended into one as their perspective changed.

It could mean only one thing: *St George* was under way of some kind, no longer anchored. Drifting? Deliberately making for the open sea?

The first was unthinkable. The three-decker had the best ground tackle of them all, massive anchors, twenty-three-inch cables. As for the other, the signal for an emergency break to sea was a blue and a red light simultaneously displayed, their ghostly glare unmistakable. It was unimaginable that their careful and highly experienced admiral would forget to signal his intentions.

Kydd's mind whirled as he tried to wring sense from it. It was impossible to make out anything in the dark chaos of the storm. Their only course of action was to stay as they were until daylight revealed the mystery.

It was a tempest of hideous proportions, the harshest he'd seen in the Baltic, and made all the worse by that sea nightmare – lack of sea-room. In the Caribbean there was a good chance to outfox a hurricane with adroit seamanship, given the distances between islands, but the Baltic was in effect an inland sea with reef-fringed land in all directions.

In the early hours Kydd sensed a lessening of force, or was he deluding himself? There was nothing he could achieve out in the open until daybreak and he left the deck for his cabin, slumped into a chair and drifted into a troubled sleep.

He woke with a start. The motion of the ship was noticeably less but the wicked drone of the winds was still audible. His watch told him that dawn was an hour or so away, but he snatched up his oilskin and made his way to the half-deck.

'Oh, sir. You're awake?' It was Smale, the officer-of-the-deck coming out of the master's cabin, looking dry and rested. Clearly he'd seen no reason why he shouldn't see out the blow in some sort of comfort.

'I am. And you?' Kydd asked pointedly, but at anchor there

was no rule that said an officer had to be on deck as long as he was within immediate call.

There was no way he could go back to sleep in the tension of waiting for dawn, and he passed the time in forced conversation with Smale.

At the first glimmering of daybreak they peered out into the grey murk, rain squalls marching in adding to the chill misery of dawn.

When visibility had reached out to a mile or more, a terrible sight was revealed. The sea was nearly empty, the convoy no more. A thin scatter of merchantmen had miraculously survived, but wrecks could be made out everywhere, dismasted, stranded, sunken.

In the centre of the wretched scene one sight brought gasps of horror. Hard aground, on her beam ends and entirely dismasted in a pitiable wreck, was the hulk of *St George*.

There were men still aboard: a flutter of colour at the stump of her fore-mast, some clinging to her sloping deck as they fought their way along, others struggling to secure gear as the battering seas threw spars and wreckage at her naked hull.

Then, from a makeshift flag-mast, a signal appeared: 'All captains, as convenient', meaning that when the seas had abated enough for boats to reach the wreck they were to go to the flagship. There were something like nine hundred men aboard *St George*, a colossal rescue by boat to contemplate, but the signal implied the admiral was still aboard and taking charge.

For an hour or more Kydd helplessly watched the seas seething in under the lash of the gale until they'd subsided sufficiently to risk the launch, *Thunderer*'s biggest boat. Coming in on the leeward side, *St George*'s entry-port was within easy stepping distance and Kydd was helped up the steeply canted deck by the side-party, soaked but unhurt.

A life-line had been rigged and he hauled himself along to the admiral's cabin spaces aft. Reynolds greeted him warmly, as did Guion, his flag-captain, the austere Atkins of *Defence* with his habitual long face rising to greet him. One or two others murmured a greeting, presumably captains of the lesser craft Kydd had seen converging on the flagship after daylight had exposed the shocking scene.

A table had been wedged into the lower corner and refreshments tastefully laid out, for all the world like a flag-officer's entertainments.

'Gentlemen. I don't have to tell you that *St George* has suffered grievous wounds in the night's gales.'

'Sir, how did it happen at all?' one of the junior captains asked, wide-eyed. 'I mean, a three-decker and—'

'A substantial-sized merchantman was driven athwart my hawse during the night and carried away my best bower.'

'Aye, sir, but—'

'L'tenant, the inshore bottom hereabouts is cobbles.' Small loose rocks, rounded by centuries of rolling together in foul weather and hopelessly slippery. The worst holding for the anchors of big ships.

'When we struck, axes were laid to the masts to ease her pounding but as it stands, our rudder has been beaten off entirely.'

Kydd felt for them: a frightful night of terror and hopeless labour in the cold wildness, relentlessly driving into the shore with who knew what awaiting them. But discipline had held and, in the howling darkness, they'd done what was needed to prevent the ship toppling. 'When shall we begin taking off your ship's company, sir? By boat some nine hundreds will take time and—'

'Thank you, but it will not be necessary.'

'Sir?'

'I intend to refloat *St George*, re-rig with jury masts and complete the voyage.'

This was either madness or inspired, Kydd reflected, but saw the flag-captain, Guion, nodding slowly.

'How can we help, sir?' Atkins asked.

'Stand by me. And I'd be grateful for the loan of your carpenter and his mates.'

'Your rudder, sir. I could have a try at a Pakenham for you,' Kydd offered. Some years ago an enterprising captain had devised a method of providing a rudder where one had been lost or dashed off, using only its remains and ship's stores. The Admiralty had been so taken with the idea that they'd printed out instructions to be issued to every king's ship to be kept for just this moment.

Reynolds gave a twisted smile but then gravely agreed. 'Do so, Sir Thomas. I would be grateful.'

'Jury masts, sir?' Atkins enquired.

'Indeed. Topmasts were struck down before the storm as usual and are to hand. I shall extract our mast stumps and substitute the topmasts, which I'm sanguine will answer.'

Half the size, but if it could be achieved, then canvas could be spread and *St George* would be no longer a dead ship. It was looking possible.

'Getting afloat?'

'The master assures me we are held only by a third of our length. Should we lighten ship, then with every man-o'-war boat a-swim and manned to excess I believe we may succeed in pulling her clear.'

Kydd couldn't help but be carried along by the tide of creative hope. This was what it was to lead and inspire, and his respect for the kindly admiral increased.

'I'm supposing you'll be as surprised as I to learn that, of our convoy of a hundred and fifty, no less than seventy-odd survived the night. I'm sending them on with suitable escort and *Rose* will press on separately to alert Admiral Saumarez as to our disposition. All sail-o'-war save her will remain with me.'

The conference broke up in a far different mood than when it had met, and the captains left with grim purpose to begin the heroic salvage plan.

As he turned to go Kydd remembered Renzi. 'Sir, would it be in order for *Rose* to carry ahead my distinguished guest? He has vital intelligence for their lordships and—'

'Of course, dear fellow. She'll put off at midday when my dispatches are ready.' In a more concerned tone he went on, 'And that Pakenham rudder. I've heard it's a beast to put together – are you sure *Thunderer* can conjure it?'

'She will, sir!'

The gale lessened as quickly as it had struck and work began without delay. Men swarmed over the cruelly dismasted *St George* to start the prodigious labour of extracting the remains.

In *Thunderer* they set about producing a three-ton, seventy-foot rudder that could be mounted securely enough to take another gale. From the depths of Craddock's ship's office the Pakenham screed was found. Just a single sheet printed on both sides but it seemed to satisfy the carpenter, Upcot, who bore it off to sketch out the requisites.

He was back soon. 'Er, sir. Here it says as we has to forge an iron plate t' take the weight, it not havin' your reg'lar pintle and gudgeon a-tall. I can't do it.'

The principle of the Pakenham rudder was robust but the actuality difficult to achieve. The rudder shank would be passed up into the trunking as usual, but instead of being supported by half a dozen pintles rotating in gudgeons bolted to the ship's sternpost it was essentially hung at the top with a massive forged shoulder bolt penetrating the two-foot-square rudder-stock, and bearing on a weighty circular iron plate. A stout tiller-bar inserted into a mortice in the rudder-head and equipped with relieving tackles provided the necessary steering capability.

'Tell the armourer to lay aft,' Kydd snapped. This was Ferne, one of the ship's artisans and seldom seen about the decks, but now about to be central to the action.

'Mr Ferne, please to consult with the carpenter concerning his needs. You and your mates are to turn to, double tides, until the job's under hatches.'

With Roscoe and much of *Thunderer*'s complement away in *St George*, there was plenty of room to spread out the workings of the huge rudder over the quarterdeck while Ferne set up his forge right forward on the fo'c'sle, the acrid stink of his fire soon spreading aft.

Renzi made his farewells and departed in *Rose*, and before the end of the day the convoy had set sail for the north leaving the warships to their exertions.

A bare three days later, all ships put every boat they possessed into the water, double-banked on each thwart, and with a drummer of the Royal Marines embarked to beat time. A ferocious heaving and straining, along with much cursing and heavy sweat, at long last had the great three-decker afloat.

Rapid soundings of her well confirmed there were no serious leaks. The last mast stumps were withdrawn and topmasts lowered into the mast steps.

In *Thunderer* the finished Pakenham rudder was swayed overside with a yardarm stay tackle and floated out to *St George* where it was fitted, to much applause.

Light-headed with exhaustion and relief Kydd kept the

deck until the first canvas was spread in *St George* and, to roars of cheering, the battleship ponderously took up on the starboard tack and headed resolutely for the open sea.

In a stroke of irony, the lessening gale dropped to a light breeze and then a playful zephyr, almost unknown at this time of the year. It was nothing that *Thunderer* and the others couldn't deal with but, burdened with an awkward jury rig, *St George* was in no shape to manoeuvre out of it. Her sails were struck, the remaining anchors tumbled down, and the flagship was once more at a standstill, threatened with the same lee shore.

It was a wicked twist in fortune and Kydd made an instant decision. 'Make to flag: "Prepare to be taken in tow".'

Not waiting for a reply he ordered, 'Mr Roscoe, rouse out a cable, double-bitt it around the mizzen-mast and out through the gun-deck sternports.' If they could get *St George* out to sea there was a good chance that there she could pick up a usable breeze.

The messenger line was taken out by *Thunderer*'s launch. *St George* took it in and hauled away valiantly until the heavy rope made its way in through her hawse to be seized around the fore-mast.

Cautiously Kydd applied small sail until the 74 had taken the first strain, waiting until the signal from the flagship indicated that her anchors were aweigh before spreading more sail until, by inches, the two moved ahead to the accompaniment of a thunderous creaking.

As if on cue, Binard appeared on deck before him, bearing a salver on which was the brave sight of brimming champagne glasses.

'I rather thought this to be your intention,' Craddock said smoothly.

Kydd proposed a toast. 'Gentlemen. To us, *St George*, and

why Boney can never carry the day while the Royal Navy keeps the seas for its own!'

Every officer first raised their glass to the flagship and then to Kydd, whose heart swelled with pride.

'And a double tot to all hands, Mr Roscoe.'

# Chapter 56

At a steady five knots the ships passed along the south of Denmark, the tow, the jury rig and the Pakenham rudder holding firm. Ahead, the fearful passage of the torturous reefs and currents of the Great Belt loomed, a hard enough beat at the best of times but for a ship under tow a nightmare.

With *Bellette* going ahead and *Defence* bringing up the rear, *Thunderer* and *St George* won through into the northern entrance to the Baltic, the Kattegat – and blessed open sea. As if at last relenting the wind turned to a brisk south-easterly, fine for the final distance to the commander-in-chief, Saumarez.

The anchorage was crowded with shipping. A convoy was clearly about to depart for England and there was every chance they could be with it.

Rear Admiral Reynolds was quick to report, his barge in the water just as soon as the tow had been cast off and *Thunderer* had found her berth.

Within the hour the captains of *Defence* and *Thunderer* were summoned.

'I've been hearing a little of what you've achieved,

gentlemen,' Saumarez opened. 'Admiral Reynolds speaks in the most handsome terms of your diligence to duty and enterprise. Might I add my own admiration to his that you have been instrumental in preserving for His Majesty a most valuable flagship. Bless you both!'

'As was my bounden duty only, sir, to stay with my admiral,' Atkins protested, in the manner of the crusty traditionalist that he was.

'Yes. Well, as it is I have a problem,' harrumphed Saumarez. 'What to do with *St George*. I will be sailing to England shortly, and patently she's in no fit condition to stay with the fleet. I would think it therefore prudent for her to over-winter here and employ the time gainfully in repairs.'

'Sir, I do protest!' Reynolds spluttered. 'With Boney setting the world upside down Britain needs every ship of force that can—'

'I appreciate your dedication, sir, but this is not to be entertained. Your vessel must be sorely tried in the stranding and I cannot allow her to risk the North Sea as winter approaches.'

'Sir! With shoring in 'tween decks and the Pakenham holding well, I've every hope that—'

'No.'

'With *Thunderer* standing by and—'

Saumarez's brow creased. 'Very well, this I'll grant: a hull survey by three, and if they allow perhaps I'll reconsider.'

Kydd was there when the report came in. Two had misgivings and one allowed that, should the vessel be spared further torments by the weather, she had a chance.

Reynolds was accompanied by Guion, his flag-captain, and in nominal command of *St George*.

'Sir. We have been with the old lady for some years and we know her qualities,' Guion said, adding, 'It's but a three-day sail to Sheerness with a fair wind – as it does today, sir.'

The mild north-easterly was indeed directly fair for England. Saumarez pondered the risk to the injured ship against its restoration to the British fleet. 'Very well. Much against my inclination. Do take *Thunderer* as a precaution and you can have *Defence* as well. I believe I'll send the convoy off with *Hero* without delay and myself sail with the Baltic Fleet separately.'

When *St George* put to sea it was without a tow, the north-easterly almost coming in from astern. Logging a good six knots, she had *Defence* on her weather beam, *Thunderer* under her lee and, with the loyal *Bellette* sloop ranging ahead, the course was set for England.

But first they had to clear the Skaggerak, the seventy-mile-wide route from the Baltic entrance across the north of Denmark and out into the North Sea, before the quick run to the south-west and the dockyards of Sheerness and Chatham.

Kydd had always distrusted the North Sea, let alone at the coming of winter, and made sure the towing cable was faked down on the gun-deck, its lighter messenger line attached ready. Who knew if *St George*, with her awkward jury rig, would need a hand to pull clear of a hazard if the wind fell or even be plucked off a lee shore in a heavy blow?

Through the night the winds stayed fair, and dawn saw them leave the shelter of the Skaggerak passage – but the treacherous weather had not finished with them. The winds began to back more into the west, whipping and moaning, with every indication of turning ugly. By now the squadron had passed some distance down the outer coast of Jutland on its way south.

Hobbs voiced his concerns: 'Better to make an offing while you can, afore you stands to the suth'ard.' Kydd was inclined to agree but sympathised with *St George* in her pressing need to get into dockyard hands, now only a day or so away.

As the light strengthened, so did the wind, backing even further. At this rate they could soon be met with winds foul for their crossing.

*St George* threw out a signal. 'All ships,' the officer-of-the-watch called, his glass up but wavering in the increasing blow. 'Fleet to return to base.'

Painfully *St George* paid off and took up close-hauled on the larboard tack, heading back up the invisible Jutland coast for the eventual turn to starboard into the Skaggerak. *Defence* took the outer, weather side while *Thunderer* lay to leeward as they clawed their way north, the winds becoming fiercer at a dismaying rate. 'Double reefs in topsails,' Kydd ordered, the viciousness of the driving gale off the open North Sea touching him with a primeval icy foreboding.

*St George* took in all sail bar her staysails and treble-reefed topsails – a precaution with her weakened jury-rigged top-hamper. Further out to sea *Defence* was conforming, but Kydd's foreboding took on a stark reality when a lookout lashed into the foretop hailed down something and a messenger raced aft.

'Sir – fore lookout reports land all t' leeward!'

In a stab of anguish Kydd knew they had not reached the critical far end of Jutland to allow them to turn and go before the wind to safety. The lookout had seen a continuous line of white where the breakers were thundering on shore and they'd clearly extended out of sight ahead. With the winds from the west it was a dead lee shore and *St George* was at hazard unless she could soon weather the point of Holmen into the Skaggerak.

'Signal – land in sight to loo'ard!' he shouted at the signals messenger by his side. 'Hoist at fore and mizzen both.'

Kydd glanced at the flagship through the stinging spray kicked up from windward. A pale flicker on her deck forward resolved into another staysail being hoisted forward, a balancing staysail at the mizzen. She'd seen and understood the message of the fearful danger to leeward and was trying to add weatherliness without throwing an intolerable strain on her spars. If they carried away it would, without doubt, mean her destruction.

The speed at which the gale had clamped in was shocking, and it was now worse than any Kydd had encountered in this part of the world. He had to look to *Thunderer* too, for she was even closer to the low coast – about ten to a dozen miles off at the lookout's height of eye.

He felt his arm twitched. Hobbs shouted in his ear, 'Sir, I mislikes what I sees, but . . . but if'n I'm not mistaken *St George* is makin' a terrible lot o' leeway.'

This meant that the mighty three-decker was falling downwind on *Thunderer* in her lee position and at the same time adding to her perilous situation relative to Jutland.

'Bear up as will keep us clear.' His duty was to his lee station with respect to the admiral. *Defence*, on the other side, was already taking in sail to slow to stay loyally in his own weather station and was uncomfortably bucketing about.

And now to complicate matters night was coming on, the racing scud overhead looking more lethal, the shriek of wind tearing at the senses.

'Sir.' The sailing master beckoned and they left the halfdeck for the shelter of his cabin where he clearly wanted to talk.

'Mr Hobbs?'

'We has a decision t' make, sir.'

'I know.' The 'we' was kindly meant but in reality it was the captain's decision alone. On this larboard tack and with the fearful leeway the flagship was making they were not going to weather the Holmen.

'In this kind o' blow we're not going t' be able to tack about,' Hobbs prompted.

'No.'

'And the Danish coast shoals well out.'

'Yes.' The utterly flat coast, hard-packed sand compacted by centuries of pounding storms, extended underwater well offshore, and could not be detected by sounding in this raging storm.

'We has t' wear about.' Hobbs's voice had an edge of quiet desperation.

He'd made it official. Brought the peril to his captain's attention. If Kydd did nothing about it and the worst happened, if he survived, the subsequent court-martial would be merciless.

On the other hand his orders were plain and direct. He was to maintain the leeward station as *Defence* would the weather and, besides, it was a fundamental rule of naval practice to stay with the admiral in battle or tempest, whatever the conditions.

'The admiral has not signalled to wear,' he said stiffly.

'No, sir, he hasn't. As doesn't mean we shouldn't, being as how it would save the ship.'

And her many hundreds of souls. At the cost of abandoning his admiral, leaving him and his near thousand men to their fate.

'I'll think on it,' was all Kydd could find to say.

A fleeting memory came to him – another place, another storm. *Alexander* and the helpless *Vanguard*: Horatio Nelson driving on shore to his inevitable doom. Ball had stayed with his admiral and, in a feat of magnificent seamanship, had at the last moment got a line across and snatched the ship from certain death in the breakers. Nelson had been saved and a few weeks later had gone on to achieve an immortal victory at the Nile.

Was this what he should be doing, not cravenly fleeing?

Out on deck again the night had come in but with an eerie twist. There was a full moon, not visible behind the flying murk and clouds. But it shone through, permeating the scene with a luminosity, touching everything with a sheen of light, turning the sleeting spray to diamonds, the mist and spume torn from wave-tops into a radiant luminescence – and revealing in piteous detail ships fighting for their lives.

'Anything from *St George*?' Kydd asked hopefully.

Roscoe shook his head. It might well be that no signal flag could survive in this.

'Any sign she's going to wear about?' In this visibility they could easily see if she began the manoeuvre.

'No, sir.'

'Lay along for wearing. Just as soon as she does, we do too and that damn quick.'

'Sir.'

Hobbs looked about, his face drawn and haggard. He knew what it would be to end life cruelly battered to death in a crashing chaos ashore – he'd survived a shipwreck before, Kydd recalled.

'He has to wear!' blurted Smale, perhaps realising for the first time the totality of what was ahead.

'Land to starboard,' reported Briggs. That it was visible from the deck meant it was some five to seven miles off and the space needed to wear was closing to nothing.

Eyes stinging not just from the salt spray, Kydd gazed at the flagship. The kindly Reynolds, what was he going through now? What desperate move was he trying to devise to stave off the death that awaited them all?

A flicker of moon-pale canvas showed at her main, mounting up to be snatched away as if by a giant hand. A last desperate attempt at sail blown to shreds the instant it met the wind. Agonisingly, on the fore-mast, another – with the same result.

He understood immediately. *St George* was trying to wear but could not, her despairing attempts denied her by the wind's blast and her own wounded rigging.

Gulping, Kydd rounded on Hobbs. 'Wear ship, this instant!'

In the brutish savagery of the storm, a few feet of water remaining under her keel and the gale now a demented shriek, *Thunderer* fought her way around, her men like heroes against the foe, her movements frenzied as those of a maddened horse. On one side the spectre of a life-ending catastrophe – and on the other the delirium of continued existence out in the open sea.

Kydd snatched a look beyond *St George*. Was *Defence* going to follow *Thunderer* to wear about to salvation? She could be made out, bucking and rearing – but still close hauled on the larboard tack, if anything closing with the stricken three-decker. As *Thunderer* won around he saw, with an inevitability that was as harsh as the gesture was noble, that her captain was going to stay with his admiral and within a very short while both ships would meet their end.

Guilt pierced him cruelly. If Atkins thought it his duty to stay, what was Kydd doing, fleeing? Then he brought to mind the hopeless attempts in *St George* at showing sail to the storm. Without a shadow of doubt it was the admiral's intention to wear about and, if this was so, Kydd was essentially following his example and unspoken orders and had no need to accuse himself. His had been a successful manoeuvre. *St George's* had not. That *Defence* had chosen the way she had was Atkins's personal decision and had no bearing on his own.

Now safely close-hauled on the starboard tack *Thunderer* stood out to sea, pounding and crashing through the violence to her deliverance . . . while astern the last moments of two great men-o'-war were played out. Mercifully, as if unable to bear the horror of the carnage below, the moonlight dimmed and failed, and they were spared the sight.

Rigid with anguish Kydd saw through his ship winning her way seawards, salvation over death, her destiny reprieve and safe harbour, while under her lee astern life was ending for thousands.

'Nothing we can do, sir,' Roscoe said gravely.

'No,' Kydd choked. 'Nothing.'

Even if they waited for respite and there were survivors, Denmark was the home of the enemy, hostile and resentful after its losses at Copenhagen and would bitterly resist any landings. But they were a sea-people and would treat any survivors well. It only remained for him, with heavy sorrow, to take the news to England of its latest sacrifice to Neptune and the gods of war.

# Chapter 57

In just the two days it took to cross the North Sea the storm faded into a spiteful scend and fluky breeze, and they finally raised the brown cliffs of Sheppey in a well-behaved south-westerly. Pennants were hoisted and answered as they passed around Garrison Point and into the dockyard anchorage to pick up moorings, where *Thunderer* went to her rest.

It had to be Sheerness, for it was best connected by telegraph to the Admiralty and Whitehall, and Kydd had news that would shock the kingdom. 'Come on, old man. Let's face it together,' he told Craddock, finding his carefully worded signal. He was grateful to have the level-headed Craddock at his side at this time.

His barge touched at the weed-slimed steps he remembered from another life when he'd mounted them as a mutineer those uncountable years before. A marine guard snapped to attention as he landed, his dress now that of the captain of a battleship, his mission the making of a thousand new widows.

'The port admiral, if you please at your earliest convenience.'

'Admiral Cuthbert,' the lieutenant answered. 'Certainly, sir.'

A plain carriage waited and, with Craddock aboard, they whirled off to the residence, with its red ensign of seniority floating above the doorway and its two sentries.

Cuthbert descended the stairs. 'Be welcome to Sheerness, sir. It's . . .?'

'Sir Thomas Kydd, *Thunderer* 74, with urgent news.'

'Not so urgent you'll refuse a bracer? Do come in, old fellow.'

They entered a comfortable, well-ordered drawing room with nautical ornaments from the seven seas tastefully on show. A fire crackled busily, throwing its warmth even to the corners. 'Now what is this news that exercises you so, Sir Thomas?'

Wordlessly, Kydd handed over his signal. 'I'd be happy to see this sent off by telegraph without delay, sir.'

'Very well.' A small silver bell was rung and a flag-lieutenant appeared, his curiosity barely concealed. 'Flags – get this off instanter, if you will. Replies to me here.'

The admiral was of an age, lines of experience deeply incised, but his manner was pleasant. 'So. From the Baltic?' he said keenly.

'Aye, sir. And the news from there grievous indeed.' To his shame, the tears he'd held back since his helpless witness of events on the Jutland shore now brimmed over.

'Good Lord! I had no idea . . . Helen, a brandy – chop-chop, dear.' His wife hurried in with a generous glass.

They sat together by the fire and Kydd managed an account of the times and a rough estimate of the appalling losses to be expected.

Cuthbert remained silent for a moment, transfixed as if in memory. 'The poor devils,' he breathed. 'Not a chance, but they played it like brave 'uns.'

'It's bad cess ashore as well,' Kydd replied. 'Boney going like smoke and oakum into Russia. I heard that Smolensk was taken, and then a smaller town called Borodino but with a monstrous pile of dead the result. It seems there's nothing between Bonaparte and—'

'Yes, but I think I have later news than you, an aviso cutter taking the northern route around your storm. Seems that it's all over, is all. Bonaparte's prevailed, conquered. He's in Moscow, set it aflame and now has the world at his feet.'

'Then . . .?' Kydd was at a loss. If Bonaparte now had his immense army astride the capital and had burst out of his Continental prison there was little that Britain, with its contemptible little army, could do to stop his final erupting into the rest of the world. It was as near as could be imagined the end of everything.

'That's not all.'

'Sir?'

'The Americans have taken another frigate, damn the rascals. It's not to be borne, the rogues.'

Kydd hunched in gloom and despondency. Since the beginning of the endless French wars in '93 there'd been setbacks and black periods but none where the whole world had been set against them.

'Oh, I'm forgetting.' Cuthbert fumbled in his waistcoat. 'I've a signal addressed to you, *Thunderer*, received only an hour ago. As through Admiral Saumarez, your commander. Saves me passing it on.'

He handed over the paper, a telegraph office form. It had to be urgent, going by this privileged and near-instant means.

Kydd took it, his mind too full of recent events to give it much attention.

It was short and to the point, the originator, Flag, Plymouth.

'Accession to your fleet: one nine-pounder, all trim and a-taunto, in due course admiral's flag.'

What the devil? The port admiral of Plymouth was advising that a nine-pounder unit, presumably a sloop, was being attached to *Thunderer* in the flippant guise of his fleet, but he was at an utter loss as to what the reference to an admiral's flag meant.

'Nothing,' he said heavily, passing it back.

Something in his tone made Cuthbert hesitate. He took the signal and read it, frowned – then brightened.

He grinned. 'Dear fellow! Do believe that in my time I've seen more than a brace of telegraph signals and I've a notion what this one means.'

'Oh?'

'Why, it's perfectly understandable to those with the wit to construe it.'

'May I know what—'

'Certainly. A naval lady of some enterprise has found a way to let her husband know of the arrival of a nine-pound infant set fair to win his admiral's flag in time. Could that in any way mean your own good self, hey?'

As with a midsummer's dawning, Kydd's world transformed. He was a father – he had a son who was his to instruct and guide, to love and cherish. To be a Kydd in the years and decades to come. To—

'As we will wet the younker's head in a bumper. Flags – the biggest bottle of champagne you can find!'

In a haze of undiluted joy Kydd bashfully acknowledged the admiral's full-hearted toast.

But there was a catch in his throat as he thought of those he'd known who were leaving their bones on a desolate Jutland beach, their families never more to see them. The even more immense numbers that were tasting death at the hands of

Bonaparte's hordes to satisfy the greed of a tyrant. And far away, across the Atlantic, the unimaginable spectacle of American frigate victories. The world was convulsed in an apocalyptic ruination and here he was, toasting the entry into it of a tiny scrap of humanity.

He composed himself and raised his glass instinctively to the view out of the old-fashioned mullioned windows. The eternal sea. And by chance his eyes focused on one ship at anchor, sea-worn and storm-battered but holding herself proud – and his mind cleared.

'Gentlemen. To . . . to *Thunderer*.' His voice was husky but he didn't care. 'The ship, as I will be proud and happy, shall take my being into the future, whatever awaits us there.'

'His Majesty's Ship *Thunderer*.'

And the world became another place.

# Glossary

| | |
|---|---|
| abaft | positioned closer to the stern of a ship |
| barky | affectionate slang for ship |
| Black Virgin | a painting held in Vilna (Vilnius) of the Virgin Mary in black |
| Brodie stove | standard stove fitted to British warships |
| carpenter's wings | space cleared against the ship's side for the carpenter, to enable access for repairs |
| cat and fish | when the anchor is clear of the water the process of securing it to the ship's side |
| *chaloupe canonnière* | single-masted 50-foot gunboat mounting one or two large cannons |
| cobbs | hard coin of value |
| Cossack | east Slavic peoples inhabiting the interior plains of Russia |
| *crache feu* | gun-brig of Swedish origins mounting up to three large guns |
| *cuirassier* | French cavalry with breastplate armour, with sabre and pistols |
| dandy prat | overly ornamented show-off |
| dark-lantern | lantern that when alight can have its light obscured or revealed at will |
| dit | curious naval yarn swapped among seamen |
| *douanier* | continental customs official |
| drubbing | humiliating thrashing |
| druxy | wood so rotten it squelches to the touch |
| fay | timber strakes laid and secured on the one below |
| *fiacre* | light four-wheel carriage for hire |

| | |
|---|---|
| Great Comet | seen in the sky for nearly a year, it was greatly feared as a portent of doom |
| guardo | as seen in a harbour guardship, notorious for sharp practices |
| gudgeon | the receiving hole for the pintle on a rudder, secured to the sternpost |
| hoy | workaday craft around a dockyard |
| lady's hole | where the 'lady of the gunroom' keeps his rags and implements |
| larbowlines | slang for the larboard watch |
| Leveller | term of abuse for seventeenth-century political belief that all men should be equal |
| messenger line | a light line tied to a larger to better enable it to be passed across |
| Mr Vice | form of address to the vice-president of the mess |
| pendant | normally a line attached to rigging blocks, as opposed to pennant, a form of flag |
| pintle | a pin fixed to a rudder to insert into the gudgeon that supports its weight |
| priddy | pretty up |
| redingote | knee-length frock coat |
| roves | circular copper devices placed inside a clinker-built boat over the nails |
| rutters | manual of sailing instructions for foreign seas |
| schuyt | galliot-rigged barge-like Dutch vessel |
| sheer | curve of the decks towards the bow and stern |
| shicer | low trickster |
| siege train | heavy guns complete with all their gear for operation and deploying |
| simkin | of low intelligence |
| spirketting | timber laid fore and aft at the meeting of deck and ship's side |
| starbowlines | slang for the starboard watch |
| stay | line used to steady a mast |
| stonachie | pocketable rope's end used by petty officers to strike laggards |
| the silent hours | during the night after lights are doused |
| tie-cleat | one- or two-armed fitting for temporary fastening of ropes |
| tie-mate | friends who take turns to plait each other's pigtail |
| vedette | a mounted sentry on patrol |
| veldwachteren | Dutch country watchmen |
| voltigeurs | military skirmishers, sharp-shooters |
| waister | seaman whose station is in the middle of the ship |

# *Author's Note*

The year 1812 is dominated by one colossal event that sets all else almost to irrelevance. It's probably the most written-about affair of the entire span of the French wars and at the time held the world in thrall – a Titanic canvas against which I set this tale: Napoleon Bonaparte's invasion of Russia. I could not ignore it, and in my long-standing desire to provide the reader with context and reason for events as they unfold before Kydd, I hope I've given satisfaction. The times were momentous, the stakes epic and the scale monumental, not least of which was the immense size of the horde that flooded across the plains into Russia, in numbers only exceeded by a very few cities on the planet at the time. That Britain was not more closely involved was almost certainly down to the untimely assassination of Perceval, the prime minister, which threw the government into chaos and paralysis.

The book opens with a pivotal event in Kydd's career. Despite his sorrow at losing *Tyger*, the command of a 74-gun ship-of-the-line was no mean achievement for any naval officer. The line-of-battle ship was a real wooden wall in a well-drilled fleet; they were proven battle-winners and Britain's history resounds to their victories. Their sheer magnitude was deeply impressive. A yacht's two-inch deck cleat translates in a 74 to a man-high fitting; her sails all set abroad could be measured in acres; and her guns were each the heft of two or three family cars. And if you stepped aboard it was possible to pace along her decks for miles before repeating yourself. A squadron of sail-of-the-line in line-ahead was a majestic and breathtaking sight, its war-like splendour never to be seen again after the vanquishing of Bonaparte.

The action of Lyngør described in these pages has to be to the undying credit of the Norwegians and Danes, particularly Captain Holm of the *Najaden* who fought against impossible odds to the end, knowing that he commanded the last and only ship of consequence left to the Danish/Norwegian Navy.

On another tack, it's not widely known that Napoleon's invasion fleet was kept fully intact after Trafalgar and, in fact, battle-fleets and invasion craft were still building when overrun just before the end of the war. My own belief is that it was the display of effortless sea supremacy at Boulogne that tipped the scales more towards a gigantic invasion of Russia rather than taking on the thin naval forces around Britain, whose empire in far parts of the globe absorbed most of her maritime resources.

Tsar Alexander was a strange and mystical creature, driven by impulses buried deep in the Russian psyche yet eager to take his country out of its medieval torpor. His fascination with the west led him to trust foreign savants, such as Renzi, in preference to his own faction-ridden and often ignorant tribe. He did, however, become central to the later nation-consuming fight-back against Napoleon and, true to his word, it was he and his peasant legions who marched on to be first at the gates of Paris, to enter as conquerors. The history of our own time would be very different if this all-powerful and autocratic Romanov had held on to the liberal Speransky and adopted his plans for the liberation of the serfs and so forth, almost certainly heading off the bloody revolutions of a century later.

The battle of Borodino is notorious for its savagery and murderous ferocity. Modern research examining artillery dockets of ammunition expended has determined that in the fourteen hours of the battle the average rate of cannon fire was three shots every second. In the square miles of bloodshed, casualties included forty-seven French generals – and it wasn't until May 1813 that the last corpse was finally interred.

The latter part of the book is devoted to the loss of *Defence* and *St George* on the wild shore of Jutland. I freely make confession that the event took place precisely a year earlier in 1811 but, such is its resonance to me of striving and sacrifice, that I felt I must include it before its time-frame receded too far. Events are as close as I can make them to what actually happened, Kydd and *Thunderer* standing in for Captain Pater and the similarly rated *Cressy*. The incident is almost unknown to a general readership, but deserves telling – the magnificent seamanship involved in refloating the flag-ship and getting her under tow for the entire distance out of the Baltic as winter closed in, the jury rig and rudder surviving all but the last and worst gale, the hopeless hours at the end played out so nobly.

What Kydd could not have known until later is that after *St George* unsuccessfully tried to wear she tried that last hope, a club-haul, as described in *Seaflower*. She was desperately unlucky for she overran the anchor and its fluke tore away the Pakenham rudder, leaving them out of control and unable to do anything further to avoid their fate. The two ships went into the crashing surf and by morning it was all over. Just twelve survived of the 865 in *St George* and six from the 560 of *Defence*. Added to the loss with all hands of *Hero*, a sister ship to *Thunderer* who was escort to the convoy and suffered shortly afterwards on the Dutch coast, the navy's toll of dead in this one North Sea hurricane was greater than the entire death roll at Trafalgar.

That night the Danes tried heroically to rescue more but were overwhelmed by the violence of the storm, taking tender care, however, of those who were saved and later repatriating them to England. The next day bodies were so thickly strewn that there was no alternative but to bury them where they lay and, ghoulishly, the local people still call their waterfront *Døde mands klitter* – 'Dead Man's Dunes'. At Thorsminde, where the drama played out, you will find a stone memorial that honours those thousands who perished and a museum filled with artefacts that are still to this day turning up regularly.

Some readers at this point will cry, 'Have you then written Stirk and his shipmates out of the series?' I can say to you that most certainly I have not! In this tale I didn't want to make it easy for our hero in his elevation but in my next book you will be making their reacquaintance . . . with a twist.

As usual, to all those who assisted in the research for this book, I owe a debt of gratitude. My appreciation also goes to my agent, Isobel Dixon; my editor, Oliver Johnson; designer Larry Rostant, for his striking cover; and copy editor Hazel Orme. And last, but by no means least, I make heartfelt recognition of the role of my wife and literary partner, Kathy, who has been at my side for every step of Kydd's journey.

DON'T MISS THE NEXT THOMAS
KYDD ADVENTURE!

# YANKEE
# MISSION

AVAILABLE TO ORDER NOW

HODDER &
STOUGHTON